SEASON OF
THE WITCH

AN EVENT GROUP THRILLER

DAVID LYNN
GOLEMON

For my best friend Gary Dog Golemon...friend, mentor and agent
...and, harshest critic.

ACKNOWLEDGMENTS

I'd like to thank J.K. Rowling, the premier influence on the greatest asset in the entire world—our children. Plus she made the subject of witches actually fun again!

PROLOGUE

LISTENING TO TCHAIKOVSKY

"Stay close by the hearth, if you be faint of heart, for the ghosts and the ghouls are at play," ~Judy Ball, *Season of the Witch*

Vostochny Cosmodrome,
Amur Oblast, Far East Russia

The latest Russian achievement in space operations, geared at protecting her secrets from the western powers, began official operational status in the months leading up to the joint Russian, American, and Chinese moon shots during the frantic chase for alien technology discovered on the moon in an effort to gain military superiority over the Greys in the recently concluded war. While not officially a secret of the hidden and shadowy Russian government, the cosmodrome's activities were. Vostochny was now referred to by the American, German, and British intelligence services as the most secure facility in the secretive and hidden Russian government. Under the cover of future missions to launch rovers to Mars and the moon, the newest Cosmodrome had become the most advanced mission control center in the world.

Operation *Tchaikovsky* had been born after a discovery of frozen water on the dark side of the moon that had been uncovered by accident during the alien technology recovery two months after the joint mission to the moon by the world's governments. The Russian find had sent shock waves through the government and was immediately hushed up by the shadow regime now governing from their hidden facilities in Siberia and publicly operated by their puppets in Moscow. In the three years since official Russian participation and cooperation had officially ended in the technology recovery of the ancient Mars built warships that had crashed on the moon's surface a billion years before, the shadow lords running Russia had authorized four secretly held launches back to the dark side of the moon. The *Tchaikovsky* mission was now to be their crowning achievement and a way to augment their newfound desire for technological domination over the western powers.

Mission control was full this day as the remote rover *Gagarin* slowly traversed the moon's darkened surface in a location that had never been mapped before the Russian discovery three years prior when an accidental low-orbit flyover had caught the photo imagery that sent Russia's secretive Central Committee ensconced in Siberia into a frenzy. A form of nervous confidence was being displayed by every technician on the control room floor of the new facility.

"Telemetry, please report the current surface temperature please?" asked Pavlov Urisky, the mission head from his perch high above the mission control center.

"Negative two hundred-and eighty-two-degrees Fahrenheit, control," called out the surface condition specialist.

"Audio and visual, are your mic's and camera's clear?" Urisky called out.

"Yes control. We had a minor buildup of frost, but the heaters automatically activated."

"Thank you." Urisky rubbed his temples trying to chase away the headache that wanted to rear its head at this most inopportune time.

He took a large swallow from a water bottle as he adjusted his mic and headphones. He was about to order his assistant to find some aspirin but was stopped when another of the technicians handed him a note. He read and then as his headache increased, he wadded up the note and tossed it in the trash receptacle. "Just what I needed," he said in exasperation.

He stood and eased into his suit jacket that had been where it normally was during a mission, on the back of his chair. He shrugged into the black jacket just as the double doors opened and two uniformed men of the new, re-created KGB, Russia's security arm, entered. They were quickly followed by four more. These next men were in plain clothes. The last closing the doors behind a fifth. The man needed no introduction as he quickly spied the mission commander at his high-rise desk in the control center.

"Doctor Urisky, I am glad I was able to make it on time." The man did not hold out a hand in greeting, but instead sat in Urisky's chair.

"Mr. Sokol, I was not informed you would be attending today," Doctor Urisky said as he slid another chair over and sat next to the tenth most powerful man in the nation. A man the world did not know existed, and one that had little love for small-time exploits of mere space travel. As the new head of the science division of the hidden central committee, he felt above such mundane things.

"Ah, it was either me or that fool Putin and I don't want that stuffed animal anywhere near one of my facilities. I am shocked the Americans haven't figured out that little game, as stupid as our fake President is. I swear that fool robs your brain blind of its IQ points whenever he speaks. Soon other arrangements will have to be made regarding our fearless leader. But, I'm only one vote in twelve—for now anyway."

Urisky had heard the rumors years before when the new Cosmodrome was in the process of its construction, but the aspect of having a puppet leader was just too unbelievable for the rumors to be true. Now he wasn't so sure. He *was* sure however that if Sokol and his other committee members thought he or his scientists would talk, they would all be joining the puppet figure head,

Vladimir Putin, in a 'planned' sudden death as so many others of recent note.

"So, how long?"

Urisky cleared his throat as he sat next to the new science director. The man Sokol had replaced had mysteriously vanished after the disastrous encounter with American and other NATO naval forces in the Atlantic Ocean the year before. He had hoped his replacement would be easier to work with, but as he looked at Sokol's dark eyes he had a deep suspicion this man would be much worse. He figured him as a 'power seeker' of major consequence.

"The rover *Gagarin* will soon crest the Krutov Rise." The director saw the confused look on Sokol's face and elaborated. "The craters rim. The remains of the vessel should be visible at that time with the assistance of the infrared and night adaptable cameras."

"If you find any retrievable material, is your plan for getting it back to Russia still viable?"

"Yes, sir. The rover will take any actionable material back to its base platform above the crater and will transfer its load to *Tchaikovsky* for its return. Transit time back home is ninety-six hours."

"When the committee chose you, I had my doubts Doctor. I see now my fears were groundless. You seem to have all under control. I just wanted to check on your progress. So, with that I have more important things to accomplish today." Sokol started to rise.

"*Gagarin* has stopped control. We are bringing up the picture of the craters interior now."

Letting out a breath of exasperation, Sokol sat back in his chair. His thought was even though he didn't like being away from the backstabbers in Siberia for any period of time, that while he was all the way out here in eastern Russia in the wastelands he may as well stay for the show, if there was to be one.

Urisky, disappointed that Sokol had decided to stay, watched as the delayed signal of the rover *Gagarin* started broadcasting. As his eyes adjusted to the darkness of the picture, he chanced a look over to the central committee member. Sokol had his index fingers templed like a church steeple as he watched, the smile never leaving his face.

"The automated program will send it into the crater and our find."

The *Gagarin* rover started moving. Its small spotlight came on and the infrared cameras were able to switch off to conserve power. The down angle of its decent made the traversing of the craters rim hard to watch as its tracks fought for purchase.

"Are you sure the rover will able to enter the craft?" Sokol asked while he stifled a yawn, after all, inspecting downed alien saucers had become routine and boring after the recent war.

Doctor Urisky reached out and snapped on a small computer terminal and brought up a reconnaissance picture taken by a low-altitude flyover of the crater eight months before on the third exploratory mission to the moon soon after the accidental discovery of the find that had nothing to do with the publicly announced frozen water deposits. The picture was from a mile above the surface and it showed the disc-shaped object. "As you can see here Mr. Sokol, the craft is in three large pieces. Due to the moon dust buildup from nearby meteor strikes over the years our astrologists estimate its age at under ten thousand years. A relatively newer craft than even those that attacked Earth."

"That is far younger than the American discovery two years ago," Sokol said, becoming concerned. "By nearly a billion years."

"Yes, quite recent in astrological terms. But one that gives us hope of viable design recovery and possibly more up-to-date sciences the craft may have onboard. In other words, a newer model car."

The dawning of understanding made Sokol broaden his smile. Then he sat forward in his chair. Now far more interested than he had been. The long private jet ride out to these wastes may just have been worth it.

"My God look at that," he said as the rover's cameras started to pick up more detail as it drew close to the bottom of the crater.

Even Doctor Urisky had to smile at the slowly pixelizing image of the downed saucer.

"As you can see, the military consultants your committee had so graciously offered were right in their assumption. There is no sign of damage other than accidental crash related destruction. In other words, sir, it was not shot down. The chance of finding viable genetic material and more advanced technology in its interior has risen to acceptable odds. The technology retrieved would far surpass that of the American discovery of the Mars built battleships near Shackleton Crater three years ago."

"Lets us hope the odds allow us to run the table then," Sokol said.

"*Gagarin* is approaching damage location AE-seventy-four, control. Permission to signal rover to proceed?"

"Permission granted," Sokol said to the surface remote controller before Urisky could open his mouth. If there was ever anyone in doubt as to who was truly in charge, that had been laid to rest by Sokol's growing excitement.

On the large screen beneath the telemetry data scrolling across its bottom, the view changed to show a giant slice of hull had been torn open as if a giant can opener had sliced into it. Pieces of silverish hull materiel lay over most of the surface of the deep crater.

"Unlike the destroyed saucers of the alien fleet and those from Camp Alamo in Antarctica after the battle there, the interior of this craft should be far more complete. Not even the Americans know what we may have accidentally discovered here on the dark side."

The rover neared the rip in the largest section of surviving hull. It stopped and the bright floodlight panned around. It focused on the saucer's damage.

"Yes, definitely impact related. No sign of weapon's fire anywhere," Urisky said, his excitement growing.

"Accident?" Sokol asked, not really caring.

"Some have speculated that with the outer damage it may be that it was intentionally brought down. You can see no trail left by a controlled attempt at landing." Urisky shook his head. He used a computer-generated cursor to highlight an area at the extreme end. "You see here that the craft came down at an extreme angle due to the 'accordion'-like damage."

"Rover has commenced its entrance into the craft, control."

"Thank you. Start a video file and order it to make a three-hundred- and sixty-degree record, please."

"Already done, control."

The view was dark. The floodlights could only do so much in dispelling the gloom. The motion and vibration of the large rover's tracks made a mist of moon dust fall from on high once the rover entered the craft.

Soon chambers of some sort started to become clear. Men and women of the technical team leaned forward to better see. The chambers were covered by thick, clear glass-like material. The enclosures looked thick and strong.

"Remote, let's get a better view of the interior of one of those chambers. Lighting to full," Urisky ordered.

"What could they be?" Sokol asked as even he had stopped fidgeting and was leaning forward, just as interested as Urisky's people. "I counted close to two hundred, but there's obviously more."

As the mission controller watched, he started to get an uneasy feeling. The camera angle was jostled as the tracks of the rover rode over chunks of debris on the flooring of the craft. The *Gagarin* moved up to the cracked glass of the first chamber it came to.

"What is that in the far corner?" Sokol asked.

"Camera two, zoom in to the far-right section of the chamber."

As they watched and after the expected delay in radio transmission, the rover obeyed the relayed signal. The angle showed what looked like a cot of some sort. The moon dust obscured much. Then one of the techs on the floor let out a gasp. In the corner, half buried in moon silt was a large body. It looked to be mummified. Although the skin was petrified and dried out, it was clear as to what they were looking at.

Sokol stood. "Our guess was right. It's a Grey."

The details were becoming clear on the large viewing screen. The long dead body of the enemy that had attacked Earth many months before had died in the impact of the saucer upon the crater's interior. Its long legs had been sliced free during impact and only its upper torso remained. But the large head was unmistakable. They knew the species well enough from the many autopsies performed on the enemy remains after the war. The mummy had the clear teeth and the empty eye sockets that were those of the larger race of beings that had attacked Earth, triple in size to the smaller Green race of slaves.

"Stabilize the camera boom and bring up the claw. What is that on the bastard's wrist?" Urisky did not bother to hold back his disgust at the old enemy for what they had attempted to do to humankind.

During the transmission delay in relaying the request, Sokol eased over next to the mission director. "What are we looking at, a barracks or dorm room perhaps of a troop transport?"

Urisky remained silent as the rover's robotic arm started moving. The headache that had begun with the arrival of the central committee member had morphed into a gut-wrenching fear of what they were possibly seeing.

On the screen the robotic arm reached out and the clamp-like claw touched the large, mummified wrist and raised it. As dust cascaded from the ancient find, many in the control center gasped. It was a chain. The creature had been chained to the back wall of what they knew now was not a barracks or a dorm facility and most assuredly not a troop transport.

"A cell," Urisky said as he tried to steady his breathing.

As the rover *Gagarin* backed out of the cell the camera angle went to wide lens. The expanse of the main deck of the saucer steadied and became visible.

"What in the name of Peter the Great have we found?" Sokol asked in amazement.

Urisky sat hard into his chair as the view on the screen expanded even more. He looked from his frightened people below to turn and see the face of the excited committee man, Sokol.

"What we are looking at is a prison ship, Mr. Director."

AFTER TWENTY-FOUR HOURS of mapping and recording the interior of what they knew now was an alien prison ship, Dimitri Sokol was preparing to leave after the disappointment of the previous day. The suspected treasure trove of technology had failed to deliver into Russian hands anything of significance that the Americans and the

British did not already possess. Sokol figured he had gained his first stain on an otherwise spotless committee record. He had decided to show Doctor Urisky the depth of his disappointment before leaving. He stepped into the control center.

He was shocked at the amount of activity still occurring on the mission floor. Curious, he spotted mission controller Urisky shouting orders from his high perch.

"What has happened, Doctor?" Sokol asked as he tried to gauge the amount of excitement he was witnessing.

"It's truly amazing. We were preparing the Rover *Gagarin* for departure back to the lander *Tchaikovsky*. Moments before it left the saucer, audio tracking picked up strange noises from the saucer's interior. Investigating to make sure we missed nothing, we sent *Gagarin* back into the depths of the craft." Urisky spoke into his mic. "Video replay, show Central Committee Member Sokol what we have discovered."

On the large viewing screen, the video was started. Sokol saw what was there and sat down, only mildly interested.

"Just what is it I am supposed to be looking at?" Sokol asked.

"The lower deck of the craft. We assume it is a specialized area of the saucer. Possibly prison isolation. Look."

On the screen was a large cocoon-like chamber that resembled an old-fashioned Iron Lung that had been used for medical purposes in earth's past. Only this one looked much larger and possibly a few tons in weight.

"What is that?" Sokol inquired.

"Speculation has run a little amok here since we found it. It's not what it *is* that is so confusing, it's the fact that whatever it is is *still* functioning," Urisky answered with a smile.

As Sokol examined the video, he did see flashing lights that were covered with dust from the moon dust that had been brought down by vibration and meteor strikes outside of the hull. They saw needles and gauges moving back and forth and audio was picking up the buzz of energy and the humming of atmospheric filters.

"Is...is something still alive in there?" Sokol finally managed to ask.

"Video, show him," the doctor said, this time the roles had been reversed. It was his time to shock Sokol.

Again, the video was rewound. The still frame stopped and Sokol felt his mouth gape open. A large window at the top of the tube-like chamber showed what was inside the still operational device. Sokol stood.

"Good God."

Doctor Urisky smiled and shook his head as Sokol just said the exact words most of his mission staff had cried earlier.

The restraints held the creature in place. Thick nylon-looking straps crisscrossed the giant of a Grey's body. This was unlike any Grey ever examined. It had long and stringy, sparse white hair covering its bulbous head. The features were slightly off, almost a more human-style quality to them. It was not in a mummified state of decomposition like the three hundred and eighty-seven chained and restrained corpses they had discovered since the rover had entered the craft.

"Is it...is it..."

"Breathing? Yes, it is. Artificially aided, but still breathing. Amazing after ten thousand years, and the damn thing is still alive."

Sokol sat hard into his chair and shook his head.

"We assume this was a prized prisoner of the Greys." Mission Control Manager Urisky moved to stand near Sokol. "Are you ready?"

Sokol looked up from the most amazing sight he had ever seen. He waited, not really knowing if he wanted to know.

"Video, move to minus footage fourteen minutes, fifty-one seconds, please."

On the screen the tape rewound and then stopped to a still frame shot to highlight a written language report on what they were seeing in the tube. The dit-dot, dash, dash and symbol language of the Greys was clearly seen.

"We have been in contact with the Russian linguist Doctor Igor Lanikov of Moscow University. He has the security clearance for just this kind of mission because he was on the United Nations team of linguists in our battle against the Greys. He translated the words on, what we here think, was the bill of lading, or manifest, that was discovered on the side of the container. It seems this very much larger than normal Grey was a very despicable character on their world. He was most assuredly one of their civilizations most wanted. A prize prisoner so to speak. And considering the ruthless nature of the Greys and what they had planned for the human race, this Bolshevik must have been a real monster."

"Among those human eating creatures, what is their definition of despicable?" Sokol asked with a disbelieving snort.

"I'm afraid until we can possibly interview this creature, we just do not know. We must make every effort to get this Grey back to Earth alive. Failure would mean we lose so much valuable knowledge. We must!"

"Rather enthusiastic, Doctor, why the sudden change over a larger than normal Grey, but still just a Grey nonetheless?"

Urisky smiled, relishing the fact that he had the power before him to finally have the upper hand over the Central Committee member.

"Well?" Sokol asked, losing patience with the suddenly overconfident and arrogant man of science.

"We have changed the programming on *Gagarin*, she has been taking readings from the thing in the capsule for the past six hours."

"Doctor, the ice under your feet is growing increasingly thin. Just get to the point."

Urisky turned and faced a large still picture of the giant Grey. Its white hair wild, framing a mouth that had double the size and count of teeth from other normal Greys.

"Mr. Sokol, this creature is drawing power from itself. Self-generating and sustained over four to ten thousand years. And we have discovered there is no external power source. In other words, the power keeping this thing alive is coming from *it*."

"Are you insane?" Sokol asked.

"If I am, so are the medical staff that designed our most advanced recorders and monitoring devices on our rover *Gagarin*."

"Why is that?"

DAVID L GOLEMON

"Because *Gagarin* is picking up not only massive amounts of electrical power from this thing, it's picking up sizable brain activity."

"What?" Sokol said with dawning understanding crossing his features.

"My people are excited, and very much frightened, Mr. Sokol."

The committee member stood and faced the doctor. He waited patiently as the mission control manager fought to find the right words he needed. Finally, he stated what everyone in the center felt.

"That creature is not only alive and producing its own life sustaining power. It's aware we are there."

PART I

CACTUS ROSES AND PIZZA ROLLS

"…Well now everything dies, baby that's a fact,
but maybe everything that dies, someday comes back…"
~ The Band—Atlantic City

CHAPTER ONE

Desert Rose Cemetery,
Las Vegas, Nevada

On the four converging dirt roads leading up to the small, private cemetery, United States Air Force Humvees stopped the few vehicles filled with hikers, dirt bike enthusiasts and campers from climbing the hills that surrounded the once peaceful setting. The state highway department, with the assistance of Nellis Air Force Base, had successfully quarantined the general area to allow the largest forensics team ever assembled in Nevada to descend on the privately held property. Blackhawk helicopters on loan from the base kept the airspace clear of any unauthorized flyovers of the small cemetery. Thus far the lid on the pressure cooker had been secured tightly. That situation could change at any time. After all, news of the vandalism had been reported by the Las Vegas Sheriff's Department, and grave robbing of any kind was indeed news. It was bound to leak out to the general public soon, so time was short.

One hundred and thirty forensics experts from the FBI and the Department of the Air Force scoured the cemetery looking for any clue as to the disposition of the vandalism that had taken place the night before. The most interested party stood aloof to allow the experts to do their jobs. The situation was beyond frustrating as they had orders to stand down by the President himself.

The large man stood off to the side of the front gate of the Desert Rose and watched silently as the government techs went about their forensics work. The approach of an even larger man with short-cropped blonde hair brought the waiting man back to the here and now.

"Just received this from the complex, Jack. The Director is throwing a fit with the President over this thing. Niles claims that because of our status as a secret department we are being kept out of something that only we can deal with. I guess there is someone in Washington making a stink about the assets being misdirected by the Department of the Air Force."

Colonel Jack Collins looked at his friend. Captain Carl Everett handed Jack a note. He read it.

"Harold Briggs again?"

"He's making a stink. Even has the Air Force Chief of Staff on his side about allocating resources from Nellis. The good Congressman is all over the President. He's been chasing rumors about us ever since the war with the Greys."

Jack wadded up the flimsy and was tempted to toss the paper away but pocketed it instead.

Carl could see the situation with the vandalism of the small alien's grave was wreaking havoc with Jack just as it was with him. "We just have to be patient buddy. We both know the little green guy just didn't wake up and take a walk into the desert. We'll find out who did this."

He could see that Jack was acting just like Director Niles Compton. He felt responsible and horrified that the Event Group had prematurely buried little Matchstick Tilly without realizing he wasn't dead. Both Jack and Niles had agreed that because of the manner of death involved in Matchstick's murder, an autopsy of their small friend was not needed or justified because the thought of cutting into their friend to see what made him tick was just too much for them to contemplate. Now that decision was weighing heavily on both men.

Jack's eyes kept moving to the empty grave next to that of the still intact Gus Tilly buried site. He bit his lip and seemed to fight back the despair he was feeling.

"Jack, why don't you take a break. Sarah is staying at Alice's house while we figure this out. She had some harsh words with the director who wanted you and her to continue with your honeymoon plans. She tore up your tickets to Bali and threw them at Niles. I think you need to go and talk to her. All her happiness about your wedding has been zapped from her mind over this."

"Sarah knows what's up. Honeymoons can wait for now and the director should have known that. Just how in the hell did Niles think Sarah would react?"

Carl was about to continue to try and convince Jack to take a break, when they were approached by a man in a blue shirt. The FBI logo on the breast pocket identified him as an agent. He held out a hand to Jack and Carl both.

"Colonel, disappointed I missed the festivities last night, congratulations on your recent nuptials. Surprised the hell out of me that's for sure. Single man Jack Collins brought down by the smallest woman I know."

"Tom, good to see you. How is Washington?" Carl asked, trying to get the conversation of Jack's recent wedding to Sarah off the table.

"That's why I wasn't able to make it to the wedding. Director Compton and the President has me tailing that asshole Congressman who is hell bent on exposing Department 5656. The man smells blood." Tom Wilkerson, FBI agent-in-charge, and a deep mole of the Event Group through presidential order, saw his comments about Congressman Briggs had no effect on Jack. He kicked at the desert sand. "Then this came up. I guess the theft of Matchstick's body is weighing heavily on everyone's mind, including the President. Thus, here I am. Your man at the Bureau."

"Thanks for handling this, Tom. I still don't understand why the President and Niles don't allow our people to conduct this investigation," Jack said in abject frustration.

"Colonel, for the exact same reasons friends don't investigate the death of a partner when a cop is killed. You and your people are just too close to make a good judgement calls where Matchstick is concerned."

The look from the face of Jack Collins made the agent hesitate and Carl strategically stepped in between him and Collins.

"Jesus Jack, I'm sorry. I'll get the Group some information as soon as I can. I know it's driving your people batshit crazy trying to get an answer. If I have to torture someone for information, I'll get whoever did this."

The three men shook hands and the agent moved off to consult with the crime scene technicians.

"He didn't mean anything by that, Jack," Carl said. "You can tell the situation about that fool Briggs and his accusations to anyone in Washington who will listen, and with what happened here last night is effecting everyone. Including fearless FBI agent Tom." Carl was about to continue when they noticed a scuffle near the empty grave of the Matchstick Man. A tall, thin, white haired man was actually rolling on the ground with a plastic-suited technician. As they watched, Will Mendenhall and Jason Ryan were in the process of running toward the two to break up the fracas. "Oh, shit!" Carl said, as he and Jack also sprinted to the scene.

As they arrived more white plastic environment suited forensics men from the FBI were nearing to join in the fight. Professor Charles Hindershot Ellenshaw III was being held at bay by a very much smaller but also stronger Jason Ryan. Will was pushing the forensics technician back from continuing the fight.

"Professor, what in the hell is this about?" Carl asked, as he and Jack took in the wild-haired Cryptozoologist. His wire-rimmed glasses were askew and he was so angry he failed to form words.

"Keep that maniac away from me!" shouted the technician being held by Will Mendenhall. The man's clear face mask had been cracked and his nose was bleeding.

"Jesus Doc, calm down," Jason said as he tried to move the tall man away. "Now, what in the hell happened?"

"First these fools don't know how to catalogue evidence properly, this needs to be treated like an archeological event," Charlie hissed and tried to break free of Ryan's grip but steadied when Carl stepped in front of him. "And then their snide little remarks about moonlight strolls by moon men. By god I don't have to put up with that crap. Matchstick deserves better than that!"

"So, the crazy bastard just attacks me? What kind of nut is he," the technician asked as his friends on the FBI forensics team gathered around their man for support while the Air Force personnel watched from a safe distance. One FBI Tech was even brazened enough to get too near Will Mendenhall.

"Cowboy, you take another step towards the Doc or me, I *will* consider you intend us harm. Then your friends can just drop you into that empty grave to replace our friend."

The FBI technician caught the not-so-very veiled threat and stopped moving.

"Come on Jack. Get your people out of here and let us do our thing, would you?"

Collins looked from the Agent-In-Charge to the still fuming Professor Ellenshaw to a ready-to-pounce Major Mendenhall. He reluctantly nodded his head at the lead agent, realizing his people were too much on edge over Matchsticks disappearance.

"Okay, my people, let's get the hell out of here."

Carl, Will, Jason, with a struggling Crazy Charlie Ellenshaw in tow, started to leave with Jack for the waiting Blackhawk sitting outside the back gate of the Desert Rose Cemetery.

As Ryan assisted Charlie into the sliding door of the Blackhawk, he smiled at the crazy haired professor as everyone crowded around waiting to hear the real story from the Cryptozoologist.

"I don't know Doc. I think you've been hanging out with the wrong crowds lately. You're turning into a crazed version of Mike Tyson."

Carl and Jack saw the change in Ellenshaw as his demeanor calmed considerably. It was Everett, with a nod from Jack who stepped up and held out his hand to Ellenshaw.

"Yeah, he's hanging out with the wrong crowd alright—you and

Mendenhall. And yes, the Doc is crazy, but crazy like a fox. Hand it over Doctor."

Ellenshaw smiled at Everett and he glanced at Jack Collins who nodded that he should do what the Captain asked. Continuing to smile he handed Carl the small notebook. During the scuffle Ellenshaw had removed the forensic notes from the technician who failed to notice his pocket had been picked.

"Sorry, they weren't answering my questions. I thought this would help us start the ball rolling as they say."

"You're one crazy bastard Doc," Mendenhall said, but everyone could see Will's pride in what Ellenshaw had done.

"Mister Everett, we've trained a pack of thieves," Jack said as Ryan started the Blackhawks rotor blades to spinning.

"I take it we're not going to wait on the FBI?" Everett said as he snapped his safety harness closed.

"Have we ever?"

Novosibirsk, Siberia, Russia

THE ALEXANDER NEVSKY CATHEDRAL was a massive stone structure erected in 1899 and was a marvel of architecture. Since the downfall of the old Soviet Union the building and its religious purpose had found new life and has since become a popular tourist destination for architectural students visiting from abroad. There was however, one aspect of the great shrine you could find no description of in any tourist brochure—that located five hundred and eighty-seven feet beneath the tiled flooring of the cathedral was housed the secret and shadowy men and women who actually ran the new Russian state. The committee hid itself in plain sight in the third most populous city in Russia. The Presidium, of which it was referred to by its members, housed eighteen floors of offices that did the bidding of the highly secretive Central Committee. The puppet committee in Moscow had no official say but for the dictates that was handed to them for public consumption. In other words, the real power of the new Russia solely resided with these powerful men and women. While each member had a name, they were referred to inside the chambers as a numbered entity. Even the numbers were never spoken outside of Siberia for security reasons. The look-a-like puppet at the head of the country in Moscow was the only person outside of the Presidium to actually know of their existence.

The council chamber was semi-dark as it usually was during the meetings that were held to govern the growing prospects of the new government. Circular in design and numbered according to power, the only empty chair was that of the new Sciences Division Chairman, Number Ten. This fact did not go unnoticed by the most powerful of these men and women, the man who held the 'Number One' position. As progress was reported on the new aspect of their latest triumph overseas, the handling and assistance in the United States for the audacious possibly getting a man sympathetic to the Russian cause elected as the most powerful man in the world—the Presidency of the United States of America.

The man known as Number Seven started to conclude his report to the committee after explaining the raging success of their radical social media blitz to split the United States into two waring sides of political strife, he had concluded by saying their campaign at embarrassing the man sitting in the Oval Office over his military expenditures during the war with the Greys was paying massive dividends and was propelling their man, Congressman Harold Briggs into the Independent Party nomination to replace the lame duck President.

"In conclusion, our efforts have doubled in assisting Mr. Briggs in our American plan, and we expect a substantial victory over his opponents in the upcoming election."

Number Seven turned to the center of the table and half-bowed to the man sitting in his powerful 'number one' chair.

"Thank you Number Seven for that very optimistic report. We, as a committee, will be watching anxiously in the coming months for the positive result you have so *optimistically* stated is bound to happen."

As Number Seven started to sit, he hesitated at the veiled threat to his safety. In other words, the American election and the positive results explained were dependent on whether he continued to serve the committee. His life now depended on the results. He sat and the other members turned their heads away with exactly that same understanding.

Number One looked to his right and lined up against the circular wall was the committee members assistants. He spied the chair of the assistant to the Science Director.

"I believe we were to hear a report on the Science Divisions recent large monetary expenditure on the front concerning the large purchases in America."

The woman representing Dimitri Sokol stood nervously. She nodded her head at the center of the table. Number One tiredly waved his hand for her to explain.

"Uh, Mr. Sokol has been delayed and is expected shorty Mr. Chairman. As for the expenditures in American real estate and equipment, the office of Strategic Sciences has no explanations at this time."

"Are you saying that the man's personal staff has no idea what their boss is doing, just who is it you work for, Joseph Stalin young lady?"

Several committee members chuckled. The only one who wasn't was Number One. He angrily turned to the member who made the comment and Number Nine, the man in charge of internal security who started the laughing, turned his head away.

"Miss Trotsky, with Mr. Sokol's familial history, it seems he would make available all information this committee asks for. His family should be seeking less suspicion, not more."

Everyone on the council knew that Sokol's grandfather had been the famous Russian spy Andre Sokol, the man who had infiltrated Hitler's inner circle during the Great Patriotic War. He had been so good at his job that Joseph Stalin had the man arrested upon war's end as he could no longer be trusted not to turn his very adequate spying skills on the Soviet dictator. After arriving home, he had been ensconced in a Gulag only seventeen miles from where the committee currently sat to conduct business. For the committee, it was seen as Sokol's duty to change the memory of his grandfather being a suspected traitor during his service to the German madman. Sokol had fought his way to the top and all in the Presidium knew the ruthless man was determined to stay there—regardless of who and what his Grandfather had been accused of.

The woman was clearly shaken and Number One could see that. Questioning her would just put him in the awkward position of forcing punishment on someone that it was not intended for. He nodded that she should sit.

"We'll move onto the next agenda item. Number Four. Our friends in Nevada. Has there been any response to our offer of peace in our times?" Number One said in a joking manner mocking Neville Chamberlain's famous quote about getting his adversary Adolph Hitler to the peace table.

"It seems their Director Compton is not a very forgiving soul," the balding man from the dirtiest department in the committee said as he stood. "He will not even entertain the offer, nor will he convey our peace overture to his Commander-in-Chief, the President." The man looked at the others around the table. "I'm afraid we're at an impasse. Compton will not soon be lowering his guard long enough for us to strike at that damnable Group. He suspects we will not be keeping our offer of peace between them and us."

"Unfortunate," Number One said as the man in charge of 'dirty tricks' again sat.

"Perhaps I may be of assistance in that regard, as in the case of many of our problems," proclaimed a voice from the back of the chamber. The tall man stepped into the light cast by the bright spots circling the table.

"Director Sokol, it is indeed good of you to join our little mandatory meeting this morning," Number One said without humor lacing his strong voice.

"Apologies to the committee," Sokol said as he half-bowed and then stood next to the chair of number Nine. "It seems some members tongues begin to wag when one isn't present to hear."

They all knew then that Director Sokol had heard the comments about his family that had been broached by Number Nine. Most would not give Number Nine the sympathetic look nor the support he needed. The man just lowered his eyes. Sokol was relatively new to the committee, but all sensed his desire to strenuously clear his families name and reputation after being falsely accused by Stalin of traitorous activity.

"We will speak of that aspect of commentary from our dear Number Nine at a later time. Please explain not only your lateness to this meeting, but also your rather bold statement on assisting us with our Event Group situation."

Sokol nodded at Number One and then pulled out his chair to sit. This was a small insult to the Number One Position as every member stood when reporting was required. He unbuttoned his coat and then took his time pouring water from a crystal decanter. He sipped the water as Number One visibly became impatient.

"Three months ago, our robotic expedition returned from the dark side of the moon. While it was widely reported that we had successfully charted a frozen water deposit inside the area reported, I can honestly state to you now of our failure. We found no such thing. The fool Putin announced our success to the world. However, it was not his doing. I reported the false success to him myself. Now I am here to explain why."

"Explanation of that and many other things I hope," said a now embarrassed and emboldened Number Nine.

Sokol took another drink of water and waited. He didn't even acknowledge Number Nine but instead ignored him.

"Continue Number Ten."

"We found no water, but we did find something of rather large import to many of our current problems and worries." He turned and smiled, smirked really at Number Nine. "Due to the incompetence of some, it was leaked to a few people with large ears that you, Number One, are particularly interested in bringing down the American agency known as Department 5656, for the reason many here suspected but never voiced," again he looked at the head of Internal

Security, "until certain men and women talked out of the security of their own offices. It seems an entity inside this Group underneath Nellis Air Force Base in Nevada knows the true identity of you, Number One, and could very well expose you. That man is Colonel Jack Collins who you met in harder times in Iraq many years ago."

Unseen by the committee members around the circular table Number One had pushed a button under the table and four plain clothed security men walked calmly through the door.

"Perhaps you better go into a little more detail," Number One said as his eyes bore into Sokol.

"I am merely saying what I've heard through investigation as to why the committee wants to bring down this rather bothersome agency. I can only report what me and my people have heard. Punish who you will, but never the messenger—of which I am."

Number Nine visibly turned a shade of white none had ever seen before. Number One looked at the security men and nodded for them to stand down. They left the chamber.

Sokol knew in his heart that his revenge against Number Nine for bringing up his Grandfather's reputation and imprisonment had been fortuitous at best and advantageous to the demonstration he was about to display.

"I propose killing three birds with one stone, as the Americans are so fond of saying. Ladies and gentlemen, we have been given a gift of a magnitude that can change the world as we know it. When I am finished with my proposal, I fully expect to be elevated to the position of Number Two. This will be voted on and I will enter that position with unanimous support by the committee. This is not an opinion, but a fact. I will achieve this by not only bringing down your foe beneath the American desert in Las Vegas, but also achieve the committee's ultimate goal of getting their desired candidate into the office of the American Presidency. Then our plan for the subjugation of Europe can proceed at a speed unforeseen by members of this august body. We will proceed with a marvelous tool and weapon that has been dealt us, and one that *I* now control."

The members went wild with accusations and many stood and

pointed angry and shaking fingers at the arrogant man from the Strategic Sciences Division. Sokol turned in his chair and smiled at his female assistant who watched on nervously, wondering if either she or Sokol would leave the underground Presidium complex alive that day.

Sokol stood. He slammed his palm down on the table three times until the committee settled. He looked at Number One. Instead of the steely-eyed glare he expected, the lead member of the council smiled and nodded his head. Either Sokol would have an interesting proposal, or the chairman would be soon enjoying watching the man executed in this very chamber.

"Mr. Sokol," Number One said, forgoing his number which meant there was no hiding the fact that Sokol was close to losing his committee designation, "this Group beneath the desert in Nevada cannot be gotten to. We have tried."

"I have plans to bring them out into the open Number One. Then I will allow our new asset recently discovered on the moon's surface to do the dirty work. Ladies and gentlemen, please allow me to introduce a new ally in our quest for retribution against the western powers for their disgraceful treatment of our nation for the past one hundred and twenty years," he said, and then nodded back at his assistant who stood and went to a side door, one that was rarely used. She hesitated. Then she nervously reached out and pulled both doors open.

Backlighted against the lights of the exterior hallway stood a shape that made every member of the central committee gasp and stand in fright. The shadowy form was over eight feet tall and its silky white hair was highlighted by the bright lighting behind it. The legs were long and powerful looking, and each member immediately recognized it for what it was. A Grey.

The Grey eyed Sokol's assistant who quickly scurried away to stand against the wall as far away as she could get. The clothing the Grey wore had been supplied by the Russian sciences division. The purplish and green pants were short. The robe was long. As the creature eased into the room it looked from member to member. The yellow eyes flared with inner fire. The clear eyelids closed and opened from the outside of the eye sockets.

The four security men rushed into the room and stood staunchly by Number One who was brave enough to stand his ground while other members cowered behind their vacated chairs. Sokol smiled at the bravado displayed by Number One as he knew the man he was destined to replace was inwardly as frightened as the rest, and why not, it had taken himself a month to sit comfortably with the large Grey until he had successfully communicated how advantageous their new union was to both creature and man. Sokol walked easily over and gestured for the Grey to advance further into the chamber.

"Ladies and gentlemen, please, he is no danger to you whatsoever. His interest now lies elsewhere. His abilities will amaze you and his power elevate us and our country to the status we all deserve."

"Why is it so large?" one of the members asked while semi-hiding behind her high-backed chair.

"Because it is a Grey in name only Number Six. Come," he said as he walked over to the blonde woman and took her shaking hand. "Please, he will not harm you."

The woman was led to the Grey who looked down upon her with its penetrating yellow eyes. The mouth was ajar, and the clear and very long incisors could be seen clearly. She shook her head and looked at Sokol. Her eyes pleaded. The white hair moved in the breeze created by the flow of air-conditioned current. The creature seemed to sense the woman's fear. It reached out with the right hand and touched the frightened committee member's cheek and rubbed it. Its scaly skin made the woman shiver. Sokol had mercy and bade her to return to the protection of her chair's back.

"Director Sokol, how do you know this enemy can be a friend?" Number One asked as he braved sitting once more. "After all, its kind had us a dinner menu item if I'm not mistaken."

"This Grey had nothing to do with the attack on our planet. It was ensconced on the very ship we recovered on the dark side of the moon. The saucer had been in that crater for over five to six thousand years. My department has spent the past month explaining the results of his races attack to our new ally."

"And what has it to say?" Number twelve asked as he took the example of Number One and sat.

The Grey answered for Sokol. It stepped forward further into the light and hissed. The mouth widened and then it hissed even louder.

"Like my Grandfather, this creature was incarcerated for being the best at what he does. Imprisoned by the very beings that could have used its help during the invasion of our world. But the Greys, like Comrade Stalin, feared that which he could not understand, and like that fool Stalin, they imprisoned it."

Again, the giant Grey hissed and semi-crouched as if to attack.

"Number One, may I demonstrate just what the Americans will be facing when we let loose this newest asset?" Sokol smiled at Number One who saw Sokol's eyes drift over to the still standing Number Nine, the Interior Security member whose department had leaked the weakness of Number One. The head of the committee understood Sokol's request. He raised his left brow high and nodded as he gestured for his four security men to stand by. They lowered their sidearms and watched.

Sokol walked up to the Grey who was still in an attack crouch. The creature saw Sokol and it seemed to relax. Sokol said something that no one could hear. Then the sciences director turned and looked at the still standing Number Nine. The overweight minister knew something was wrong when the Grey turned and looked at him. The yellow eyes flared to a brightness that suggested an interior flare had been ignited. The creature hissed and then stood straight to its full height of over eight feet tall. First its bulbous head tilted left, and then right and it hissed again. This time spittle flew from the mouth as it studied Number Nine who was now backing away. The creatures right hand came up and the crystal nailed fingers waved through the air. Number Nine turned and started to run. Number One's security men started to stop him but was again ordered to stand down.

Before the startled committee members, Number Nine stopped in mid-stride. He grabbed his throat and started clawing at it like a crazed, choking animal. When their eyes went from Number Nine to the Grey, they could see the creature still hissing and spitting but its hand had closed into a clawed, choking position mimicking as if it were actually touching the man's throat. Then the Grey's other hand came up and with an elongated outstretched index finger swirled it through the air in a circle. Number Nine was lifted free of the polished floor. As the man tore at his own neck for a snatch of air, his body started spinning. Soon the gravitational pull of the powerful spin snatched his arms and hands from his throat as the centrifugal force made him pinwheel like a top. Then the Grey used both hands to shove Number Nine as he spun through the air ten feet up and his spinning form smashed into the paneled wall where his body turned into a bug on a windshield and virtually disintegrated.

There were gasps of shock. There were screams and moans of sickness from the most powerful men and women in Russia as their eyes were wide and stunned at the magic produced by the powerful Grey.

The creature turned and faced the men and women. Again, it lowered to a crouch and hissed as Sokol eased his hand over its back to calm it. He turned and looked at his female assistant who reluctantly stepped forward and took the giant Grey by the hand. It hissed at her and then calmed. She swallowed and then led the creature from the chamber. Sokol smiled and then buttoned his suit jacket and returned to his chair as he absentmindedly stepped over bits of remains of the man who had insulted his family. Sokol once again poured a glass of water and sipped nonchalantly.

"You have my apologies for what you just witnessed. It wasn't arrogance on my part as I assumed number ten would eventually meet and untimely death anyway."

"A harsh demonstration, but a just end to the man. Number Ten, how soon can this committee expect an outline of your plan?"

Sokol didn't have to look at Number One. He waited a moment until his assistant returned and handed him several sheets of papers.

"Number One, the initial stages of the plan is being transmitted by computer to you for your approval and distribution to those you deem fit for its consumption. I caution however that the abilities of the Grey are classified and for your eyes only."

"You need not explain security protocol to me, Number Ten."

"Of course not," Sokol said, but had an inner smirk that only he could feel.

"Your starting point?" Number One asked.

"As I said, eliminate your nemesis in the desert in Nevada and the only organization that causes even myself and the Grey a danger. Department 5656. We will go about this in two phases. First, continue to order our new friend Congressman Briggs of Louisiana to assert pressure on the public exposure of this secretive group."

"And?" Number One asked as he began to see Sokol's plan come together in his mind's eye.

"To bring the Event Group out into the light of day."

"As I said, we can't get into their complex for full-scale operations."

"We don't need to. We bring them to us. We kill all those they hold dear. I have read their compiled dossiers. Once I start to move, there is no way this Director Compton can ever control that American boy scout, Jack Collins. Collins will be the first domino to fall. If I read this Colonel correctly, he will expose his own Group through his temper after our new friend does its work."

"Why Collins? I thought he was the one person we would steer clear of," Number One said. "I have met him in the field, he is most formidable."

"Without knowing it Collins has always been this Group's weakest link."

"How?"

Sokol smiled. "We meet him and his capable men on the ground of our choosing."

"Again, Number Ten, how?"

"By eliminating in the harshest terms those friends of his we *can* get to."

CHAPTER TWO

Event Group Complex,
Nellis Air Force Base, Nevada

The sixteen department heads met in the large conference room on level seven inside the cavernous underground complex. The man sitting at the head of the table, Director Niles Compton, was silent throughout most of the reports from his people regarding the incident at the Desert Rose Cemetery the night before. The director had darkened circles under his eyes, as did most of the department heads who attended that day. All saw him rub the long scar that ran from his eye-patch to his jawline. All knew the Director was still self-conscious about the wounds he sustained in the war.

After the report from the security department delivered by Major Will Mendenhall claiming that the FBI and local authorities were still baffled by the theft of the body of the Group's friend and adopted member, the Matchstick Man, the men and women of Department 5656 started to lose hope that this was just a prank and started to seriously believe a horrid mistake had been made after the murder of the small alien. Blame was readily volunteered by all, and guilt for not truly understanding the small alien's amazing bodily capabilities.

As Will finished his report, the double doors opened, and a naval signal man entered to give Assistant Director Virginia Pollock a note. She read it, and then excused the young man who left. She cleared her throat, not once but twice, as if she were choking back some awful shot of alcohol. With one last attempt, she looked at Niles Compton. Niles nodded. It was Alice Hamilton, sitting to Compton's left, who visibly encouraged Virginia to continue.

"This is from the lab. The DNA recovered from the empty grave has been confirmed to be Matchstick's." Virginia's eyes moved as she finished reading, and then she placed a hand over her mouth. Suddenly standing from her chair, she turned her back on the gathered department heads. Alice saw her distress, and went to her as she sobbed behind her hand.

Jack Collins, Carl Everett, and Will Mendenhall all exchanged looks. Virginia was about one of the strongest women the men knew, and whatever news she had gotten had shaken her to the core. Jack looked over to his new wife, the former U.S. Army Lieutenant Sarah McIntire, who exchanged worried looks with the people sitting next to her, Charlie Ellenshaw and Major Anya Korvesky. Jack could see they all three wished to join Alice in consoling Virginia, but held back.

Virginia, with encouragement from Alice Hamilton, the oldest living member of the Event Group, wiped her eyes and turned back to face the Group.

"Apologies. The report continues to state that the DNA recovered was from an active and still viable alien specimen."

"You mean he *is* alive?" Charlie Ellenshaw asked what everyone else feared.

"My God, what have I done?" Virginia let loose with tears and a moan.

Alice decided enough was enough She looked at Niles who just nodded his head, and she took a now openly sobbing Virginia Pollock out of the conference room.

Jack and everyone knew Virginia made the final call on forgoing the autopsy which would have found that Matchstick had not succumbed to the bullets that they all thought had ended his life.

Collins' eyes went along the table until they lighted on the Director. Compton had confidently signed off on a straight burial, and the decision not to dignify cutting the small alien open for study. Jack could see that it was not only Virginia near collapse for the decision, but the Director as well. Secretly every member of the Event Group, including Collins himself, had felt relieved at not having to go through the gruesome science of discovery with an autopsy.

"Mr. Director, perhaps it's time we take a break, and get some rest," Jack said from his end of the table.

Niles started to speak, but then just nodded his head in agreement.

As everyone started to leave, Jack nodded at Xavier Morales suggesting the computer genius stay.

"Carl?" Jack said as he and Will were getting ready to join the others.

"Yes."

"I need to talk to Niles and Doctor Morales. I didn't want to get anyone's hopes up here, but I would like you, Will, Ryan and our new Lieutenant Tram to get your asses out to Chato's Crawl. If our little green friend is alive, he may just try to get home. It may be a distance for the little guy to travel but you can brief the security detail there to be on the lookout. Put extra men on all sites, the town, Gus's old house, and the Superstition Mine."

"You got it, Jack. But do me a favor, tell Niles and Virginia it's not their fault. Tell them we need them on this."

Jack nodded. He had never seen Carl or will without a snappy comeback or a witty comment. The event was affecting everyone at the Group, and Jack didn't care for it, because it was effectively eating at him also. He watched until the room was empty.

Collins walked over to Niles, who was deep in depressive thought. Jack started, and then stopped to put his hand on Niles' shoulder to get his attention, but then sat in the chair usually reserved for Alice Hamilton. Xavier Morales adeptly moved Virginia's chair, and rolled into place on Nile's right side. Unrestrained like Collins, Xavier did place his hand on the director's back, and attempted to comfort him. Compton looked up from his closed-eyed thoughts.

"Rough night," Jack said.

Niles removed his glasses and looked back at him. "I'm sorry, Colonel. We managed to turn what should have been the happiest night of your life into this nightmare."

"It wasn't as if it was done intentionally. Besides, Sarah just may be sick of me already. I tend to wear on those who love me."

Niles feigned a smile.

"Should we send someone out to Arizona to see…"

"Already ordered, Niles. Everyone knows what they have to do. As a matter of fact, with Virginia so upset, I have the next in command here to order some mandated rest for the Director. Do you agree, Doctor Morales?"

"Exponentially."

Jack just looked at the young computer whiz.

"I mean, yes," Xavier stuttered.

"Perhaps you better see this," Niles said as he flipped a switch on the small console on the table. "Europa play news footage of this afternoon please. Baton Rouge rally."

Jack became curious as he saw Xavier shake his head.

'Yes, Doctor. File 8967.03, recorded this date,' said the Marylin Monroe-voiced supercomputer.

Jack turned when the monitor at the center table rose and the footage started. It was the view of a large crowd standing in light rain in front of a covered stage. A rather bulbous-nosed man in a black suit that Jack recognized as the minion of the man who assumed the presidency after the alien attack on Camp David, was speaking, and American flags were prevalent everywhere. Placards that read *'No more secrets!'* and ones declaring *'Briggs for Order and Oversight!'* were everywhere.

"…and I swear that once in office, I will expose this hidden agenda by my past predecessors inside the Oval Office. From Republican to Democrat, I will prove to the American people that we have all been lied to for over a century by the very men who claim to be our protectors. How can one man in power hide a large agency, and not have approval for such from the Congress of the United States? The men of the Presidency do not believe in Congressional oversight just as they don't believe in the Constitution itself. How can any agency be hidden and prove to be working for the American people as the Constitution calls for? I say they can't, so believe me, my fellow Americans, I will expose this corruption for what it is—an assault on the rule of law from every President from Woodrow Wilson to Barrack Obama. Corruption as they steal from other needed agencies for their budgetary needs. Ladies and gentlemen, I promise you this one thing: jail time for the criminals that so blatantly disregard our Constitution!"

On the screen, the crowd in Baton Rouge, the capitol of the congressman's home state, went wild. Europa shut down the footage.

Jack leaned back in his chair, and Xavier rubbed the attacking headache assaulting his brain.

"The president can't do anything about this maniac. You can imagine the fight on our hands if he pulls off the nomination of his party. But what can the president say? Defend that which he officially has no official knowledge of?" Niles shook his head and replaced his glasses. "With this mess and that of the Matchstick situation, I just don't know."

"Mr. Director, with Europa's rather sneaky ability, I could…"

"Don't even think about it, Doctor. We don't play this particular game *that* way. The day we interfere in an election is the day I shutter this place. Understood?"

Xavier looked from Niles to Jack with disappointment etched on his face. "Yes, sir."

"Now, let's try something that *is* in our charter, shall we." Niles turned to Collins.

"Orders, Mr. Director?"

Niles stood and went to his large desk. He opened a locked door, and brought out a thick manila envelope. He walked over, and offered it to Jack.

"I have a favor to ask, Jack. I need you to send Sarah to do a distasteful chore. One that you won't like more on a personal basis than professional."

Jack took the thick envelope. He placed it on the table, waiting.

"I usually don't like anything coming out of this room, so shoot, Niles."

"Who is the greatest tracker of valuable assets in the world?"

Jack got a sick feeling in his stomach as Niles failed to look at him.

"I need Sarah to go to London. That's where an associate is clearing something up with our friends from MI-6 as per the deal we made. Tell Sarah to give him that, and bring back Colonel Farbeaux. I need him as well as I need you. That envelope should go a long way in convincing him."

Jack felt the eyes of Xavier Morales on him as he reached for the envelope. He opened and saw the cash inside.

"That's from my private holdings. Family money. Five million dollars."

Jack pulled out another smaller sheet of paper, and scanned it.

"Henri's complete pardon for crimes committed in the United States. No stipulations, no small print. That's the President's contribution. After all of this time, he has officially kept his word to Farbeaux. He was reluctant to let Henri completely off, but he knows how much we need both you and him for what's heading our way."

"Niles, are you sure? We could be working on this Congressman Briggs debacle."

"Jack, find Matchstick. To hell with everything and everybody else."

Lake Charles, Louisiana

CONGRESSMAN and presidential nominee Harold Briggs faced the large crowd, who seemed to anticipate his next comments and the buzz began. The prop flag slowly rose behind him and the gathered throng cheered wildly. The flag was one of America's most enduring symbols which had recently been seized by far-right and far-left wing zealots for purely political purposes. The coiled snake with the banner 'Don't Tread on Me' rose high, and Briggs turned and saluted while it traveled to the top of the flagpole. He turned back to the angry attendees, and awaited the quieting of the large assembly.

"Now, a subject that should concern all Americans. That subject is: what is too much secrecy? I'll tell you when it is too much, and that is when agencies or departments are created by people in power that have no Congressional oversight, and who refuse to answer to the American people. Men and women that work behind the scenes in a shadow government, and only answer to one man—the President of the United States. Yes, you know the rumors. And I guarantee you and I have witnessed this so-called group in action during the unpleasantness of war. Such an agency actually exists—one among a possible many that usurp much needed funds from deserving areas of lawful government. I am going to expose this criminal front, and eliminate them from the national foundation. No more lies, no more stealing, and no more Presidential powers that seek to undermine the legitimate intelligence and military goals of the nation..."

TEN MINUTES LATER, Congressman Harold Briggs was hustled from the stage, and into a dark limousine for his next rally in Houston, his third for the strenuous day. He was met in the back seat by his chief of staff, Conway Fleming. When Briggs saw that Fleming had joined him after a quick flight from Washington, he excused his campaign manager, and told her he needed alone time with his chief of staff. She angrily stepped out.

"Conway, what brings you south?"

Fleming waited until the stretch limo was moving. The bearded man looked anxious. Briggs saw that as an opening to voice his feel-good moment.

"Well, did you come all this way to tell me how much you liked the speech? I would damn near give up the Presidency to see the face of that self-righteous son of bitch in the Oval Office. Next up Houston, and then on to California." He slapped Fleming on the thigh. The friendly gesture was hard enough that the assistant jumped. "Is the president still claiming his standard line?"

"That he is," Fleming said as he rubbed his leg. "Think-tank, privately owned and funded."

"Yeah, well that dog just won't hunt," Briggs snapped, and looked out of the tinted window. "A think-tank with government subsidized military personnel and a scientific community absconded from every prestigious university in the country. Yeah, right. And I'm a Yankee from that cesspool in New York."

"Oversight is not what brought me down here, Congressman."

"What then? Someone hang the wallpaper upside down in election HQ?" Briggs said with a chuckle at his own wit.

"Our friend in Europe has passed along a request. He would like you to spare a friend of theirs some time—this afternoon."

"As much as I like our new friends in Europe, do they realize we are in the midst of a presidential run?"

Fleming turned and looked out into the misty afternoon. He had warned Briggs not to get involved with a foreign entity this close to the election. But he knew the arrogant man had his stubborn ways and an infinity to self-grandiose his power. He turned back to face the congressman.

"Turning the man down is not an option."

"To hell it isn't, does he know..."

"Congressman, this is a trap you saw coming and stepped in anyway. I warned you that once you accept help from these people, it leaves the door wide open for them to ask for favors." He looked angrily at Briggs. "Favors that they expect you to grant."

"What am I supposed to do? Cancel a major rally in Houston because my European overlords says to?"

"To put it bluntly, sir, yes. You'll claim the weather got you down today and you have to postpone. I've made arrangements with the networks to rework their schedules so it shouldn't cause too much concern."

"What if I just say no?" Briggs asked as he glared at his chief of staff.

Fleming faced down Briggs and his expression told the

congressman all he needed. Fleming told him anyway. "As I said, not meeting our friend's friend is not an option."

Briggs bristled at being told what he could and could not do. He pounded the seat between he and Fleming.

Chief of Staff Fleming hit the switch, and the partition between the front and backseats slid down. "Driver, we have a change of plans. Inform security that the Houston rally has been postponed a day. Get us to Houma right away."

The driver just nodded his head and then the glass partition slid up.

Fleming opened his locked briefcase. He removed a small computer disc.

"What's that?" the congressman asked angrily.

"It's what our friends requested. Perhaps it will be enough to satisfy them for a while so we can get down to political business. Try to make that point to whoever this person is you'll be meeting. This is a dangerous favor. If the President gets wind of it, we may just vanish like so many others that mess with this strange group under the desert."

Briggs reached out and started to take the shiny disc from Fleming, but the Chief of Staff held it firmly, making sure the congressman was looking into his eyes to see the seriousness of what he was about to say.

"These are the names of American citizens, and if the rumors are true and our investigator at CIA is correct, the names here are known only to the President of the United States." He relinquished his tight grip on the disc. "You must understand Congressman, if this list gets into the open with all of our hollering and scandal talk about hidden agencies, they'll rightly suspect where the list came from."

"This deal is getting worse by the damn minute."

The limo turned off and started south toward the oil town of Houma, and a meeting that would explain in minute detail how Harold Briggs life was no longer just his own.

Apache Junction, Arizona

THE U.S. AIR FORCE LEARJET CHALLENGER 350 had gently set down at a small airstrip in Apache Junction only an hour and thirty minutes after the order from Colonel Collins had been given. The airstrip was small, and mostly unmanned with the exception of the refueling truck that had been ordered before the Learjet had left Nellis Air Force Base. After landing, they had met their contact who had delivered the Bell 700 helicopter from Phoenix-Mesa airport. Ten minutes later, Jason Ryan had them speeding toward the legendary Chato's Crawl.

Carl, who rode in the co-pilots seat next to Ryan, turned and saw Will Mendenhall arguing with the newly installed Vietnamese expatriate Van Tram. The new man in the Group officially no longer had a homeland, a punishment meted out over his cooperation with American forces during the war with the Greys, as well as the incident in Mongolia. Carl raised the right headset from his ear to hear Will explaining why Tram needed his harness on, especially when Commander Ryan was at the controls. He shook his head as the quiet Vietnamese sniper just stared at Mendenhall without saying anything. The harness was still on the seat, untouched.

Ryan, his sunglasses reflecting the light of the late afternoon sun, watched the desolate terrain slide by the canopy window. He shook his head as the scenery brought him back to the bitter time they had all faced in the summer of 2006 during the Event in the desert involving their friend and missing comrade, The Matchstick Man. It was in this general area where Ryan's life with Department 5656 had begun in earnest.

"This is why I rarely go outside at the complex," Ryan said as he adjusted the speed of the Bell helicopter.

"Why is that?" Carl asked through his mic.

"I step on the sand, and expect something to reach up and grab me to pull me under. It's the only Event file I have ever had nightmares about."

"Mr. Ryan, believe me, you're not the only one," Carl replied.

Ryan looked over at the naval Captain. He saw the sadness there.

He mentally kicked himself for even bringing it up. He half-turned in his seat, and saw a concerned Will Mendenhall who had heard the conversation over his headset.

"Sorry Captain. I have a big mouth, and even smaller brain."

Carl took a deep breath and smiled at Ryan, basically saying, *'Don't worry about it.'*

When he had brought up the battle in the desert, it also brought down a cascade of memories for Everett. The face of his deceased fiancée Lisa Willing was so associated with the desert sands it was quite impossible to separate the two. The manner of her death was a nightmare Carl faced alone.

In the back, Tram listened and looked at Will who just mouthed the words *'later',* intending to fill the team's newest member in on the story some other time.

"Okay, there she is," Ryan said, grateful to have the subject dropped.

Three miles away, they could see the house the Event Group had built for Gus Tilly and his ward, Mahjtic Tilly, better known as The Matchstick Man. Off to the side, was Gus' original desert shack he had been living in when he had discovered the injured alien in the crash debris found high above in the Superstition Mountains. The newer guard shack was the only operational building on the property, now owned by William Dawes. Young Billy had been Gus Tilly's only friend before Matchstick, and was now the brilliant business owner of Tilly Enterprises of Phoenix, Arizona. Billy had inherited everything after Gus' murder, and had instantly become a rare responsible billionaire.

The staff of sixteen guards were quartered in the large Victorian house built for Gus and Matchstick, but kept their activities limited to the bedrooms and the main floor. Carl remembered that Gus refused to live in the comfort of the new place, preferring his old shack as he dug for the rich gold strike that was found by the Event Group and given to Gus and Matchstick. The three men sitting in the chopper who had lived through it all watched as the old property came into view, and they all had the same, sad feeling of remembrance over the extraordinary Gus Tilly and his little friend, the Matchstick Man. Each man, Will, Ryan, and Everett, became silent in tribute to the friends that had died in and around Chato's Crawl and the Superstition Mountains during the opening battle with the Greys.

Carl watched as the single on-duty guard walked from the shack and waved at the incoming helicopter. The U.S. Marine guards had been informed that the famous and regulatory ruthless Captain Everett was paying them a visit today.

The Bell helicopter sat down on the pad between the house and the shack. As Carl stepped out, he ignored the salute from the Marine private who was in plain clothes. Military protocol was not foremost on his mind as he looked around. Ryan stepped up beside him, as did Mendenhall. Their eyes went to the single spot all three swore they would never look at. It was the area just off the helicopter pad where Matchstick, Gus Tilly, Pete Golding, and Dr. Denise Gilliam had been gunned down and murdered by cowardly assassins. The area showed no trace of the slaughter, but that didn't stop the ghosts of memory from rising up to greet them. Carl placed the aviator sunglasses on, and turned away toward the old ramshackle house Gus and Matchstick had once called home.

Will pulled the guard aside.

"You got our communique about the situation with Matchstick?"

"Yes, sir," the Marine said. "Been quiet here. Of course, at night, well, you hear things."

Mendenhall looked around as the evening sun washed over the desert. His eyes moved to the mountain range high above, and he shivered. He did not ridicule the Marine as he knew the place here was indeed haunted, and you would never catch him making fun of anyone who feared it. He patted the young private on the back. After the hell they lived through that long-ago summer, Will had no appreciation for the desert. Like Ryan, he didn't even like the Nevada terrain as it reminded him of the Superstition Mountains.

"We're desperately hoping Matchstick shows up here. From now on, order fifty percent alert for all guards and double the scheduled patrols. Get me a breakdown on the available manpower before I leave. There is also the situation about this Congressman Briggs and his people. Place the 'kill' signs up. No one comes near this place. If they do, place some well-aimed bullets in their asses. My orders, my responsibility."

"Yes, sir."

"Excused."

Carl and Ryan moved to the old shack while Will and Tram inspected the Victorian house, as well as checked in with Europa through Matchstick's private terminal in the house's basement.

As Everett pulled on the old screen door, the rusted spring and hinges popped free and the door flew off. He reverently picked it up. "Gus had always been meaning to get a new one as I recall."

Ryan started to say something witty and out of place, but stopped short of opening his mouth as he saw the gentle way Carl picked up the screen door and laid it against the clapboard wall.

"Maybe we can..." Carl started to say, but stopped when Ryan cut him off.

"I'll get a hammer and nails, and have it back on before we leave."

Carl sadly nodded his head, and then entered the old shack. He removed his sunglasses as he and Ryan took in the dusty furniture, the dilapidated and broken couch, and the springs of the old cast iron bed. Carl wiped the sweat from his forehead as he saw the small baby-like crib that had been Matchsticks as it sat next to the Gus larger bed. Carl cleared his throat and examined the bent and warped wood of the floor. The dust was thick and undisturbed. No one had been inside for a very long time.

He spied something on the old dresser that Gus had salvaged from some old house in Chato's Crawl. He walked over and picked up a faded picture in an old-fashioned bubble-type glass frame. He smiled as he saw Gus as a handsome twenty-year old Marine second lieutenant. His saucer cap was tilted jauntily on his head and he looked every bit as formidable as any man ever to wear the uniform. He saw the young, cocky smile on his face, and knew from his history that would be the last photo of Gus that he would ever be spied smiling in. A year after that photo had been snapped, Gus had lived through the most gruesome battle of the Korean War—the Chosin Reservoir, where Americans had to strap the bodies of their frozen buddies and comrades onto the side of tanks to bring them home again from that frigid, desolate valley. As Carl looked at the photo, he was reminded of Gus saying that was why he always loved the desert. He never wanted to be cold again. His eyes moved to another frame on the dresser. He reached out and lifted a smaller, far more recent picture. He swallowed as he looked at a stern Gus Tilly, and in his arms was the child-sized Matchstick Tilly. A young, smiling Billy Dawes, Gus and Matchstick's only friend besides the men and women of the Event Group, was beside them. Carl cleared his throat again, and then handed both photos and frames over to Ryan.

"These go back with us," Carl said as Ryan saw what had made the Captain go silent upon entering the shack. "No one's been here. Let's take a ride up the mountain and see if any of the miners have seen or heard anything."

"Matchstick never could have made it this far. We should concentrate our efforts closer to home," Ryan said sadly.

"We cover all the bases. We owe the little fella that."

"Uh, have Will take one of the SUV's up. I think I'll hang out here and fix that door."

"You alright?" Carl asked as Jason wiped his nose.

"Yeah, sure. It's just the dust in this place," Ryan said in self-defense.

Carl slapped Ryan on the back as he left the shack, knowing that the feelings Ryan had was the exact reason he wanted to leave. The ghosts here *were* overwhelming.

Two hours later, the Bell helicopter lifted free of the helipad and the silent crew started their journey back home to Nevada. They had only managed to bring the haunting nightmare of Matchstick's, Gus, Pete's, and Denise's death back to the forefront of their minds.

SOON THERE WOULD BE MORE than just ghosts haunting the men and women of Department 5656.

Houma, Louisiana

THE SIKORSKY S-92 heavy-lift helicopter was ready for takeoff immediately after Congressman Harold Briggs stepped aboard. Briggs was on a cell phone, and ignored the crew chief's offer of a set of protective headphones.

"Just tell them I'm a little under the weather after the Baton Rouge rally. No, this is something I have to take care of privately." Briggs saw the large passenger compartment door close much to his surprise. He hurriedly ended the call to his campaign manager in Houston, and pocketed the phone. "What are you doing? We were supposed to be joined by a Mr. Sokol. Or are you just wasting my valuable time?"

The crew chief did not say anything in answer, but insisted the congressman take the offered headphones. Briggs reached for them.

"If this means the bastard stood me up, he needs to be informed I am missing a substantial rally in Houston. Your bosses said this man is very important. I have given him the courtesy of this meeting, and he stands me up like some lowly congressional aide?"

The crew chief just raised his brows underneath his crash helmet, and moved away to one of ten empty passenger seats without explaining. There was plenty of room on the flight as the large crew chopper was normally maintained and operated by Felson Air Services, a large company that supplied transport for oil field crew personnel to offshore drilling and production platforms in the Gulf of Mexico. As the Sikorsky shot into the overcast air, Briggs angrily placed the headphones over his ears, meticulously aligning them as not to muss his perfect hair.

"Now, where is he, this Mr. Sokol?" he said into the mic.

The crew chief still refused to say anything. His eyes looked out of the window at the passing grey-colored Gulf of Mexico as if Briggs wasn't even present.

"Good afternoon, Congressman."

Briggs pressed the headphones harder into his ears as the voice came across.

"Sorry about the misdirection, but since you attract so much attention these days, I had little choice."

"Who are you and where?" Briggs asked.

"Oh, I couldn't pass up the opportunity to pilot this wonderful Sikorsky. Did you know he was a Russian immigrant to your country?"

"Who?" Briggs asked, totally confused as to what the voice was referring to. He stood, angrily stalking past the crew chief, and went to the separation panel between the passenger compartment and the cockpit. His eyes widened when he saw a man in, not a pilot's coveralls, but a rich satin suit. The stranger was piloting the large helicopter without the assistance of a co-pilot.

"I speak of the engineer who designed this aircraft. He was Russian. Small trivial fact I know, but I dare say a prideful one."

"Uh-huh," Briggs said, not very interested at all. "May I ask just what in the hell you're doing? And where is the pilot?"

The man at the stick applied power, and the Sikorsky shot higher into the air. He adjusted his microphone, then flipped a switch, and turned a knob.

"Houma Center, this is Felson flight 102, climbing to four thousand feet. ETA ten minutes to platform *'Mystery Deep'* exploratory well number three." All communication was done in clear and concise English.

After the pilot received a response, he removed his right headphone, and looked to his right. "Join me, Congressman. I have some questions I want to ask."

"Not before you tell me just who in the hell you are!"

"Why, I'm the man you came here to meet. My name is Dmitri Sokol."

Briggs was shocked to see the man in the expensive suit as he manipulated the complicated controls without much effort. The man was dark haired, and fit the description he was given on who he would be meeting. There was no explanation as to this man's value to his campaign.

Harold Briggs struggled to fit through the tight opening, but finally managed to squeeze his rotund frame into the vacant co-pilots seat. "Now, what is this about?" Briggs saw the arrogance of the man as he smiled. "I cancelled a very important rally because..."

The Sikorsky banked sharply to the right, slamming Briggs hard into the firewall and window. The pilot straightened the ship out, and looked at Briggs. The Congressman didn't like the way he had been cut off.

"Apologies, old man. It's been a while. Now, I believe you have a few questions to answer regarding your ongoing efforts to expose a certain group in the Nevada desert. There are a few things I need to know before I can assist you in this endeavor."

"I go through higher contacts than you. I don't even know who the hell you are."

Sokol turned and faced the fat man from Washington. The smile was noticeably absent. "The ball has been handed off to me, Congressman. That is all you need to know. Any assistance from us that you need will now go through me and my offices."

Briggs didn't like being on the defensive, no matter how dangerous his chief of staff said they were. He stared straight out of the windscreen as splatters of rain danced against the glass.

"Our aims have always been three-fold, Mr. Briggs. Number one, assist you in your goal of becoming the most powerful man in the world," he smiled as he considered the saying a bit out of date. "Number two, in exchange for that assistance, we expect you to find certain men and women that can assist in securing a more prosperous working relationship with your country. One that will benefit both nations. Number three, to help bury the hatchet, so to speak, between east and west. The men I represent are not satisfied with the status quo. You will assist us in changing this." He looked over at Briggs. "Now, as your American saying goes, Mr. Briggs, the gloves have to come off. You will give us what we want or that elusive group in the desert will not be the only thing exposed to your countrymen. You will be also. I don't think your fellow countrymen would appreciate another scandal as far as foreign assistance in a

Presidential election. I think that would be just a tad detrimental to your goal."

"Just what is it that you want?"

"You have a list that was compiled of former and current agents of this mysterious Group. I and a colleague of mine need those names. Of course, our concern in this matter will have no adverse effect on your determination to expose this group. Names, just that simple."

Harold Briggs felt his heart speed up. He swallowed his newfound fear, now knowing why this meeting had been called, and why the extreme security measure of meeting in the air.

"The list we have is very protected. Some may not even be former members. I have to say no. I will not expose members of this Group even to you and your bosses."

"I believe that is called 'you're missing the point', Congressman."

"This was not the agreement. We only put a period on this deal *after* I become President. You attempt to blackmail me, and I go straight to the FBI."

Sokol laughed. This time Briggs could see real mirth in the man's eyes.

"Soon you will meet someone who will dissuade you of all treacherous action, Congressman."

"What do you mean? Are we to meet another cockroach like you coming into the light?"

"Mr. Briggs, if you plan on winning this election," Sokol reached over and harshly grabbed the congressman in the crotch area, squeezing as hard as he could, "you have to grow a pair of these!"

Briggs felt his stomach do rolls as the pain hit his testicles. He grabbed the area and rubbed.

"My home office believes it time for you to understand what is at stake here for all concerned, Harold. I need that list of names, and I have just the person to get it out of you." Sokol hit the radio transmit button on the collective. "*Mystery Deep*, this is Felson flight 102, requesting permission to land on platform one. Over."

"*Felson 102, cleared to land. Over.*"

With his testicles aching and his heart once again racing, Harold Briggs looked up and saw the oil platform.

"What is this?" he asked, pain lacing his question.

"This is called international waters, Mr. Congressman." Sokol smiled and this time it was genuine. "And you're here to meet a very close associate and advisor of my very special group who can explain things in much greater detail than myself."

The oil platform was large. Briggs could see many men in hardhats roaming the steel decks as they approached.

"Welcome to *Mystery Deep*, Congressman Briggs."

CHAPTER THREE

London, England

The red flags that hung outside the modest building were the only consideration toward advertisement and company designation the operators deemed necessary for one of the world's oldest and most prestigious auction houses. Famous for the crowded galleries that were always choked with the rich and famous as they bought up the world's heritage. These patrons, for the most part, never knew the finest works were never viewed by the public. Instead, they were held in trust for private perusal and bidding when legal circumstances called for a more cautious approach to dealing in rare finds. Privacy is what some buyers craved, even more than the treasures they sought to own.

"As you can see, Mr. Constantine, this piece has been appraised at a most reasonable twenty-six point five-million pounds. The reason for such a valued piece going for so little is the fact that there has been some difficulty in acquiring a proper line of ownership dating back to the fifteenth century. While this object is still verifiably authentic, the current owner would prefer to avoid any legal entanglement in its auctioning. His preferred method is for a private discussion of its sale. In other word's Mr. Constantine..."

"It is stolen."

The well-dressed auctioneer lost his smile. "Well, sir, perhaps that would not have been my choice of words."

"But it is my choice," the bearded man said from the ornate chair in the darkened office. The man looked over at the display table and the well-lighted object sitting upon it. "Let's not play games here, Mr. Chenowith. You have my letters of introduction. My privacy in these matters is of utmost importance. The names on that letter of introduction should demonstrate how dear I hold my relationships to friends in high places. The gratuity I have given to your house should also attest to my seriousness in acquiring the object in question." The bearded man slowly rose from his chair and once again stood before the private exhibit. His right hand removed a pure white kerchief from his suit pocket, and placed it over his hand as his fingers caressed the blade in its jeweled encrusted sheath.

"You must admit, the item is mesmerizing, is it not, Mr. Constantine?"

The bearded man turned, and looked at the auctioneer who conducted these clandestine meetings once every two weeks for private buyers. He adeptly removed the curved blade from its sheath and examined it.

"The reward placed by the Vatican is now nearing the cost of the item itself. I believe the archivists want the thief who stole it more than they want the dagger back."

The Englishman didn't like the comment, and he showed it by setting the blade next to the sheath, and then placing a white silk covering over the knife. He moved to his desk, sat down, then picked up a pen, and started acting like he was working.

"Good day, Mr. Constantine. I see you're not as serious a buyer as I was led to believe."

The bearded man smiled as he faced the crooked auctioneer. "I only bring up Vatican interest because I am the thief who stole it, Mr. Chenowith."

The man at the desk looked up, the blood slowly draining from his face.

"Actually, the blade never belonged to Lucius Pontius Aquila. It is a well-known fact that according to Vatican archives, and verified in an obscure and small passage in a letter from Mark Antony to the Roman Senate. It proclaimed that immediately after the murder of Julius Caesar, Senator Lucius Pontius Aquila threw his knife into the sewers of Rome for fear of retaliation after the murder had been derided by Mark Antony himself in his famous *'friends, Romans, countrymen, lend me your ears'* speech. So, you see Mr. Chenowith, the blade *always* has been a fake."

"Impossible," Chenowith said as he angrily stood and stormed to the viewing stand. He ripped the covering off the blade and its ornate sheath.

"You know, I never met the person responsible for actually getting the forgery out of the Vatican archives. I only dealt with his go-between. It wasn't until I met this mousy little computer whiz in America—who works with some very disturbing and not very friendly people, I might add—that told me who really stole the item in question."

The man turned and stared at the smiling, bearded man in front of him. He was about to protest in what his opinion was the most ridiculous statement he had ever heard, when the double doors to his office opened and several men in suits entered.

"Your name isn't Charles Chenowith, but Gaspésie Marzetti, formerly a lowly clerk in the Vatican archives."

The four plainclothes men from Scotland Yard took the stunned auctioneer by the arm as the bearded man took the blade from its stand and then slammed it tip first into the viewing holder. He snapped the blade off in a clean and vicious snap, then tossed the handle to the man formerly known as Chenowith, who bobbled it, nearly dropping it to the floor.

"It wasn't even that impressive a fake. I felt very insulted when I examined it twenty years ago."

As three of the officers led the thief out of his office, a fourth stopped and faced the bearded man.

"Her Majesty's Government thanks you for your assistance in this tasteless matter. Lord Durnsford also sends you his regards. What MI-6 had to do with you, I'll never know. But there you have it."

"Let's just say I owed a debt, and it is now paid in full, shall we? Just ask Lord Durnsford to please forward the results to his friend in America; that part of my debt is hereby settled. And to also thank Doctor Morales for his assistance in tracking this rather unsavory thief."

The man from Scotland Yard smiled, and dipped his head.

"As you wish, Mr. Constantine, or should I say, Colonel Farbeaux?" The inspector smiled again and walked out of the office.

Henri smiled, and then saw the sheath still on the display shelf. He reached out and took it, feeling the rubies that encrusted it. His smile grew. He pocketed the very real jewels and gold of the forged knife sheath that was used to make the fake look authentic to the naked eye. The sheath and jewels were on loan from Christies Auction House, but that fact seemed to slip the officers' minds in their haste to make the arrest.

Henri Farbeaux walked out three hundred thousand dollars richer than when he had walked in. If Henri was anything, he was an opportunist.

COLONEL HENRI FARBEAUX prided himself on his ability to vanish whenever the need called for it. Having just stolen a very valuable item from the Christies collection was one of those times. For Henri, hiding meant staying in some very disreputable establishments, which made him, for the most part, feel right at home.

Shamus O'Brien's was about as disreputable as taverns come. For the colonel, it not only afforded a certain comfort in hiding, but also a hidden bedroom on the third floor. O'Brien, a wanted man from his days supplying weapons to the now-peaceful Irish Republican Army, had assisted Henri numerous times in the past in escaping the London authorities after transactions of a less-than-legal origin.

It was O'Brien who came to Henri's table with a brown paper bag. He slid into the booth beside the world's greatest antiquities thief and smiled. Without a word, Henri slid over a tightly wrapped piece of white jeweler's paper, and O'Brien placed the paper bag over it.

"I think you'll find this covers my current bill," Henri said.

"I'm sure it does, old friend. You have never failed to amaze your friends and influence your enemies." O'Brien was a heavyset man who had lost all political desires for his once violent world. He reached under the paper bag and pulled the four small jewels away before pocketing them.

"Don't you want to appraise them."

"Colonel, I have known many thieves in my life; I being one of them. You have never undervalued any payment to me. You are by far the most honorable thief I have ever dealt with. And that includes me." O'Brien lifted a bottle, poured Henri a drink, and then himself. "I'm curious, Henri."

"Oh, oh, when an Irishman gets curious, people of the world get nervous," Henri said with a smile as he sipped his freshened drink.

"It's your eyes, Henri. In stealing from idiots and top of the line thieves like Christies, you used to take immense pride. Now your eyes tell this old Irishman that you don't enjoy it. Hell Darlin', I don't think it was ever about the money or the artifacts or the bank accounts you have spread all over the world. It was because you could take from people you have always considered undeserving. If they owned it, you took it, even though I doubt you ever really desired it. Now, the light and thrill has gone from you, my boyo. It's a woman, is it not, laddie?"

"I miss the old Shamus. Never asked questions. Never pondered the honesty of others."

O'Brien swallowed the shot of whiskey in one gulp, then burped. Henri shook his head in mock distaste. "I'm far too old to care anymore, Henri old man. If it is a woman, she's stepping on your game. You just don't have the desire anymore. The old Henri is gone." Shamus poured himself another whiskey. "I believe I'll miss the old

Henri," he drank, and then stood up as he slid the paper bag over to Farbeaux.

"There was once a dream of a woman, quite ordinary but magnificent. But I woke up from that dream, Shamus. She haunts another's waking and sleeping hours now." Henri smiled and then finished his drink.

"Well Colonel, I wish you luck in all that you do, Laddie." He leaned closer to Henri. "I suggest you use that new shaving kit in the bag, and cut that beard off quickly."

Henri got a confused look on his face.

"That's what I mean Henri old boy, you're losing your touch for the game. You think that beard is a disguise, but *she* tracked you down anyway." Shamus laughed. It was a deep reverberating sound inside the small pub. He stepped back and waved at a small figure at the bar. "Maybe you haven't woken completely from that dream old friend."

Henri looked up just as the woman hopped from the stool and approached.

"Hello Henri."

Colonel Henri Farbeaux stared in shock at seeing the newly married Sarah McIntire Collins.

SARAH WAS SITTING at a small round table that overlooked an alley through a sliver of a window. Her eyes moved from the window to the bathroom door where Henri was shaving. She heard the water shut off, and the door opened. Usually she would have been terrified Henri would pull an old Farbeaux stunt by exiting the bathroom without a shirt, or worse, any clothing at all, but this time he was completely dressed and well-shaved.

"Not interested." Henri tossed a white towel into a chair.

"Henri, we need your help with this," Sarah said as she stood and faced Farbeaux.

"My days of getting shot at and assisting those that would rather have me deep in the ground are over, my little Sarah." Henri poured two glasses of white wine. "Sorry, this is all I have."

"Kind of sacrilegious...wine in an Irish Pub, isn't it?" Sarah said, taking the offered glass.

"What can I say? I'm a rogue as you've said many times before. Now, I have a chartered plane to catch," he said as he drank from his glass.

Sarah placed her glass on the table, and approached Henri. "Colonel, this is important. We think Matchstick may still be alive and lost out there. You're the best tracker, outside of Jack and Carl, and the best investigator of historical mysteries this side of Charlie Ellenshaw."

Farbeaux walked over to his suitcase, and placed cufflinks in his expensive shirt sleeves. He shook his head. "I must admit to never having stolen a dead body before, and that is what happened you know. Your small alien was stolen by thieves. So, tell me little Sarah, what besides some unreliable DNA test says he's alive. What kind of expertise do you think I have that could possibly assist you?"

"Henri, I'm maybe the only person in the world that does have a higher opinion of you. Only because for some reason you have shown me a side of you that few have ever seen. If others have seen what I have, I think that low appraisal of your career might be different. Why only me, Henri?"

Farbeaux stopped fiddling with his cufflinks, and fixed Sarah with a sad look. "If you have to ask Sarah, you're not as perceptive as I have given you credit for all of these years."

Sarah swallowed hard, then picked up the glass of wine, and drained it as Henri had done before. She knew why Niles had suggested Jack send her to London. For having just been married, Sarah was feeling she had been used because the Frenchman always had a soft spot for her. She understood, but she felt like a jerk for playing along while knowing Henri saw things differently. She was hurting him, and Jack and even Niles may or may not care. Even for the sake of Matchstick, it was a step too far, and it was just now that Sarah realized it. She sat hard into the chair.

"I understand this ill-advised wedding has cost you your military rank and your career?" Henri asked as he shrugged into his suit jacket.

Sarah didn't answer, she just stared at the small tabletop.

"I'll admit, my little Sarah, when I heard Jack was going to ask this of you, my heart sank. It has not resurfaced. I may be a lot of things, but a man that interferes with another's marriage is not one of them." Henri closed and latched his suitcase. "So, on that pitiful note, I bid you *adieu*."

"Henri, Director Compton said to give you this, in hopes we can persuade you." She held out the large, manila envelope.

Farbeaux took a deep breath and then reluctantly accepted it. He broke the seal and peered inside. His brows rose.

"The money is from Director Compton's private family account. The complete pardon letter is from the President," Sarah said as she bypassed her glass and chugged the wine straight from the bottle. She swallowed and then watched as Henri read the Presidential pardon. When finished, Farbeaux tossed the envelope full of cash back to Sarah, who fumbled it and then caught it. He did, however, pocket the pardon from the president. Then Henri did something Sarah had never expected him to do. He reached down, pulled her up from the chair, and kissed her deeply. Sarah pushed back, but then her lips met his more willingly. The Frenchman slowly released Sarah and she sat back down hard into the chair.

"That is the only payment I have ever desired from you Sarah. Tell Director Compton, this one is on me."

Sarah was stunned as she watched Henri lift his suitcase and turn for the door.

"Well, I suppose you have a tracker and thief back on the payroll. What you do with him going forward is up to you, *Mrs.* Collins."

Sarah smiled and followed Henri out of the hidden room.

Mystery Deep, Exploratory Well # 3,
sixty-eight miles off the coast of Louisiana

AS THE LARGE Sikorsky sat down on the helipad on the uppermost platform of the immense rig, Briggs was amazed to see men and women in varying uniforms and outfits. Some wore oilfield clothing complete with hardhats while others wore white, blue, or yellow laboratory coats. As the landing team secured the wheels of the giant helicopter, a large man in tan work-clothing slid the crew door open, and gestured for the congressman to follow him. Of the mysterious Mr. Sokol, he had already left the helicopter pad, and was nowhere to be seen. The escort reached for the congressman's briefcase, but Briggs held it tight and glared at the hard-hatted man.

As Briggs was led to a steel staircase, he was surprised to see men working at drilling. The high derrick above their heads was for far more than window dressing. It looked as if this was a working drill platform. The congressman dealt with a lot of oil company contracts, and had inspected many platform's during his time office. He knew a working structure when he saw it. So, if the *Mystery Deep* platform was some form of ruse, it was an expensive one. The man led Briggs to a large square shaft five levels above the helipad. He pushed a button, and two sliding doors opened. When they stepped in, Briggs had to force his ear drums to 'pop' as the elevator closed its doors, and became hermetically sealed.

They started down. As they descended, the congressman's ears adjusted and he became more comfortable. Then his eyes widened when he realized they had entered the elevator on the extreme bottom level of the platform. By the time their descent stopped, he felt they'd traveled at least ten floors beneath the sea.

"I have been in Louisiana politics for many years son, and know just about every drilling outfit in the Gulf, but why is it I have never heard of this operation before?"

"Sir, I only work here. I'm sure your host will answer any questions you may have." The man waited a moment and then the double doors slid open. He gestured for Briggs to step out.

The congressman did not like the smirk on his escorts face. "You're not coming?" he asked, holding tightly to his briefcase.

"I am not cleared for the subsurface levels, sir. However, you will be met."

Briggs hesitantly stepped out. The doors closed and he heard the pneumatic whine as the elevator rose. He looked around, and was astonished by the scene before him. The area in which he stood reminded him of an exceptionally large reception area. Only it was void of any administrative greeters or welcoming accoutrements. The floor was polished steel that reflected the wavy aquatic light from outside. He could see the Gulf of Mexico mere inches from the hardened glass of the rig. He stepped up, and peered through the eight-inch-thick glass. He saw fish and divers as they welded bracing for the ongoing platform construction.

When a hand touched his back, he jumped and turned. He was looking at a beautiful dark-haired young woman dressed in a business pant suit and tie. She held out her hand to the congressman.

"Congressman Briggs, I would like to welcome you aboard the *Mystery Deep* exploratory platform." She waited for Briggs to accept the welcoming gesture, which he hesitantly did but not before admiring the beauty before him with his roaming eyes. The woman, Russian or Ukrainian by her slight accent, finally managed to pull her manicured fingers from Briggs sweaty grip.

"If you'll follow me, Mr. Sokol has arranged for an early supper." She turned and gestured to an industrial looking set of double doors. They opened automatically when approached. She again gestured for Briggs to precede her into the closed off area. He hesitated, then walked through.

What he saw was a dining area that could have been ensconced in any fine hotel or private billionaires' residence. The long table had chairs at each end, and there were place settings for two. Fine crystal ringed even finer china and bright, shiny silverware.

The woman walked to one of the chairs and pulled it out. "I hope you are fond of Chilean Sea Bass, Congressman. Mr. Sokol likes to stay local in his choice of menu."

Briggs said nothing, but he did sit. The briefcase was securely placed beneath the table near his feet.

He heard a loud hiss, another set of double doors at the opposite end of the large room opened, and his host came through wiping his hands on a towel. He had changed suits, and when he approached, he tossed the towel across the room where it landed on a bronze bust of Vladimir Putin and draped over its dark features. He went to the table where the woman had pulled out his chair and he sat. Then she started to pour wine.

"Thank you, my dear. Mr. Briggs, this is my assistant Vexilla Trotsky."

The woman bowed her head as she poured a nice white wine for the congressman.

"I imagine the name sounds familiar?" Dmitri Sokol said, as he opened a cloth napkin and placed it in his lap.

"Vaguely," Briggs answered as he sipped the wine, and then looked closely and appreciatively at the glass.

"Her Great-Grandfather was Lev Davidovich Bronstein, or better known to you and your countrymen as Leon Trotsky. Soon after the Bolsheviks came to power in 1918, he became a very powerful man. However, after Lenin's death, he fell out of favor. Stalin sent him into exile where he was murdered on his orders in Mexico. The strange dialect you hear from my assistant is a bastardized form of Spanish and Russian." As the woman placed the bottle of wine down, her hand was taken by Sokol and squeezed. "We have that in common, you see. She is very loyal because both of our families were ruined by the great Stalin. We have both sworn that men such as he will never rule our lives, nor the lives of our people again." Sokol kissed the woman's hand, then shooed her away. Sokol sipped the glass of wine just as six men in red waiter's attire entered. They placed a large china plate with steaming Chilean Sea Bass. "I hope you enjoy—luxurious meals are one of my weaknesses."

Briggs waited while the waiters left the dining area. Then he placed the fork he never intended to use down on the polished tabletop.

"My people failed to realize we were dealing with Russians," he said as he drained the crystal glass of wine.

Sokol, after biting into his meal, wiped his mouth, then stood. He retrieved the bottle and walked to the far end of the table, and poured Briggs another glass. "That's the problem with the world today,

Congressman. The separation of the human race by men that aren't worthy to make that decision." He set the wine bottle down, then went back to his chair, and placed the napkin back onto his lap. "You see, men like you and I need to realize that there is a much better way." Sokol started to eat again as Briggs watched the confident man before him.

"What is this about…Mr. Sokol is it?"

The Russian wiped his lips again. He sipped more wine, and fixed Briggs with an unsmiling glare.

"When you achieve your goal in the political arena, I expect you and I will work closely together in changing the status-quo." Sokol downed his glass just as his assistant made another appearance. "Until we are ready, I need to satisfy certain elements back home, namely the very men you have been dealing with. My eventual elimination of these gentlemen may be the only way that you are ever truly free of them."

His assistant walked to the table, and poured her employer another glass of wine.

"That is what this is for," Briggs held up the briefcase and then sat it back down. "I plan on fulfilling their request and that will end our relationship."

Sokol chuckled, then placed a fork full of Sea Bass into his mouth. "I am always amazed how easily it is for Americans to lie to themselves. I guess it's a form of delusion, as if you can control elements around you by telling yourself something that doesn't meet the requirements of reality. I've learned from past experience that is a misnomer, sir."

"If I wanted to listen to someone's warped opinion on delusional leadership, I would just turn on the television and watch that fool in the White House. His embarrassment over this hidden Group in Nevada, and my election is the only reason we are even talking."

"As I was saying Congressman, as soon as I am in a position to please the men above me in power, the sooner I can remove them and insert my own play of the cards. If what you have in that case is what was requested by these men, the sooner I can achieve their goals, and then eventually, mine. That goal is to take charge, and then you and I can make a new world. Together. When I eliminate certain enemies of my enemies, they will have no choice but admit to my growing power, Congressman. The names you have will help me achieve this. Trust, you see. If my superiors trust me, they will never see the knife that plunges into their backs. More wine?" Sokol smiled and finished his dinner.

CONGRESSMAN HAROLD BRIGGS, Independent nominee for his party to run for the highest office in the land was near panic as he watched Dmitri Sokol eat his desert. After the extraordinary claim made by his host, Briggs realized he was so far in over his head he saw no way to ever draw a free breath again.As Sokol placed his napkin onto his plate and watched as the waiter took it away, he fixed Briggs with a calm and collected look, as if he had not just delivered a speech that would rival anything Adolph Hitler would have given to his cronies in 1933. The man seemed not concerned in the least about divulging his plan, and that was because Harold knew he was already in the rabbit's snare. If he gave over the computer disc inside his briefcase his life would be over, and he was just realizing deservedly so.

"So, I believe my superiors requested something from you. I assume it's in that case you so reverently guard."

"You intend these people harm just so you can gain the confidence of men as low-handed as you?"

"An unfortunate way to put it, Congressman, but in short, yes. What is your American saying, you can't make a cake without breaking some eggs?"

He held the case up once more. "These *eggs* are still Americans. Men and women not responsible for the illegal situation our presidency has placed them in. If I refuse to go further with you and your plan, it seems you may be placed in a very leaky boat, my friend."

Sokol stood, lifted the bottle of wine, and walked to the far end. He started to pour, but Briggs placed his hand over the glass as if this would say, in no uncertain terms, that the pleasantries were now over.

The Russian smiled, moved back to his chair where he poured himself more wine, and then sat.

"In case you haven't noticed, Congressman, you are at the tiller of that leaky vessel. Perhaps you need to meet my ace in the hole," he chuckled at the American saying. "My new friend that will make all of this, and so much more, possible. I hope sincerely he becomes your new friend also."

Briggs watched as Sokol downed the rest of his wine, then placed the empty bottle upside down in the ice bucket as if putting a period on a very long and disturbing sentence in a horror novel. He stood again, and walked to the double doors on the opposite end of the large dinning room. He opened them and then vanished.

Briggs looked around nervously. He heard the creaking of steel against steel as the large platform was brushed by the angry sea growing around them. The feeling of movement made the congressman quite nauseated.

The lights went out, and even the outside sea view was cut off as steel blinds crashed down and sealed the windows. Briggs was so startled that when he suddenly stood, he knocked over his wine glass. He heard the sound of pumps and the soft hum of the air conditioning system as he felt around in the pitch blackness.

"Hello? This is very amateurish, I assure you. I haven't been afraid of the dark since..." He stopped mid-sentence when he heard the double doors open again. He tried desperately to peer into the darkness. "Sokol, stop these silly games."

Silence.

"Turn on the damn lights!" he called out angrily.

He heard shuffling noises coming from the direction of the double doors. The unplaceable sound was growing closer.

"It's very disconcerting being stalked by something you can't see, is it not Congressman?"

"Where are you, Sokol?"

"Safely out of the way of the predicament you find yourself. We never really know how our new associate will take to someone."

"What predicament? I insist you turn on the lights, and get me back to my people."

"I'm afraid that is no longer up to me."

"Then who is it…"

The long fingers caressed the left side of Briggs' face and he yelped, jumping away, and knocking over his briefcase. What ever had touched him was sickeningly warm, and he could still feel the trace of something that felt like slime. He viciously wiped at his face.

"Please, you've made whatever sadistic point you wanted, now turn on the goddamn lights!"

"My associate thinks you are in need of more persuasion, Congressman. He wants assurance you will continue down the path of cooperation," came the voice through what Briggs now knew were speakers arrayed around the room. "I would like you to meet the gentleman whose power will make all of our desires move from mere wishful thought to reality. Congressman Briggs, his actual name is damn near impossible to pronounce correctly, so we just call him, Asmodius."

Briggs felt his legs twitter as if the start of a leg cramp. Then he felt his feet slowly come free of the floor. He tried in vain to keep contact with the polished steel but was helpless to anchor himself. Then he felt static electricity course through his body, and his hair stood on end. He tried to call out, but felt his throat tighten as if being choked, all the while his black shoes kicked out trying to find some form of purchase. He felt as if he were nothing but a child's doll being held at arm's length. Then his nostrils caught the stench of something wholly unpleasant. It was as if a dead fish had lain too long in the Louisiana heat. Then, he heard the shuffling sound again, and his eyes widened as he realized that he wasn't being held by whatever had entered the chamber. He was suspended in the air by some power that was merely projected by whatever had joined him in the dark. After a while, he was slowly lowered to the floor where he grabbed the back of a chair for support. Slowly, the static electricity drained from his body. He breathed heavily trying to get his fear under some form of control.

The lights suddenly flared to a brilliance Briggs wasn't prepared for forcing him to close his eyes. He blinked several times when his vision finally cleared, and he saw only Sokol's assistant, Vexilla Trotsky, standing by the double doors. She was holding a small laptop computer, and wasn't even affording him her lovely smile, which she had been showing all evening. He started to relax believing it was all just a put-on show just to scare him. He let go of the chair back, and then gathered what courage he had remaining, brazenly puffing out his chest. But that was when he sensed the movement behind him. He slowly turned, and that was when Congressman Harold Briggs suffered the first near stroke of his life. The entity known as Asmodius was towering over the smaller man. His yellow eyes penetrated to his brain, and he noted the recognition in the horrid creature's face and body. It opened its mouth, and then leaned down as its long, dark tongue came free of the scaly lips, and licked the congressman's left side of his face. He cowered when the moistness made his gorge threaten to rise. As he opened his eyes, he saw the Grey's long, clear teeth, and he cringed in terror. Then the creature moved back three steps and watched Briggs. Its head moved from side to side as it examined him like a bug under a microscope.

"My God! Are you people insane?" Briggs stuttered.

The creature slowly brought up its left arm, and extended the long digits of its hand, palm up. A ball of blue light started spinning as if it were a small globe of bright electrical flame. He was forced to step back when the spinning ball of neon-like light slowed, and then blue and green sparks exploded. Briggs went to a knee as the ball changed shape into bright red lines that shot free of the Grey's hand. They formed first into a large star that expanded into a glowing four-pointed star, and then as Briggs eyes widened in fright, a green circle of electrical light circled the star. Then the creature closed its large four fingered hand, and the sparks flew and the pentangle vanished as if it had never been. The Grey gave Briggs a sickening grin, exposing his long, clear canines. The yellow eyes bore into his own, and he had to turn from the sight.

"The briefcase, please, Congressman," said the woman who watched on as if this whole thing had been planned from the outset.

He started to bend over when the Grey moved swiftly, knocking the congressman from his feet. It stood over the case. Then to Briggs' amazement, the creature's hand rose, and then waved over the case. It rose into the air. With his eyes bulging, Briggs heard and then saw the case's clasps pop one at a time. The lid slowly opened, and the disc came floating free into the air. Briggs jumped when the case fell to the flooring of the dining area. On wobbly legs, the congressman backed up so fast, he stumbled into the long table, and fell down next to the case. With a flick of the long-nailed fingers, the disc flew across the room, and the woman deftly caught it. The Grey's yellow eyes never left Briggs.

As she inserted the disc into the laptop, she moved to the table, and sat down as the drive warmed up. Briggs never noticed this because he was staring into the most frightening visage he had ever seen. He had been debriefed on the Greys after the war, had even attended an autopsy of one of their casualties, but until now he had never seen a live specimen in person, and it sickened him. As he lay on the floor, the creature leaned over. With a curled hand the grey-colored finger rose into the air, and so did Briggs. He floated as if he were lying on his back in the water.

"Asmodius, put him down, please," the woman said absentmindedly as she was giving the laptop commands.

The fingers circled in the air and Briggs felt his body cartwheel as if he were spinning around the sun. Then he was thrown into a chair, and the giant Grey hissed as if in warning. Its white, stringy hair flew from side to side as its entire body shook. Then Briggs heard the doors open, and his eyes gratefully turned that direction. Sokol walked in with a glass of amber liquid, and handed the glass of whiskey along with his smile over to a stunned and visibly shaken Congressman Harold Briggs. Sokol patted the man on the back in a mocking comforting gesture.

"I believe Asmodius is attempting to say, 'welcome to the team', Congressman."

"Wh…what is that thing?" he stammered as he tried to keep his heart from bursting through his chest. "It...it... looks nothing like the dead Grey's that I have been briefed on."

Sokol only smiled as he looked over at his assistant, and saw the first few briefing photos Briggs had delivered come onto the laptop's screen. The creature was still looking threatening at the frightened congressman. Then without moving the burning yellow eyes from him, waved a clawed hand toward the laptop, it shook and made both Sokol and his assistant jump in reverence to its power. A swirling ball of light appeared, and spun as Earth would in its gravitational rotation. Then the image pixelized, and the Grey opened its hand wide. Amazed, the three humans watched as the faces started to appear from thin air, rotating in five-foot projected representations around the darkened room. The Grey smiled, making Briggs want to void the wine he had consumed.

The unidentified photos absconded by Briggs' private investigators, himself and several traitorous entities inside the intelligence agencies, was that of the Matchstick Man and spinning beside it was a photo of Alice Hamilton, Anya Korvesky, Virginia Pollock and a man from Jack Collins security team, Sergeant Pete Sanchez.

CHAPTER FOUR

**Lake Mead National Recreation Area,
Ninety-Four Miles, East of Las Vegas**

Chain lightning crisscrossed the night sky sending most campers into fear-induced hiding spots. The lake, normally calm, was sending waves of Colorado River water crashing onto the ragged shoreline. Boats, normally sitting calmly at anchor, were tossed about as if they were at sea instead of the manmade lake created by the construction of the Boulder Dam. Tents were shaken and knocked down as the summer storm struck in earnest. The owner and operator of one of the smaller bait, tackle, and convenience stops was no different than the tourists when it came to fear of summer storms in the desert. He closed his store early, and made for the apartment he owned above the shop.

Bob Davies watched from an upstairs window as the lightning increased. Every boom that thundered from the sky told the men and women who called the desert home that there may be flash flooding in the area, and that was what the denizens of the lake area feared most. On instinct, Bob, the sixty-three-year-old owner, ducked as the thunderous roar crashed overhead as if ducking would have made a difference. As the store beneath shook under his feet he could hear cans and bottles falling from his stocked shelves. Every sound of crashing and breaking made him cringe at the potential loss.

"Bob, honey, what was that?" his fifty-seven-year old wife Emily asked as she came up behind him and held him for comfort.

"It's our damn profit margin shrinking again, that's what. Goddamn desert! If it's not one thing it's another in this godforsaken wasteland."

"That's not what I mean. Listen."

"To what, our inventory being smashed to pieces?"

"That wailing. Do you think an animal got into the store? A Coyote or something?"

Bob cocked his head after the last chain lightning passed across the black sky, and the thunder dwindled. He was about to tell his wife she was nuts when he heard a screech, and what sounded like running footsteps. He moved quickly to get his small twenty-two rifle he used to scare varmints away from his property. "Damn frightened animal will shit all over the damn store." He made sure the small weapon was loaded in case it wasn't something as frightened as a mere coyote. Large cats have been known to frequent the trash receptacles ringing the lake. "You stay put now."

His wife cowered by the window as Bob moved to the stairs. He switched on the downstairs lights for the store as his feet hit the top steps. Nothing. "Damn fuses popped again. Honey," he called over his shoulder, comforted that the upstairs lights were still on. "Go to the fuse box and reset the breakers. Damn storm has blown the circuits again."

He started moving down the stairs, and had to stop when the most powerful lightning bolt of the night streaked across the sky. His eyes saw the flash of electricity from his high vantage point on the stairs. Then he heard the mewling sound again. This sounded more like a regular house cat, of which they didn't own. He shook his head, and made sure whatever it was could hear his progress down the stairs. He felt somewhat foolish for the demonstration, but rather safe than sorry in his estimation. After all, it could be a nut job from Los Angeles or Vegas down there, and not an animal at all. He cautiously made the bottom step. He eased into the store in the rear by the bait and tackle section. The chain lightening highlighted the chrome lures and the nylon fishing line. Bob raised the small rifle.

The thunder rumbled and he realized the storm had seemed to settle right over the western shore of the lake. In between the roar of thunder and the flash of lightning, he could hear the waves crashing into the shoreline. He could imagine a lot of damage was being incurred by the massive amounts of tourists' boats still anchored just off the shoreline.

He heard the mewling again. He swung the twenty-two up and over to his left. The sound had come from the grocery section of the store. He could only wonder if a coyote or a bobcat was devouring his bologna and packaged ham. He heard movement. Then the sound of a sliding door, and knew it was his lunchmeat that was being raided. Just as he turned a corner into the grocery section, the store lights finally flared to brightness. What he saw made the finger on the trigger jerk. He scared himself bad as the small bullet exploded out of the barrel. The slug 'pinged' off the tiled flooring, and crashed through the plate glass window. The glass held momentarily, and then came crashing to the floor. Bob cursed himself for causing more damage than any small animal could have.

"Bob, what happened? You alright?" came his wife's worried call from upstairs.

He could tell by her voice she was as frightened as he was. With the rain entering the shattered window, he knew he was causing himself more of a headache in water damage. He shook his head and started forward. He passed the luncheon meat cooler, and saw that everything looked undisturbed. He felt even more of a fool than he had before he shot his own window out. Then he saw the frozen food case. The sliding top was open to its stops. He saw a lot of his frozen products were missing, but most notable of them was the frozen pastries. Hot Pockets and pizza roles along with frozen burritos were gone, and he knew this because he had restocked them before closing. He jumped in his skin when he heard steps behind him, and when he turned, he saw his wife. He almost fainted dead away when he saw she had an old-fashioned Colt .45 Peacemaker, and had it terrifyingly cocked in her shaking hands. It was pointed directly at his nose. He ducked and cursed.

"Jesus, lower that damn thing!" he cried out.

She did, only hesitantly. "Well, you didn't answer, I thought maybe a bobcat got your old ass."

"Here, give me that hog-leg before you shoot you and me both."

She looked at the shattered window as more chain lightning streaked across the sky. When the building shook and the thunder played out, she turned to him with raised brows that made the curlers in her hair almost look like they were highlighting a strange form of antenna.

"Oh, like I'm the one shooting out a two-hundred-dollar pane glass window. Don't you ridicule me Buffalo Bill!"

Before either could react and just as a powerful bolt of lightning illuminated the night sky through the empty windowpane, a blur of green shot from a hidden corner behind a rack of sunglasses. The screech of terror came from both husband and wife, and whatever it was that used their heads as a steppingstone to get out of the window. The leap was amazing, and Bob and Emily would both later swear it had to have been an escaped green monkey.

"That does it, we're moving back home to L.A. They can take this desert, and shove it up their asses!"

His wife sat down hard onto the wet floor. She saw the spilled bags of pizza rolls and other frozen snacks the little monkey had dropped in its headlong flight to escape.

"I hope that monkey thingy has a microwave."

Outside of the small convenience store the storm started to abate.

Event Group Complex,
Nellis Air Force Base, Nevada

XAVIER MORALES RUBBED HIS EYES. As he looked around the computer center, he could see his technicians were just as tired as himself. He went back to the screen at his personal station halfway up the theater-style center. Europa was scanning for anything in the news that was out of the ordinary, while many of his people were busy researching the man out to expose them, Harold Briggs, Congressman from Louisiana. His phone buzzed. He picked it up, and in a joking manner to lighten up whoever was about to be disappointed with their search results, said; "Department 5656, top secret agency of the hidden government. Xavier speaking."

"Not funny, Doctor."

Xavier sat up straight in his wheelchair when he heard the voice of the director.

"Sorry, sir. We're running on caffeine and donuts down here."

"Yes, but let's try and set an example, Doctor. Anything on the Matchstick front?"

"No, sir." Xavier cleared his throat. "However, we found out that our intrepid congressman Briggs made an unannounced visit to a small town called Houma after claiming illness to get out of a Houston rally. Whatever it was must have been a priority."

"Houma? Houma, Louisiana?"

"Yes, sir. Europa read the official FBI report, and a Secret Service memo confirmed it. It seems he boarded a helicopter there, and that was where the FBI tail ended."

"Flight plan?"

"No sir. The FBI said nothing was filed." Xavier heard the release of breath, telling him that his news wasn't well-received on the other end of the phone.

"Any word from Carl and his team in Arizona?"

"They reported Matchstick hasn't been anywhere near Chato's Crawl. The house, shack, and mine were all cleared. They'll be landing at McCarren in five minutes. Colonel Collins is on his way there now to get them. As for Sarah and our special guest from London, they are about an hour out."

"Good. If someone has a plan for finding something that's lost or missing, it's Farbeaux."

Xavier was about to express his doubts comparing the Frenchman's abilities to Europa's, when he was approached by a young female tech and handed a note. He scanned it. "Excuse me Doctor Compton." Xavier looked at the woman. "When was this?"

"Three hours ago. Europa picked it up before the report aired on Las Vegas television."

"Why would Europa correlate this with the Matchstick search?"

"It's what the owner claims was stolen and the description of the intruder, sir."

"What is it Doctor Morales?" asked Niles on the other end of the phone.

Xavier nodded his head, excusing the technician. "One of those strange stories the news stations uses for fillers. It seems a small bait and tackle shop at Lake Mead was broken into and items were stolen during the same storm that hit Nellis about three hours ago. The owner and his wife claimed it was a small monkey. A green monkey."

Silence on the other end. A sharp intake of breath was heard, and then Niles spoke as calmly as he could. *"Just what was stolen Doctor?"*

"Believe it or not, pizza rolls, hot pockets, burritos, and frozen pastries. Sounds like one of my people if you ask…"

"Doctor, get Europa to contact Jack and give him this report. Tell him to gather Carl's team, and to get their asses out to Lake Mead immediately!"

"Did I miss something here?" Xavier asked. "I mean, yeah, a little green monkey, but that's nothing to pin our hopes on and send the team out on the basis of a wild story. There must be more to what you're thinking."

"Doctor, believe me when I say, that store owner has encountered the Matchstick Man. What else breaks into a store and steals something like frozen pizza rolls but a creature who ate nothing but? Now move Doctor."

. . .

NILES HUNG up the phone and turned on his private Europa terminal, watching the report and the interview with the store's frightened and angry owner. He watched it three times with his hopes rising with each and every viewing. He looked over at Alice and Virginia. At that moment his office door opened, and in walked Professor Charlie Ellenshaw and his new crypto-assistant, Anya Korvesky.

"Tell him, Charlie," Anya said quickly.

"Niles, Xavier told us what the plan is. We can get there faster. Let us secure the store, and the witnesses until the Colonel and his team get out there. Matchstick may still be close, but if we wait on the full discovery team to get out there, we may lose a good shot at getting to the little guy."

"Permission denied. I need both of you working on the Congressman Briggs line. That's the priority."

Niles saw the disappointment. Charlie actually kicked at an empty chair.

Virginia opened her mouth to say something.

"No, I need you here to assist with Farbeaux when he arrives."

"But..."

"No." Niles looked at Alice. "You have something to say?"

"Well, I can drive out there and..."

"No."

The look on Alice's face became stern and Niles tried his best to ignore it.

"Look, don't you think I want to go out there to see if we can find him? I'm the damn director and I have a job to do—so do you, now get to it." He looked at a glaring Charlie Ellenshaw. "Now."

"Permission for a dinner break?" Alice asked.

"Granted. Now go," Niles said.

The four left the office.

Niles Compton threw his glasses and shook his head.

OUTSIDE THE OFFICE, Virginia and Charlie saw Alice waiting for them with her arms angrily crossed over her chest, tapping away at the carpeted floor with her high-heeled toes.

"Are you driving, or am I?" Virginia asked with a grin.

"We have an hour and a half before Niles becomes suspicious. We'll get Gonzales in security to fly us out there. It's faster. We'll bring Pete Sanchez also. After all, when Niles gets us for disobeying orders, he'll have the standby security chief on hand as a witness."

Anya shook her head at both Alice and Virginia.

"I knew I liked you two ladies from the start."

Mystery Deep, **Well # 3,**
sixty-eight miles off the coast of Louisiana

NOW THAT THE initial meeting with Congressman Harold Briggs was done and out of the way, Vexilla Trotsky sat in front of the laptop, and got down to business. Unlike her employer, she had no love for alcoholic spirits. She only had water and an electronic pad on her desk as she had left Sokol to give the farewell speech to Briggs. She had the steel shutters on the underwater windows open as she felt the reflection offered by the Gulf waters relaxed her. Most of the science department and alien welfare unit had closed down for the night after securing the Grey in its comfortable cell. While not having bars didn't qualify it as such, Sokol figured as long as the alien wasn't in chains it would not know the difference.

As Trotsky ran through the images of the men and women they would be targeting for the committee's part in Sokol's scheme, she started to get an uncomfortable feeling. Her eyes roamed to the thick glass, and she stood to see if any divers were out. She scanned the area, but all she could see in the underwater lighting was one of the steel support legs of the rig. She felt the waves start to crash against the facility, and knew that the storm was ready to start in earnest high above their accommodations. As she turned back to her desk, she still couldn't shake the feeling that she wasn't alone.

She started scrolling through the photos again of the suspected members of Department 5656 that Briggs and his team had compiled over the years. They had no names to put to the faces. She shook her head wondering how they were going to find Briggs' investigation useful.

The overhead lights flickered.

Vexilla watched for a moment, but the lighting remained steady. She bent back to her task. She opened a connection with Siberia and the committee's supercomputer 'Red Ice.' With the connection made, she entered the disc, and then started the facial recognition program. Some of the photos were easily discerned, but only the men and women wearing a military uniform. The civilians, she knew, would be much harder to identify.

The lights flickered again.

Ignoring the interruption, she continued typing out her commands.

The lights went completely out.

"*Maldita ingeniería*," she said aloud, reverting to her Spanish roots from the time her great grandfather had been exiled to Mexico. Her complaint was with the rig's engineering department. She watched the laptop to see if the electrical situation was affecting her program, but the screen remained clear of any interruption. She bent to start reading again, when the laptop spun and faced away from her. She was shocked and started to reach for it, when a clawed four-fingered hand slid the computer to the far side of the desk. In the light from the outside floodlights, her eyes locked on the yellow orbs of the Grey. The creature was staring right at her. She stood suddenly and the Grey hissed. She slowly sat back in her high-backed chair. This seemed to satisfy the Grey.

"Asmodius, what are you doing on this level?"

The Grey seemed intent not to answer as it started scrolling through the photos that Briggs had supplied. With the tip of a crystallin claw-like nail, it ticked the glass sending the photos scrolling. Sokol's assistant watched, tempted to reach for the phone, but decided against it.

Suddenly the Grey hissed loudly as it took two quick steps back. It shook its head wildly sending his sparse grey hair flying. Vexilla stood and backed away. The Grey, never easy to be around at the best of times, was looking right at her as if she had caused some form of offense.

"What is it?" she asked, eyeing the electrically operated door and contemplating a run to escape whatever had caused the frenzied reaction from Asmodius.

The Grey held a hand over the laptop, and it spun in a circle three times on the desktop before stopping. The Grey stomped away six feet before turning with its large mouth agape, and spittle flying freely.

Vexilla Trotsky swallowed as she finally looked down at the photo that had irritated the Grey. It was the photo of the famous Green alien that had been shown to the world leaders just before the initial attack on the planet. She remembered its name from their briefings by the committee. Mahjtic. The small alien tasked at giving assistance in the war effort, and one who even by Russian military accounts, had helped save the world.

"The Matchstick Man?" she said.

The Grey hissed again, this time taking a menacing step toward the desk and her.

Vexilla had made the decision to run. She turned, but some invisible force held her in place. It was if her spine had been severed. The Grey waved a hand and the desk went flying, shattering against the steel bulkhead. As her eyes moved to the left, she saw that the laptop was still there, nothing at all was supporting it. It floated and she nearly fainted. The next thing Vexilla knew, she was being pulled toward the Grey. Then her expensive shoes came free of the steel deck. She felt the weightlessness take over, and the next thing she realized she was facing the snarling face of the Grey. A single finger with its clawed tip pointed to the laptop, and the clear photo of the Matchstick Man.

"Where?" it hissed in a cotton-filled voice that didn't come from its scaly lips, but somewhere in Vexilla's own brain.

She tried to speak, but her voice was just as frozen as her body.

She struggled but finally managed to shake her head. When she did, she felt pressure on her throat, and when she looked up, saw the Grey was using its right hand and its fingers to curl into a pinching, choking gesture. It started to smile as Vexilla became frightened she would die right there and then.

"Asmodius, let her down!"

Vexilla hit the floor, and started fighting for breath. The laptop also struck the deck and shattered. The Grey hissed at Sokol who had entered a split-second before Vexilla's life was choked out of her.

"What is this about?" Sokol asked as he hurriedly helped his assistant up. "And why have you left your room?"

The Grey crouched and Sokol began to wonder if the Grey could be handled at all.

"Are you okay?" he asked a white-faced Trotsky.

"How did...he get...out?" she struggled to say as her throat was aflame with pain.

Sokol turned on the Grey who was rocking back and forth hissing its displeasure.

"He killed his two guards. Security cameras caught him walking straight here as if he knew what he would find. What set him off?"

Vexilla pointed down to the smashed laptop. "He came across a photo of that small alien the allies used during the war with the Greys. The one they called the Matchstick Man. Mahjtic Tilly."

Sokol took an angry step forward toward the Grey, who stood and stepped toward Sokol.

"He's dead you fool! Murdered, if the reports from the committee are to be believed. Dead and buried!"

The Grey seemed to go insane as it grabbed Sokol by his throat and lifted him. Vexilla smashed her hand into the alarm panel on the wall, and a blaring siren started sounding throughout the rig. This didn't deter Asmodius as he shook Sokol. The Grey was vigorously shaking his head, enough so Sokol felt the sickly strands of hair as it struck his face.

The Grey stopped and brought Sokol close, his feet fighting for purchase on a floor he was being held four feet above. He saw the large mouth open and the crystal teeth. The threat was real, and Sokol wondered if his long-range plan for getting what he wanted—in ending the committee's reign—would end here and now.

"Not...dead!" The Grey shook Sokol two more times violently.

"He's dead! Shot and killed!"

"Not dead. Never dead." He threw Sokol into the wall just as security broke into the room.

The Grey hissed, then started for the double sliding doors. He ruthlessly knocked the five security men clear of its path by just using a gesture of a swipe through the air, and left the lower section of the rig.

"Go after him!" Sokol screamed at his men as Vexilla was the one this time assisting him to his feet.

"Dmitri, we have to kill that goddamn thing. It's insane! If the committee finds out how unstable it is, we could be their next target."

Sokol angrily threw off her supporting hands. "I need him for our plan. To hell with the committee! Did you see that power?" Sokol screamed and ran after his security ream before they killed the greatest asset in world history. "I was right all along!"

Vexilla watched Sokol follow, and she decided there and then that she would not be a part of this insanity. She scrambled and finally retrieved the phone from her shattered desk.

The phone on the other end was picked up immediately.

"This is the night officer, operating number please."

"Operator 569015. Inform the committee that the asset known as Warlock has been re-evaluated and deemed unstable. Request instructions not go through Number Ten. Just me."

"Number One will be immediately informed."

Vexilla tossed the phone down to the deck and closed her eyes. She had just betrayed the man she loved, and was glad of it. She didn't fear his wrath or the wrath of the committee. She feared for her immortal soul over the being they were dealing with.

SOKOL MADE his men lower their AK-47's. He saw the Grey just standing on the helicopter platform staring out to sea. The aggressiveness had left the large creature as the rain seemed to sooth the beast. Lightning streaked across the dark sky as Sokol approached.

"You do know that without me, the committee will kill you?"

The Grey turned; its bright yellow eyes blazing at Sokol. It lifted its hand and pointed north.

"Not dead. It is danger to Asmodius." The Grey smiled at Sokol, then poked him in the chest with a sharp, clear nail. "Danger to you. It knows I am here. His kind know all. This is why we enslaved them." It hissed, and then turned back to look at the distant horizon. As for Sokol, his face drained of color as he realized the Grey's voice was coming from his own mind. "It is time you understand Asmodius. I can make anything come to pass in your desires. But there will be no more orders to follow. No more lock in room. Me, same as you."

"Partners?"

"Asmodius does not...know this word." The Grey turned and its large hand encircled Sokol's smaller head. The creature closed its eyes. Sokol felt the power of the Grey as it entered his mind. He saw the Grey smile and nod as if he found what it was looking for. He released Sokol just before the guards reacted. The Russian ordered them to stay away. "Yessss, partners."

"What are you going to do?" Sokol asked as he joined the Grey at the railing.

"Attack. Attack Matchstick...attack his friends...make dead all."

Sokol smiled for the first time since the strange disturbance had started.

"That's a start."

"Then Asmodius wants what it wants."

"What do you want?" Sokol asked, not liking the confident way the Grey turned away from him.

"Revenge for my kind."

"The Greys? They locked you away."

The smile again, and this time Sokol felt the blood drain from his face.

"Revenge for *my* kind. Not Grey." It spit into the rain. "They lock my kind away for what we were."

"What were you?" Sokol asked apprehensively.

The Grey only smiled and didn't answer. It did however stretch out its large hand and then closed its eyes. Sokol saw that its concentration was focused northwest—toward Nevada, and the unsuspecting group of men and women searching for a lost friend.

CHAPTER FIVE

Lake Mead National Recreation Area,
Ninety-Four Miles, East of Las Vegas

ormer United States Air Force Captain and complex security man, Henry Gonzalez was having a hard time setting the large UH-60 Blackhawk down on the sand just one hundred feet from the lake. Alice Hamilton, a pilot herself, didn't envy the hardship the Captain was having with the high winds and lightning storm that circled the lake. He finally felt the wheels strike the sand, and he immediately powered down. He angrily pulled his helmet off, and tossed it to his crew chief who was near to vomiting.

"I hope what you people are after was worth that!" he shouted over the Blackhawk's twin turbines powering down. He looked at Will Mendenhall's temporary replacement in security, Pete Sanchez, and shouted at him. "How did you allow them to talk you into disobeying the Director's orders?"

Charlie Ellenshaw was about to say something about the importance of what they were after, but was stopped by Sergeant Sanchez who was pulling site security for the mission. He just shook his head at Charlie, stopping him from even trying to explain Alice Hamilton's influence over the entire Group.

"Look Gonzales, if you receive radio communications from the complex, delay them with static." Sanchez looked at Alice and winked.

As Anya Korvesky opened the sliding door, they were immediately pelted by stinging sand and sideways rain

"Where is the store?" Alice shouted into the wind.

"About two hundred feet up that bluff," Sergeant Sanchez said, consulting his GPS system on his Group cell phone. He immediately placed the device into the pocket of the protective rain gear they had been issued. He had to smile at Alice, who looked like an old-fashioned seafarer with her droopy rubber hat, and knee-high boots.

"I think you and Charlie should interview the store owner while Alice and I will start a grid search pattern to see if we can find anyone else out here. Someone camping maybe, and ask if they saw anything strange," Anya shouted while holding her rain hat in place.

"Right," Sanchez said. "Are you armed?" he asked the former Mossad Major.

She just smirked at the Sergeant, making him feel foolish for asking such a naïve question. As soon as Sanchez and Charlie moved off over the sand dune, Anya, Virginia, and Alice started moving toward the rough shoreline.

"We would have a lot better visibility out here if this storm would hurry up and pass," Anya said over her shoulder at Alice, who for her age, wasn't having as nearly a difficult time as she would have thought. Virginia Pollock, on the other hand, seemed to stumble in the sand every five feet or so. Both women were amazed at Alice and her durability, but when it came to finding Matchstick, they understood where her inner strength came from.

"Look! A camping area," Anya said, pointing up another small rise.

Alice and Virginia started to follow Anya toward what looked like a sparsely populated campground for trailers and motor homes. Lights inside were bright as campers waited out the storm in a far more comfortable setting than the few tents closer to the shore.

After forty-five minutes, they had canvased the entire campground. They had not found a single witness to the night's strange events at the bait and tackle shop other than harrowing tales of chain lightning and windblown camper damage. As they exited the last Winnebago, they were met by Sergeant Sanchez, and a soaking wet Charlie Ellenshaw.

"Any luck?" Sanchez asked, shouting into the wind as he tried to keep his face from being sand-pitted.

"No, everyone's cowering in the comfort of their homes on wheels."

"Yeah, I remember when you actually left the comforts of home, at home, when camping. I guess times have changed," Charlie said as his rubber hat flew from his head. He started to go after it, but then decided not to as he was already miserably wet.

Sanchez looked at his watch. "The Colonel's team will be here soon.

I think we should wait in the Blackhawk until we get more boots on the ground."

"You're probably right," Anya said, and then was cut short by Charlie Ellenshaw tugging on her raincoat. He pointed down toward the water.

Walking away from the gathered group and obviously unwilling to wait on Jack and his people, Alice Hamilton and Virginia Pollock were moving toward the windblown tents of the hardier campers.

Sanchez shook his head. "The Colonel's right, no one listens to anyone around here."

"Well, neither of them are armed, so I guess that makes the decision easy as to what we do."

Sanchez looked at the drowned rat named Charlie Ellenshaw, and they moved off, following the stubborn women.

The first three tents were empty. It seemed the campers had decided to make a stand at Bullhead City, instead of riding out the storm. Charlie and Sanchez checked out one other tent and came back with a shake of their heads.

"Look, if I know Matchstick, he doesn't like weather like this. I know he's close, I can feel it," Alice said, unwilling to call an end to their limited search.

"The only one in the area left is that large tent down the shore. It's dark. No lanterns or movement. I don't think anyone's home," Sanchez said, hoping that would dissuade Alice from going there.

"We don't stop searching because of some damn rain, Sergeant. I know you didn't learn that from Jack," Alice said as she started to walk away through the sideways rain. The others followed.

As Charlie passed Sanchez, he looked at him and said, "Ouch." He smiled. "She still has a bite, don't she?"

"Now I know who probably trained the Colonel and Mister Everett," Sanchez said, but started to follow anyway.

Alice finally made it to the large yellow tent. The flaps were drawn and tied down. There was no light at all. Her hopes started to dwindle as she turned and saw the others waiting. She started toward the main tent flap. She scratched at the nylon fabric. Nothing.

"No one's home Alice," Charlie said, cupping his hands over his mouth to be heard over the wind and the thunder.

Alice started to turn away when she stopped, and tilted her head. She reached out and untied the flap.

"Oh, great, now we're breaking and entering," Sanchez said. He wasn't joking.

Alice slowly opened the tent flap and the wind immediately took the material, tearing it from her hand. She heard the scream of a small child, and immediately regretted her actions. Whoever was in the tent was scared and whimpering.

"I'm sorry. We were just checking to see if everything was alright. This storm is really bad." Alice waited for some form of answer. "We're looking for a friend who is lost out here. Where are your parents?" she asked as kindly as she could, but she knew her shouted words were anything but soothing.

Sanchez was right, they needed more manpower for a search of this size. "I'm sorry, we'll look somewhere else." She was about to turn away when an empty box hit her and bounced to the sand. The wind took it, and it flew into the waiting group where Charlie Ellenshaw caught the piece of windblown trash. Charlie brushed his wet, stringy white hair from his face. He adjusted his glasses and examined the torn open box. He immediately ran, and stopped Alice. He held out the box for her to see.

Alice turned as white as Charlie's hair.

"Gino's Pizza Rolls!" Charlie said as Alice turned hurriedly back to the tent. She slowly opened the flap. She swallowed as she took a tentative step inside the darkened area. Her eyes roamed over the inside. It was so dark her eyes failed to adjust as the sides of the tent bowed in and out from the force of the wind.

"Matchstick?" she called.

Nothing.

"It's time to come home. Are you hurt?"

Suddenly Alice's heart froze as a scream reverberated inside the dark tent, and she was grabbed around the thighs. She fell backward through the tent flap, and into the driving rain where she fell onto her back.

Anya, Sanchez, and Virginia were stunned. Charlie even had to step back momentarily as he thought Alice had cornered some kind of desert cat inside the tent, and was now being attacked.

They all ran toward the encounter fearing the same as Charlie.

"Alice, Alice, Alice, Alice," came the words over and over again.

The group stopped in shock as they heard Alice Hamilton start to laugh. Charlie was the first one to see what it was that had attacked Alice. He started to laugh and cry at the same time.

Mahjtic Tilly looked up from his position on Alice's chest and screamed. He jumped five feet from Alice to Charlie. He flew onto Ellenshaw's neck and squeezed as if he were trying to wring the breath out of his body. Matchstick was still wearing the small, specially made Complex jumpsuit the security team made for him. It had been the one he had been buried in. The silver captain's bars bestowed on him by Will Mendenhall were still pinned to his collar.

"Crazy Charlie, Crazy Charlie, Crazy Charlie!" Ellenshaw went down as the rain soaked both Matchstick and himself. He started laughing, and he knew it might take days to stop after finding the friend they had come searching for.

Virginia Pollock placed both hands over her mouth and started to cry. It was a deep, crushing heart cry as she watched the overly excited Matchstick.

"Unbelievable," Anya Korvesky said, amazed the little alien was actually alive. Most people in the Group were of the same conclusion as herself that Matchstick didn't miraculously dig himself from his own grave. That it was outside forces that had stolen his body. As she watched, she couldn't help but join Virginia in her amazement.

Everyone was still crying and laughing, slapping each other on the back when Matchstick stood up and started pulling on Charlie and Alice's arms.

"Home. Must go home…home. Alice, we go home. Charlie, we go home. Must go now!"

"Take it easy buddy," Sanchez said as he bent over to calm Matchstick.

"I'm afraid we can't let you take him," said a voice from behind them. "We thought the little guy ran off. But I guess he just went lookin' for more food. That boy can eat some, let me tell 'ya."

As they turned, they saw a boy of no more than sixteen years of age standing there. He had a shotgun leveled at the Group.

"Now wait a minute," Sanchez started to say when the first shotgun blast tore up the sand just inches from his boots.

"Look, I don't know who you are, but Matchstick is coming home with us. You'll have to kill us all," Alice said as she pushed by Charlie Ellenshaw to confront the teenager with the long black hair holding the shotgun on them.

"Grandma!" the boy shouted into the storm. "I found the green fella. I guess his friends too."

Sanchez' hand was inching closer to his nine-millimeter, as was Anya's. They both saw that the boy was unsure of himself. His eyes were wide in fright. The barrel of the shotgun was wavering up and down and from side to side. Another world-shaking bolt of lightning reached for the earth below, and that made the teenage boy jump. Sanchez saw his opportunity.

"Boy, lower that gun 'afore you blow your own foot off," shouted a voice behind all of them. "You, the big Mexican fella, and you, gypsy girl, don't pull those guns, or we'll have a real mess on our hands. A mess that will outright ruin everyone's night."

As they turned, they were shocked to see an old woman. She had at least ten men on her right and ten men and women on her left. Everyone but the old woman was armed. Some with automatic weapons. Anya and Sanchez both moved their hands away from their hidden weapons. The boy moved off to stand next to the old woman who placed an arm around him. She held him close, and with her free hand rubbed his wet hair as one of the men in her company disarmed both Sanchez and Anya, then searched the others.

"Go stand by your pa," the old woman with the heavy wool coat said.

Alice, Matchstick, Charlie, Virginia, Sanchez, and Anya watched as the teenager moved away and stood by a large man who was more than six and half feet tall.

"Look, ma'am, this is no joke. We're from…"

"I knows where you're from, young man," she said, cutting Sergeant Sanchez off. She started to come closer to the startled men and women of the Event Group. "Jim Bob, we can't have these good folks followin' us."

"Yes, Granny," the largest man with the teenaged son said as he came forward with plastic ties.

"You can't tie us up and leave us here," Anya said as the man turned her around and slipped the plastic wire-tie over her wrists before tying them behind her back.

"Oh, I 'spect your friends will find you soon 'nough, I reckon."

"We have to take Matchstick back with us," Alice said to a woman in shabby secondhand clothing who was tying her up as well. "He's our friend and you have no right to take him."

The old woman finally advanced in the dark. She walked up to Matchstick who was holding firmly onto Alice's legs. His eyes were wide, and he was shaking. The old woman placed a withered hand onto the side of the lightbulb shaped head of the small alien.

Alice wanted to strike out at the white-haired woman, but with her hands being tied she saw no opportunity.

"We have no intention of harmin' this sweet thing. You had all of us worried little fella, runnin' off like you did." With effort, the old woman bent over. Alice saw that she had to be at the very least in her late nineties. She looked at Alice. "But someone *is* comin' to see harm does befall him." She smiled genuinely at Matchstick. "I guess I don't have to call you Gary no more." She looked at Charlie Ellenshaw. "You call him Matchstick, do ya?"

"Gary?"

The old woman stood with difficulty, shoeing away the teenaged boy who tried to assist her to her feet. "We had to call him somethin'. Now that I think about it, Matchstick is far more apt than Gary." She cackled like a hen laying an egg. "I just always liked that name and thought it fit the little thing."

Charlie exchanged worried looks with Virginia, and pursed his lips as if saying, *'okay, we just entered nutsville.'*

"But, with the distance we have to travel, I 'spose it be best if the green child had someone other than strangers to keep him company. Someone he knows." She stepped up to Charlie Ellenshaw. "You seem like you be best. Kind of spindly lookin'. Probably far less trouble than the rest."

"Ma'am, whoever you are, we have resources you wouldn't believe," Sanchez said as the old woman turned toward him.

"I 'spect you do. Being from the gove'ment and all."

"How do you know that?" Alice asked.

She turned toward Alice.

"I imagine with all of those resources this young man says you have at your 'sposal, you'll figure it out, Mrs. Hamilton. That mean old fella, Garrison Lee, would have in no time 'tall."

"Just who in the hell are you? And how do you know these things about us?" Virginia asked again as her ankles were bound.

"Oh, the same way I knew that little fella weren't dead," she laughed again, this time not as hardy as her earlier jovial cackle. "Imagine my thoughts when he came a poppin' up out-a that grave. Just 'bout made poopy in my pantaloons. But pop up he did, and now we have a fightin' chance with what's headin' our way."

"And just what is heading your way?' Alice asked as she was led to the interior of the tent where she was placed on the nylon floor out of the rain.

The old woman stuck her head in the tent and smiled. Her teeth even and straight. Her blue eyes seemed to be illuminated from within.

"Even with all the amazing things you have seen in your young life, Mrs. Hamilton, you would find it hard to believe what's comin' for us all."

Alice wanted to ask more, but the strangers left as the others were pushed into the tent, and their feet wire-tied, all except Charlie Ellenshaw and the Matchstick Man.

"We found him and lost him again in less than five minutes. The Colonel's going to have my ass," Sanchez said, shaking his head.

"Not after I tell him who we ran into, he won't."

In the darkness of the tent and through flashes of lightning, they saw Anya Korvesky.

"You know her?" Virginia asked as she tried to force her way out of the plastic wire-ties.

"Back in Romania, my Grandmother used to tell us stories, you know old gypsy legends. One was about a cult of sorts in America."

Alice got a sickening feeling in her stomach at the mention of the word 'cult.' "Of sorts, what do you mean?"

"Did you catch her accent? I did. She tries to hide it with a country twang. But she's not country at all."

"What does that mean?" Sanchez asked, frustrated with his restraints.

"From the stories told, I believe we were just introduced to the most powerful conjuror in the world."

"Who?" Virginia persisted.

"According to Grandmother, I think that was Elsbeth Barlow, known as the Witch Queen of Salem."

AIR FORCE CAPTAIN Henry Gonzalez was sitting in the pilot's seat of the Blackhawk and reading a paperback novel. His co-pilot was stretched out in the back trying to doze, but found it hard to do with the lightning and thunder roaring across the desert skies. Gonzalez heard the sliding side door open. He closed his book.

"Any luck?" he asked. He started to turn, when an old-fashioned, ball and cap Navy Colt was shoved into his face. His co-pilot was on the seat with a gag in his mouth, and was in the process of being wire-tied.

"Sorry I have to do this young fella, but we can't have you followin' us."

The man was a giant. His checkered shirt was rain soaked, and his balding head shiny with rainwater. The man cocked the pistol, and fired the Navy Colt's rounds into the Blackhawk's control panel. Sparks flew and ozone permeated the air.

"What the fu—" Gonzalez started to say.

"As I said, sorry." The large man backed out of the helicopter just as Gonzalez was pulled from his seat, and yanked into the back where he soon joined his co-pilot in captivity.

The large man walked to the old beat up Ford station wagon. Behind it were several old and rusted cars and pickup trucks. The man walked to the station wagon, averting his eyes from the strange alien riding in the backseat with a bug-eyed Charlie Ellenshaw next to him. He faced the old woman in the front seat while she ate a handful of Oreo cookies from the package.

"Okay Granny, that whirlybird ain't goin' nowhere."

"You didn't hurt them fellas, did you?" she asked as she removed the top half of a cookie from the bottom, and licked the crème-filled center.

"Granny, you knows I only hurts them that tries to do us harm."

The old woman patted the large man's arm as the rain started to finally diminish.

Suddenly, a driver from one of the trailing cars rushed forward just as the morning sun started to rise in the east.

"Granny, we have another one of those dragonfly-lookin' choppers coming right at us!"

The old woman shook her head, and leaned forward through the lessening rainstorm.

"Damn, it's them folk's friends. I was hopin' to be far from here by the time they showed." She opened the door to the station wagon and stepped out.

"Uh-oh," the large man said as he started backing away. "Look out boys! Granny done got her dander up."

The old woman closed her eyes, and faced the large helicopter coming at them from the north.

"SEE ANYTHING?" Jack asked through the intercom.

Ryan shook his head. "We have a group of cars close to the lake, that's about it. I see the Air Force Blackhawk, so Sanchez and his advanced team is still on the ground. Want me to set it down there, Colonel?"

"Yeah, Anya and the others shouldn't be that far."

After Jack had picked up Carl, Ryan, Will and Tram at the airport, they used an available Blackhawk to fly out to Lake Mead. An angry Niles Compton had been fooled for as long as fifteen minutes after Alice, Virginia, Charlie and a coerced Sergeant Sanchez had left the complex. He informed Jack on where they were headed.

Before Ryan knew what was happening, the Blackhawk jinked to the left. Everyone in the back was thrown.

"Get off me!" Mendenhall shouted at Tram. "That's why you wear your harness when Ryan is flying!"

Ryan fought the stick, then just as suddenly, felt the control column get yanked from his gloved hands. The Blackhawk swerved right. Then left. It was as if invisible hands were wresting control from him.

"We're having major issues here," he shouted.

Everyone tensed. Even Jack was holding on for dear life in the co-pilots seat.

Ryan watched the control switches that electronically sent signals to the engine as they started flipping down to the 'off' position. Then he felt his rudder pedals being forced in the opposite direction of the pressure he was applying. All this happened just as an electrically charged blue wave hurled across the sky, and hit them.

"I don't have control!" Ryan said as calmly as he could.

"Get over the lake!" Jack called out.

Ryan tried with all of his strength, but with the hydraulic system failure he had literally no control. Then an amazing thing happened. He felt the pressure on the foot pedals go limp, and for a brief moment, he had control of the tail rotor again. He swung the giant Blackhawk into a tight turn left. Then both G.E. turbines stopped cold, and the helicopter started to auto-rotate, meaning the Blackhawk was allowing the powerless rotors to give them enough lift to keep them upright and level.

"I think we're about to go swimming," Mendenhall yelled.

Later all would describe the strangest crash landing any had ever known. It was if a cushion of air hit the helicopter from below, buffering it a moment just before it struck the water.

As THE SUN rose in the east, dispelling the last of the great storm, debris started to float to the surface of the now still and calm lake.

On shore, the old woman watched the helicopter go down into the lake. She shook her head and with great effort, as if sapped of all energy, slowly opened the car's front door. She hesitated before entering, looking again at the spot the flying machine had vanished. She saw one person break the surface of the lake, then another. She smiled, and nodded her head.

"Gettin' old, I guess. Took far more workin' than it used to."

The caravan of cars with the old Town and Country station wagon leading the way, left the state park at Lake Mead with their guests Charlie Ellenshaw and the being they now knew as—The Matchstick Man.

CARL, the strongest swimmer was the first to reach the calm shoreline as the sun made its first full appearance. As he started to stand and check on the others, a hand took his and assisted him to a standing position. He looked up into the face of Anya Korvesky. He started to say something, but she cut off his words when she hugged him, sapping his anger before it was released. He gave in, and hugged her back. After releasing her, he saw Alice and Virginia, looking like drowned rats, help both Ryan and Mendenhall out of the water. Jack, helping Tram, fell to the sand lining the beach, exhausted from their swim.

Jack automatically felt something was wrong. With hands on his knees, he tried to catch his breath before asking. Alice beat him to it.

"We found Matchstick. He's alive."

"Where is he?" Carl asked, seeing the strange look on Anya's face.

"Where is Doc Ellenshaw?" Jack asked.

"It's all my fault," Alice said. For the first time since they had known her, the men of the security department saw Alice's eyes tear up as she looked east. "They took both of them. Both Matchstick and Charlie."

"Who? Who took them?" Will asked, nearly losing his cool.

Alice shook her head, not wanting to bring up the subject of witches, and that of Salem, as Anya had put it.

"What do we do now?" Virginia asked.

"We go and get our people back."

They watched as an angry Jack Collins left the beach, not caring if anyone followed.

CHAPTER SIX

Event Group Complex,
Nellis Air Force Base, Nevada

Jack, Carl, Will, and Jason rode the elevator in silence. The doors opened on level seven, and they immediately marched into the director's reception area. They came to a sudden stop when they saw the supervising men and women of the varying departments standing idly while waiting outside the conference room.

"What the hell is going on?" Everett asked one of the three assistants to the director as he tried to scramble by.

The harried assistant stopped and spoke softly so the other managers couldn't overhear.

"The Director has Mrs. Hamilton, Assistant Director Pollock, Major Korvesky, and Sergeant Sanchez in his office. He doesn't want to be disturbed." The male assistant leaned in closer. "I don't think I've ever seen the Director this mad before."

The assistant slunk away as a conspirator would.

"Niles has breached protocol and ethics by bypassing the security office and bringing one of our security men without informing us," Everett said, looking at Mendenhall to make sure he hadn't given

Niles permission to pull in their man. Will slightly shook his head, not really wanting to add to Mister Everett's anger.

"We'll drop the issue for now," Jack said. "They disobeyed the director's orders, and with this Congressman Briggs scandal developing, Niles didn't need his most experienced people going rogue."

"But..." Jason Ryan started to say.

"But nothing, Commander. Not only did they lose Matchstick, they allowed Doc Ellenshaw to be snatched. That's why we don't breach the subject of not following protocol."

Ryan, after seeing Jack's point, didn't pursue the subject.

Jack heard the pneumatic elevator behind him stop, and the doors slid open. He half-turned and smiled as Sarah stepped out. The smile quickly faded when he saw who came out next—Henri Farbeaux. Sarah walked up, and hugged him.

Will Mendenhall noticed immediately the reception area had grown as quiet as a church. Most were polite enough not to look at the trio, but you could tell the subject of Collins, Sarah, and Farbeaux wasn't far from the management team's mind.

Sarah stepped back, and Jack decided then and there on how he would act. He held out his hand to the Frenchman.

"Colonel, I appreciate you coming. Sorry to come after you this way."

Henri took Jack's hand after only a brief hesitation.

"I figured if you could swallow your pride and send such a valuable asset to make the offer, the least I could do is come and see what mess your Group has gotten into now," he said with a smirk. "My rather tardy congratulations on your recent nuptials. It seems the Jack Collins luck has been proven once again."

Jack eased his hand from Henri's and his eyes drifted to Sarah. "Thank you, Colonel."

Carl felt the tension between the two. The last they had seen each other in Mongolia hadn't been a tense parting. Now there was. It had to be Jack and Sarah's wedding that had now driven a new wedge between the two men.

"Henri," Carl said curtly offering his hand.

The large former SEAL intentionally cut the handshake off short. Farbeaux did, however, smile at Will Mendenhall. This handshake was more cordial. After all, during the battle of Antarctica, the two men had resigned themselves to die together. Now they had that shared experience, and both felt the bond. The greeting between Ryan wasn't as such. The handshake was so quick it was almost unnoticeable.

"Jack, what's going on here?" Sarah asked, breaking the uncomfortable silence after her homecoming.

Jack looked briefly at Henri. "We'll get into that later. The short story is Matchstick was found alive, but now he and Doc Ellenshaw both have been taken." He looked around at the gathered department heads. "By who, we're not sure yet."

Sarah walked over to Ryan. "I heard you had some problem out at Lake Mead?"

Ryan looked at the Colonel briefly, and Jack nodded his head, indicating that he could talk.

"Problem my ass, we were knocked right out of the sky."

"What?"

"Look, I can't explain, but whoever was controlling that Blackhawk wasn't named Ryan."

"I know you like to joke, but I'm not getting it," Sarah said looking from Jason to her new husband.

"We were all there. The Commander's right. Someone, or something, took control of that bird, and sent us into the drink."

Behind them the doors opened again, and out stepped three security men from their own office. Marine Staff Sergeant John Calhoun stepped forward, and stood close to Jack and Carl.

"What's up?" Collins asked, curious as to why his men were there.

"The director called down, and said he wanted a security detail to come to the conference room."

Jack and Carl exchanged confused looks.

"What's this about, Colonel?" Calhoun asked.

"I guess we'll see. Carl you come too."

The five men walked to the double conference room doors, and opened it. Once inside, Jack saw Niles standing and Alice, Anya, Virginia, and Sergeant Sanchez were sitting at the empty conference table.

"Doctor, what's going on?" Jack asked as if it were a mere question, but his blue eyes told a different story.

"Colonel, you and Captain Everett have a seat. I understand you had quite a swim this morning. Also lost a rather expensive UH-60."

"Yes, sir. Now, can we have an explanation as to why you have sent for a security team?"

"Yes, you can. As of this moment, Major Korvesky is under house arrest." His eyes met Carl's, and didn't blink as if challenging him to say something. Everett just raised his brows. "She is to be limited to her private quarters where her meals will be delivered to Crypto on level eighty-seven. The only reason I am granting her that privilege is for the simple reason Professor Ellenshaw is now missing."

"Niles..." Jack started to protest.

"Sergeant Sanchez is also under house arrest. As a courtesy, I will allow you to set the parameters of that arrest. Assistant Director Pollock is relieved of her duties, and suspended pending my consultation with the President."

Jason Ryan started to stand up.

"Sit, Mr. Ryan. I'll get to you soon enough." Niles tossed his thick glasses onto the conference table. "Sergeant Calhoun, you will escort Mrs. Hamilton to her home in Las Vegas where she will immediately commence her official retirement." This time Niles Compton showed his first emotion outside of anger. He placed a hand on Alice's shoulder and squeezed. "I'll keep you updated as best I can within regulations."

"May I speak?" Carl asked, slowly standing up.

"No, Captain. The decisions made here were not mine to make. This comes directly from the President."

No one noticed, but Jack almost imperceptibly nodded his head.

"We all know you could have persuaded him to go a little lighter," Carl continued, holding the director's angry eyes.

"I could have, but I didn't. Because they disobeyed my direct orders, we have lost Matchstick and placed Professor Ellenshaw in a situation that may cost him his life."

Niles challenged Everett directly by making him look away first. None of the security men had never seen Compton this way before.

Jason, Will, and Carl couldn't believe Jack had given in so easily without a challenge to the director. They all looked away from Compton, focusing on anything or anyone but him.

Niles reached out, and pushed a button on the table. "Mr. Jefferson, please send in Doctor Morales, Colonel Farbeaux, and Mrs. Collins, please. And inform the department heads that today's meeting is to be rescheduled."

"Yes, sir."

"Permission to be excused?" Virginia said with her head lowered.

"Granted. Sergeant Calhoun, escort them out please."

The four disciplined staff members stood. Anya looked at Carl, and shook her head as if warning him not to say anything at the moment. Sergeant Sanchez started to walk toward his friends in the security department, but lowered his head and left. Alice slowly walked away from the table without a word. She stood at the door for a brief moment as security held it open for her.

"Mrs. Hamilton?" Niles said.

Alice half-turned.

Niles started to say something, but stopped short. All could see the love the man had for Alice as he shook his head. It seemed for the first time in the director's life, he failed to find words he could use.

Jack, Carl, Will and Ryan all stood, and watched as Alice turned away and left the conference room.

Niles Compton sat hard into his chair, and for the first time the men of the security department had ever seen, the director swiped at his eyes as he stemmed the flow of tears.

"Sorry, gentlemen. I hated doing that," he said, taking his time wiping the lenses of his glasses. Then he attempted a smile. The attempt failed.

"A little damned hard on them, weren't you?" Ryan asked, standing angrily just as Sarah, Morales, and Farbeaux came through the door.

"Commander, at ease," Jack barked.

"Sit down, Mister Ryan," Carl echoed.

Will Mendenhall tugged on Jason's sleeve and the naval aviator finally relented and sat. His eyes told everyone that he was far from being over his anger. Then a curious look crossed his face when he glanced at Collins, and the Colonel had a small smile on his lips.

"You didn't inform the White House, did you Doctor?" Jack asked.

Niles looked up, and a hint of a smile appeared.

"Are you suggesting I need acting classes, Colonel?"

"If you're going to bluff like that, that may be necessary."

Ryan and Mendenhall exchanged confused looks. "Don't mind us mushrooms in the room, but could you big brains explain just what the hell's going on?" Will asked, looking from the director to Collins and Everett.

"I already briefed the Director on what happened out at Lake Mead, and he explained in detail about other matters. Although I wish the Director would have mentioned his intent earlier than he did," Jack said as he stood, "I didn't guess at his plan until just a few moments ago." He looked at Sarah as she and Farbeaux took seats, and Xavier Morales wheeled up and placed his chair next to the Director. "Niles, I think you better explain your story."

"It's simple gentlemen. By the way, Colonel Farbeaux, thank you for coming." Henri just nodded his head. "I was informed by the President that our good friend Congressman Harold Briggs has a few names he can forward to the press about the Group. One of them is already missing—Matchstick. The others are Alice and Virginia. I wanted them out of here for their own protection, and I knew they would give me nothing but grief. And Alice may have just pushed me down an elevator shaft if I ordered a guard to babysit her. Virginia the same thing. By the way Jack, I need a twenty-four-hour guard on Alice's house." Collins smiled, and nodded.

"That doesn't explain Sergeant Sanchez and Anya," Carl said.

"That part you won't like. Colonel, would you explain my reasoning?"

Jack turned and looked at Carl. "It's just a small matter of concern. Congressman Briggs has gotten his information from somewhere."

"Now wait a minute, you can't be suggesting..." Carl started to protest.

"No. However, there's something you didn't know. The President has learned, with a little help from Doctor Morales and Europa," Collins nodded his head in an appreciative manner at the computer whiz, "that Briggs has gotten a hold of several reports about our operations against the Greys during the war. We don't know how yet, but Anya was mentioned. Probably because of the Congressman's close ties with the State of Israel and her uncle in the Mossad. We're not sure yet. And Alice because of his investigation into Garrison Lee. Now, Sergeant Sanchez was my fault. I sent him to Washington during the conflict to keep an eye on Virginia when she was dealing with Congress. I accidentally exposed him to Briggs. We're sure he noted the name associated with A.D. Pollock during those hearings."

"Now the President has full and truthful deniability when it comes to those names," Niles said. "Call me a stickler for detail, but I will never give anyone the chance to hang the President over us. I will send the President word about this so if and when he's asked, he knows for a fact that these four people are not on any current government payroll."

"As I said, I didn't know how the Director could protect our our people, knowing how stubborn about their own safety they can be." Jack smiled at Niles. "But he came up with a doozy of a plan. I just hope we can explain to Alice why it had to be done that way."

"I think that is a job for Mister Ryan since he decided to talk to his director the way he did," Niles said.

"Appropriate," Collins said. "I think Major Mendenhall should go also to keep an eye on his wayward buddy. I just hope Alice will be in a forgiving mood when they explain why it had to be done."

"Now that their security is settled, let's figure a way to get Matchstick and Charlie out of the mess they're in." Niles looked over at Carl. "Mister Everett, perhaps it's time for you to ask Major Korvesky if she has a moment to explain her witches' theory concerning Matchstick's abduction. Perhaps you can also ease her mind about why she's been exiled to the eighty-seventh floor?" With that out of the way, the director turned his attention to the Frenchman. "Now, for the real reason I asked Colonel Farbeaux to join our merry band of fools."

"I would indeed be interested to learn," Henri said.

"Are you familiar with Louisiana, Colonel?"

Hotel Icon,
Houston, Texas

THE CHIEF of staff ignored the knocking door by an angry staff and continued to pace the large executive suite in one of Houston's most luxurious hotels, the Icon. Congressman Harold Briggs was on his third glass of straight Jack Daniels and still had not uttered a word to any one of his staff since arriving in Houston from his clandestine meeting in the Gulf of Mexico. He went straight to his suite of rooms, even bypassing the gaggle of reporters that were there to get brief interviews. Now he was ensconced in his room where no one was allowed other than Conway Fleming.

"I can't help you if you don't tell me what went on out in the Gulf. Were you threatened or coerced in any way?"

Briggs downed the glass of bourbon he was holding and then reached for the ice bucket. When he saw that it was empty, he angrily slid it across the wet bar knocking three other bottles off its shiny top.

"Look, we already have reporters beyond curious about the way you're acting, and your opponents are going to pick up on that sooner or later."

Briggs ran a hand through his once perfectly coifed hair and then shook his head. But he still remained silent.

"If it will help, I received an assist from the Pentagon they didn't intend to give. It seems Nellis Air Force Base has actually refused to renovate a section of the old army airfield on the northern quadrant of the base that the Corp of engineers had recommended. When have you ever known a branch of *any* service to turn down funding for improvements? Seems a part of the puzzle about this mysterious department may have fallen into place. If you can prove they are hiding something out on that old firing range, a hidden compound perhaps, it may go a long way to forcing the President's hand and admit to his hidden agenda."

Harold Briggs simply looked at Fleming as if he were someone he failed to recognize. His eyes were red, and his suit was a mess. He poured himself another glass of bourbon.

"Okay, it obviously has something to do with this strange meeting. What happened. Didn't the information on the disc satisfy them?"

With the drink halfway to his mouth, Briggs stopped and started to laugh uncontrollably.

Conway Fleming wasn't amused as it looked as if his boss were having a breakdown.

Briggs finally got his laughter under some form of control and then finished his drink. "Russians. Our new friends are Russian." His glare at Fleming was absolute. "You failed to find that out in your extensive vetting process. If the press gets wind of the assistance and who gave it to us it won't matter in the least what past presidents have hidden from the public. All they'll see is Russian conspiracy. Get it genius?"

Fleming was speechless. He walked to the wet bar and poured himself a glass of straight vodka. When he lifted it to his mouth, Briggs suddenly swatted it out of his hands. The glass struck the wall and shattered.

"I'm fighting for the presidency and instead I could be going to fucking jail, and you're drinking vodka of all things. Tell me, do you have any common sense at all?"

"Now I'm suddenly a Russian agent because I was drinking vodka? You're the one that was approached with the offer of help and financial backing and with all of your foreign experience you didn't see who was really behind your benefactors. Give me a break."

"Do you know what they have planned with that information?"

"Exposure," Fleming said, this time reaching for a bottle of whiskey and a fresh glass.

"Our original backers would have used it that way, but there's a new player in the game. This ruthless bastard isn't out to expose anyone. He's out for himself. This Dmitri Sokol is a man I don't want to screw with."

"What does he have planned?"

Briggs drained his fifth bourbon and then slammed his glass down. "He's going to kill American citizens and we just became accomplices in that!"

Fleming looked at the drink in his hand and then slowly sat it down untouched. He moved to the couch and then sat heavily. "We have to get in touch with his superior. Are you sure he's not a part of this Sokol's plan?"

"I'm not sure of a damn thing."

"Well then, that's the way we'll play. If it is Russia we're dealing with, their history tells us they don't take to traitors to any one of their causes too lightly. We trade getting the hell out of the agreement we have by giving them their traitor. They have to deal."

Briggs paused before pouring another drink. He sat the bottle down. "Do you think it will work?"

Fleming had gotten up from the couch and was once again pacing the suite. He was thinking and thinking hard.

"Yes. Only you don't make the offer. I don't want you anywhere near these bastards again." He faced Briggs with a hard look. "Now, is there anything you're *not* telling me about this meeting on the oil rig other than this Sokol's plan?"

Briggs felt the blood drain from his face. If he told Fleming the truth, he knew he would lose his chief of staff for good. The memory of the power of the giant Grey was still foremost in his mind and even that memory was enough to drive him insane.

"No. Just what his plans were to deal with this group."

"Okay," Fleming walked over to the bar and forcefully removed the glass and bottle from Briggs hands. "Enough of this. I need you clear headed for the rest of the Houston gig. Do not, under any circumstances, deal with the press. Those fascists have a nose for crap like this. Tomorrow you give your speech and then you go on to California."

"And you?"

"I've got a call to make. And I'm not going to settle for this *'we'll take care of it'* shit. I want to be there when they crucify this bastard, Sokol. Then and only then will I be satisfied that we're in the clear. Now, get yourself cleaned up. Meet with the organizing staff about tomorrow and get some rest. Leave it to me." Fleming walked from the room.

Briggs, instead of doing what he was told, poured a last drink, and quickly downed it as he picked up the phone to have his campaign manager join him. The memory of the Grey and its ancient power still haunting his thought process.

"I hope you don't get to meet Asmodius, or you just may regret your bravado."

Novosibirsk, Siberia, Russia

THE STEAM ROOM was silent as just the hissing of cold water on brick could be heard. Number One sat alone as he soaked in the moist heat of the steam. Gone was his hairpiece and the corset he wore for appearance sake. He was deep in thought about the strange alert he had received earlier from the night shift control officer. The message had been cryptic and had been from Sokol's assistant Vexilla Trotsky. Number One had to think about if this was just a ploy or an actual betrayal. He knew Sokol had many enemies on the committee that could be framing him, but he himself didn't personally fear the young ladder climber. He knew the boy could be useful in future committee endeavors. If he could help it, he would rather avoid killing the young man and possibly losing the powerful Grey.

Without seeing, Number One felt the temperature change as the steam swirled around in a vortex. He knew someone had joined him.

He straightened the large towel around his waste and waited. It was his personal assistant. Behind him was Number Seven, the committee's foreign affairs officer and the man specially chosen by Number One to conduct the Congressman Briggs operation. He saw the uncomfortable way both his assistant and Number Seven looked as they stood before the reclining head of the Presidium as the steam and humidity began soaking their suits.

"Sir, Number Seven has received a call from the United States. Houston to be precise," his assistant said.

Number One looked up and wiped his sweating face with a towel. He knew it had something to do with the Briggs situation as he knew the Congressman was in Houston. He didn't like the way things were adding up. First Sokol asks to meet their American political asset, and then the strange call from Number Ten's own assistant saying Sokol may have gone rogue.

"Go on," he said as he took a long pull of water from a clear bottle.

"Sir, there is definitely something going on with our friend, Number Ten, and the new asset of his."

Number One looked at his assistant and then gestured for him to leave the steam room.

"Continue."

"Our Mr. Sokol has plans that go far beyond your orders sir. I was informed by the Congressman's front man that he plans on eliminating members of the covert American Group for his own gains and those of his new asset."

"The Grey?" Number One asked as he lowered the steams flow.

"Miss Trotsky say's the Grey is now called Asmodius. Now Fleming says that Sokol threatened Briggs so badly that he asked out of our arrangement as a reward for turning in a traitor."

"Is that so?"

"Yes, sir. Vexilla Trotsky's suspicion is now confirmed. We could lose control of the whole plan."

"Not only that, if he kills members of the Event Group, he'll be unleashing a man that could personally cause me very serious problems."

"Colonel Collins?"

"What have I said about mentioning that name in this building?"

"Sorry, sir."

Number One stood and walked to a phone on the wall. He swirled his hand in the air to clear it of steam. He picked it up. "I want to see Lieutenant Colonel Leonid Petrolovich immediately. I don't care if him and his unit is on maneuvers. Inform him I have actionable intelligence he needs to act on, and I want a viable plan on how to deal with it." Number One hung up the phone and turned for the shower area.

"Sir, there is one other thing."

Number Seven saw the look on his superior's face knowing the man was close to showing his anger, something he rarely did.

"Our friend Fleming, Briggs chief of staff, wants to be present to make sure we deal with this problem properly and then he wants our guarantee that we never contact the Congressman again."

"Is that so? Does the fool actually think we'll just wander off into the American sunset like one of their cowboys in those terrible films? No, Briggs is our man going forward. I think the good congressman needs to be reminded of just who and what we are capable of." He smiled. "Of course, Mr. Fleming can join our Spetsnatz Commandos in dealing with Sokol and this Asmodius. He'll serve as a good example of what happens to people who think we are fools."

FIFTEEN MINUTES later the 15th Special Guards Brigade, the most specialized unit of killers in the Russian military, was alerted in Moscow. They would soon be traveling north, over the pole in a flight destined for the United States of America for action on the Gulf coast.

Santa Fe Reginal Airport,
Santa Fe, New Mexico

THE LINE of cars sat idling at the guard shack just east of the main terminal. The rusty and sun faded red Town and Country Ford station wagon was in the front with the other eleven vehicles behind. The guard for the private plane terminal was leaning beside the burly driver of the station wagon.

"I'm sorry, you have to have a clearance pass from security inside the main terminal. Get that and I'll allow you through."

The old woman, Elsbeth Barlow, watched from the passenger seat as her driver made as if he had misplaced his pass. Elsbeth became bored at the situation, and with a small glance into the backseat to make sure the small green alien was covered completely with the blanket, she leaned forward to make eye contact with the uniformed security guard.

"Young man, we have a plane ready for us. Now, I be afraid of flying and this delay isn't helping. As you can see, I'm not the only elderly person in this vehicle," she turned her head indicating Charlie Ellenshaw who sat silently with a reassuring hand on the covered Matchstick Man.

"Ma'am, as I was saying, you have to have clearance to get into the private aircraft area." He looked closer at the shabbiness of the occupants and then looked up at the line of battered and rusted automobiles behind the first and knew these people didn't belong. "Now, you yokels don't look like you belong here, so why don't you turn yourself and these other cars around and head back to the hood?"

"Who you be calling a yokel?" the large man behind the wheel asked as he started to go for the door handle. Elsbeth placed her old and wrinkled hand on the man's arm and he relaxed.

"No call to be rude," she said as Charlie Ellenshaw winced in the backseat.

"I think you should just allow us to pass," Ellenshaw said.

"Okay, playtime's over. Get these cars moving or I'll call for assistance."

"Warned you," Charlie said as he slumped lower in the seat making sure Matchstick was covered well.

As the security man watched, Elsbeth placed a package of butterscotch pudding cups she had been opening on the seat next to her and raised her right hand toward the guard. Suddenly his head slammed forward into the doorjamb of the station wagon. He rebounded like a basketball bouncing off a backboard and went flying backward into the guard shack as the sliding door slammed closed.

"Oh, man, you got a way about you Granny, I swear you do," the driver said as he laughed.

"I hope I didn't hurt the boy too bad," Elsbeth said as she peeled the aluminum lid off one of her pudding cups. She turned and offered it to Charlie who just shook his head from side to side quickly with his eyes wide behind his wire-rimmed glasses.

The driver looked through his window and the glass of the shack. He saw the guard's booted feet propped against a desk where he had landed. They twitched and then became still.

"Nah, he ain't hurt none too much Granny. Wake up with a powerful headache though."

"Well, I'm not for puttin' up with insultin' folk like that young man. Yokels indeed. He won't remember a thing other than he bumped his head some." She took a plastic spoon full of pudding and put it in her mouth. Then with the spoon outstretched she waved it through the windshield. The gate magically swung up. The cars drove through.

They drove directly onto the taxiway. Charlie Ellenshaw was wondering what they were up to when he saw the sparkling, new, Boeing 737 waiting with boarding ramp already at the door. The station wagon and other cars parked. Elsbeth Barlow tossed the empty pudding cup into a trash bag dangling from one of the radio knobs and then turned to the driver.

"Now, them fellas out in the desert are no fools. Won't take 'em long to know what to look for. Get the folks back east after you split up. Go separate routes. That evil bastard will eventually start getting' an idea where we are at anyways. So be watchful."

"Yes, em."

She turned and looked at Charlie Ellenshaw. "You ain't feared of flyin' are ya beanpole?"

Crazy Charlie looked from Elsbeth to the shiny new Boeing

aircraft, confused as never before. He saw the female pilot walk to the door and wave at the cars on the ramp and saw arms poke from windows in a return wave. Ellenshaw just shook his head and watched as the crazed, white-haired lady cackled.

"How 'bout you, Matchstick, you 'fraid of getting' in the air with old Granny?"

Matchstick popped his head from where he had been hidden under the blanket. He saw the plane and he just looked at Elsbeth while blinking his eyes. Elsbeth shook her head and cackled again.

"I'm not sure if I'll ever get used to your eyelids slidin' in from the sides of that lightbulb shaped head of yorn." She cackled laughter again and Charlie and Matchstick both exchanged worried looks.

"Well, let's get goin back to old Massachusetts. Fuel for that plane is costing me dearly. Sorry I ever bought it. Only used it this once."

"Is this your aircraft?" Charlie asked, amazed that someone who looked as if she couldn't rub two nickels together could actually own a huge airplane like the Boeing.

"What did you 'spect skinny, me ridin' a broomstick?" Again, the cackle as she opened her door and got out of the battered Ford. Charlie and Matchstick watched as the female pilot came down the rolling stairs and hugged the old woman.

Ellenshaw turned to Matchstick.

"And I thought you digging yourself out of that grave was the strangest thing I've ever seen."

TEN MINUTES LATER CHARLIE ELLENSHAW, the Matchstick Man and Elsbeth Barlow were streaking toward Salem.

CHAPTER SEVEN

Event Group Complex,
Nellis Air Force Base, Nevada

Most members of the Event Group never ventured down into the realm of the Cryptozoology Department on level eighty-seven. With a staff of only fifteen men and women, Charles Hindershot Ellenshaw III kept the strange club as exclusive as he could. The main reason for this was that most of the sciences on staff still believed the entire department was a joke regardless of how many of the theories expounded by 'Crazy Charlie' had been proven by their own sciences to be just more than correct. Now, since the abduction of Professor Ellenshaw, the limited staff saw the dark chambers of their work environment even darker than normal.

Major Anya Korvesky was far more depressed than the young men and women around her as she and them created a search plan going on her theory that Director Niles Compton seemed to dismiss out of hand because of the subject matter—the Witch Queen, Elsbeth Barlow. Thus far Niles had her on the subject because when Xavier Morales ran Barlow's profile in Europa, not even the Cray supercomputer could find any official accounting of her actual existence.

"Major, I don't want to get on your bad side here, but Professor Ellenshaw always demanded we look at any outrageous theory with a dose of skepticism before we even begin," said Ellenshaw's long-time confidant, Lisa Ingram, a female anthropology major from the University of Main at Orino.

Anya laid down her pen, frustrated that she couldn't delve right into the subject, but then again, she realized these people had learned the hard way not to allow personal feelings to get in the way of actual scientific research.

"Please, never be afraid to speak up if you think I'm going down a path here that someone disagrees with. I've been around Charlie long enough to know how thorough he is."

"Well, is it possible your grandmother in Romania was only passing on an old legend? I've read your grandmother's file. We know she was the Gypsy Queen in Europe, but may I ask Major, did you believe her?" Ingram asked, hoping she didn't offend the Israeli intelligence officer.

"I always took my Grandmother's tales with a sensible dose of skepticism growing up. But when it came to the occult, yes, she has been proven more right than wrong. I did believe her. Perhaps it was when she spoke about Elsbeth Barlow of America, there was a reverence as if she wasn't telling us about a legend but telling us about a life that she actually witnessed."

"Excuse me," said Jake Witherspoon, a boy with glasses so thick they could have been used for a window in a pressurized submarine, "are you saying your Grandmother knew this woman?"

"I can't say that. Frankly the story was so unbelievable at the time I didn't think about it twice." Anya stood and paced Charlie's office.

"Europa is the best at finding people. Yet she has not found one historical reference in regard to even a legend or old wives' tale concerning an Elsbeth Barlow," said Lisa Ingram.

"Although I proclaim it from time to time, perpetuating a myth began by your old friend Pete Golding, Europa has never been infallible."

The members of the crypto team turned and just inside the door was Doctor Xavier Morales in his backless wheelchair and alongside him was Carl Everett. How long they had been there was anyone's guess.

"Captain, Doctor, sorry we didn't hear you come in. We're not used to visitors down in the dungeon," Lisa Ingram said.

"What are you saying Xavier?" Anya said as she exchanged looks with Carl. This was the first she had seen him since her reprimand and had started to wonder if he shared the same opinion as the Director of her duplicity in Charlie's kidnapping. "Are you saying you believe me?"

Doctor Morales used his strong arms to wheel over to the center of the room. His eyes wandered over jars filled with the strangest animal specimens he had ever seen. It reminded him of old Universal black and white movie props. To his brilliant mind it was a tad off-putting.

"No, I don't particularly have any reason to believe a non-eyewitness account, especially when Europa can't find any reference to Elsbeth Barlow. However, Director Compton does believe you. He sent us as sort of a peace offering. Captain, please explain." Xavier's words dwindled away as his eyes caught sight of the hand and forearm of the creature specimen that was found in the Amazon rainforest twelve years before.

"You, Alice, Virginia and Sergeant Sanchez aren't in trouble for your actions, although an official reprimand has been placed in your files for disregarding Niles' orders. No suspensions or retirement has officially been ordered."

Anya stared at Carl. "In English, please."

"Your faces have been exposed to this Congressman's, excuse the term here, witch hunt. Niles had to get you officially off any active roster so if the President is confronted with your faces or names, he can honestly say he has no knowledge of you and the others ever being on a government payroll. It's called…"

"Plausible deniability," Lisa Ingram finished for the Captain.

"Right." Everett walked up to Anya and smiled at her. "I guess you can say Niles has offered up Xavier here as a peace offering. He's here to help you find your elusive witch queen," Carl turned to leave. He couldn't help dig at the men and women looking at his retreating form. He stopped. "So, I'll leave you to it. It's too damn weird down here for me. It's like the old mall store, Spencer's Gifts, only stranger. Get some blacklight posters down here or something people."

They watched the naval Captain leave the room.

Xavier, his eyes still on the weird display of extinct creatures or animals that legend says couldn't exist residing in their specimen containers, shook his head and clapped his hands.

"Well, shall we get started?" Morales rolled over to the computer terminal and brought the mic down to his level. "Europa?"

"Yes, Doctor," she said, her Marilyn Monroe voice coming through loud and clear.

"We have some people here that think you're wrong about the existence of Elsbeth Barlow."

"Is that right?"

"That's right Europa," Xavier said with a smirk while looking at the men and women of crypto who couldn't believe Europa actually sounded indignant.

"Then Doctor, shall we prove it one way or the other?"

"Indeed."

Mystery Deep, **Exploratory Well # 3, sixty-eight miles off the coast of Louisiana**

DMITRI SOKOL WATCHED as the video link was completed. The face that began to appear was one he recognized immediately—Number Seven. He noticed immediately that the man in charge of the Congressman Briggs team was on an aircraft. The shaking of his surroundings explained in no uncertain terms that it was also a

Russian military plane. Sokol wanted to smile for the way these men constantly underestimated his intelligence.

"Number Seven. How nice of you to contact me to check on how my meeting went with the American asset you have worked so hard on. I admit you were right—he will be a most useful fool in acquiring eventual American cooperation in Russian expansion in the future. Tell me, is Number One available, I would like to also submit my report to him."

Number Seven made a foolish show of turning and looking around as if he were actually in Siberia. "No, I'm afraid he is conducting business elsewhere at the moment. I just wanted to relay the content of a most disturbing phone call I received from the Chief of Staff of the Congressman. He said you had a rather aggressive plan that does not coincide with what we have discussed at the Presidium of merely exposing this American Group. Is it true that you may have another direction you wish to venture down?"

Sokol, again wanted to laugh at the amateurish way Number Seven approached the subject of his betraying the committee. He really didn't care as he already knew he himself had been betrayed by his own assistant, Vexilla Trotsky, and that Briggs would go directly to the committee superiors after his meeting on *Mystery Deep*. The delay in their response time to his treason would be the committee's very undoing.

"Mr. Briggs is mistaken, my friend. All I wanted from him was more extensive cooperation if I am to assist Number One in exposing this Group. The material delivered by the good Congressman fell well short of the extensive list of people we need. I merely informed him. I may have bluffed some on the extent of our displeasure, but that is all. Inform Number One that everything is well in hand. I will of course reach out to the useful American fool and calm his nerves."

"Yes, that would be appropriate. I'll immediately inform Number One of the misunderstanding. I have a personal meeting with him in five minutes. Rest assured my friend—I will handle everything."

"Thank you, Number Seven."

The monitor clicked off.

Dmitri Sokol looked over at Vexilla Trotsky. She was bound hand a foot to an ornate chair in his office. He smiled at her as the Grey stood over her menacingly. It had been the Grey that had informed him of Vexilla's treacherous call to Siberia.

"It seems we have to advance our plans somewhat. I didn't actually think Number One would have the balls to come at me so soon. But Number Seven is obviously onboard an Ilyushin-Il-476, jet transport and also needless to say has a commando team in his accompaniment." Sokol looked at his watch. He hit an intercom switch on his desk. "Captain Tomsky prepare your men for an air assault on *Mystery Deep*. Time frame within the hour. If I know my superiors, prepare for a maximum effort by Lieutenant Colonel Petrolovich and the 15th Special Guards Brigade. Plan accordingly."

Sokol stood and walked to where Vexilla sat with tape over her mouth. He again smiled down at her. "Now the game truly begins." He looked at Asmodius the Grey. "The three ladies on the list provided by Congressman Briggs, you can begin." He turned as the Grey became excited. "Your choice of which. Just one of them for now until you prove to me your long-distance abilities."

The Grey spit in anger at only being allowed the one target. It angrily stomped from Sokol's office.

The Russian turned and watched the automatic door slide closed. He looked at a bound and frightened Vexilla.

"That is what is so encouraging about our new friend. He is very excitable about performing his duty."

Logan International Airport,
Boston, Massachusetts

THE LARGE BOEING 737 eased slowly into the private hangar on Logan's north field. As Charles Hindershot Ellenshaw III and a sleepy-eyed Matchstick were taken from the aircraft by two very large and better dressed men than those in Nevada, Elsbeth Barlow continued to face out of the window. Her eyes were closed. She wasn't aware she had been approached by the pilot of the Boeing plane. She reached out and gently nudged the old woman.

"Granny, we've landed. Your guests have already been taken to the cars. Your escort is ready."

Elsbeth Barlow didn't move. The pilot threw her captain's cap to the left-hand seat and then again, gently touched the old woman's cheek. She let out a sigh of relief when she felt the old woman still breathing. But then her relief faded when her own mental abilities picked up on a vibe that came from the far-off mind of Elsbeth. That was when the female pilot realized the old lady was off on a trip of her own and unlike the private jet, had yet to land.

The pilot reeled backward when Elsbeth sat straight up as if waking from an intense nightmare. Her eyes were wide, and her entire body was shaking.

"My God, what is it?" the pilot asked, quickly sitting in the vacant seat next to Elsbeth.

"It is calling itself Asmodius now." The old woman looked at the pilot with wild eyes. "It's going to attack someone. I feel it."

"What do we do?" the younger woman asked as she gestured for her co-pilot to assist.

"Take skinny and Matchstick to the compound. I need to be alone. Seal up this flying bucket of bolts. You and the others stay clear of what's goin' to happen. This could backfire and send that evil bastard right to me."

"Granny, maybe we can..."

"Go child, it's moving closer to its prey!"

**North Flamingo Road,
Las Vegas, Nevada**

VIRGINIA POLLOCK CLOSED her cell phone. She half-heartedly smiled at Alice Hamilton as they both sat at Alice's kitchen table.

"That damn Niles just said for us not to worry and that things aren't the way they seem. He said he will come over and personally see us to explain."

"When did that Brainiac start being so mysterious and cryptic about everything?"

Virginia smiled again and finished off the glass of wine that her and Alice had been sharing as they perused through a personal photo album of Alice's life with former Event Group Director and Senator from Maine, Garrison Lee. For Virginia it was if she were viewing the personal history of Department 5656 through the images of the famous couple.

"You know, regardless of the reasons, Niles is right. Garrison would have fired all of us for doing what we did. Maybe it's time I turned in my security clearance for good."

"You mean really retire?" Virginia asked, shocked.

"This Matchstick situation put a burden on my heart, and for the first time it took something out of me I don't think I can get back."

Virginia placed a hand over Alice's which was still sitting atop the closed photo album. "I think we need more wine. Maybe we can get drunk enough to kick the shit out of Jack's guard detail and escape our imprisonment."

"To tell you the truth, Dear, I think something a little stronger is called for."

Virginia patted Alice's hand once more and stood. "Have no fear, the intrepid assistant director is here. Where did Garrison keep his private stash of whiskey?"

"In his study on the second from the bottom bookshelf. He always thought the hollowed-out copies of 'War and Peace' and 'The History of the United States' fooled me when it came to hiding his liquor. There's a forty-year-old Scotch and a twenty-five-year-old Kentucky bourbon."

Virginia shook her head as she left the kitchen to get the added strength of the alcohol.

Alice took a deep breath, grateful for the brief respite of comforting memory about Garrison Lee, a person she missed more than life itself. Wanting more such respite, she opened the photo album.

Alice started perusing the photos she had mostly absconded with from Event Group files. Most were unofficial and of a more personal nature depicting her and Garrison on various missions through the years. Her own visage had changed throughout the time she had spent with the Group. From a young nineteen-year-old girl to her time with Garrison on their last mission together down in South America where he had passed away. She smiled as the years peeled away. She turned the page, and something caught her attention.

"I don't remember this picture," she said aloud, as she lifted the acetate cover and pulled out what she knew was a faded and very old Polaroid print, and not one of the professionally done photos by one of the Event Group archivists.

In the faded photo her and Garrison were in a pit with several staff members she remembered from days past and looked to be in the middle of a dig. It had to have been from very early in her career with the department. She looked closer at the time stamp on the very bottom edge of the Polaroid, 9/14/56. Alice shook her head as she was starting to doubt her memory in her old age. Then she snapped her fingers. She had pinpointed the obscure dig through the cobwebs of time. It was Boston. If she remembered clearly enough it was a dig at the site of old Boston Common. She could even see the marker where the first shots of the American Revolution had been fired during the infamous Boston Massacre. The city had allowed them in under the guise of the Daughters of the American Revolution sponsored search for artifacts during routine street repairs. She shook her head as she now remembered nothing of interest had been found. She placed the photo down and started thinking about how and why this picture had gotten into her personal album.

Alice was reaching for the photo when she stopped. Her hand started to shake, then she was overcome by the most powerful sense of Déjà vu she had ever felt. Nervous, she turned feeling she was being watched. All she saw was a mist outside of the sliding glass window.

The glass was fogging over as the outside temperature rose and the air conditioning system inside started to fog the large glass in the window, she turned her attention back to the album. Her fingers again touched the picture and that was when she saw it. She shakily placed her glasses on and examined the photo.

It was her in the bottom of a shallow trench with a small trowel in her hand and behind her was Garrison wearing his ever-present brown and battered fedora. He had his hands on his hips as he always did when reprimanding someone for cutting corners. Alice, even though upset, had to smile at her lovers rough-as-a-corncob attitude even now. The hole in the street was surrounded by Event Group staff as she recalled some of the familiar faces. It was the silver haired woman standing somewhat aloof beside some of the others. The face and hair was as if she were looking at the exact double of the woman from Lake Mead who had taken Charlie and Matchstick—Elsbeth Barlow. Alice dropped the photo as she realized it couldn't be the same woman because the photo was over sixty-five years old. The woman depicted couldn't have been the same because her body and features had not changed at all. Alice stood up and backed away when she came to the conclusion that no matter what she thought was possible or impossible, the woman was the exact double of Elsbeth Barlow.

"My God, Anya was right!"

As Alice braced herself against the kitchen counter, she heard a 'squeaking' noise coming from her left. She turned her head and in the condensation from the colder air striking the warm glass, she watched as a symbol started to be etched into the watery surface. It was if a child was writing in the fogged glass. Her eyes widened as several more symbols started to magically appear. There were straight lines with ovals. Circles with arrows through them. Also, what looked like ancient middle eastern Sumerian writing which Alice had studied in her youth. Soon the entire window was covered in the strange symbolic writing. The letters and symbols started to run with condensation.

"I chose the History of the United States and the bourbon,"

Virginia said as she came back into the kitchen. She stopped when she saw Alice was standing near the counter with her hand over her mouth and the other over the left side of her chest as if to still a racing heart, and for the first time in the twenty-six years Virginia had known her, Alice looked absolutely terrified.

"You look like you've seen a ghost," she said as she placed the bottle of aged bourbon onto the table over the photo that had scared Alice. Her eyes went to the glass and that was when Virginia saw the writings through the running condensation.

Virginia stopped cold when she saw the symbols and then hurried to see about Alice. Then she saw her reflection in the sliding glass door and the strange writing and that was when the Event Group assistant director screamed and turned so fast Alice jumped. In the reflection was a sight that froze her blood in her veins. The largest Grey she had ever seen, and Virginia had seen more than just a few after the war. She spun around and was shocked to see nothing but the kitchen wall and hallway leading to the study where she had just come from. There was nothing behind her.

Virginia felt her heart return to somewhat of a normal beat pattern as her eyes searched everywhere for the vision that had suddenly vanished. She felt Alice's hand on her shoulder.

"You didn't see anyone standing behind me?" she asked.

"No Dear. You came back alone. Now the writing on the glass is gone. What did you see?"

"I..."

Alice was suddenly slammed to the kitchen counter where she rebounded and fell to the tiled floor. Virginia screamed again as she moved to help her. Then she grabbed at her throat. The pressure was tremendous as she was lifted free of the floor. Alice, stunned, fought to her hands and knees and through a painfully racing heart attempted to reach for Virginia's foot as both of her shoes went sailing through the air during her struggles to free herself from a force that wasn't there. Alice was then rocked by a brutish kick to her chest and thrown back again as Virginia fought for a lifesaving snatch of breath. Alice rolled and nearly crashed through the sliding glass window.

When she shook her head to clear it, she saw Virginia in the reflection off the glass. This time it was Alice who screamed when she saw the assistant director wasn't alone. A giant Grey standing over eight feet tall was strangling her friend as it shook her as if she were nothing more than a ragdoll. The creature was hissing and smiling at the feeble attempts made by Virginia to free herself.

"What the hell?" came a loud shout, as four Group security men came crashing through the kitchen door after hearing the screams from outside.

Alice turned, still trying to stand after the brutal assault, but felt the sharp pang through her chest as she did so. When she finally managed to get up to her knees, she saw what the security men were seeing. Virginia was floating in midair with her hands at her own throat.

The first security man, Alice didn't remember his name but knew him to be a young Marine, reached for Virginia as the other three went for their nine-millimeter semi-automatic pistols. The Marine suddenly flew backward and crashed through the dry wall in a spray of bloody mist. Then Alice screamed again as two of the three security personnel were struck by an invisible wave of hatred and devastating force and thrown up and then through the ceiling. The fourth fought with what he couldn't see as Virginia began to slowly lose her fight for air. Then as the security man grabbed out for the only thing he could see, Virginia's own hands, a blow was struck that crushed his head and neck down into his shoulders and chest. Blood sprayed across the kitchen so hard Alice had to turn away which spared her the last moment of Virginia's Pollock's life as she was casually tossed onto the kitchen table as if she was nothing more than a sacrificed lamb. When Alice opened her eyes, she was seeing the reflection in the glass once more. The Grey slowly walked toward her. She turned and nothing was there. When she again glanced at the window, she saw the Grey smiling at her as it raised its right hand. Then she saw it scribble with a bloody clawed finger a four-pointed star on the wall above Virginia's lifeless body. Then it drew a circle around the star and then with a hiss of pleasure it drew the number one within the pentangle. Alice closed her eyes and screamed.

Then as Alice once more turned away in terror of what was coming for her, she felt another presence in the kitchen. Suddenly she heard the Grey hiss in anger and then she heard the words 'leave her be!' in a woman's voice. A final hiss and an animalistic roar from the giant rattled the dishes and glasses inside the kitchen cabinets.

When Alice opened her eyes, the creature was gone in the window's reflection. The dripping condensation was there but the symbols were also missing. She turned and that was when she saw the footprints in blood on the tiled floor. Mixed in with the prints of the Grey was that of a much smaller person. The bloody prints were all over as if a tremendous fight had ensued in the seconds Alice had heard the womanly voice.

Alice Hamilton felt the pain in her chest and wanted to reach for the countertop but failed as her body gave out. She reached with her outstretched hand into the bloody prints on the floor and she grasped the faded Polaroid photograph and crumpled it into her hand as the pain of the heart attack struck in earnest.

The house that Alice Hamilton and Garrison Lee had shared out on North Flamingo Road in Las Vegas became deathly still and silent.

Logan International Airport, Boston, Massachusetts

THE FEMALE PILOT and her crew waited at the bottom of the rolling stairs as suddenly the large Boeing jet started to rock as if it were in flight and fighting through harsh turbulence. A shock wave of power slammed into them and the four men and one woman sprawled onto the concrete inside the hangar as an invisible wave of air actually lifted the wings of the aircraft. The wind stopped and the plane bounced several times on its landing gear and then settled. Then the overhead lights went out, came back on, and then several blew out with a loud banging noise. The pilot, Millicent Krensky, one of the first female fighter pilots to fly combat missions in an actual war, flew up the stairs as the Boeing 737 settled. She opened the door and ran inside. Elsbeth Barlow was laying in the aisle far from where the pilot had left her moments before. Running to her side she lifted the old woman's head and placed it in her lap. Millicent feared the worse until she saw Elsbeth's eyes flutter open.

"Granny breathe damn it. Tell me you're alright!"

"Don't have to shout child. I'm old as hell but not deaf. Help me to my feet."

As she slowly assisted Elsbeth up and placed her in one of the large seats, she took her pulse. It was rapid but safe for now. That was when she saw Elsbeth's bloody tennis shoes. Bright reddish-green liquid poured from the pink soles.

"What happened?"

Elsbeth tossed her head back and closed her eyes.

"The bastard is back and he's loose. This time we won't be able to stop him. He's grown in power. The defeat of the Greys has intensified his strength somehow."

"Whose back Granny?" the younger woman asked.

Elsbeth opened her eyes as a single tear wandered down the creases and crevasse of her aged face.

"Asmodius. In our history he was known as…"

"The King of Demons," Millicent answered for her. The name in necromancy circles was a famous one and a legend most scoffed at.

"Yes," Elsbeth said closing her eyes once more. "But he is so much more than that. Asmodius has whoever is handling him fooled. The king of liars and the killer of children has always been far more than just a demon, and my hope that the little green guy could help without drawing others into this mess was badly mistaken."

"What are you saying Granny?" Millicent asked.

"Never you mind child. I have a task for you."

"What?"

"I think it's time to call in allies to the cause. I think through my failure they may be more receptive to our cause after tonight. Go on now. You have another long flight ahead of you."

"Where am I going?" Millicent asked.

"Nevada. We need help far sooner than I thought."

FOR ELSBETH BARLOW, her plans for dealing with the greatest threat to humankind had to be changed. That change involved a small Group of men and women that comprised the Event Group.

PART II

ASMODIUS MODAI

"The prince of darkness rose up from his sleep.
He unfurled his wings and stretched his dark limbs,
before swooping down on the world beneath…"
~Amit Rahman, The Prince of Darkness

CHAPTER EIGHT

**_Mystery Deep_, Exploratory Well # 3,
sixty-eight miles off the coast of Louisiana**

The elevator stopped at the lowest level of the rig. Dmitri Sokol nodded at one of the two fully equipped guards and one of them ruthlessly tore the tape off of Vexilla Trotsky's mouth. She dipped her head in pain, refusing to show that Sokol nor his thugs could hurt her. She had resigned herself to the death she knew was coming.

Sokol stepped from the elevator and went directly to the new chambers assigned to Asmodius. The two guards followed with the woman between them.

"You men, go back and join your unit. We should be having company very shortly."

The men did as they were told and left for the upper levels. Sokol looked down at Vexilla and smiled. "Let's see how our friends first foray into the real world fared, shall we?"

Vexilla didn't answer, she only glared at her former boss. She knew Sokol now as the real king of lies for the way he had in recruiting the unsuspecting and using their own anger against them as he had done with the history of her family. She now had a hard time deciding who was more despicable, the monstrosity he had under his power, or the man standing before her. He tapped in his security code. The doors slid open.

Sokol hesitated when he saw that the only lights came from the several differing candles that Asmodius had asked for. The windows to the sea were shuttered and the room sparse. He took Vexilla by the arm and entered. That was when he saw Asmodius for the first time as the creature stepped from the shadows. He was shocked to see the Grey was bleeding. Several long scratches flowed from its cheeks to the jawline. Asmodius wiped a white towel across the wounds and then tossed the towel away where it landed by Sokol's feet.

"What did you do to yourself?" Sokol asked as he angrily pushed Vexilla aside. Her eyes watched the Grey and knew immediately something he did most definitely didn't go according to its plan. She hid her joy now knowing the bastard in some way could be hurt. She backed off when the Grey hissed and took a menacing step toward her. It was if it sensed she was hiding her pleasure at its discomfort.

"Well?" Sokol insisted.

The Grey turned away and then angrily swiped its long arm through the air and then the outside windows to the underwater world opened, giving them more light to see by. Then it swiped its clawed hand through the air once more and a brief flash of light morphed into a picture of a nice-looking woman with black hair. Then the Grey angrily swiped it through the depiction, and it vanished, exploding into a million sparkles of light.

"Good, who is she?" Sokol said.

Asmodius shook its head. Either he didn't understand Sokol's question or it just didn't care. Both the Grey and Sokol turned when they heard Vexilla, her hands still handcuffed behind her back, chuckle.

"What's so funny?" Sokol asked.

"I don't know who she is, but I do know that she's well known in Washington circles. She was a part of the team that dealt with the congressional hearings during the war."

Vexilla glanced at the Grey who turned away as if it weren't interested in the least.

"So. I couldn't have asked for a better example be made. Asmodius did well. Now, with the committee no longer our concern, we can move on. We don't have to pretend anymore about satisfying their fear of this Group under the desert. Not our concern. With Asmodius doing what was asked, we have successfully laid the suspicion of this woman's murder on the committee's doorstep."

Vexilla laughed again. The Grey became angered at her arrogance. "Why don't you ask the Grey bastard what went wrong?"

Sokol turned as the Grey advanced on Vexilla. It started to reach for her but Sokol stepped in front of her. He turned on Asmodius. "What does she mean?"

The Grey again, turned away and stormed to the far side of the chamber.

"I asked a question," Sokol persisted.

"Ask the bastard who else was killed and who bloodied it up? That may be interesting."

The Grey turned and its yellow eyes glowed in fury. It swiped its arm through the air.

"I kill who I...wish...to kill!"

Sokol felt like he was gut punched. He shook his head and then a thought struck him. "Well, you'll soon get your chance." Sokol paced as he thought. "It doesn't matter, we're done doing the committee's bidding anyway. I don't care who he killed."

Again, the laugh. He angrily turned to his former assistant. "You're not thinking this through Dmitri. He, as we suspected he had the power to do, projected himself to his attack zone. It would have been impossible for it to be hurt if his physical presence wasn't there. Who, or *what* injured it?" Vexilla laughed again. "I think you may have someone out there that knows more than you do about your new friend."

Sokol turned and looked at a furious Asmodius. "Well?"

The Grey, from across the room lifted Vexilla off the floor. It pushed her against the steel wall and started to twist her neck. The only thing that saved her was the alarm buzzer that sounded.

"All hands to defensive stations. We have an intermittent radar contact coming in from the North."

"We'll take this up later," Sokol said as Vexilla was suddenly and ruthlessly let go where she fell to the deck. "Now, go do some killing for me!" He paced to Vexilla and helped her up. "As for you my dear, it's time for you to pay for your treachery. It's time you die with the men sent to kill us."

Throughout the rig, one hundred specially chosen commandos prepared to ambush their fellow countrymen who came to end the career goals of Dmitri Sokol.

North Flamingo Road,
Las Vegas, Nevada

JACK HAD BEEN at McCarren airport to see Will Mendenhall, Jason Ryan, and Colonel Henri Farbeaux off on their mission to get a closer look at the man out to expose the Group—Congressman Harold Briggs. Xavier Morales had informed them that he suspected Briggs was getting his information from someone who knew far more about Department 5656 than they should and that left out most American citizens and possibly shed more light on who the main suspects were without it being said. Outside of confronting the Congressman directly, Jack had given Henri, Jason and Will free reign as to how they went about gathering the information. Tram would run as their back-up from a hotel suite in New Orleans.

Jack's cell phone buzzed.

"Collins," he said curtly as he left the airport's private access area.

"Colonel, we have a stage one 'purple' alert issued by Europa. We have a cover team heading there now. The situation is critical according to Captain Everett," Xavier Morales said.

"Address?" Jack asked.

"Colonel, it's Mrs. Hamilton's residence," Morales said.

Without another word Collins tossed the phone onto the passenger seat and then screamed toward Flamingo road. A stage one purple alert told him that Event Group personnel were down.

AS JACK TORE into the circular drive, he saw the Event Group cover vans in front. They had various logos on the sides proclaiming emergency house repairs. They even had a falsified Nevada Gas Authority van with flashing yellow lights. Just as he opened the car's door, Sarah was there. She took Collins in her arms and started to cry.

"Sarah, what happened?" he asked as he held her at arm's length.

"Virginia, your men, they're all dead!"

Jack took Sarah by the hand and they sprinted to the open front door of the house. They were met by Carl. He just held out his large right hand and stopped them from entering the house.

"There's nothing you can do in there, Jack."

Collins locked eyes with his friend. The question didn't need to be asked.

"A massacre. Virginia, all four of our men," he said as he saw the shock in the colonel's eyes. Carl stepped out of the way when a man in a gas service uniform and another in a cleaning service coverall stepped up with a stretcher. Carl moved aside. Jack reached for the sheet covering the body and pulled it back. The serene face of Virginia Pollock greeted Jack and Sarah's horrified stares. Jack balled the corner of the sheet up as his anger built and then he calmed and allowed the sheet to finally slip from his grasp. He lowered his head.

"Alice?" he asked.

"They took her to the closest trauma center. Desert Springs Hospital. Niles is with her. Heart attack they think. It's bad Jack. I don't think she's going to make it."

Carl lowered his head and shook it. He and Collins knew when they were helpless to do anything. "Jack, what about the Master Chief? Should we call him in Paris?"

"God, I forgot about Jenks. He'll flip out." Collins thought a moment as he looked from Carl to Sarah. "No, we need time. If Jenks finds out, we'll have him to worry about as much as our killer. When is he due home?"

"Five days," Sarah said shaking her head knowing that the gruff Master Chief was going to take the loss of Virginia very hard.

"We'll brief him when he get's home. My responsibility," Jack said.

"No," Carl interrupted. "I'll do it. God knows he'd kill anyone else. I brought him into the Group. It has to be me."

Jack could only nod his head knowing that Carl was right.

Jack turned to look at Sarah. "Go, be with Niles. We'll come as soon as we get a grasp of what in the hell happened."

Sarah swiped tears away and then turned and ran for Jack's car.

Collins took Carl by his large shoulders and lightly shook him. "Hey pal, I need you."

Carl nodded his head. "Jack, our men were murdered in a ruthless way. No one man has the strength to do what was done."

Jack patted Carl on the shoulder and stepped inside of the house. He was immediately approached by a man he knew well. He was part of the medical staff at Group and was a specialist in crime scene analysis. His eyes went from him to four covered bodies lying on the living room's hardwood floor. Jack intentionally looked away as he knew more of his men were under those sheets.

"Colonel, you have to see this. I can't figure out what in the hell took place here." Jack watched the technician turn and return to the kitchen area.

The first thing Jack saw was the pentangle etched in blood over the kitchen table. The number one stood out as his eyes went to the table itself.

"Assistant Director Pollock was found there. It was like her death was some form of sick ritualistic sacrifice."

"Could you tell the cause of death?" Jack asked as he tried to swallow the taste of bile in his throat.

"Without an autopsy, I can't be sure. But it looks like strangulation by a powerful hand. Her larynx and spinal cord were pulverized."

Collins heard a chair being moved. He turned and saw that Carl had entered and had sat down. Jack had never seen Carl so distraught. He completely understood.

"Colonel, we also discovered this," the technician said turning to the sliding glass window. "We couldn't recover much, but what we did…I just don't know what in the hell it is."

On the glass, men were working with a heat gun as they fogged the glass while a female tech outlined with a white grease pencil what looked like words and symbols."

"Get what you can for Charlie…" Jack stopped himself before he could say the name Ellenshaw, forgetting they didn't have him at the complex. He cleared his throat. "Make sure they get pictures and get them to Cryptozoology. Make sure Major Korvesky is made aware."

"Yes, sir."

"Jesus Christ!" said a voice from the entrance hall.

Jack turned and was looking at the stunned face of Tom Wilkerson, FBI agent-in-charge of the Las Vegas field office.

"What the fuck happened here?"

Jack angrily turned on Wilkerson. He was still angry over the confrontation at the Desert Rose Cemetery. He took the FBI agent by his blue windbreaker and brought his nose to his face.

"I don't want to hear any FBI bullshit on how you're going to handle this. My crime scene. Our people are dead!"

Carl took Jack and forced his arms away from Wilkerson. When freed the FBI man backed away from the blazing blue eyes daring him to say something.

"Jack, I'm here to assist. The President is aware of what happened. He said not to get in your way. You have a basic free hand to do what needs doing."

Jack deflated. He reached out and lightly tapped Wilkerson on the shoulder.

"Sorry, Tom. But we have five dead and a very special woman in the hospital who may not make it."

"Our labs at your disposal. I have a team posted outside to keep the Las Vegas locals at bay. We will seal this scene, Jack."

Collins nodded.

"My crew here needs time, Tom. Give them that. Then report fatalities from a gas leak."

Tom Wilkerson looked around at the blood and the symbol on the wall.

"Go get the sick son of a bitches that did this Jack, and I'll hold them down for you while you beat them to death."

This time it was Carl who thanked the FBI man. "We'll be at the hospital. Call if anyone gives you a problem."

"Will do, Captain."

Looking at the crime scene, special agent Tom Wilkerson sat hard into the chair Carl had just vacated. He shook his head at the terror at what must have happened in the quiet house on North Flamingo Road.

"And I thought dealing with terrorists was bad."

Cambridge, Massachusetts

Two MILES from the Harvard University campus, stood a magnificent house built in 1678. Once belonging to the family of a little-known French and Indian and revolutionary war hero, John Alston Barlow. The home was rarely seen by the citizens living close by. The woods that surrounded the estate acted as a natural barrier that not only kept people out, but the family in. The Barlow's have always looked at their home as a virtual prison where they had been kept out of public view since the time of the witch trials almost three hundred and forty years ago.

Charles Hindershot Ellenshaw III watched as Matchstick had slowly come around from his delusional and basically silent state since he had been found alive. When they first encountered the small alien at Lake Mead, they had not realized that their friend wasn't all there. It was like unwrapping a toy at Christmas without all the parts included in the box. As Charlie watched from their comfortable area where they were being held, Matchstick would doze and then suddenly awake as if he had a horrible dream that bordered more on night terrors. Mahjtic had shown no memory of how and when he was shot and supposedly killed that night in Chato's Crawl. Charlie felt he wasn't nearly qualified enough to start reassembling the small alien's dysfunctional mind even though thus far Matchstick showed no memory loss when it came to Charlie or those friends he had encountered at the lake. He dare not bring up the subject of Gus Tilly, Doctor Denise Gilliam, or Pete Golding.

As he watched the dozing alien's eye's fluttered open. Charlie went to the large bed and sat on its edge.

"How you doin', Matchstick?" he asked watching him for any sign of panic.

He remained silent. Matchstick sat up in bed and looked around. The small nose, almost imperceptible, moved as if he were smelling something familiar.

"Wa...wa...ater," he said in his typical cotton filled voice.

Charlie reached for the pitcher and glass on the small table. He poured a glass and offered it to Matchstick. The thin fingers came up and gently pushed the glass away. Then Charlie realized what Matchstick was saying. It was the same observation he had when they first put them in confinement.

"Yes, I smell it too. We must be by a river or lake."

"Moving...wa...wa...ter."

"A river then." Charlie put the glass down and assisted Matchstick as he sat up on the ornate bed. "Let's go about this with what we know," Charlie said as Matchstick's eyes roamed around the room they were in, not really locking on anything. "We know we landed at Logan International."

"Bos...tonnn."

"Yes, Boston. If we are smelling water, and as dank as that smell is, I think we're in a basement." Charlie looked around at the antique setting. "A very nice basement, but a basement. Must be a low water table in the area. Any ideas?"

Matchstick stopped looking around the room and his almond shaped eyes settled on the cryptozoologist. "Char...lessss."

"Yes, it's me, Charlie."

Matchstick looked at Ellenshaw and the eyelids closed from the sides of his head and then the black orbs rolled in exasperation. It took Charlie a moment to realize his mistake.

"Oh, yes, of course. The River Charles you mean."

Matchstick made a clicking noise with his tongue and cheek as if saying, *'now you got it.'*

"Old friend, what do you remember of the past nine months?"

Matchstick pushed the covers off its small legs and stood on the bed. He was still wearing the small blue coveralls of the security department. To Charlie's dismay, the little guy still smelled of earth— or, *'the grave'* he corrected his thinking.

"Gussssssss. Peeeeeat. Doc...tor...Gill...Gilliam." His eyes went down to look at Charlie. His large head tilted to the left, and then to the right. Then his eyelids closed, and he squeezed them shut for the longest time. When he opened them, Ellenshaw saw the tear run down its green skin. Charlie just nodded. That answered his question.

"Matchstick, how in the world did you survive those bullets?"

"The mysteries of the universe are vast Professor. Of all the people on earth, you and your associates should know that better than most."

Ellenshaw turned and stood from his place on the bed. Matchstick backed as far away as he could until its small back was against the wall. Both were staring at the old woman who had entered the basement unseen. Gone were her shabby street clothes and they had been replaced with a modern, if not out of fashion full-length flowered print dress. Her silver hair was placed in a bun with a pink ribbon.

"Sorry to have startled you." Elsbeth Barlow walked further into the large room and looked around until she found a chair and then she sat. She closed her eyes and took a deep breath as if she were exhausted. When she opened her eyes, she gave her 'guests' a small smile that was anything but applicable in their current situation. "In answer to your question about Mr. Stick, his body is far different from ours as I am sure you know, skinny."

Charlie noticed the old woman had lost her backwoods sounding dialect and she now spoke in clear and very precise English.

"We learned a very long time ago that when a Green has massive trauma done to its system, that system will shut down to repair itself, or regenerate if you prefer. Depending on the form of trauma, this process may take as much as two years. I am sorry, but the cause I represent could not take a chance on waiting that long. I need Mr. Stick here to assist in finding *him*."

"Who are you?" Charlie said as Matchstick still kept his distance.

This time a little of the backwoods in the woman came out as it had before. She laughed. More of a cackle like she had voiced at the lake. "That is a complicated question."

Charlie stood up and looked from the old woman to Matchstick who still stood as far away as he could get on the limited size of the bed. "Well, I think we deserve an explanation, so why don't you un-complicate it for us."

"My name is Elsbeth Barlow."

"Are, are you like, one of them? An alien I mean?" Charlie asked. After what he had seen what this woman was capable of at Lake Mead the question didn't seem at all outlandish.

Again, the laughter. "Lord, no." She looked from Ellenshaw to Matchstick who had closed his eyes as if in deep thought.

"There's no use in searching that enormous brain of yours for a memory of my name, Mr. Stick. You're never heard of me before. At least your collective memory with your race won't allow you to remember."

"You, Madam, are not un-confusing the situation at all," Charlie said as he saw the questions in Matchstick's face as he thought about what the woman said.

"In other words, Charles Hindershot Ellenshaw III, me and Mr. Stick have met many times before. But due to some chicanery by me and others, he won't remember. Neither him nor the many of his kind from the past." She smiled kindly at the small alien. "Without him and his race my kind would not have been able to fend off our enemy in the past."

"As I said, I am not following you," Charlie said, wondering if he had totally lost all of his imagination or was this woman just that insane.

"Charlie, may I call you Charlie?"

"Call me a fool for thinking you have a reason for doing what you've done."

She smiled. "Well, Charlie, you and your friends always thought that the war with the Greys was the real threat. I never gave it a second thought you see. Humankind has always been able to fight off the bad side of his race or that of any physical entity, be human or otherworldly. But for thousands of years man has had an enemy that cannot be fought off with brute strength and bravery like your small Group under the desert has in abundance. The real enemy has returned. How? I do not know. But the bastard *is* here. I saw him just tonight."

"Again, just who in the hell are you?" Charlie asked as he watched Elsbeth stand from the Queen Anne chair.

"Some call me Granny. Mostly my followers that have chosen the solitary life. Some call me the old one, like John Adams, George Washington and even that rapscallion Thomas Jefferson, all of whom I assisted in the past and the very men responsible for hiding my old ass away from the world in expectation of this day." She started for the door and then stopped and turned. "Even your old friend, Garrison Lee."

"How old are you?" Ellenshaw asked.

"That's not very chivalrous of you Professor. Never ask a lady how old she is. No wonder you never married."

"We need to contact our Group. We need to let then know we're being held by a mad woman," Charlie said defiantly.

"Already in the works, Slim." She reached for the door.

"I am sorry for your loss." She opened the door and that was when Ellenshaw saw two guards outside the open door. Elsbeth Barlow shooed them away.

"What loss?" Crazy Charlie asked.

"We'll talk later Slim. You're free to move about the estate. Breakfast in twenty minutes."

Charlie sat hard onto the soft, down filled bed, and Matchstick flopped down next to him.

"I think we may be in a little trouble here my friend."

All Matchstick could do was nod his head at a fast rate of speed.

Desert Springs Hospital,
Las Vegas, Nevada

NILES COMPTON PACED OUTSIDE of the intensive care as the doctors and trauma specialists worked on Alice Hamilton, when an eruption of noise sounded from the upper areas of the hospital. Sarah looked at Niles and both were worried the commotion had something to do with Alice. They were relieved however when they saw security and other employees of the hospital run through the hallways and then up the stairs. Sarah felt the relief and continued to fight back the despair she was feeling over the possible loss of Alice Hamilton and the sudden death of her friend, Virginia Pollock.

Niles stopped pacing after the noise had subsided and then sat next to Sarah and placed his arm around her. The small geologist saw the redness of the Director's eyes and knew he was having a difficult time with what had happened. Coupled with the Matchstick disappearance, the abduction of Charlie and now this, she could tell Niles was close to the breaking point.

They both heard the automatic doors to the emergency room open with a click and Sarah was relieved to Jack and Carl walk in. Both men had the good sense to wash up before coming in. Sarah stood along with Niles and withheld her desire to hug Jack. She did indicate however that he should see if he could bring Niles back from the despondent state he was in. She walked over and took Carl by the hand so Jack could speak with the director.

"Tom Wilkerson of the Nevada field office is allowing our people to make the first forensic run at the house. We should have an idea what happened soon."

Niles started to say something but stopped. He just nodded his head.

"Alice?" Jack asked. He turned and saw that Carl was already being informed by Sarah about her condition.

Compton cleared his throat, started to speak, and then just simply shook his head. Collins understood. He knew because of her age it was never that good.

"That is by far the toughest woman I have ever met. Hell, she's tougher than most of the soldiers I've known. She'll fight, Niles."

Compton was about to speak when several people came through the double-automatic doors. Men in black suits and ties were moving hospital orderlies out of the way as several more men came in. Jack, Niles, Carl, and Sarah all saw what all the commotion had been about upstairs as the President of the United States came in following his security detail. With hair that was almost totally grey and a face that held the lines of worry generated by the eight long and tough years of his administration, he walked up to Niles and forced the man into his arms. He patted the director on the back and nodded at Jack over the director's shoulder.

"What's the word?" he asked as he continued to hold Niles' shoulders.

Niles shook his head. "Not good. Total cardiac failure."

"What in the hell happened?" He was now looking at Collins as Sarah and Carl joined them.

"We're still working on that," Jack said as he exchanged looks with Carl.

The president reached out and took Collins by the shoulder and Jack could see up close how the war with the Grey's and his injuries from the battle of Camp David had aged Compton's best friend. The president also glanced at Everett and Sarah until they joined them. The five people standing in the intensive care waiting area looked far beyond mere conspirators.

The intensity in the look of the president said volumes about how he felt about his people at the Event Group. "Honest opinion here, and don't hold anything back. Did Congressman Briggs have anything at all to do with this...this...."

"Hit," Niles said without hesitancy. "Mr. President, I have not one shred of proof, but as you've known since college, I am not a believer in coincidence."

"Leads?" the president asked.

"Nothing other than the fact that Doctor Morales believes that Briggs is getting his information from someone who knows the Group intimately."

"The damn Russian outfit?" the commander-in-chief asked.

"Or someone else," Carl interjected, ignoring the warning look from Jack.

"Meaning?"

Niles looked at his friend. "Major Korvesky said that the old woman and the people that snatched Matchstick and Charlie at Lake Mead is known to her Romanian family. Elsbeth Barlow."

The president looked closely at Niles. "Barlow? Are you joking?"

"That's what the Major reported," Carl answered for Niles.

"Old ghost stories?" the president said as he turned away from the four people in the hallway.

"Wait a minute, are you saying you've heard about her?" Jack asked, wondering if even the president was going off kilter over Alice and Virginia.

"Yeah, Colonel. They're what we call part of the Camp David ghost stories told by President's and their staffs through the years. But that's all they are, ghost stories about a mysterious lady that comes out of the woodwork from time to time to help the country. Pure bull if you ask me. If it was true where was this mysterious savior when we needed her with the world's fight against the Greys?"

"Is that all you know?" Niles asked in all seriousness.

"No, the story goes, and I hate even bringing this up, because, well, come on, it's not even that entertaining."

"Jim?" Niles said as if reprimanding a child.

"The story says she's a witch. Not just a normal witch, but *the* witch queen."

The four members of the Event Group exchanged looks as that

description was the exact one given to them by Anya and her wild gypsy tale.

"Oh, come on. Are you people thinking there's a shred of truth in that?" the president asked, incredulous.

"Like the truth that there isn't a Bigfoot, or a mysterious and highly advanced submarine that plowed beneath the sea for hundreds of years and one that eventually guided us to a place called Atlantis. Or that a small little green man named Matchstick saved our lives in a war with space aliens?" Niles looked angry for the first time in days. "Do you want me to go on?"

"I get the point baldy," was all the commander-in-chief said.

The five people in the hallway surrounded by fifteen secret service agents stood as they thought about the next step they had to take when the door to intensive care opened and a young doctor stepped out. He was immediately surrounded by men in black suits with radio connection's in their ears. His eyes widened as he took them in.

"Doctor," Niles said pushing through the cordon of agents, "how is she?"

Even Jack Collins had to choke down his emotions before the young man could answer the director.

"All we can do is keep her stable. What in the hell has that lady been through? I counted seven old bullet wounds and at least three stab marks."

"Prognosis?" the president asked.

Again, the doctor's eyes went wide in shock at who was standing before him.

"Sssssir, ...all we can do is watch her."

"No Doctor, we can do much more than that." The president nodded at a secret service agent near the door who turned and opened it. The person that came through was a burly man in a black naval uniform. The stars on his shoulder boards announced exactly who he was.

"Your name, son?" the man with beard asked as he removed Alice's chart from his shaking hands.

"Hanson. Kevin Hanson," the young doctor answered.

"Good, Doctor Hanson. That's a good start. My name is Admiral James Dennison, they call me the Surgeon General of the United States. The President has asked me to supervise your additional caseload. Do you have any objections?"

"Nnnno...sir."

"Good, shall we go in and consult with your team, sir?"

Both the Surgeon General and the young doctor turned to go into the I.C.U., but the Doctor turned and quickly approached Niles Compton.

"Excuse me, sir," he said with new-found respect for whoever these strange people were, "but Mrs. Hamilton had this in her hand when they brought her in." The doctor quickly placed a small object in the hand of the director and then hurriedly turned and joined the head physician in all of the nation.

Niles unfolded the crushed photo and looked at it. It was an old woman next to several other men and women and who looked like a younger Alice and of all people, Garrison Lee.

"Doctor, did she say who this was?" Niles called out before the doctors could vanish.

"All she mumbled was something...something, Barlow. Sorry, that's all she said.

"Mr. President, I think we have a better than average lead beside that of Congressman Briggs."

"Go to it baldy, I've got to get out of here before some dickhead politician finds out I'm missing." He smiled at Niles and hugged him. "I'll be praying for Alice."

Niles could only nod his head as he gathered his people together for a return to Group.

"Colonel?"

Jack stopped with the others.

"The gloves come off on this one," the president turned and went in the opposite direction of the Event Group.

Jack looked at Carl.

"You heard the man, let's go find the old woman that hurt our friends."

CHAPTER NINE

***Mystery Deep*, Exploratory Well # 3,
sixty-eight miles off the coast of Louisiana**

D mitri Sokol stood underneath the umbrella held by one of the rig engineers. His eyes looked toward the roiling rain clouds that hit the Gulf on a regular basis. He spied the rented Bell 525 sleek and speedy executive helicopter. The wind buffeted the streamlined craft until its Russian pilot sat it down gracefully on the helipad high above the main deck. Sokol smiled as he watched the four men step into the rain. Then Sokol nodded his head for his deck crew to offer the men cover as they converged with umbrellas, delaying just long enough for the newcomers to be soaked by the slashing rain. The four men were escorted to the main deck. Sokol stepped forward, never losing his calm demeanor nor the arrogance he had toward the man in the front of the pack.

"Number Ten," the rotund man from the committee said as he held out his hand.

After a moment's hesitation Sokol relented and shook. "Number Seven, this is a rather opportune time for you to visit our facility.

Unexpected to say the least without us being informed, but very much opportune."

Number Seven glanced around him at the oil workers moving from place to place as he eyed for any armed security. He saw none.

"You may not think it is so opportune when you hear what it is, I have to say."

Sokol chuckled as if the man had just told a small joke. Instead of commenting which caught Number Seven totally off guard, he held out his hand to the bearded man standing beside Number Seven.

"I don't believe I have had the pleasure," he said.

The bearded man looked to Number Seven when Sokol's hand was offered. A barely perceptible nod of his head told his guest to shake.

"Yes, this is a rather valuable friend of the committee. May I introduce our liaison with Congressman Briggs, his Chief of Staff, Mr. Conway Fleming."

"Ah, the man behind the curtain. Tell me Mr. Fleming, what would make an important man like you brave the Gulf weather in the heat of summer?"

"Perhaps we would be better off discussing our situation inside," Number Seven said.

"Where are my manners. Being in America has offered little time for the social graces. By all means, follow me."

As they walked toward the elevator that would take them into the bowels of the giant rig, Number Seven looked at the darkening skies one last time as he switched on a small digital locator beacon on his cell phone. As his eyes left the sky as he stepped into the lift, he hoped that very same sky had its ears on.

Ilyushin-Il-476 Military Flight,
Operation *Rasputin*

THE OPERATION WAS to be accomplished in two phases. One, the sea operation which had just departed the giant jet aircraft, was to HALO (high altitude, low opening) jump from forty-two thousand feet over the Gulf of Mexico. A unit of commandos would use rubber Zodiac boats to assault the *Mystery Deep* platform from the sea. The fifty-three other Spetsnatz would come at the rig from the air. The second phase was far more dangerous than that of the first as they would be required to land on the rig in other than nominal weather conditions. This specialized assault element had been specially trained for this type of mission due to the ongoing tense situation in the Persian Gulf. The 15th Special Guards Brigade was the best in the world at seaborne assault with the parameters laid down by the shadow government in Siberia. The rules of engagement—eliminate all personnel and the asset known as *Asmodius*.

The man commanding the 15th Special Guards Brigade, Lieutenant Colonel Leonid Petrolovich, closed his eyes as the jet's engine whine wound down as it slowed for the last element to start their free fall to the sea below. Not a religious man himself, he watched as several of his Spetsnatz crossed themselves in preparation for one of the most dangerous jump assaults of their lives.

The sound of a buzzer sounded and the large green light over the ramp was illuminated. The ramp started opening as the rain started to fly in and around the interior in earnest. Petrolovich lowered his goggles and then stood. He gestured with his hands for his team to stand. Twenty-five men on each side of the craft stood. They turned, facing the ramp. The Colonel gave them all a small salute.

As the sun sank beneath the storm clouds into the western Gulf of Mexico, Operation *Rasputin* had commenced.

As a waiter in a red vest and silky white shirt offered Number Seven and his guest, Conway Fleming wine, Number Seven turned his crystal wine glass over. Fleming did the same. Sokol smiled and held out his glass to be filled.

"I admire that, business first. So, what can I help you with, or should I say what can I assist the committee with?" Sokol smiled and then sipped his wine. As he did his eyes ventured to the two men standing behind Number Seven. Obvious they were here to protect such a valuable asset as the Congressman's chief of staff.

"We are here because there is a concern that you went far beyond our instructions in assisting our friend Congressman Briggs in his quest to expose our main concern in the Nevada desert. Can you explain the deaths that were a result of this failure?"

Sokol again smiled at Number Seven as Fleming raised his brows, as the American became concerned that their visit may not have come as big a big of a surprise as they thought it would. Sokol nodded at the waiter and he placed the bottle of wine on the table and left the dining area.

"Wherever did you come by that information?" Sokol asked, feigning concern.

"Number Ten, we have many resources that you may not be aware of. The deaths that may have been incurred by our nemesis in Nevada, may backfire and send their rather capable security forces in our direction."

"Plus, you threatened the very man who will soon become the President of the United States," Fleming said hurriedly, quickly tiring of the silly game being played by the two Russians. "I insist that all communication between your people and our man cease imm—"

"Again, it's amazing how misinformed you are," Sokol said as he swallowed the rest of his wine. "Allow me to get to the bottom of this misinformation campaign against my project, gentlemen." Sokol poured another glass of wine and at the same moment pressed a small buzzer on the tabletop.

The automatic double doors opened. Vexilla Trotsky wasn't bound this time, but she was held by the arm. When the two guards saw what was holding the woman, they reached for sidearms but were immediately thrown brutally against the steel bulkhead. Blood trailed them to the deck. Both Number Seven and Fleming stood as the Grey, seemingly satisfied with his action, relaxed. It stepped into the room and pushed Vexilla harshly into a vacant chair.

"Gentlemen, may I assume this woman is your source of information?" Sokol stood and poured Vexilla a glass of white wine.

She angrily turned her head away in disgust. "Oh, and excuse Asmodius, he really isn't fond of sudden movement. I apologize for his quick reaction toward your men."

"Get that thing out of my sight!" Number Seven said, gritting his teeth.

Sokol sat back down and just raised his brows at his two guests. Then both men backed away when Asmodius eased into a chair next to Vexilla, who leaned as far away as she could. The Grey smiled as if he were merely joining them for dinner.

"Please, feel free to ask him to leave," Sokol said in all seriousness.

Asmodius turned and looked at the two frightened men. It leaned back in the chair and then with its right hand he waved over the two men and they were picked up and then sat in their original chairs. Fleming turned his head and vomited onto the steel deck. Sokol tossed him a towel.

"Clean that up please. Things are rough around here as it is. But soon we won't have to be cooped up like chickens on a farm. Asmodius wants to see a little of the world. It's been quite some time since he's been here."

When the two men looked at the Grey it just smiled.

"Now, Asmodius would like to ask you a few direct questions Number Seven, I hope you are honest in your answers."

"Go to hell. You have just placed a price on your head that will send you straight to the same hell that your great-grandfather was sent to."

"Where…is…the Green?" Asmodius said.

Number Seven shook his head and pressed his temples as the shooting pain shot from his brain to his inner ear.

"What is it?" Fleming asked, wild-eyed.

"Get out of my head!"

"I suggest you answer my friend," Sokol said as he poured himself another glass of wine.

"I don't know what you are talking about!" Number Seven screamed.

"Evidently he has a concern about two very worrisome enemies.

One is a Green alien, of which you have most assuredly heard of, the other an ancient enemy who may or may not have joined forces with the little green man. Now, answer my partner, please. I have enough of a mess to clean up in here."

"Go to hell," Number Seven yelled as he pressed harder into his temples.

Asmodius raised his right hand and extended the four fingers of that hand. He slowly balled it into a fist. Number Seven started to scream as blood started to flow freely from his eyes and ears.

"Stop!" Fleming said as he started to shake in terror of what he had stepped into. "The Green, he's been dead for months! The other I know nothing about!" Fleming turned and saw Number Seven as he fell from his chair. Even Sokol was frowning at the display of power from the giant Grey. "The very people you attacked with this...this creature, are the only ones that can tell you anything. Now let him go!"

Asmodius stood and closed its fist harder as Number Seven started to flop on the steel decking.

"Asmodius, stop. We can always throw him into the sea later." Sokol looked at Fleming and smiled.

The Grey suddenly opened its hand and the screaming stopped. Vexilla stood and was suddenly grabbed by Asmodius. She winced as her arm was nearly broken.

"Let me help him!" she yelled in pain.

With a crystal tooth smile, Asmodius let her go. She ran to Number Seven's side and was relieved when the man took a large breath. He struggled up to his knees and then spit out blood. Fleming once more fought to control his stomach after the brutal display.

"A reckoning...is...coming...for you!"

"Number Seven, don't give away the surprise before the applicable moment arrives, you'll ruin it for everyone. If you mean the element of commandos arriving from the air, we may have a surprise in store for *them*. Asmodius, I believe the time has arrived to sever our relationship with the Motherland."

Asmodius stood. Its smile was horrid as both Number Seven and the American Fleming realized they had been had.

The large Grey turned and left the dining room.

THE TEN ZODIAC rubber boats flew high into the air as waves buffeted the assaulting force. The darkened sky opened up in earnest with lightning and rain. Through the flashes of the newly arrived Gulf storm, the lead boat saw the *Mystery Deep* platform emerge from the mist and rain. The leader of group one held his gloved hand high in the air and swirled a closed fist and then the ten boats started to disperse into a circular pattern as they neared the rig.

LIEUTENANT COLONEL LEONID PETROLOVICH broke through the clouds, grateful to see the ashen grey breakers striking the legs of the rig. The wind pushed he and his fifty-two men slightly off course, but with their precise body movements they were able to correct.

He glanced down at his altimeter and was satisfied that he was still high enough to correct any angle of attack he chose. He saw the helipad through the streaking rain and the mist covering most of the large rig. He adjusted his fall and then flared as his altimeter reading started to go into the redline. He chanced a look at the men closest to him and saw the competent way they were handling the high altitude drop. They also adjusted. After studying aerial photos of *Mystery Deep*, it had been decided that thirty-five of the specially trained commandos would shoot for the three boat ramps at the base of the rig while the rest would attempt to hit the helipad. The danger was of course the tall derrick that was placed in the middle of the platform. If a gust of strong wind came up it could be disastrous for any member of the team that even slightly missed their mark.

The buzz sounded in his earphones underneath his black helmet. He pulled the stainless-steel handle and his chute deployed with a loud bang. He looked around just as others started their own deployment. He saw the large 'H' on the surface of his target landing zone. It was coming up rapidly. He smiled as he saw no resistance forming below.

THE ZODIAC'S neared the giant legs of the rig. The squad leader that would arrive first was relived not to see anyone through his night vision goggles. He smiled knowing that the way would be clear to reach the ladders that ascended to the lower decks. Like his commander landing on the decks above, the leader of the second team knew they had caught their targets unaware. Now their targets were caught between one team coming down and one going up. The slaughter would commence in the middle.

After thirty minutes of searching, the Spetsnatz found the lift that descended far beyond the numbered decks. The Colonel knew that was where Sokol and his band of traitors would be. Sending half of the command down the fifteen stairwells and the other half down the two lifts, the strike force made ready for battle.

The team struck simultaneously. Some from the stairwells, others from the two lifts. They stopped. They saw two men and one woman as they faced the arriving strike force. The three looked shocked and bewildered.

Petrolovich came forward when he recognized Number Seven. "Where is he?" he shouted.

"They went up top to wait for you. The bastard knew you were coming," Number Seven said.

"There was no resistance there."

The lights went out and only the sea was seen through the thick glass. Vexilla closed her eyes knowing this was the last moments of her life.

AS THE LAST of the Spetsnatz moved into the stairwells and the lift, their actual targets had been only feet away from them. In a wavering haze of moving air, Dmitri Sokol stepped from the camouflaged cover that was generated by Asmodius. The Grey swirled its large hands through the air and the redirected light defused and then vanished as if it were fog that was lifted and chased away by the sun, and then the fifty men of Sokol's defense force became visible. The men made ready to cover them if the Spetsnatz returned suddenly before their ruse had been discovered.

"Very inventive," Sokol said as he looked at Asmodius. He looked at his Rolex watch. "We have little time. Our ride will be here shortly. Deploy to the lower area. The ship should be waiting."

The security force moved off toward the stairwells.

Five minutes later the men of Sokol's command boarded a crew ship that serviced offshore drilling rigs. It sped away as the sharp bow cut through the growing waves.

Asmodius was in the ships cockpit and looked to be enjoying the rough ride through the churning Gulf.

"Asmodius, I think it's time to show me exactly what you can do," Sokol said as he opened the cabin door and stepped out into the rain. Asmodius followed. His goat-like legs balancing perfectly in the rough seas.

As the giant rig grew smaller, Asmodius closed its yellow eyes. The right hand came up slowly as in its mind it saw the *Mystery Deep* platform. Suddenly it closed its right hand. It squeezed so hard that its crystal nails dug deeply into the sickly skin of its palm. Blood flowed and the wind took it immediately away.

When the explosion came Sokol ducked as the tremendous heat blossomed out like a flower blooming. Giant sized pieces of steel flew into the air as the oil rig ignited and then punctured the fuel and natural gas tanks lining the entirety of the platform. The night sky lit up for several hundred miles and broke windows in Houston, Galveston, and New Orleans.

When Sokol looked back, the *Mystery Deep* platform was gone, vanishing into the Gulf storm.

"Now we can start our real work and save my country from the fools who wish to subjugate it."

The Grey watched Sokol duck back inside the ship's wheelhouse. It turned and looked at the spot where the *Mystery Deep* platform once rose from the Gulf. Then it turned back to see Sokol inside the warm and comfortable cabin and in the rain of the storm, Asmodius raised the scaly skin over its non-existent brows as it studied the fool Sokol and then the warlock slowly smiled.

Algiers, Louisiana

THE BAD REPUTATION New Orleans has in the general view of most of the nation was nothing compared to the view the citizens of New Orleans held for the enclave of Algiers, the closest neighbor to the more touristy and very much larger city. Most citizens of New Orleans steered clear of the seedy underbelly that was Algiers.

One man who felt comfortable in the darkened streets and seedy bars of Algiers was Colonel Henri Farbeaux. While Jason Ryan and Will Mendenhall had their heads on a swivel looking out for their safety, Henri strode the streets confidently. When he saw the poorly maintained neon lights of green and blue and the flapping Parrot blinking in its oval sign, Henri stopped the two men before entering.

"Perhaps you gentlemen would feel more comfortable waiting for me in the café across the street. As filthy dives are concerned, the Blue Parrot gives those establishments a bad name."

"Perhaps you better let us do our jobs, Colonel," Will said as his cell phone sounded. He raised it to his ear while watching Henri trying to decide if the Colonel's heart was really into finding the real story on Congressman Briggs. "Mendenhall," he said into the cell.

Ryan watched Will's face and then saw him stagger and lean heavily against the ivy-covered exterior wall of the Blue Parrot. He watched his friend hang his head and then he lowered the cell. He raised it to his ear again.

"Keep us informed on her condition. Yes, sir, he's right here. Give me a second." Mendenhall rubbed his eyes and then looked at Jason and Henri.

"Virginia is dead along with four of our security men. Murdered at

Alice's house. Alice is in the hospital in critical condition and her prognosis isn't good." Will rubbed his eyes until they turned red.

"What?" Jason said allowing his temper to lead the way.

"They don't know much." Will held out the phone to the Frenchman. "The Colonel wants to speak with you."

"Yes," Henri said into the cell. He listened and Will and Jason knew that Collins was making the call a one-sided conversation.

Ryan took Will's shoulder and gave it a squeeze. "Is that all Jack said?"

"They have a lead on that old woman that snatched Charlie and Matchstick. Also, that we are to continue here. They're not discounting that Briggs didn't have something to with Virginia and Alice."

Henri handed the phone back to Mendenhall. "I am sorry for your loss. I always thought Ms. Pollock was one of the classier people I have ever met. As for Mrs. Hamilton, if anyone can pull through this, it's her. Now, are you ready to do as your Colonel asks?"

"What's that?" Ryan asked with anger lacing his words. "Go after what now looks like a secondary target in Briggs? Not even that asshole would have the balls to go after Alice and Virginia. If you ask me..."

"I didn't ask you, Commander. I did ask if you're ready to do what Colonel Collins has ordered."

Ryan, after Henri had brought him around, just nodded his head. Henri glanced at Mendenhall who also nodded.

"Good. Things are bound to get a little ugly in here. It seems the Colonel has finally decided that some things you can't fight with rules." Henri held their eyes for a moment and then turned into the Blue Parrot.

The club was so dark only the lights surrounding the stage were seen. Black lights illuminated the exotic murals of a false Caribbean landscape, and the people occupying the tables and booths were anonymously hidden in the shadows. Henri watched as Ryan and Will exchanged worried looks. Finally, Henri turned to a cage with a woman who looked to be a cross between a very much older Bette

Davis and the wicked witch of the East. He walked to the cage. The woman popped a bubble with her gum and then finally looked up.

"Three, that's sixty dollars cover."

"We're not here for your...entertainment. We need to see Madam Prudhomme."

The woman in the cage snorted. "No Madam's here, buddy. You want *that* you need to go across the street."

When no answer came from Farbeaux, the woman with the extreme coifed curls in her obvious blonde wig looked up. Henri wasn't smiling. She recoiled somewhat when she saw the green-eyed intensity.

"I do not like repeating myself. If you do not pass along my request, as unpleasant as it would be, I will reach into your little cage and rip out your right eye."

The woman started pressing something the three men couldn't see.

Ryan and Mendenhall were pushed out of the way as two very large men who appeared from the darkness of the club appeared.

"You men, out."

Henri turned into the chest of the first man. He was at least six foot five inches tall and had a chest resembling a beer keg. The second man wasn't that much smaller. Henri turned back to the woman who stared back at him wide-eyed.

"You look lonely in there, my dear," he said as his right hand went out and took the larger man by his jacket collar and hurled him through the tight bars of the protective cage where his head became wedged.

The second man moved toward Farbeaux and that was when he was stopped cold by Will Mendenhall. He struck the man in the back of the right knee and he stumbled into Ryan who, when the man looked up as he grabbed Jason for support, the naval aviator just smiled down and punched him in the area between his nose and his eyebrows, sending the man directly to the floor where he lay face down in the filth.

The first man was struggling to free himself as the blonde-haired woman turned and fled through her small door. The Frenchman assisted him in his extrication. The large Cajun immediately took a swing at the Colonel. Henri easily stepped aside and then used the brute's momentum to sling him headfirst into the tinsel hung wall.

"I see you haven't lost your graceful touch, Henri."

Farbeaux turned to see a woman enter with the terrified blonde standing far away from the entrance. The woman, nearly three hundred and forty pounds of her, held out her hand. Farbeaux smiled and kissed it.

"Liza, you haven't changed a bit," Henri said as he straightened and then viciously lashed out at the largest man as he attempted to rise from the floor. The foot caught him in the sternum, and he went down and didn't move.

"Number one Henri, you're still a liar of major proportions. I have changed, I've lost twenty-seven pounds since we last saw each other. Second," she looked down at her two bouncers, "those are hard to come by in Algiers. No one wants to work anymore."

Henri smiled and turned to Will and Jason. "Liza, may I introduce you to Major William Mendenhall and Commander Jason Ryan. Gentlemen, Madam Liza Prudhomme, a very old and dear friend."

Both Mendenhall and Ryan nodded their heads in greeting. Ryan was unable to keep his eyes from the largest bust he had ever seen on a human being.

Madam Prudhomme blushed like a schoolgirl as she dipped her head and could barely bend for a curtsey. "Henri, you have never shown up here with such handsome specimens before. Why I could take these boys home and feed them nothing but love and gumbo, fatten up a little."

Will and Ryan exchanged looks that bordered on terror.

"Now, Henri, you've made my clientele a rather nervous bunch as we were already visited by the Parrish Sheriff earlier tonight for his... gratuity. What brings you to my place of business?"

"Liza, nothing goes on in the south that you don't know or hear about. As I know European rumor and innuendo, you are my opposite number here in New Orleans. Perhaps we can speak more privately?"

"Look Henri, I don't conduct business in your field of endeavor any longer, so if you…"

"In reference to a certain Congressman from your lovely state, Liza."

Suddenly the woman's rosy cheeks changed from a nice blush to one that was drained of all color.

"Come with me Gentlemen," she said.

"HENRI, you stay clear of that man, you hear me? He is a snake hiding in plain sight."

"We're aware of that ma'am," Will said as Henri shot him a warning look about how he and Ryan needed to remain silent as this woman was famous for clamming up when talking to the wrong people.

"Anything more specific, Liza?"

Madam Prudhomme slid her top drawer out and pulled out a pistol. It was an old fashioned two shot derringer. "Henri, if you go snooping into that man's business, you better be packing one of these. You see, I may not know much, but the man that wants to win that God-awful White House has a new set of friends. He may not know it, but those friends do quite a lot of business here in Algiers. Hell, even our distinguished Mr. Briggs doesn't know, or at least he didn't at first, who he was dealing with. My people do."

"Madam, who are these friends?" Ryan asked and then he stared back at Henri as if challenging him. "Sorry Colonel, we're short on time."

"Let's just say they're not the sort of people you go messin' with."

"Liza, as the Commander just said, we're pressed for time. If it makes you feel better, by the time he gets wind we're after him, his influence here and his quest for the Presidency will be over. Now, please, who are his friends?"

Madam Prudhomme looked at Henri. That look said that she had decided to say the words he wanted to hear. "I have an investment in construction as you may or may not know. Oh, just a small outfit out of Metairie that builds and equips oil platforms. This small outfit likes to stay clear of the limelight because, well, they like to skirt certain construction codes and licensing when it comes to offshore platform construction." Liza took and pen and paper and scribbled a note and gave it to Henri. "The main office is in Lake Charles, but you will be better off going to this place, Maritime Welding in Metairie. It's not far. Ask for Bobby Joe. It seems he isn't too keen on the men who subcontracted his welding shop for a big job in the Gulf."

"Liza, who is Briggs working with?" Henri asked as he gave the address to Ryan.

Madam Prudhomme reached for the derringer and then placed it into her bodice underneath her ample breasts.

"The Russians."

CHAPTER TEN

Event Group Complex,
Nellis Air Force Base, Nevada

Xavier Morales studied the holographic three-dimensional diagram of the symbols that had been copied from the sliding-glass window at Alice Hamilton's home. Niles Compton stood by the Doctor inside the cleanroom with his arms crossed.

"Well?" Niles asked impatiently.

Xavier took a breath and rubbed his tired eyes. He knew the Director was under extreme pressure, not by anyone from above, but on himself.

"Europa is having a difficult time with the symbols. It's as if she knows what they are, but it's almost as if her memory bubbles are being attacked every time she assembles the images in the hologram or any program she has. It's as if the symbols themselves have some form of self-destruct code inside the shape of the structure of the design. It's like some outside program is running and every time she gets close, the memory bubble fails. Diagnostics show nothing other than her normal processing parameters." Morales shrugged his shoulders. "I just don't know."

Niles pursed his lips and fought his own memory on the subject of a deteriorating program. He pulled out a chair and angrily tore off his protective gloves and head-cover. He adjusted the microphone at the terminal.

"Europa, are you accessing foreign databases for the meaning and design of the symbols?"

Xavier looked at Niles as he wondered at the director's line of inquiry.

'Yes, Doctor Compton.'

"We're accessing every database across the globe, Doctor. She has broken into every system of higher education the world over. Hell, we even crashed the archives at the Vatican and any nutcase on the web. Nothing."

"Europa sever all outside influences. Confine yourself to Event Group file database only."

"Severed, Doctor Compton."

"Now, reconfigure the symbols as noted and copied by Group forensics."

The hologram changed from the meaningless scramble of strange and broken symbols produced by whatever interference the symbols produced. Soon, the green hologram had all of the symbols as copied from the watery streak lines on the glass window.

At first the symbols held. The most dominate set were two triangles with a straight line through both. The second most used was the four-pointed pentangle but with a slight difference from the historic design. Instead of a circle around the star another triangle wound around its points.

"The symbols are holding," Morales said. "Europa, make your investigation quick."

'Processing.'

Both Xavier and Niles hoped that whatever influence stopped them before was waning as they were only using the closed-looped system of Europa without the need of other databases.

The enthusiasm was short-lived as the symbols started to disassemble and break apart. Xavier cursed.

"Europa why are the symbols changing shape?" he asked, losing patience with the Cray.

'What symbols are you referring too, Doctor?'

"Are you kidding?" Morales asked as he slammed his gloved hand down on the table, knocking his microphone off its stand.

Niles placed a calming hand on Xavier's shoulder. He closed his eyes and thought. Morales was right, the symbols were creating their own tapeworm and scrambling any attempt at deciphering them. Niles watched as the robotic arms made to insert and remove stored bubble files stopped moving. He decided to take a chance.

"Europa, check your last command"

'Processing request. Last command requested was historical file search of department 5656 symbolic files.'

"Display symbols, please."

As they watched, the symbols reappeared. Then just as suddenly broke apart into a meaningless jumble.

"Europa, does your memory have an imprint of the symbols?"

'To what symbols are you referencing, Doctor?'

Both men were lost as to how this could be happening. When the cleanroom door opened, they both turned and saw a young female computer tech enter.

"Excuse me, Doctor Morales," her eyes widened when she saw Niles Compton sitting next to Xavier. "Director."

"What is it?" Morales asked.

"Doctor, I know I'm only a grad student and a freshman intern from Pepperdine, but I think I may have part of the answer to Europa's problems with the symbols as they were copied."

"Why didn't you take it to your supervisor, Professor Thompson?" Niles asked, and then they saw outside the cleanroom window in the waiting area that her computer department supervisor was pacing and looked very angry. "Oh, I guess you did," Niles said. "I gather you have a different point of view, so you decided to go over his head?"

The girl looked sheepish.

"Well, at least you have *something*," Niles said. "Shoot, before your supervisor takes that very same advice and shoots you."

"May I?" she asked, as she pulled out a third chair on the terminal counter.

Niles nodded. She sat. Compton and Xavier exchanged looks.

"Although we don't have a clue as to why the symbols magically break apart and Europa has no memory of our requests, I may have stumbled across something that Europa can assist with."

"Not following, specialist," Niles said, placing another restraining hand on Morales shoulder who was becoming agitated.

"Europa, hologram the design for earlier inquiry for symbols recovered from the Hamilton crime scene."

On the hologram pad, the symbols once more came on. The young tech just waited patiently. The symbols started to disassemble almost immediately.

"I think we established that Europa is having a hard time retaining the symbols and her memory of them. It has to be some form of tape worm in the design of the symbols," Xavier said as he waived the girl's supervisor into the cleanroom to gather up his grad student.

"Doctor, please allow me to explain," the girl said as she saw her angry supervisor enter the room and stand with his arms crossed.

Xavier exhaled in exasperation and then gestured with his hand for her to continue.

"We're concentrating on the symbols and wasting time," she said to a shocked trio of vastly more experienced computer technicians. "Europa, place the crime scene photos of the glass into the existing hologram, please."

On the pad, overlaid on the disassembled symbols, a photo of the sliding glass door appeared complete with the condensation as created by the air-conditioned house meeting the warmer outside air of Las Vegas.

"Europa, please enlarge and enhance the glass."

Europa did as she was commanded. With the blowup you still couldn't discern where the symbols had even been drawn in the fogged condensation.

"I told you this was a waste of time. As soon as you overlay the symbols, Europa goes into shutdown and we still have nothing."

"That's because you're looking for the meaning of the symbols, Professor Thompson, and whatever program is overriding Europa's abilities at deciphering them starts its interference."

"Isn't that the idea?" Niles asked before Xavier could.

"Forget that aspect," she said, almost becoming exasperated. "Europa, on the hologram go to infra-red please and look for trace elements other than condensation and regular household impurities."

"I told her this was a waste of time. Without the symbols in the hologram, I don't know what it is you are hoping to achieve," her supervisor said.

"We won't know what the symbols mean, at least as of yet, but how about the identity of who or *what* wrote them on the glass?"

"Ridiculous theory," her supervisor said angrily. "You're wasting our time here. The symbol written in blood came back as having been written without any trace of how it was done. What makes you think…"

"Display the print Europa," she hurriedly said before she could be interrupted again.

'Identification fingerprint is now added.'

The look on the faces of three most experienced computer men in the world were priceless as the infrared hologram started showing trace lines of a fingerprint through the watery condensation.

"As I said gentlemen, the symbols remain a mystery, but the person or *thing* that wrote them is hiding in plain sight."

"Thus far you have made two references as to the author of the symbols as, *who* and *thing*. Explain," Niles said.

"Europa, the points of identification on the print, can you identify them from the FBI's IAFIS database?"

Everyone in the cleanroom knew the FBI IAFIS database was short for Integrated Automated Fingerprint Identification System.

'The print is identifiable, but no record of the person responsible for the print is currently on file.'

"Told you. This is a waste of time," her supervisor said, getting ready to remove her from the cleanroom.

"Europa, I understand the individual responsible for the print isn't on file, but is the style of the print available in the database?" The young woman felt the hand of the supervisor on her shoulder.

'Yes.'

Everyone froze.

"Is the print human?" she asked.

'Negative.'

"Identify fingerprint origin, please," Niles asked, standing up.

'Yes, Doctor Compton. The print origin is that which has been dubbed—extraterrestrial—Grey species.'

"My God!" Xavier said, shooting an angry glance at the supervisor of this rather extraordinary young technician. The supervisor pulled away and decided silence may just actually be the better part of valor.

"Thank you for your assistance young lady," Niles said, smiling for the first time since Jack and Sarah's wedding three nights before. "Professor Thompson, please escort your tech back to her station and issue her a full Europa security clearance. Do you agree Doctor Morales?"

"Most assuredly."

Niles and Xavier watched Thompson display a new-found respect for the extremely young and talented grad student as they left the cleanroom.

"You know Doctor, I feel ashamed I don't even know that girl's name."

Niles started for the door as the intercom started making a short chime indicating Compton call into security. He turned and smiled at Xavier Morales.

"Well, there's a reason why she's so smart, Doctor. She came to me last year after she completed her thesis. Her name is Loretta."

Compton opened the door and then turned once again.

"Loretta Golding. Pete Golding's niece."

NILES SAT at a station outside the cleanroom and dialed the extension for security. "Colonel, what do you have?"

"We have identified the photo Alice had in her possession."

"Go ahead."

"Boston, 1955. Small dig there concerning Boston Common. Permission to send a team there."

Niles took a deep breath. "I want a full meeting of the department heads first, Jack."

"What's up?"

"Sound an Event alert and inform the President by coded message. We know who killed Virginia."

"Who?" Jack asked, his rage burning through the comm system.

"The Grey's are back."

Two minutes later the computerized tones of four bleeps and one longer bleep sounded throughout the complex. Department 5656 went into Event mode.

Baton Rouge, Louisiana

CONGRESSMAN HAROLD BRIGGS was sitting and staring into the storm filled night. His campaign manager was talking at a rapid pace as to what subjects would be covered at the next rally set for Northern Michigan. The day before, he had been ambushed when he found himself losing his place even with a teleprompter. The days polls had shown he had slipped by eight points and was now in a virtual tie with both of his Republican and Democratic opponents.

"Congressman, did you hear what I just said?"

He turned from the window inside the suite at the Hyatt Place hotel. "Yes, I heard you say my numbers were down."

"That's not what I just said, Congressman. I said Senator James Booker just rescinded his endorsement of you."

"Uh, huh."

"Look, if you're worried about Mr. Fleming, I've got a call into his office in Washington. With your debacle in Houston I'm sure he's got his hands full putting out fires in the capitol."

The campaign manager looked at Briggs and she grew angry. She gathered up her briefing materials and placed them in her briefcase.

"I better go to bed before I end up resigning right here, right now."

Briggs didn't react to her comment as his mind had shut down. Instead he walked to the bar and again poured another drink. The woman left the suite, slamming his door as she did.

With drink in hand he turned and faced the window again. The lights of Louisiana's capitol were diffused in the rain and for the most part all he could see was his own reflection. As he lifted the glass to his lips he suddenly froze as his reflection wasn't the only one he was looking at in the glass. Asmodius was right behind him. Briggs screamed and dropped his glass and fell to the floor as he turned to see nothing. He started to cry and placed his hands over his eyes. He tried to stand and fell. His eyes roamed to the large television. This time he found the sudden energy to stand as he ran for the remote control. He turned up the sound.

'...the reason for the disaster has yet to be determined. Rescue boat were on the scene within five minutes of the explosion that rocked the entirety of the Gulf region. Thus far the United States Coast Guard claims the casualty list will be in the extreme. At this time not much is known as to the bottom-line ownership of the Mystery Deep platform, but the Maritime Industries Management firm said the investigation is ongoing.'

Harold Briggs again collapsed into the divan facing the television. When he turned toward the window, again he saw the image of the giant Grey. It was smiling at him. He squeezed his eyes shut as tight as he could and then threw the remote control and struck the window. The plastic device shattered. That was when Briggs knew if he wasn't careful, he would end up like his campaign manager—a victim of Sokol and his Grey ally covering their tracks. His cooperation with the Russians would be forced to continue as the threat from Asmodius in the window's reflection was clear and precise a warning about his silence and his further relationship as he would ever receive.

Coast Guard Cutter, USCGC *Resolute*,
Eighty-six Miles South of Louisiana

THE GULF SEAS WERE FURIOUS, adding to the difficult task of looking for survivors of the disaster on the *Mystery Deep* platform. Thus far, other rescue elements had only recovered eighteen bodies, mostly burned beyond any form of identification without the use of DNA and dental records.

The Coast Guard Cutter *Resolute* out of Galveston Texas, had been on a routine patrol east of their base of operations when the distress calls were sounded. It had taken them nearly two hours to get to the scene due to the radical weather shift in recent days of mystical storm patterns that developed suddenly and from nowhere. By the time the *Resolute* had arrived, just the few bodies had been recovered. She stood on station while other rescue vessels steamed home with their sorrowful results.

As the large cutter broached the high seas the alarm onboard was sounded.

"Captain, lookouts report body in the water!"

"Where-away?" Lieutenant Junior Grade, Wendel Acheson asked, raising the field glasses to his eyes as the *Resolute* dipped into a large sea trough.

"Four degrees starboard, eight hundred yards distance, Captain."

Acheson couldn't see anything from the bridge windows. He shook his head as he knew he couldn't use his most valuable life-saving tool, his HH-65A Dolphin helicopter. It was sitting in its deck hangar tied down due to the rough seas.

"Helm, dead slow, steer one-five-nine. Make ready lifelines and let's see if we can get a boat in the water."

"Aye, Captain," answered his Master Chief.

"Captain, lookouts report swimmer is signaling."

"Alive through this mess and from a platform that is burned down to its stanchion legs?"

"Aye, Captain, second and third lookouts report same. Swimmer is alive."

"Okay, let's do what they pay us for ladies and gentlemen."

TWENTY MINUTES later USCGC *Resolute* did the job the nation paid her to do. They pulled out of the stormy seas the one and only survivor of the disaster on *Mystery Deep*—a woman name Vexilla Trotsky.

Metairie, Louisiana

"I SWEAR I don't know how this state stays above water!" Will Mendenhall said as he fought to see through the rain and the darkness. The windshield wipers were on high and still he was forced to travel frustratingly slow.

"There it is," Henri Farbeaux said from the backseat of the rental car.

"Yep, Maritime Welding," Ryan confirmed as he squinted through the water runoff at the old and battered sign.

It wasn't as large as most welding outfits, but they were made aware by their link with Europa that some of the more profitable companies flew under the radar as far as labor pricing went. Maritime Welding of Metairie was one of the lesser known but established shops.

The main workshop was a light as was the second, and only a single light shown in what they assumed was the office. Will pulled up and parked.

"It doesn't look like anyone's home," Ryan said as he heard Henry in the back seat chamber a bullet into his nine-millimeter. "No one's home Colonel. What are going to do, shoot up the joint for fun?"

Farbeaux didn't answer. His eyes went from the office to the surrounding workshops. His eyes tried in vain to penetrate the rain.

"Okay, you're managing to creep me out," Will said, tempted to pull out his own service weapon.

"Something is wrong here," Henri said as he opened the car's door.

"The Madam said this is a small operation but runs twenty-four hours a day while they have contractors in the field. Plus, do you see that?"

"What?" Mendenhall asked, growing nervous at the accurate way the Frenchman had by way of intuition in dangerous situations.

"Cajuns aren't typically trusting like us French. They usually don't leave their office doors ajar. And if you can hear through the rain, for a twenty-four-hour place of business, there doesn't seem to be any noise."

Will looked at Ryan. This time he did pull out his Glock nine-millimeter. Ryan did the same as Farbeaux left the dry confines of the car.

"I almost hope he's right," Mendenhall said. "Because if he's not, I guarantee you that most Cajuns here 'bouts can outgun *and* outshoot anyone of us."

"Oh, great," Jason said as he followed Mendenhall out.

HENRI REACHED the office door as he sent Mendenhall and Ryan to the two workshops. The colonel eased into the office. He aimed his weapon as he scanned the area. No one home as Ryan had said. He saw a coffee cup and sandwich on the desk and a name plate—Bobby Joe Prendergast. Henri reached out and felt the ceramic cup. The coffee, while not steaming, was still warm to the touch.

Next, he checked the bathroom and the superintendent's office. No one. He reached out and tuned off the CB radio used to communicate with the welding companies field teams. He saw the diagram on the wall and walked over. It was a blueprint of a platform in the Gulf. The name was instantly familiar because the news on the radio had been blaring its name for most of the day—*Mystery Deep*.

"Interesting," Henri said.

Farbeaux left the office and spied the backdoor. He eased into the rain, weapon extended. He saw Ryan and Mendenhall exit the first of the two workshops, hesitating only long enough to glance into the windows of a large step-van parked near a fence. He quickly joined them.

"Anyone in the office?" Will asked.

The Frenchman shook his head. He dipped his head at the workshop they had just exited.

"No. But whoever was there must have left in one hell of a hurry. A cutting torch was still lit and leaning on a sawhorse and a radio was blaring country music. Several lunches were still out in a break room. It looked like someone's meal was interrupted."

Farbeaux started for the last building. The door was of the large sliding variety. Henri pulled it open. The three men entered. Farbeaux suddenly held up his left hand into a balled fist, stopping both Ryan and Mendenhall immediately.

Henri scanned the room with the high overhead fluorescent lighting creating shadows everywhere. The pistol went right, indicating one of them go that way and an index finger left for the other. The trio split up. The shop was silent as Henri checked the darkened corners where steep fabricated for offshore rigs sat finished ready for painting.

"Oh God!"

Henri nearly collided with Ryan as they ran to the sound of Will's voice. They skidded to a halt on the wet cement floor as the vision of what Mendenhall had seen stopped them full force as if striking a brick wall.

Eight men were hanging upside down from the old wooden rafters of the workshop. Their stomachs had been eviscerated as cleanly as chickens. Their arms hung low and each man had a symbol cut into their chests just below their necks. Stepping over the soiled intestines of the welders, Henri spied the double triangle with the line through it. It was as though the men had been sacrificed in some form of brutal ritual. All three men, Will, Jason, and Henri, had all seen the most horrific battlefield wounds, but this was something they were never prepared for. Farbeaux shocked both Mendenhall and Ryan when he used his cell phone and started taking pictures.

"Jesus, Colonel," Jason said shaking his head.

"Commander, do you want to wait until the authorities arrive and use their photos. Or do you want to get these to your complex as soon as possible. If you insist on waiting for the police, by all means. If not, I suggest we allow the local authorities to take over and for us to leave this place now."

Jason quickly saw the colonel's point. He was envious that the Frenchman could think so clear-headedly in the roughest of times.

All three turned to go as thunder rumbled and shook the corrugated steel of the roof. They froze.

"What the…"

Another clap of thunder drowned out Ryan's exclamation.

Standing at the now closed door was the largest Grey any of them had ever seen, and they had seen a lot. Standing next to the Grey was the smaller form of a man. The dark-haired man was smiling, the Grey was not.

"Gentlemen, our Russian. And it looks like he has a friend," Henri said and began firing almost immediately. Will and Ryan, shocked at first, quickly caught on that the thing and man in front of them were responsible for the sacrificial slaughter of the men hanging in the rafters. They too laid down a withering fire as they ran for cover. The Grey stepped in front of the much smaller man and swirled both of its four fingered hands in a circle. The air was moist with a watery haze as the alien spun a vortex. The bullets from the Glock nine-millimeter's stopped mere feet from their target. They reversed in midair and then screamed toward the very men who had fired them in the first place.

As Farbeaux raised his head above several wooden pallets he saw the Grey stride a few steps into the workshop. It raised both hands and then the corrugated tin roof started shaking. The Grey slammed his arms and hands downward. Finally, the nails holding the roof in place were shot from the tin like bullets leaving a gun barrel. The roof crashed onto the three men.

All that was heard was strange laughter and the rain striking the fallen tin.

Event Group Complex,
Nellis Air Force Base, Nevada

As THE DEPARTMENT heads spoke among themselves, Jack Collins was growing frustrated. While they debated the meaning of the photo Alice had passed on, Jack felt valuable time was being wasted with the various departments bickering over where to start looking for Charlie, Matchstick and their captor, Elsbeth Barlow, whom the world's informational systems, including the most advanced computer on the planet, Europa, says doesn't exist. For Collins and the security department the departments had virtually nothing to go on. With Alice clinging to life in a Las Vegas hospital and not being able to provide any advancing clues as to the whereabouts of Matchstick and Charlie, Jack was anxious to get out to the east coast to start the investigation the old-fashioned way.

Collins was just getting ready to pull he and Carl from the meeting, when Xavier Morales rolled into the conference room.

"Quiet please," Niles said as he instinctually turned to his right and left and the two painfully obvious empty chairs. To his left, Alice's vacant spot, to his right, the chair belonging to Virginia Pollock. He cleared his throat as Naval Ensign Helen Torrez sat uncomfortably in the seat to the directors left side. She had her electronic notepad out and ready to record the minutes of the meeting. Ensign Torres felt sheepish and very much out of place in her replacement of a legend. Niles looked at Xavier and the head of the computer center nodded his head. "Before we begin with a report from Doctor Morales, I have an announcement to make." Niles cleared his throat and his eyes went down the table to each of the sixteen department heads. He stood up.

Jack exchanged looks with Carl as Niles looked to be having a hard time doing what he had planned. Again, the director tried to clear his throat.

"Sarah Collins," Niles said. He then pulled out the large high-backed chair to his right side. "I know you don't want this, but through previous discussions with both Alice Hamilton, and...," Niles coughed, as it seemed his words were choking him, "...Assistant

Director Pollock, you are hereby appointed to the position of Assistant Director, Department 5656, salary package and security clearance to be adjusted at a later time. Please come forward and take your chair please."

Sarah was wide-eyed as she turned to look at Jack. With a barely perceptible nod of his head she could see that he agreed with Alice, Virginia, and Niles assessment. She began to stand but hesitated. Her legs felt weak and rubbery. She looked up and fixed on Niles who gave her a slight nod of his head. Sarah finally regained the strength in her legs and stood and slowly walked to the front.

Jack looked over at Carl and Anya. Both looked almost as proud as he was. It was Carl who started the soft hand slap on the conference table. Soon all department heads lightly tapped their hands in agreement. As she approached Virginia's chair, Sarah wanted to turn and run from the conference room. Niles held the chair out and nodded that it was alright to sit where her good friend had for many, many years. Niles placed his hands on her shoulders and patted lightly his encouragement. He leaned over and whispered. Jack couldn't hear what the director said but he could see his new wife of three days swipe a tear from her cheek. If he knew Sarah, that would be the last tear she would ever shed in front of the assembly.

"Sorry Colonel Collins, I feel like I'm interfering in your marriage already, after all, I just promoted your new wife over you and that makes her your boss at home and place of business. Apologies." Niles joking manner gave the Group a chance at a rare smile and then he sat down.

"Quite alright Mr. Director, if you think I have it bad, just wait until she disagrees with *you*."

The lighthearted moment from the roughest man in the Group went a long way in breaking the black spell cast by Virginia's sudden death.

"Doctor Morales, I suspect you have some news?"

"Yes, sir. I have managed to decipher some of the symbols using non-historical records. It seems whoever we are dealing with is quite knowledgeable in ancient Sumerian Sanskrit. I have pinned down the symbols as having come from Northern Iraq and has been considered a dead language for at least seven thousand years. This is why there is no documented historical context to the symbols."

"You said you deciphered some of them, Doctor?" Sarah asked, immediately jumping into the fray just as readily as Virginia Pollock would have done. Jack smiled inwardly as Sarah proved him to have been right about his choice of loves from the beginning.

"Europa, please display research paper 190-224."

In the center of the room a large, ten by ten pad rose from the floor as the new and ingenious holographic display system was used for the first time, replacing the antiquated misting-projection hologram from years past. Soon Europa had the symbols displayed in a blue, red, and yellow replica of the symbols found at Alice Hamilton's house. Xavier rolled his backless wheelchair straight into the revolving display.

"Now, you'll have to excuse Europa, it seems out friend doesn't care for the symbols all that much as it interferes with her entire system as if the symbols themselves were acting as a mode of electrical interference. As soon as I know how this is possible, I will inform you all. Europa, suspend your audible and visual systems please. That's for her own protection until we find out exactly what we're dealing with."

'Yes, Doctor Morales.'

"Let's take the most prevalent symbol first, shall we?" Xavier moved his wheelchair to the right and the hologram showed the four-pointed star with the triangle surrounding it. It slowly spun in a circle as the view was augmented for all to see clearly.

"A Pentangle?" Niles Compton asked.

"Yes. That is what I and the ancient languages department thought. But through her knowledge of gypsy lore, Major Korvesky," he nodded his head at Anya, "says that while there are many versions of the ancient symbol, the basic design has always been that of a four-pointed star surrounded by a circle. As you can see, this pentangle has a triangle around it. Major Korvesky says that modern cults and devil worshipers use this more modern symbol because, well," Xavier smiled and shook his head, "frankly speaking, they're idiots. Gypsy lore says that the triangle pentangle is far more ancient than this modern version. Seven to fifteen thousand years old."

Whispers and talk began immediately.

"You say the original is ancient Sumerian?" Niles asked, keeping the meeting on track.

"Yes. A variant, smaller, larger, more detailed has been found on ruins that date back to the time before Moses and even before Babylonian society. Some historic markers have been found in cave systems in Iraq between the Tigress and Euphrates rivers. The late and brilliant Doctor Halpern of the University of Akron describes the symbol as mostly a symbolic symbol by early civilized man in reference to a subterranean deity, or God if you will. But he never developed any proof of his thesis before his death."

"What is the name of this God?" Sarah asked.

Jack was proud as he knew Sarah spent most of her professional life deep in the underground world of the planet and had come across many strange and wondrous thing in our geological past. The woman knew caves and geology.

"Europa come back online please," Xavier said as he rolled further away so he could view the next hologram.

'Online, Doctor.'

"Access the Halpern thesis from January of 1937, please. Please name the deity in correspondence to the symbol."

A new hologram of a rotating cave opening appeared and circled the room. Then the CGI display morphed into a view deep inside the cave itself. *'Ancient Sumerian text decipher the symbol as representing the deity known ten thousand years ago as Asmodius. This name corresponds with modern texts from ancient Egyptian and a lessor known Hindu form of the same name. This has been confirmed in Greek, Sumerian, and ancient Hebrew texts. Asmodius—known as, the Prince of Demons.'*

"Okay Europa identify the double linked triangles with the horizontal line piercing both, please," Xavier said and then watched the gathered department managers for their reactions.

'The symbol is known for ancient royalty and was sometimes associated

DAVID L GOLEMON

with biblical text from the earliest age of man and retranslated in the old testament. The two triangles represent father and son. The horizontal line has been known to depict the relationship to royalty. Father and son in this context as explained by Professor Halpern, suggests that in his opinion is misleading at best. His description is as follows. The father and son reality is of King and Subject. This father and son symbol represents a passage from the Old Testament described in Ezekiel 28:12 and Isaiah :14...'

"Europa, summation please," Xavier said, trying to keep his supercomputer on point without reciting the entire biblical passage.

'Yes, Doctor. While many biblical scholars concede the modern point of view that the references from the old testament refer to a real human king of Babylonia being cast aside from the sight of God, it is Professor Halpern's opinion that the biblical account was right from the beginning and that the more redux version by modernists is wrong. Halpern then was influenced by a text that has been met with skepticism that was originally placed in the old testament claiming that the archangel Asmodius Modai was cast from heaven for rebelling against God.'

"Doctor Morales are you suggesting that the symbol is describing a fallen archangel named Asmodius Modai? It sounds suspiciously like you're describing Lucifer and his fall from grace."

"Correct Professor Freeling. That is exactly what I and Europa are claiming. You are a theology professor and you know as well as I that Asmodius means prince of demons. What greater demon and villain in human history is more so than Lucifer himself? Place the symbols back to back and you have the name Asmodius Modai, an alias for the men and women here that are skeptical. Ladies and gentlemen, I may not believe in the fairytales a lot of people in this room do. But I do believe in facts. Are we dealing with someone, or something that is in all actuality, Lucifer? Probably not. Are we dealing with an insane entity that that it believes that very thing? In my opinion, yes."

"Then you *are* saying that our friend and colleague, and Colonel Collins' four security men were murdered by some nutcase that thinks he's the Fallen One, or should I say the Prince of Darkness?" Professor Freeling scoffed.

178

The room erupted and Collins exchanged looks with Everett who merely shook his head.

"Regardless, Doctor Morales and Europa has put a name to our enemy. Suggestions Doctor?" Niles asked.

"No evidence other than the ancient symbols left at the crime scene. Four of Colonel Collins more experienced security men caught off guard and crushed to death? I'm leaning toward a more fantastic reality than your normal criminal type. I believe the miraculous rising of Matchstick and the kidnapping of Charlie, coupled with what happened at Mrs. Hamilton's home, have to be related somehow."

Suddenly three tones sounded, and the complex inner-communications system came on.

'Colonel Collins, a disturbance is being reported at Gate number one. Complex Security is currently observing an intruder. The intruder is currently being detained by Air Police elements from Nellis. Please advise.'

Jack looked at Carl after the intercom had gone silent and both men stood and left the conference room. He had hoped to be flying to Boston, but an intrusion at one of the Event Group access points was a serious affair. Behind him he heard the Director call an end to the meeting as he rose to join Carl and Jack.

IN THE SECURITY department the one-hundred-inch monitor showed the old hangar that was gate number one. The camouflaged main entrance to Group was the most heavily guarded point of egress that was manned twenty-four hours a day. As he, Carl and Niles watched, the Air Police had a single person stopped and detained on the desert sands of the northern firing range a mere fifty feet from the dilapidated and secrete entrance to the complex. A helicopter was winding down and they assumed the intruder had come onto the firing range in that manner. Both the intruder and the Bell Jet Ranger were surrounded by ten Humvees.

"What in the hell, someone fly off course?" Carl asked.

The security camera zoomed in and the three men saw that the intruder was a woman. All three, Niles, Jack, and Carl raised their brows when they saw the dark-haired woman point to the dilapidated hangar.

"Mister Everett, tell our men to break cover and bring that person in."

"You're not afraid of letting this person know about gate one," Niles asked.

Jack shook his head as he stood from his spot on the desktop.

"For some reason Mr. Director, I have a suspicion this lady knows exactly what's under the camouflaged hangar."

"My thoughts exactly," Carl agreed. "Anya always said that old lady didn't look the type to work alone, and the thugs she was at Lake Mead looked a little inept, but this one looks like she knows exactly what she's doing."

"What are you suggesting?" Niles asked as Jack moved for the door of the security department. He stopped and faced the director.

"I think we're about to get a message from our mysterious Elsbeth Barlow."

THE TWO SECURITY men holding an arm each were dressed in desert BDU's, and although the woman couldn't see them due to the hood over her head, she knew they were heavily armed. In the dark she felt and heard a large lift and by the twitter in her stomach she knew she was heading downward. The mechanical noises stopped, and she heard a large gate slide open. The two security men from Gate number one eased her out politely from the large transport lift. Suddenly the hood that had been thrust over her head in the desert above was removed. She tried to blink the brightness away as her eyes adjusted. When she finally looked up, she saw two men standing in front of her. Both were wearing blue coveralls, and both had military ranks displayed on their collars. She was being greeted by a dark-haired man who was scarred in many areas of his face and who wore the silver eagles of a full-bird colonel. The second man was blonde. He was also sporting a silver eagle on his collar, only this one was one she more readily recognized. The blonde was a Captain in the US Navy, the same branch that she was still part of.

"Excuse me for the intrusion gentlemen, but I was wondering if you can loosen these handcuffs as a professional courtesy?"

Jack Collins looked at Everett and both said nothing. Instead Carl took the woman by the arm and he and Jack started walking her past the logistics center where the trespasser had a good view of the Group hangar deck. The woman was impressed seeing the thirty-five Humvee vehicles, the four UH-60 Blackhawks and several other transports. She was about to comment when she was led into a small room with three chairs, a table, and a large mirror. She smiled knowing exactly what was behind the mirror and wondered who would be observing her interrogation.

"Let me guess, the waterboarding room?" she asked, only semi-jokingly as Carl pulled a chair out for her and then forcibly sat her down. Jack and Carl sat opposite her. The room was silent as the back-haired woman looked from face to face. "Is this the part where I state my name, rank and serial number?"

"Probably wouldn't be a bad start Lieutenant Commander Krensky," Jack said.

"You know my name?" she asked as she squirmed with her hands still cuffed behind her back.

"We knew the moment our security cameras got a close-up of your face. Our computer has the best facial recognition software on the planet," Everett answered for the colonel. "As an active member of the Naval Reserve, I suppose you know you're still liable to the oath you took, Commander? And that charges could include breaking onto a highly secured military reservation?"

"Such is the nature of the beast."

"Meaning?" Jack asked.

"I knew what I was getting into when I was chosen to make our first overture to your Group, Colonel Collins."

"Chosen by Elsbeth Barlow?" Jack asked as he examined her face for any surprise. As he had suspected before, he saw none.

"Yes."

"Millie, may I call you Millie?" Carl asked. "Millicent seems so formal for someone who seems to know us almost intimately."

The woman looked Everett up and down and then Jack. "I think I would rather be addressed by my military rank. I earned it."

"Okay, Commander, I agree. Let's do away with any pleasantries." Jack's blue eyes dug mercilessly into the woman's green ones. "You and whoever Elsbeth Barlow is took two of our friends from us. We want them back immediately. And what you said about waterboarding? We have much better methods. As of right now you are in a place that doesn't exist. That means Commander, you don't exist."

"After you're done with torturing me gentlemen, if you still want, you can have your friends back. Alive and well and very much unharmed." She smiled. "Although I believe it was *you* who buried your little green friend alive."

"And how did you and this Barlow woman know Matchstick wasn't really dead, just dormant," Jack continued.

"That as they say, is a long story only Elsbeth can explain. I believe the answer is above my pay-grade."

"Why did you and your boss take them?" Carl asked.

"Number one, we needed to get your attention. Number two, if you failed to see our point of view, we needed...Matchstick I believe you call him?"

"For what?" Jack asked.

"I'll get to that, Colonel," she said as she leaned forward and slightly turned left exposing her wrists and the cuffs that secured them. Her dark eyebrows rose in question.

Jack nodded at Carl who stood and used the small key to unlock the cuffs.

"Now, a friendly gesture has established trust, at least that's what our book of torture says," Jack said with a smile that didn't reach his eyes.

The woman rubbed her wrists. "Thank you. Not used to being handcuffed, now I see why people don't like it. "Now, we don't have a lot of time, so..."

Suddenly the lights dimmed and then went out, but before they did both Jack and Carl saw the woman raise her now freed hands off the tabletop. Then the lights flared back to life. Through the sound of running boot-falls outside the room, Jack and Carl exchanged looks. Then Jack held his right hand up and saw that he and Carl had been handcuffed by the same set they had just removed from the woman a moment before. The door opened and two security men entered with drawn weapons. Niles Compton was right behind them.

"Jack, what happened?" Compton asked.

Collins and Everett both held up their hands and Niles saw the cuffs binding the two men together. He looked from the two to the visitor to the complex. He faced the woman, leaning as close to her as he could get without bumping noses.

"Nice trick, or sleight of hand, whichever magician's vocabulary you choose to prefer, but if you want to play games I can surely oblige. Five of my people are dead. I will not have one compunction in shooting you in your lovely head if you don't release them immediately. Then if you still wish to play your little game, I will warn you now that I will track this Elsbeth Barlow down and she will personally pay for what she has done."

Jack and Carl had never once heard Niles Compton threaten anyone. His words were some of those you would never have associated with the director.

The woman looked from Niles to Jack and Carl. She lifted both hands and then spread her fingers. The cuffs clicked open. Jack tossed them onto the tabletop. Niles turned and stood by the door after excusing the two Marines.

"Doctor Compton, Elsbeth Barlow had nothing to do with the murder of your friends and associates. As a matter of fact, you owe her a debt of gratitude for intervening before the real killer had a chance to finish the job with Mrs. Hamilton."

"What do you mean by that?" Jack asked.

"Mrs. Hamilton was seconds away from falling to the same fate as Ms. Pollock. Elsbeth expended a lot of energy in stopping it."

"It?" Niles asked.

"I suspect you have already deciphered its name?"

"Asmodius Modai," Niles said, not as a question.

"Elsbeth said you people were worthy of hearing the truth. By the way Colonel, Captain Everett, I was impressed when Elsbeth explained your part in the battles for Antarctica and Houston. And Doctor Compton for your part as well. I guess we all lost friends and comrades in the war."

The door opened slightly and a marine in blue overalls stepped in. "Colonel, Will Mendenhall's on the line, says he needs to speak with you ASAP."

Collins stood and went to the extension on the wall. He punched a number. "Collins," he said and then slightly turned away.

"Okay, now that the mutual admiration society moment has passed," Carl said, "who was it that murdered our friends?"

"You'll have a hard timer believing it. But what I'm about to say is true. You're dealing with an entity that thinks it's the Prince of Darkness. A lie he has perpetrated since the dawn of civilization. One it thrives on. A thing that is responsible for the world's religious communities' belief in good and evil, heaven and hell. He hides behind the false front of Asmodius Modai, but you call him Lucifer. But you may know him as a…"

"Grey."

Carl and Niles turned and watched as Jack hung up the phone. "That was Will, he and Henri and Ryan have just checked out of our safe house in New Orleans where a doctor had to stitch them up. They tracked down a lead on Briggs and some offshore deal he had. They were ambushed. Almost taken out by a giant Grey. Will said he doesn't know how, but the bastard brought down a building around them. He said it was like the Grey used some form of magic. Our in-house skeptic, Colonel Farbeaux, confirms the Major's account."

Jack stood over the dark-haired woman. "Strange how these magic tricks keep appearing."

"If you buy me a drink, I'll explain some of it."

"Try it right now!" Niles said, not in good enough humor to be friendly.

"Okay, but you *will* need that drink soon enough," she said.

"Commander, our patience is wearing so thin right now it's damn near transparent," Jack warned.

"Magic?" The woman stifled a laugh. "I guess you could call it that. The manipulations of surrounding air, the combination of sounds and letters. The use of both hand gestures, words, or a combination of both. Yes, magic if you will. I prefer one of the more ancient sciences in the history of the world. But if you want, you may refer to it as magic. That's what the Grey is you see. The great liar taught the human race thousands of years ago when it decided to leave his own race and world for a backwater planet where the barbaric people there could be manipulated easily. Asmodius Modai, the first and only Warlock."

"And Elsbeth Barlow, the Witch Queen of Salem."

Carl, Jack, and Millicent Krensky looked at Niles. They could all see that Compton was slowly becoming a believer.

**Event Group Safehouse,
New Orleans, Louisiana**

"Damn Doc, what are you using there, a steel cable?" Mendenhall hissed, leaning away from the needle and thread.

"Oh, come on Major. Six little stitches. You never complained this much when I was at Group. I think maybe you've grown soft since becoming an officer. I guess a staff sergeant means tougher, huh?"

Will looked closely at Doctor Neal Forester, M.D., retired. He decided not to argue the point of who was tougher, officers or enlisted men.

"Well, I think you've lost your touch since retiring, Doc."

"Complain, complain."

As Will was getting stitched up from the incident at Maritime Welding, Ryan and Farbeaux were in the retired Group doctor's study. They watched the report being broadcast from Metairie on what the local authorities were calling the mass ritual execution of local laborers. After digging themselves out of the collapsed building, the trio had come within seconds of being caught by the local constabulary which would have created somewhat of a scandal at a time when the Event Group needed even less attention than before.

"...Many in the sheriff's department believe the ritualistic murders is either tied to organized crime or the international drug trade. We'll have more on this story as details become available."

Ryan was getting impatient and started to turn off the television when Farbeaux held his hand up.

"...meantime in a news filled day, the lone survivor of the Mystery Deep oil platform disaster has been transferred to University Medical Center in New Orleans. The woman, who has yet to make a statement, has thus far been the only employee recovered from the largest platform disaster since the Deepwater Horizon explosion of April 2010...,"

"Commander, where did Director Compton say that the FBI lost the tail on our good Congressman?" Farbeaux asked as he turned the television off.

Ryan pulled out his notebook as he smiled when Will cursed the doctor once more. "It says they lost him after he boarded a helicopter in Houma Louisiana."

"There was a blueprint in the offices of Maritime Welding of the *Mystery Deep* platform." Farbeaux walked to the window of the Group safe-house and watched as the sun started to rise out of the east. The clouds were slowly starting to burn off as the storm began to clear.

"What are you connecting here, Colonel?" Jason asked.

"I am of the same mind as your director and your friend Colonel Collins. Coincidence is a scenario I rarely ascribe to. I think we need to go see a certain survivor of this so-called accident at sea."

"I suspect she'll be guarded rather heavily being the only witness to a mystery."

Farbeaux walked over to a coat rack the retired doctor had near his small office where Mendenhall continued to complain about his stitches in an army sort of profanity laced tirade. Henri pulled three white lab coats off their hooks and tossed Ryan one of them.

"Your amazing Europa field link can produce identity badges I presume?" the Frenchman asked.

"That's her specialty," Ryan quipped.

"Shall we go and see exactly what language this survivor speaks. My wager is that she has a bit of an Eastern European dialect." Henri placed the white coat under his arm. "If the Major is through being poked and prodded, let's see if there's a connection, shall we?"

CHAPTER ELEVEN

Cambridge, Massachusetts

As Charlie and Matchstick watched from their chairs around the large, highly polished table, Elsbeth Barlow was speaking on the antique phone on the credenza. Matchstick's large obsidian eyes never left the silver-haired woman even as he plopped four sausage links into his small mouth. He stopped chewing when the old woman turned to the table and held the phone out.

"Slim, your boss would like to speak with you. I guess he's doubtful we haven't boiled you and your little friend in a caldron of toil and trouble."

Charlie placed his napkin down on his plate of untouched breakfast. He stood as Matchstick reached over and took his sausage and placed those in his mouth with the others.

"Yes, Niles, we're fine." Charlie's eyes went to Elsbeth who was watching Matchstick eat and wondering just how much food could fit in the small alien's stomach. "No, sir, I haven't observed any ill effects from his recent dormant state. He seems overly hungry, but I guess after a few months in the ground that should be expected. No Niles, no memory of what happened to him after the..." Charlie turned away from both Elsbeth and Matchstick. "...incident." Ellenshaw looked at his wristwatch. "It will be good to see some friendly faces. Yes, sir, I'll watch him." Charlie handed the receiver to a large man and then returned to his seat and silently placed the napkin in his lap. He began to eat immediately. He soon found he was famished after being reassure by the director that help was on its way.

"Well, Slim?"

Charlie slipped a piece of toast into his mouth and faced Elsbeth. "If you're expecting our Director to automatically give you a pass and say everything is forgiven, you don't know Niles Compton." Charlie for the first time in years took a sip of coffee. "So, if you don't mind, I and Matchstick will remain your captives until our friends arrive. Keep things in perspective, so to speak."

"Prudent of Doctor Compton. So, when will your friends arrive?" Elsbeth asked as she stood up, forgoing the effort by the large man in black to assist. She poured more coffee for Charlie. She smiled when Matchstick held out his cup. Charlie shook his head before she could pour.

"You don't want to offer him any coffee. It would be like giving a child candy just before bedtime," Charlie said as he buttered another piece of toast.

Matchstick looked at Ellenshaw and angrily placed the china cup down on the table. Charlie, without looking at Matchstick's accusing glare, slid his small bowl of fruit over to the alien as a peace offering. Elsbeth Barlow returned to her chair.

"We've met many times before—you know that my small friend?" Elsbeth said as she sipped her own coffee.

Matchstick paused with a slice of cantaloupe halfway to his mouth and stared at the silver-haired woman.

She cackled. Not as loud and annoying as before, but the laugh was still like scraping fingernails across a chalkboard to Ellenshaw's ears. Even Matchstick winced at the irritating noise.

"Oh, not you personally, but your ancestors. Without them my kind would have been extinct many thousands of years ago."

"That's the third time you have said, 'my kind.' As a historical freak and immensely curious at all times, may ask what *kind* you are?"

"Oh, Slim, you haven't really figured it out yet?" Elsbeth looked from Charlie to Matchstick who chewed his food as he listened. "Why, I'm a witch. We all are here. Don't you see all the black cats and broomsticks laying around?"

Charlie stopped eating and glanced around the beautiful dining room. He looked at the large man by the credenza filled with food. The man was trying hard to control his smiling and looked as if he was about to burst with laughter.

"I'm having fun at your expense Slim I apologize. No, you don't see those things. I haven't picked up a broom in centuries and I'm afraid I'm allergic to cats." Elsbeth smiled as she sipped her coffee. "Professor, you'll never comprehend what a real witch is. As they say, you'll always be a skeptic. You're a man of letters and higher education," she paused. "Please don't get my wrong, I admire folks such as yourself. As a matter of fact, I'm much like your past and present Directors. I insist that the men and women who follow me keep up their studies. We need to know about the outside world as much as possible."

"You said centuries," Charlie said. "How old do you claim to be?"

"Why does every male in my lifetime fixate on my damn age? I'm old Slim. Very old. A curse of my choosing, but a curse, nonetheless. My only regret is that your little green friend and his ancestors didn't teach me the spell for immortality until I was this old." She looked at a startled Matchstick and winked. "I could have been taught that little trick back when I was a little more youthful. Now I got all of the old age pains and ills with none of the benefits of my youth." She cackled that irritating laugh again. "Tell me Slim, what will it take for you to become a believer? Even your ancestors believed enough to burn not just a few of us at the stake."

"A little before my time," Charlie said, pushing his breakfast plate away where Matchstick immediately took the bacon from it.

"Don't worry. If I held grudges, there would be a few people far ahead of you on my revenge bucket list."

Charlie studied Elsbeth Barlow. Her demeanor was that of

someone who learned many years before that you can lead a horse to water but couldn't make him drink. Through her attitude she looked like she had tried to convince skeptics for most of her long life. For the time being he would let her insanity and ambiguity slide by.

"What's your plan?" Charlie asked, removing his wire-rimmed glasses and using his napkin to clean the lenses.

Elsbeth turned her head and watched Matchstick eat for the longest time. Her wrinkled face grew serious. Serious enough that the small alien placed the bacon on the plate unfinished.

"I can't win the fight that's coming alone. Even with the power of all of my people. I need this little guy. I've got to get him to remember just exactly what his race is capable of. You know Matchstick, your kind weren't slaves all through your history. At one time the Grey's treated you as equals. Many thousands of years ago. They relied on your knowledge to stop our enemy the first time. When you became mentally more powerful than them, that was when you and your people were enslaved. Now I need you to remember from the collective memory you share with your race on how to defeat the very being that developed the powers we share."

"Who is this being you speak of?" Charlie asked.

Elsbeth stood. "Randall, I need your assistance, please."

The large man with the black shirt and black sports coat left his spot by the door and assisted Elsbeth up from her chair.

"Thank you. Now I need your help with something very distasteful. Slim here wants to be introduced to the Fallen One."

Charlie looked from Elsbeth and her minion to Matchstick who had stopped eating and was watching intently. Elsbeth raised her right hand and moved it from right to left through the air. The heavy, thick drapes covering the leaded glass windows shot closed. Charlie and Matchstick both went wide-eyed. Then Elsbeth took the large man's arm for further support. She closed her eyes. "Ready Randall?"

"Yes, Granny."

"Okay, *nnahno-suportum-Modai!*" she said as she balled her hand into a fist as the large man closed his eyes and mumbled and repeated the spell Elsbeth had just voiced. His dark hair acted as if it were filled with static electricity and his and Elsbeth silver hair was pulled toward the now darkened corner of the dining room. Charlie started to rise form his chair, but Matchstick leaped from his seat to Ellenshaw's lap, successfully pinning him.

Suddenly a burst of electrical sparks, cartoonish in looks, burst outward from the corner of the dining room and then Charlie did stand and scream as a full, life sized version of a giant Grey appeared as if summoned into the room by a spell Elsbeth had just cast. The large creature looked shocked. It looked around the dark room until its yellow eyes fixated on the three humans and one alien. Its eyes widened and the Grey hissed in anger and stomped its goat-like legs. As it started forward Charlie and Matchstick fell down onto the carpeted floor. The Grey came on as if it were going to tear both of them to pieces.

The large man let go of Elsbeth's arm and tried to get in-between Charlie, Matchstick and the charging Grey. Elsbeth reached for him but it was too late as the Grey turned on the man Elsbeth had called Randall. The creature swiped at him and he went flying through the air. The Grey turned and once more started for Charlie and Matchstick.

"Tarness-expectai-Modai-susecpatus!" Elsbeth screamed and then went to her knees.

Just as the Grey roared and lifted its clawed hand to strike at a cowering Matchstick, the image burst into a million blue, green, and red sparks and the room was silent.

Randall came to and immediately ran to Elsbeth who was struggling to get to her feet. He hefted her as he also used his right hand to open the drapes in a magical swirl of his own small power.

"I'm sorry. That's the first time I've seen Asmodius. I'm afraid I didn't handle it too well," Randall said to Elsbeth. She patted his thick arm.

"Makes me a little weak in the bladder my own self, Randall," she smiled as the man led her to her chair. Then he helped Charlie and Matchstick up.

"What in the hell? Are you saying your ancient enemy is a Grey?"

Charlie said as he tried to relax Matchstick as the alien put a choke hold on Charlie's neck for support.

"Yes, Slim. His name is Asmodius Modai. Or if you prefer, the Prince of Darkness. But the name it prefers no matter how false its claim, is Lucifer, the fallen angel, a lie it has perpetrated since the dawn of civilization."

"What does it want?"

Elsbeth smiled and accepted the small glass of brandy from a bloodied Randall. She downed it quickly.

"What he want's, my good Professor, is the world he created long ago back in his possession before it was taken away."

"Who took it from him, you?" Charlie asked, incredulous about the entire tale.

Elsbeth said nothing. Both the Elsbeth and Randall simply turned and looked at Matchstick.

University Medical Center,
New Orleans, Louisiana

RYAN TOOK his turn driving as Will was still fuming over being treated like a pincushion at the safe house. If the truth be known all three, Will, Jason, and Henri were still in shock after seeing the Grey in Metairie. As they drove into the hospital parking lot it was the Frenchman's hackles that rose first. He looked around from the backseat at the brightness of the day. After so much rain the clear skies should have made anyone feel better. The sky was as blue as Henri could ever remember seeing. Still, something had caught his attention, but he couldn't place it. It was like they were walking into a situation where they did not have the upper hand.

"Park as close to the main entrance as possible," Farbeaux said.

"Expecting us to have to leave in a hurry?" Will asked, barely able to turn his head due to the soreness of his body from having a roof nearly crush him to mush. He saw Henri pointing. He looked up. "Oh," was all he said.

Parked on the side near the main parking area was a large bus. The charter was painted in a garish montage of Louisiana bayou scenes complete with fishermen and hunters and Spanish Moss laden cypress trees. On the side was the slogan, *'For America and the World— Harold Briggs for President.'*

"It seems our fearless Congressman is also interested in our lone survivor."

Henri only nodded his head at Ryan's observation.

"How do we go about this?" Will asked. "I think we better check in with Doc Compton on how to proceed." Mendenhall placed the call. Both Farbeaux and Ryan were shocked when the call lasted only a minute. Will shook his head.

"Well?" Ryan asked, but Henri had a suspicion on just what instructions the Major had just received.

"The director said for us to use our own discretion on who we kill to get information."

"Funny," Jason said.

"I don't think he was joking, pal."

"Then let's see what we see, shall we?"

The three men with their white lab coats strode confidently through the main door and straight past several State Troopers on guard in the lobby. They went to the information desk.

"Excuse me," Ryan said, leaning confidently over the desk and the elderly volunteer manning it. "We're visiting here from Dallas. We're looking for…"

"Congressman Briggs has asked us to consult with the rescued survivor of the *Mystery Deep*. Perhaps you can point the way." Ryan looked at Henri. Then he realized the faint. If they asked directly for the survivor's room number that would have set off alarms in the lobby. But asking for a famous Louisiana Congressman was not as suspicious. After all, wherever Briggs was, the woman they wished to talk to would be close by.

"Well, the Congressman and his people are in the waiting area near the nurse's station on the fourth floor," the silver haired lady said with a smile.

"So helpful, thank you," Henri said as the trio moved to the elevator. On the way past a cart Will snatched a chart and hid it close to his coat.

As the elevator doors closed, Ryan turned to Farbeaux. "That was pretty indirect," he said.

"Never go straight at the desired target, Commander. Come at that target from the flanks or rear. You should have learned that by now."

"Excuse me for being a little lax on my burglary and deception skills, Colonel. I'll try to make amends for that."

"Please do."

The doors slid open and Will braced for security to catch them right off the bat. They immediately saw a woman and several men standing near the nurse's station debating something. All five people were animated as they seemed to be arguing some point or other. Henri watched for the briefest of moments and saw the woman whisper and look at a closed door with two Louisiana State troopers on either side. The women was saying something she didn't want whoever was in the room to overhear. Ryan and Mendenhall were shocked when Henri bypassed the nurse's station and went directly to the room's closed door and the large state troopers standing guard near it. They both prayed the French Colonel knew what he was doing. Henri turned to the two men just as they reached the closed door. Farbeaux knew they had caught a break when he saw the secret service detail assigned to the presidential frontrunner were standing at the coffee machine. He knew how local authorities in a state had a natural aversion to any federal officer. Henri smiled at the two state troopers.

"Glad to see our federal tax dollars are hard at work," he said with a nod toward the coffee machine.

One of the officers smiled and mumbled to his partner. "Ain't that the truth?" The larger of the two actually opened the door for the trio of circumspect physicians.

"Damn, but you're good at this crap," Mendenhall said as they entered the nearly silent room.

Will stopped as did Henri and Jason when they heard the beeping of monitors, and then as they turned the corner near the bathroom, they saw a man standing over a woman with bandages on her head and both arms. The portly man with the Elvis grey hairdo turned and saw the three doctors.

"I just need a few more minutes."

Farbeaux looked at the man and he noticed him shaking.

"We just need to check her vitals."

"A nurse just took Ms. Trotsky's vitals a minute ago," Briggs said, taking a closer look at the three men.

"Yes, well, we're specialists from Dallas, you won't mind if we do our own examination do you?" Farbeaux asked confidently. Briggs held his ground.

Henri stepped around him. Ryan and Will took up station on either side of the bed. The woman looked badly burned in several areas but looked like she would survive.

"This is awful careless," Farbeaux said as he leaned over the black-haired woman. "He pulled a small syringe from her I.V. tube and held it up for the others to see. Briggs stepped back from the bed.

"One of the nurses must have left that there. I'll chew someone's ass for that."

Henri smelled the needle at the syringe's tip. He looked at the congressman. "Are you this young lady's father?" he asked.

"Why, uh, no. Just an interested party," Briggs said, suddenly looking like a rabbit ready to bolt at the sight of a hunter.

The Frenchman looked at Ryan and nodded toward the door. Ryan walked over and silently slid the bolt closed hoping it went unheard in the noisy hallway. Briggs saw this and started to back away more assuredly. Henri quickly reached out and took Briggs by the nose and mouth, cutting off his air supply.

"Oh, shit," Mendenhall said aloud as Ryan returned.

"Tell me, as an interested party Congressman, exactly what that interest is?" Henri shook him as Briggs eyes started to flutter as he fought for air. Farbeaux let up slightly on the man's nose but not his mouth. "Quietly, Mr. Briggs."

"Mummamuhma," Briggs said under the pressure of Farbeaux powerful fingers.

"Maybe if you move your hand slightly, we can understand what the good Congressman is saying," Mendenhall said, afraid he was going to watch a United States Congressman murdered right before his eyes.

"It was a threat. The first words from men like this is always a threat," Henri said as he did let up on the grip over Briggs' mouth.

"Who...are you?"

Henri reapplied the fingers over the mouth. "You don't know, Congressman?"

Briggs vigorously shook his head as he was staring at Farbeaux.

"You think we're your Russian friends?" Farbeaux asked.

"Mummamuhma," Briggs tried to say.

"Well, that's a start," Farbeaux said with a smile.

"What did he say?" Ryan asked, amazed at Henri's technique at questioning, as it kind of reminded him of Jack's method.

"He thinks we're Russians. Assassins." Farbeaux let up only slightly on Briggs mouth. "Me and the men accompanying me are not Russians, Congressman." Henri straightened the man up and then guided him to a chair. He placed his index finger on his lips and made a sshhh, gesture. "Now, why did you try to kill this poor lady lying helpless in her bed with succinylcholine."

"What is that?" Ryan asked.

"A small dose will cause the body into paralysis and the patient dies as a human body would naturally shut down after a trauma. Untraceable."

"That's a lie," Briggs said as his eyes were wild, going from face to face.

"Okay Congressman, perhaps we better bring in the authorities and allow them to decide," Farbeaux said with not very much sympathy in his eyes. "Your fingerprints on the syringe and this," he reached into the Congressman's pocket and produced a small rubber stopped vile, "may give you pause for seeking assistance from outside this room."

"Who are you?"

"The little bald man you seem to be fixated on from that private think-tank in the desert sends his regards," Henri looked at Ryan and Mendenhall and winked.

"You work for Compton?"

The three men remained silent when the director's name was mentioned by Briggs. "Congressman, allow me to guess. You seem to have gotten yourself into a bind with some eastern European types. Am I correct?"

"Why would this Compton want to help me, a man out to expose him and the President?"

"Congressman Briggs, if you wish to avoid wearing a federal prison number for many, many years to come, I suggest you allow us to ask the questions," Farbeaux said.

Briggs just nodded his head. His eyes were wide and terrified as he was watching his political future being stolen from him at that very moment.

As Farbeaux was explaining things to Briggs, Ryan went to the door and placed an ear to it. He listened. He turned and nodded his own head at Henri that thus far, no alarm had been sounded. He then clicked on the recorder on his cell phone and the conversation would stream directly to Europa and the complex.

"Now, since we are extremely short on time, why were you willing to murder this rather lovely lady?"

"She and her boss were blackmailing me." Briggs eyed the syringe and the small bottle in Farbeaux's hand. "This man turned on his own people and went rogue. At first all they asked for was for me to expose...," he looked around at the three men and his eyes expressed just how frightened he was, "this mysterious department in Nevada. I only had a suspicion, but these Russians knew far more than I did. They know everything and that was how I was able to have a file on this Niles Compton. It was only that promised. After that they said they had no further requests."

"So, you decided to kill the only person who knew you were working with the Russians?" Ryan asked ahead of Farbeaux.

Briggs became silent.

"Was this rogue Russian killed in the *Mystery Deep* explosion?" Farbeaux asked.

"I don't know," Briggs finally said.

"But the Grey did survive. Is that correct?" Henri asked with brows raised.

Briggs was shocked and stunned that these men knew what they knew. "How...how did you know?"

"Because the son of a bitch dropped a damn building on us last night," Mendenhall said angrily.

Briggs lowered his head. "I didn't know what this madman Sokol had in mind. He's completely nuts!"

"Sokol? Dmitri Sokol?" Farbeaux asked.

"You know him?" Mendenhall asked.

"I know of him. He's not a very nice man."

"Strange how many not very nice people you know," Ryan quipped as he looked at Henri.

"What is this man's plan with the Grey?" Farbeaux asked, ignoring Ryan's remark.

"Look, that Grey bastard is just as insane as Sokol. It's not like the other Grey's."

"We kind of noticed that, Congressman," Mendenhall said, rubbing the bandage on the back of his neck.

"They call him Asmodius. He can do things. Strange things. As I said, it's not like the Grey's from the war. This one is powerful and under Sokol's control. His bosses in Russia tried to eliminate them both. I was hoping they succeeded when *Mystery Deep* went up in flames."

"Well, we can definitely say that one of them survived," Ryan said.

"Congressman, may I suggest that you walk us to the door and smile as you show us out," Farbeaux said as he stood Briggs up. He pocketed the syringe and the small bottle so the Congressman could see him do it. "I may also suggest that your health may have taken a turn for the worst. Perhaps you're really not up to running for such a stressful job as President." Henri smiled.

"Blackmail again?" Briggs asked.

"No, we just offered you an alternative to *other* solutions," the Frenchman said as he angrily pushed Briggs toward the door.

"Other federal authorities will be by to transfer Ms. Trotsky to a more secure location. I suspect she may have a lot to say about not only her employer Mr. Sokol, but also the men he betrayed. It might be what you call, in her best interest."

"You bastards!" Briggs hissed. The he straightened his coat and used his fingers to rearrange his hair.

Ryan unlocked the door and the three men stepped out with Briggs smiling and shaking their hands.

"Thank you, gentlemen for traveling so far. Your prognosis is very encouraging."

Ryan, Mendenhall and Farbeaux smiled in return and then turned to leave when the hallway was filled with a scream. They all went back to the room. The State Troopers along with Briggs security detail were trying to open the door, but every time they came close the door was pushed back with enough force to toss the troopers backward. They started to ram their bodies into it and finally the door flew open. Ryan reached for his weapon but then remembered they were left in the car before they came in. He cursed himself.

As the door was forced open, a blur passed them as the body of Vexilla Trotsky was thrown out into the hallway. Nurses screamed and orderlies fell trying to avoid the crushed body of the lone survivor of the *Mystery Deep* disaster.

As the State Troopers looked on wide-eyed, one of the secret service men yelled to *'watch out.'* As they turned, the Grey was standing by the large window and was grinning. Then just as suddenly, it started to fade to nothing.

"Did you guy's see that?" the first trooper asked as his shaking hands pointed his service weapon at nothing.

"What went on in there?" the second asked, looking directly at Briggs. Then both troopers turned to ask the three doctors.

They were gone.

CHAPTER TWELVE

Desert Springs Hospital,
Las Vegas, Nevada

Inside the I.C.U. all was quiet. Niles Compton sat at the side of Alice Hamilton as the on-duty nurse checked her I.V. drip. Niles turned away and choked down his anger at what had happened to Alice and Virginia. He felt he had failed his two most trusted people. The nurse turned to him and gave him a reassuring smile.

"I've never seen a woman fight so hard. Every time her vital signs take a dip, she seems to struggle back." The nurse saw the pain in Niles face and patted his hand. "She must be a very important lady to have the Surgeon General on the case."

Niles nodded. "She's important to quite a few."

"Take heart, she's a fighter."

Niles looked down at the serene face of Alice Hamilton as the nurse opened the curtain and then left. Compton reached out and took Alice's hand and squeezed it tight, hoping in some way that one of his oldest friends would know he was there. He lowered his head as the respirator beat a lonely note.

The curtain was pulled back again and Niles saw Jack Collins and Sarah standing, afraid that they were intruding. Niles nodded his head that indicated they were doing anything but. He removed his glasses and acted as though he were cleaning them while not really hiding his red eyes.

"We just wanted to check on her before we left," Jack said as he watched Sarah move to the opposite side of the bed to sit and take Alice's hand just as Niles let go of her other.

"So, you ready?" Niles asked.

"We'll get to the bottom of this Niles. On that you have my word."

Niles nodded at Jack.

"I suppose you heard the news?" Jack asked as he saw Sarah lower her head as she said a silent prayer for Alice. He gestured for Niles to step out of the area.

"What news?" Niles asked.

"After you left the complex, Henri and his team checked in. You know what happened at the hospital in New Orleans, but one thing you don't know is that immediately after our French friend spoke with Congressman Briggs, the bastard called a press conference for tonight. The speculation is running wild in the press, but Henri seems to suggest the good Congressman is contemplating stepping out of the race for the presidency due to health reasons."

"Let's get a cup of coffee, Jack," Niles said, turning to Sarah who nodded that she was staying with Alice.

Out in the corridor, Niles ignored the coffee machine and faced Collins.

"The Congressman doesn't know it, but he may well have just saved his own life. You wouldn't believe what the President was contemplating."

Jack looked toward the closed off section of the I.C.U. "Well, the President knows what that lady in there has done for her country. I think he may not have really cared what he had to do to protect her and us. After all, he's the still the President, he can pretty much get away with what he wants. I don't think he really gives a damn about the consequences."

Niles just nodded.

"Excuse me gentlemen."

Both Jack and Niles turned to see a rather large and rotund man standing near them. He stepped forward with outstretched hand.

"Yes?" Niles said, ignoring the handshake offer.

"I represent some colleagues that you may have had dealings with the past year and a half. I believe the last time they spoke to you they offered a settlement of sorts about differences of opinion in national and historic affairs. Opinions regarding the Atlantic Ocean incident and perhaps more recently in Mongolia?"

Jack tensed and Niles placed a hand on his arm to calm him. The rotund man held up his hands in mock defense.

"I don't wish any unpleasantness gentlemen," he said, taking a step back from the withering glare of Jack Collins. "My associates asked me to come by and offer our sincere condolences for the loss you have sustained in Ms. Pollock and your security personnel. I understand Ms. Pollock was a very great woman and one of the best engineers in the world." The man looked sheepish and he refused to look Jack in the eyes. He concentrated solely on Niles Compton. "We also want to express our hopes and wishes for a speedy recovery of Mrs. Hamilton. Her exploits in her representation and defense of your nation is legendary beyond measure."

"Quit playing games, Russian, why are you here?" Jack said, ignoring the warning look from Niles.

"The peaceful overture offered by my associates after the incident in Mongolia last month. I have come here to reaffirm that offer of peace between our organizations. The incidents proceeding the death of Ms. Pollock and your men and the injury of Mrs. Hamilton, was not perpetrated by any current member of my organization."

Silence met the man's proclamation of the shadow government in Russia's innocence in the matter. Jack took a menacing step forward.

"The man you seek is in Louisiana and his name is Sokol."

"We know who he is. Dmitri Sokol. The number ten man in the falsity you call a government," Niles said, his proclamation stunning their Russian visitor.

"Director Compton, we wish to proceed in this matter and remain neutral. We will take care of our internal problems if you would allow us to, and we would be more than happy to..."

Jack moved to strike the man from Siberia, but Niles stopped him and actually pulled the gun from Jack's sports coat before Collins knew it. He turned on the Russian just as Sarah came out of the curtained off area of the I.C.U. She froze just as Niles Compton, one of the gentlest men she had ever met, cocked the Glock nine-millimeter, and placed it squarely under the heavy-set man's chin.

"Tell this to your superiors," Niles said, "we will take care of Dmitri Sokol and his pet Grey ourselves. And then tell them to make arrangements for their replacements, because we're coming after them with every fucking thing we have at our disposal." Niles pushed the pistol into the man's double chin. He was tempted to start the war right then and now, but Jack eased the gun down.

"Go on, get," was all Collins said to the Russian.

"I think I missed something," Sarah said as she forcibly tried to still her heart.

Niles turned away as the Russian hurried down the hallway looking back as if Collins would be on his heels.

"Frankly Niles, you're beginning to scare me a little," Jack said as he placed his arm around Sarah.

"Jack, get Charlie and Matchstick back. Kill that son of a bitch Sokol and that murderous Grey. Then I need all of my people here." Niles turned away as he wanted to sit more with Alice. He stopped and turned. "I think I just declared war on a bunch of assholes that won't take my threat lying down. Good luck you two. Will, Jason, and Farbeaux will meet you in Boston."

Jack and Sarah watched Niles turn and open the curtain. The last thing they saw was Niles bending his head and speaking with Alice.

"Come on short Stuff, we have some work to do."

Novosibirsk, Siberia, Russia

NUMBER ONE SAT in his customary spot at the long table. The toast points and caviar sitting untouched on his china plate. He listened to the banter around the table as he watched the members of the inner circle of the shadow government far more relaxed than they had a right to be. For a man that prided himself on keeping a firm grip on any situation, he felt the loss of control for the first time since their plan went into motion twenty years before. An hour before dinner, a video report had come into his private quarters from their man in the American west, Vladimir Malchivich. The man was a bloated fool of major proportions, but one that would never contemplate inflating or lessening a threat to the committee. The threat laid down by the man who controlled the only organization in the world that actually knew about the Presidium and the Committee, the Event Group, was now foremost on Number One's mind. He picked up the unused butter knife and clinked it against his crystal wine glass. His dark, angry eyes informed the red-coated waiters that they should exit immediately.

"Number Three, has there been any word from our sources on the ground in America regarding Sokol?" his face soured as he said the name of the man that had cost them well over a hundred highly trained commandoes and betrayed the Committee.

Number Three stood up and wiped his mouth with a napkin. He swallowed. "Our consulate liaison in New Orleans has heard rumors he and his people are held up somewhere outside the city. Location unknown at the moment. We have dispatched twenty of our staff from their current missions in Germany to investigate."

Number One toyed with the fork, moving sturgeon caviar from one side of his plate to the other. Number Three remained standing, not sure if he was required to say more. Finally, he eased down into the chair.

"It seems that Sokol's murderous action against this Group has inflamed the situation to the breaking point. Instead of the Quid-Pro-

Quo we had hoped for after Mongolia, it seems that this Director Compton isn't in the mood to treat our recent proposal with any validity. After Dmitri Sokol and his Grey is found and dealt with, we must consider the prospect that the situation with Department 5656 will escalate. We must plan accordingly. I'm afraid we have to bloody them somewhat even more than the fool Sokol to make them see reason. With us losing our chance at a friendly President thanks to Compton's and his peoples recent visit to our cowardly Congressman Briggs, we have lost a tremendous opportunity and many, many months of planning."

"What are you suggesting?" Number Nine said from her chair.

"We strike while the iron is hot. With their problems dealing with Sokol, they may not see us coming."

"Kill even more of them?" the woman called Number Nine asked.

Number One silently looked up. He knew this woman was watching him closely. She was a long ago graduate of the old Soviet ways and she, like many others in the room, were sad the good old days had vanished.

"Do you have an aversion with that prospect, Number Nine?"

"On the contrary, sir. In the completely foolish attempt at skullduggery and diplomacy in offering this Group a form of peace after Mongolia, we have delayed what in my opinion was the inevitable. We should have shown from the start our true inner-strength and resolve in the matter."

"Then we are in agreement," Number One said as he placed his knife down loudly. "And number Nine, I want to commend you for holding your opinion on my docile ways until you saw an opening and opportunity to exploit it."

The woman blushed. She knew then that what she had said would forever color the way Number One looked at her. She, like a few others around the table, was now on Number One's list of people on the Committee to watch.

"The minute we hear from our sources that either Sokol has been dealt with by Compton and his people, I suggest we strike at the heart of the Group even more ruthlessly than the idiot Sokol."

"Orders?" Number Nine asked, partially standing.

"Cut the heads off this foolish chicken."

"Heads?" Number Nine asked.

"This Event Group is like a multi-headed Hydra, it has many heads. So, start by cutting off the most dangerous ones first. I want Doctor Compton and Colonel Collins eliminated. Then maybe we can come to some form of negotiating point that the American's will understand."

The Committee and Presidium chamber grew silent as most looked at their appetizers as if someone had placed a cow patty on the china dishes.

Number One looked from face to face and then angrily slid his own plate down the table. He then stood and angrily angled toward the door. He stopped and faced the Committee.

"Colonel Collins first. Without him, their sword isn't as sharp."

Barataria Bay, Louisiana

THE ISLAND just off the coast of New Orleans was famous for one thing—it was the base of operations for a man that assisted in saving New Orleans and the American south during the War of 1812. The bay was the home waters of Jean Laffite, a privateer of some renown who was influenced by Brevet Major General Andrew Jackson to side with America in a battle that placed the final knife in the belly of the British Empire and their desirous designs on the new continent. Barataria had been a major concern in regard to security and a home base for his ships for the pirate until, as history often proves, you are only as valuable as the assistance you give and when you give it. Immediately after the war the United States reneged on the promise of a pardon for Lafitte and his men and soon a bounty had been placed on the privateer until he and his loyal followers were chased out to sea by the U.S. Navy, never to return to New Orleans or American waters again.

The sun was starting to set when the large yacht eased into the bay only a mile from the national park called Laffite's Island and dropped anchor. Sokol excused the Panamanian captain and his three-man bridge crew to join his own men below decks as he would use this time to reassert some authority over an increasingly unstable Asmodius.

Sokol heard the heavy footfalls coming up the stairwell from far below in the darkened spaces of the hold. Sokol closed his eyes as he stared out of the large bridge windows growing more apprehensive as the pounding of footstep grew closer. Since the attack on his former assistant Vexilla Trotsky in her hospital bed in New Orleans, the Russian had sensed a loss of control over the Grey. Instead of eliminating a voice that could lead the American authorities straight to him personally, Asmodius and that fool Harold Briggs had drawn the attention of the very men and women the Committee and himself would prefer to avoid at all costs—the Event Group. Gone was the Committee's interest in just exposing the Group in the American desert, now both he and the Siberian Group may have inadvertently declared war on the only people in the world that could prove the government in Moscow was nothing more than a sham regime who was controlled out of Siberia. As much as Sokol himself wanted to take over the Committee, he knew that making an enemy the likes of Department 5656 may just make his takeover moot if the Russian people found out that Vladimir Putin was nothing more than a puppet and imposter. Now Sokol found himself in the same exact predicament that Number One found himself in. Dodging the likes of Colonel Jack Collins.

Sokol closed his eyes and geared himself for confronting the Grey who was showing more and more independence, when he heard the bridge door open. He opened his eyes again as the footfalls entered the bridge. At the same moment all the lights went dark as they were in the hold where Asmodius had been sitting and not speaking for the thirteen hours it was down there. Sokol knew the Grey was mentally speaking with someone and just the thought of who it may have been gave the Russian pause. Sokol could feel Asmodius behind him. Its breathing, deep and menacing. Sokol put on a brave face and turned to face the Grey with every intention of setting the alien straight on just who was in charge.

"Why are we here? I have an aircraft waiting in Mobile to fly us to the Ukraine where we can continue our work against the Committee and where I have access to the financing we need to eliminate the fools in Siberia. Instead you insist on coming here. You said you needed to think. What in the world can you have to think about other than how to attract more attention to our plans? Even here in the backwaters of New Orleans people will be looking for us!"

Asmodius ignored the question and stepped up to the bridge windows, pausing only a moment until the sun's flaming orb ducked behind some early nighttime clouds in the west. The bridge was now completely dark and silent with the exception of the Grey's heavy breathing.

Asmodius walked to the navigation console and then reached out with a four-fingered right hand. The Grey used a small ball imbedded there to scroll the local map away from their current location inside of Barataria Bay. The Grey leaned over the map and with the tip of his clear claw he clicked it on the glass. Sokol leaned over and looked at where the Grey was pointing.

"No...Ukraine...yet. We pause here...until...we...talk."

Sokol looked up from the map and into the yellow eyes of the Grey.

"Look, as a strategic ally in my operations against the Committee, I need to know what you're thinking. You attacked Vexilla right in front of the very people we now wish to avoid. We are no longer trying to expose this Group for the Committee. And what possessed that fool Briggs to try and assassinate a guarded witness? I know it was you Asmodius, and that was why you were forced to project yourself into her hospital room. Now, the longer we stay the more probable a confrontation. Instead of blame landing on the Committee, it's us that Colonel Collins and Niles Compton will examine."

Suddenly Sokol felt a jolt of electrical power course through his body. His muscles froze in the most painful way. It was if very one of them cramped at the same moment. Then the pain moved to his head.

It flamed brightest in the frontal lobe of his brain. His arms went straight to his side. The Grey reached out and lightly ran a clear-tipped claw gently across Sokol's forehead and then his right temple. The Russian could follow its movements by his eyes only. Then he heard the words coming deep from his brain as if his memory was replaying a voice from his past.

'You...fear...this enemy...in...the desert?'

Sokol tried to speak but his vocal cords were as frozen as much as his body.

'You...should...human.' Asmodius moved behind Sokol as it placed a little more pressure on his temple area. *'This...Group...they...will... eventually...interfere...with...Asmodius...Modai. They...have...a great...and... ancient enemy of my...kind. They will...soon...have...another, stronger...ally.'* Asmodius moved its claw from Sokol's temple. *'It is time...we make an adjustment to...our relationship....'* It smiled, exposing its clear teeth.

"What are you talking about? I make adjustments, you follow orders. That's how this partnership works, Grey," Sokol said menacing Asmodius with a harsh look.

'Your men are below...decks?'

"You asked me to place them out of sight until we reach the Gulf waters." Sokol took a menacing step toward the Grey who irritatingly enough continued to be amused by Sokol's anger.

Sokol turned when he heard a small motor launch come along side the large yacht. Asmodius turned and smiled.

'Our company has arrived...we...will...depart.'

"What are you talking about? I'm not leaving anywhere without my men."

'Your men?' This time Asmodius' smile was so wide its facial muscles were seemingly stretched to the breaking point.

Sokol had had enough. He reached for the mic on the navigation console and clicked the small button. "Colonel, come topside and remove this creature from my ship!"

Asmodius laughed as it held both arms in the air and then held them out straight as it closed its yellow eyes.

Sokol heard the doors on every deck of the large yacht slam

closed. He heard his soldiers below banging on them and smashing their bodies against the steel and wooden hatches.

Sokol turned to scream at Asmodius but the Grey magically lifted his body into the air and threw him out of the bridge and onto the deck where the Portuguese captain and his three men helped him to his feet. Then they unceremoniously lowered him to a small skiff. Asmodius instead of stepping onto the ladder simply floated down from the main deck to the small boat. Without orders the captain set the skiff off toward the island of Barataria.

Sokol struggled as Asmodius settled at the front of the skiff. Its yellow eyes concentrated on the yacht. Then to Sokol's amazement, a waterspout started to spin crazily over the ship. The tunnel acted as a giant tornado as it engulfed the yacht. Sokol could only imagine his men fighting with the magic that kept them entrapped in the ship's lower spaces. The waterspout dipped the bow of the yacht and then he watched as the fantail rode high into the air and then the large private yacht slid down into the murky waters of Barataria Bay. Only tale-tale bubbles marked the watery grave of over one hundred Russian commandos.

Asmodius turned and looked at Sokol as if daring the human to say something. The smile was still on its face.

The filthy captain turned the small boat away toward the island. As for Sokol, he knew then that he had released hell on earth.

AN HOUR later the small party stood on the sands of Barataria Island. The old ruins were still visible from the beach. Sokol had heard of the island. The dwellings, as haunted as they looked, had seen a lot of American history. This was the former home of one of the more colorful men in the American past—the Privateer, Jean Lafitte.

The pirate, at the height of his power had used Barataria as a base for his squadron of raiders and it wasn't until his men and weapons were needed in the fight against the British in the War of 1812 that Lafitte had seen a chance at redemption with his adopted country— the United States.

The adobe buildings were for the most part a shamble of their former selves. As the sun sank in the west Asmodius watched the glassless windows as if he were waiting for something. Sokol for his part felt eyes on them. As the cypress trees blew in a freshening wind, Sokol watched the Spanish Moss sway back and forth. Then he saw them. One light at a time. Out of the forty remaining skeletal frames of dwellings every empty window was now illuminated. Sokol felt his legs go weak as he was tempted to turn and run into the surf. Asmodius was still smiling.

The chant started deep in the old buildings. The voices in their harmonious chanting would come and then go with the breeze. Asmodius held its arms out wide as if accepting grace from a million followers.

"What is this?" Sokol said looking from the back of the Grey to the smiling Portuguese captain and his men.

Asmodius finally graced Sokol with a look as he faced the Russian. "This...is my...army," it hissed as it turned back just as the beach started to fill with men, women, and even children. They came from the old dwellings as if they had been waiting since the time of Andrew Jackson. They surrounded Asmodius reverently as if he were a god finally come to set their kind free. Sokol could see they were from every race on the globe. Every nation, every country.

As Sokol watched, he felt his bladder grow weak as an old man stepped forward from the group of over two hundred worshipers in black robes. Now Sokol knew why the Grey had been alone in the deep recesses of the yacht. It had been calling its followers forth. Followers who had waited thousands of years through generation after generation for their master's promised return. The old man stepped forward and fell to his knees in the sand and Asmodius touched the grey hair of the man and gently caressed it. Then he bade the old man to rise. He was holding a black garment and held it for Asmodius. He accepted the robe and placed it on as his followers all collapsed at the same time and bowed their heads as the chant started.

'Asmodius Modai...Asmodius Modai...Asmodius Modai.'

Then the crowd charged Asmodius and he accepted their

worshiping embraces. Even the captain and his men acted as though Asmodius was the second coming of Jesus. But as Sokol watched, he knew immediately that his analogy and description was miles off.

The Russian was watching the second coming alright. But it was the second coming of the biblical Fallen One.

CHAPTER THIRTEEN

Grady's Tavern,
Boston, Massachusetts

W ill Mendenhall sat across the booth from Ryan and Van
Tram. Will shook his head as he scratched at the stitches
under the bandage. Ryan reached out and pulled his hand away.

"If you don't stop that, you're going to pop those stitches," Ryan
turned and smiled at Tram, "and we really don't want to hear you
crying again when they re-stitch you."

"It's just this damn waiting crap that's driving me nuts."
Mendenhall looked at his wristwatch. "Where in the hell is he?"

"You know Will, for as long as we've been dealing with Colonel
Froggy, I don't think he cares much about keeping us waiting."

As the Irish patrons eyed the three men suspiciously, Will, Jason,
and Tram were beginning to wonder if Henri had gone bonkers
making them wait in one of the filthiest dives in all of Boston.
Characters the likes of which none of the three wished to tangle with
seemed to be taking a rather blatant interest in the trio. Ryan was
positive that he must have been wearing a Yankees ball cap with the
way the men and women in the tavern looked at him.

"Is there anywhere in the world the Frenchman doesn't have contacts?" Will asked, tempted to scratch his wound once again.

"You know, for American soil I sure do feel out of place," Ryan said as he lifted his club soda just as a waitress in wrinkled pants and stained white blouse flopped a large drink down in front of Tram. Ryan was shocked to see the small Vietnamese had ordered a boilermaker. A beer and a shot.

"Whoa buddy, when I said try to blend in, I didn't mean become a drunk like the rest of us."

Tram looked from the large mug of beer. And the overflowing shot of Irish whiskey to Jason. "Not order."

"Compliments of those boys at the bar," the blonde waitress said with a smirk and then popped her gum as she turned away.

Will, Jason, and Tram turned to look at the bar where several men with grey hair and thick beards that were basically the size of any NFL lineman were smiling at the trio in the booth. Then Ryan saw what most were wearing. Some had Levi vests that had numerous patches on them that declared the men were part of a group of locals that had survived the war in Vietnam. One had a t-shirt that said that he would most assuredly go to heaven because he spent his time in hell—Vietnam.

"Oh, boy," Ryan said, as Will placed his face in his hands. Ryan looked at his friend. "maybe if you tell them you're an officer, it might make a difference?"

Will looked up and then placed his face back into his hands.

Van Tram stood and half-bowed at the waist. He reached over and gestured at the boilermaker and nodded his head in silent thanks. Several of the large men lost their smiles and pulled away from the bar and started walking toward the darkened booth area. Tram remained standing. The leader of this adventurous group looked down at the three smaller men. The hat he wore was filthy and on it was scrawled the logo, Vietnam Veteran. On his vest was the local union patch for the pipe-fitters local 18.

"You know, a lot of folks around here can't tell a chinaman from a jap. But one thing most here know is Charlie Cong. Why you here, Charlie Cong?"

Tram eyed the man who was obviously referring to him as "Charlie," or Viet Cong. Tram nodded his head as he took the shot of whiskey and quickly downed it. He then followed it up by taking a swallow of beer.

"Thank you for the drink," was all Tram said as he sat back down.

"Gentlemen, we didn't come here looking for trouble," Mendenhall said, trying his best diplomatic approach.

A smaller, but not by much, man leaned over the table. "The problem is my friend you chose to come at all."

"This man is our guest. He's on temporary assignment to our country. I would expect a little more respect from a veteran," Ryan said.

Will tried to lightly shake his head in an attempt to get Ryan to curb his growing temper.

"And just who in the hell are you shorty?" the largest man asked.

"I'm a United States Naval Commander. This is a Major in the U.S. Army and this gentleman is a Lieutenant in the Peoples Army of North Vietnam." Ryan stood up as his smile faded. "You know, the same army that gave you boys all you could handle a few years back?"

"Oh, shit," Will mumbled as the largest man grabbed Ryan by the shirt collar. "I'm going to kill Henri!"

"Well, excuse us all to hell," the largest said smiling. "A swab jockey and an officer," he said as he drew his giant's hand back and began to explain to Ryan just why he had little respect for his branch of service.

All talk ceased when a small hand shot up and out and took the large man's wrist and twisted. Tram was standing and leaning across the table. He twisted the large man's hand until it was in danger of snapping. He finally let go and the brute stumbled backward into his friends. Ryan and Mendenhall knew they had to prepare to defend Tram. The Vietnamese sniper calmly picked up the glass of beer and drank half.

"Please, gentlemen, sit," Tram said as he looked from Ryan to Mendenhall.

That was as far as Van Tram got as the five men pounced.

COLONEL HENRI FARBEAUX was driving up to Grady's Tavern when he saw the four Boston police cruisers in the street fronting the tavern. After picking up his contact at Logan International airport Henri had hoped Ryan, Mendenhall, and Tram could hide out inconspicuously in the dank and dark dive his contact had told him about. Henri pulled into the alley across the street. He reached for his cell phone, but his hand was staid by the man who had assisted him in Britain, Shamus O'Brien.

"The local constabulary is leaving," O'Brien said as he nodded toward the tavern. "As I see it, they don't appear to have any lads in their custody.

"I should have never had you do the recommendations for a rendezvous," Farbeaux said as he opened his car door. "I tend to forget you didn't hang out with the most reputable of characters when visiting the States."

Shamus O'Brien, tired from his hurried flight from London, just looked at the Frenchman and shook his head. "Present company included?"

Henri smiled and winked and then started across the street with the former Irish Republican army soldier. Farbeaux was grateful for the nine-millimeter in his coat pocket as they smelled the interior of the tavern long before the door was opened. As he stood looking into the dank bar, he saw the wreck of the hatcheck station and also the smashed and broken bars of the cashier's box. Farbeaux exchanged worried looks with O'Brien.

"This is worse than the establishment you own," Henri said as Shamus wrinkled his nose.

"Cousin Shaune was never one to be overly fancy in his place of business. But back in the day he was an excellent source of funding and weapons that transited from America to Ireland."

"Well, I would say those days are over for cousin Shaune O'Grady."

Henri stepped over smashed beer advertisements and even had to duck under a Bowie knife that was stuck in the fake wood paneling. Again, he exchanged looks with the Irishman who had flown here at his request.

Shamus knew Boston as if he had been born and raised on the mean streets. Having been the liaison with Irish American sympathizers to the troubles back in his home country, Shamus knew every underground organization in the state and just what factions were still aligned with the organization who still fought for the unification of Ireland.

"I hope I didn't lead my associates here to have them buried in one of your landfills," Henri said, not seeing Ryan, Mendenhall or the small Vietnamese Lieutenant, Tram.

"Oh, you tiny ballerina of a man, how long has it been!"

Farbeaux stepped back and nearly pulled his weapon when a giant of a man with a beard down to his Adams Apple, picked Shamus up from behind and bounced him several times in a bear hug. He finally placed the even larger Shamus down and then eyed his cousin from across the pond.

"Shaunny boy, glad to see the yanks haven't starved you to death yet!" Shamus screamed as he took O'Grady in.

"Ah, the locals know better than to get in between me and my porridge!" O'Grady turned to Farbeaux. "And what is this with you. Smells like a copper to me."

"Well, now boyo, he's what brings me here." Shamus took his burly cousin by the arm and leaned into him. "Shaune, we were supposed to meet three associates here. Tell me you and the boyos didn't kill them?"

Shaune O'Grady made a face and then slapped his cousin on the shoulder. "One of the boys you looking for have a small man's attitude toward the larger human species? The other a man of color and yet another, the kind which has communist leanings?"

O'Brien looked from Shaune to Henri who knew they were too late, that more than likely Will, Jason, and Tram were already floating face down in Boston Harbor. Farbeaux sadly shook his head.

"Yeah, they be here cousin. Follow me."

Shamus and Farbeaux followed the giant Irishman into the bleakness of the tavern. Henri became alarmed when he heard men chanting somewhere in the dark reaches of the bar. Then he saw a circle of men around a booth and that was when he noticed Van Tram being picked up and hugged by a man that resembled the Creature from the Black Lagoon. The large man shook Tram and then placed him back down into the booth and patted him on the back as more beer and shots were delivered.

"These the boys you're lookin' for?" Shaune asked.

Henri was shocked to see the battered and bruised faces of what amounted to a group of Hell's Angels in dress and style. They were laughing and smiling even as they were still wiping blood from their noses and mouths.

"What in the hell happened to them?" Henri asked.

"Oh, they were just getting to know the boys a little." Shaune leaned into his cousin. "Stay away from the little Communist bastard, he's got a mean kick and even meaner punch. Just ask the boys."

Farbeaux was amazed that there wasn't one mark on Tram, Will or Ryan. They were all taking turns drinking beer and downing shots. The Frenchman shook his head in admiration.

"And to think, most of us here may have been shot at by your grandpa or cousin. Small world ain't it?" The larger of the men said as he slid more drinks over to the three strangers. Then he slapped Tram on the back. The small sniper was glad he had been able to demonstrate that small men could actually take care of themselves. Not that you would have to prove that to any Vietnam veteran ever to have fought in the long-ago conflict. Henri could see that the respect shown to the Vietnamese was equal to Tram's own for the men his family had once fought against.

"I hate to break up the good times, but we have work to do gentlemen," Henri said while removing the shot glass from Van Tram's hand.

The burly men that were buying the drinks turned and gave Henri withering looks. When Tram stood and offered his hand to the original patron who had attempted to tear his head off at the shoulders, the man with the vet's hat on nodded his head and then shot Farbeaux an angry look once more. The three men moved off to join Henry and the two Irishmen.

HENRI SAT down in the darkened back room. Shamus and his cousin Shaune sat silently by as Henri made the introductions. Suspicion crossed the faces of the two when Will's, Ryan's, and Tram's military ranks were explained to them. Needless to say, neither of the Irishmen shook hands with the three. Farbeaux handed Mendenhall an address torn from his notebook.

"Colonel Collins is to meet us here within the next two hours."

Will read the note and then passed it to Ryan.

"So, why are we sitting in a bar talking with Britain's most wanted?" Mendenhall asked, eyeing the two large Irishmen.

"Because gentlemen, they know this city better than anyone in the world. If they wanted to hide, they could never be found. If they wanted to kill, they would never be caught. If they…"

"We get the point, Colonel. They're your kind of guys," Ryan said, cutting off the Frenchman.

"Yes, they are. Major, do you have the package?"

Mendenhall eyed the Irishmen suspiciously once more and then reached into his coat and slapped the yellow envelope on the table. It was just in time that they saw it was only an envelope as their hands were already caressing the handguns they had hidden under the table.

Shamus reached out and took the envelope and opened it. He slid it over to his cousin Shaune.

"That's a lot of bleedin' money," he said eyeing the Americans.

"Well, we need a lot of information," Farbeaux said as he waited for their hands to relax and appear above the table again.

"You brought me all the way to Boston for information?" Shamus asked, again looking suspiciously at the French Colonel.

"Yes, I needed you and your contacts. Now either you can help us, or you won't."

The American Irishman, O'Grady, slid the envelope back to Henri. "If you have come to us the odds be that whoever you need this information on straddles the line when it comes to the law. We don't hurt our friends."

"We are not asking you to hurt anyone that wouldn't deserve it." Henri said before Ryan could say something irreparable. "This person isn't above the law, but she seems to be above everything else in this city. That means that the odds are that you know her."

"Now, our friends out west know where we can find her. We just need to know *about* her."

Jason relaxed as Henri seemed to have laid at least one of the Irishmen's suspicions to rest.

"Then this person isn't associated with the troubles. In any way?" Shamus asked.

"Not that we know of. But if this woman is as powerful as we think she is, she could never hide out in your city without you knowing something. If we're wrong and you *don't* know everything in and around Boston," Henri reached for the envelope full of cash, "then we obviously need to seek our information elsewhere."

Shamus exchanged looks with Shaune and then reached out and stopped Henri from removing the offer. Mendenhall shook his head knowing then that the Frenchman really knew his scum of the earth.

"Well, let's not be hasty. If we have any knowledge of someone who isn't a friend, then we can possibly do business," Shamus finally said as he slid the envelope over to his cousin. "What do you want to know my French friend?"

"Elsbeth Barlow. Who is she?" Mendenhall asked, not waiting for Henri this time.

This time it was Shaune who hurriedly slid the envelope back to the Frenchman. He stood up as did his cousin.

"Keep your money, Colonel darlin'," Shamus said as he started to turn away.

"Then she is a friend of yours?" Ryan asked, ready to stop the two men from leaving. Even Tram tensed, ready for another go at the largest Irishmen he had ever seen.

Shamus turned and faced the four men. He started to say something, but O'Brien stopped him. They once more turned to leave.

"She may be responsible for killing one of the most brilliant scientists this country has ever produced. She also injured an old woman that has saved this world, as fucked up as it is, countless times. If you know something you damn will better tell us."

Shamus looked intently at Ryan. "Or what, boyo?"

Ryan was about to explain when the unseen voice stopped him dead in his tracks.

"Or you and all of your organization will cease to exist within six months. Anyone you ever knew in life will regret the day you didn't answer our inquiries. Regard it as a favor to a friend if you like. Or regard it as a threat. Justify it anyway you wish. But answer the question or we can start thinning out your heard right now."

The voice was so calm and smooth it gave all who heard it cold chills. When Henri, Ryan, Will, and Tram looked up, it was Colonel Jack Collins and Carl Everett standing in the open door. Jack walked in and took the offered bribe from the table and slipped it into the pocket of Shamus.

"I'm sure you will be more comfortable sitting as you talk." Jack sat in a vacant chair while Everett folded his arms and waited by the door. The Captain saw Will start to rise but a simple shake of the head stopped him, and the Major eased back down. "Colonel, I'm happy you were able to convince your friends that cooperation is always in their best interest."

Farbeaux looked from cousin to cousin. "Gentlemen, Colonel Jack Collins, United Sates Army. His Doctor Watson there is Captain Everett, U.S. Navy."

"I must say Henri, you have definitely changed your taste on your working associates," Shamus said as he gave in and sat. O'Brien did the same. "You know this burns the last bridge with us?" he said to

Henri as he eyed the newcomer with small scars lining his tanned features.

"I believe the question was about Elsbeth Barlow," Ryan said when the room became silent.

Shamus nodded his head at his cousin Shaune to speak for them.

"Look, that woman would have never hurt your friends. That much I do know. If she did, she had good reason to."

O'Brien saw by Jack's face his answer wasn't sitting too well with him.

"Okay, you want the goods on her?"

Silence greeted the obvious question.

"We have much Irish silliness in our history of tales. Legends of witches and warlocks. But Elsbeth Barlow is no legend, nor is she an old wive's tale. I know you Americans are a hard bunch to believe in things you can't touch or use scientific reasoning on. But when it comes to the old woman, let me just say this, she's real and she can end your life with a snap of her fingers. I dare say that there are very few we don't mess with in this city. We are never frightened of most things." O'Brien leaned in close. "But we leave Elsbeth Barlow alone."

"The Witch Queen of Salem?" Jack asked. The non-belief was apparent in his voice. It wasn't in Henri's, Will's, Trams, or Ryan's after they were attacked by the Grey in New Orleans.

Shamus stood slowly looking at Farbeaux. "You already know about her, but you drag us into this anyway?"

"Details Shamus. That's what we need. Barlow says she needs something from us, and she has already taken it. What we need to know is if she's trustworthy," the Frenchman held the Irishman's eyes until he sat back down.

"I am sorry for your friends, but as I said, if what you say is true, Elsbeth Barlow would never hurt them. If you knew the power she wields, you yanks would have had her caged many, many years ago and gone about your business of ruling the damn world. If she's on a mission, do not get in her way." This time Shamus removed the envelope from Shaune's shirt and tossed in front of Collins. "As I said, keep your money, we will not be involved." He turned and faced

Farbeaux. "As I said, Colonel, this burns it with us. The next time me or mine see you, we'll kill you for dragging us into these troubles."

They watched the cousins stand and leave.

"Well, that was helpful," Mendenhall said as he took a shot of whiskey and then downed it with a hiss. "What now?"

Jack stood up and pocketed the money.

"We've been invited to dinner. I think we'll attend."

Everett opened the door for them.

"Let's go meet the mysterious Elsbeth Barlow then."

Baton Rouge, Louisiana

CONGRESSMAN HAROLD BRIGGS was in his second-floor study. Ever since his arrival back home, he had been inundated with interview requests regarding his sudden cancellation of all political functions planned by his campaign. Speculation was running wild and even the rumors dropped by his campaign manager about Briggs suddenly coming down with an illness only prompted wider speculation as to the real reasons. Some had even suggested that the President of the United States had something to do with his sudden retreat from the active running of his campaign due to the congressman's insistence on his 'hidden agency' investigation.

His wife of forty-two years tried once more to get him to talk to her, but he still refused to go into detail. Even with the obvious breakdown of his usual vanity for his dress, hair and demeanor, she felt she didn't know the man she married back when he was just the Mayor of Lake Charles over forty years before. Ellen Briggs had been so worried about him that before his arrival back home she had hidden the two guns they had in the house for their protection. She had failed to find the third. The two she had found were now in the possession of the Secret Service who stood watch outside the house.

"Harold, you're scaring me," she said in a last attempt to allow her into his head.

Briggs turned and smiled even though she could tell he had been crying. This was a development she had never once seen the man from Louisiana do in their time together.

"I'm scaring you?" he asked.

Ellen Briggs could see that her husband was getting ready to lose control as he was torn between laughing and crying. She watched him raise the glass of liquor to his lips and saw that he shook so badly that whiskey spilled on his white shirt.

"What in the world is there anything to be scared about in this wonderful world of ours?" This time he finished off his drink without incident.

"Harold, come away from the window. Your security detail will think you insane. There's rainwater coming in everywhere."

As Briggs poured another drink he watched as a new storm made its way in from the Gulf. It seemed since this whole ugly thing had begun it was constantly raining. He snickered to himself as he heard his wife stop short of hugging him from behind. When he capped the crystal decanter of whiskey, he turned back to the balcony and the increasing electrical storm outside the open French doors.

"Honey, I think I need some food in me. That may make me feel better." He turned and smiled. For the briefest of moments Harold Briggs looked like his old self. "Would you mind making something?"

"I'll call down and have someone from the staff bring up a sandwich right away."

Harold still had the smile on his face as he stepped away from the rain and the open doors. "No, make me some of that shrimp and grits like you used to in the old days. You know before we had a staff."

Ellen Briggs was shocked when Harold leaned down and kissed her on the forehead.

"Alright. Just like the old days," she said as she started for the door.

"Ellen?" he said, stopping her at the double doors to the study.

"I never could have made it this far without you. I should have listened to you all along."

"Harold, whatever it is, we'll fix it," her smile was hesitant but truthful.

He paced the five steps and faced his wife. He reached into his back pocket and gave her an envelope. Scrawled on the front was a name and an address in Las Vegas, Nevada.

"This is a personal note for a man I know. After I leave for D.C. tomorrow, would you make sure he gets it? Don't let anyone from my staff read it. Just this man. Okay?"

Ellen looked at the letter and then nodded her head. This time Harold kissed her with passion.

Briggs watched his wife leave the study as thunder shook the foundations of the house. As soon as she had closed the doors behind her, Briggs lost his smile.

The phone buzzed. He ignored it.

"Congressman?"

Briggs tried to also ignore the intercom on the top of his desk. He heard the voice of an assistant once again. He strode to the desk and saw the newest poster design for his campaign on top. He picked it up and looked at it. *'For truth and justice in an out of control world—Briggs for President.'* The congressman swallowed the last of his whiskey and chuckled. He casually swatted the poster from the desktop and then reached for the upper desk drawer. His fingers felt the cold steel of the small thirty-two caliber pistol his wife had missed and he removed it from the desk as he placed his empty glass down and then picked up the phone from its cradle.

"Yes?" he said as his eyes roamed over the blue steel of the small semi-automatic.

"Congressman, a gentleman calling himself Roderick Smith says he is returning your call."

"I don't know a Roderick Smith," he said as he sat on the edge of his desk. Another flash of bright lightning didn't faze him as he toyed with the pistol.

"The gentleman said to tell you the game is still viable."

Harold stopped playing with the gun and smiled. "Interesting, put him through please, I may have something he would want to hear directly from me." Briggs listened as the call was put through. The congressman reached over and flipped a small switch that turned off the recorders and one that also scrambled the incoming call to a sound that was irritatingly similar to someone forcing a phonograph record backward.

"Congressman, how good of you to accept my call. I understand that after your encounter with our Mr. Sokol you have had doubts enter your thinking. I am calling to reassure you that although mistakes were made on our part in relying on Mr. Sokol and his other worldly partner, we have a strong desire to see our plans though. My sources have informed me that you are having doubts. Please don't my friend. We have a marvelous opportunity here to..."

"You have an *opportunity* to die if you get in that man's way. I watched him and his Grey do things that are physically impossible. They are both insane. You know this and still you promise pie in the sky estimates. Do you think after he killed all those so-called specialists you sent to the Gulf you can control him and his little pet?"

He heard the man breathing on the other end of the line. He knew he wasn't speaking with a go-between as he had in the past. He was speaking with the designer of the bold plan to put him in the Oval Office.

"Admittedly, we sorely underestimated Mr. Sokol, but as soon as our business is concluded, we will hunt this man and his Grey down. He will pay for his..."

"Now we have that department you seemed so worried about on our," Briggs cut the man off and then he laughed and corrected his thought, "on *my* tail. That means the President knows and by this time his intel people."

"We have made a decision on Department 5656, my friend. In a few days you won't have anything to worry about where they are concerned. We will remove the brains from the head. The Operation is in action even as we speak."

Briggs laughed again. "Let me give you another option." Briggs placed the phone down on the desktop and then looked over at the fallen campaign poster. He shook his head and then placed the barrel of the gun in his mouth and pulled the trigger just as thunder crashed across the dark skies of Baton Rouge.

· · ·

TWENTY MINUTES later as Ellen Briggs opened the door with a plate of Harold's favorite snack of Shrimp and Grits and smelled the residue of gunpowder, she knew the campaign for Harold R. Briggs, Congressman from Louisiana, for the office of President was officially over.

Novosibirsk, Siberia, Russia

NUMBER ONE LOOKED at his two top assistants. The gunshot was still echoing in his head and memory as he had just listened to five years of hard work cease to exist in the time it took for the coward Briggs to pull a trigger.

The two assistants exchanged worried looks as they had never seen their boss turn this shade of white before. They knew the man to be ruthless and one that never second guessed himself on any subject. But things had changed for Number One after he devised the plan to go after the secretive Group in the American desert. This Collins and Compton had the man most feared in Siberia apprehensive and frightened. No one knew the reasons for this but Number One himself. Now, something had happened that set off alarm bells in the committee halls.

Finally, one of them stepped forward. "Sir..."

"Do we have assets on Director Compton and Colonel Collins?"

"Only Compton at this time. Colonel Collins is off the grid on a field assignment."

"Do you fools have any idea just what field assignment Collins could be on?" Number One asked angrily as he shoved everything that sat on his desk off the edge, and then standing up and facing his two cowed assistants. "He's hunting Sokol and the Grey. If Collins finds them before we find Collins, this committee is doomed. The world will have proof that the idiots in Moscow are nothing more than puppets to our will! And now, because of Sokol and his out of control Frankenstein, our one hope of pulling this mirage off is dead! Another trail for Collins and Compton to follow!"

The same man started to say something but the second stopped him from receiving more rage from Number One.

The portly man who once served as a young Lieutenant in the K.G.B. in the seventies grabbed the closest of the two assistants and shook him by his lapels. Number One seemed to have lost his mind.

"Get me the location of Collins, Sokol, his little pet, and I want every agent we have in the States to converge on them. I want them dead!"

"Director Compton?" the bravest of the two asked an infuriated Number One.

"Kill him immediately!" Number One smiled and seemed to relax for the briefest of moments. "That may get Collins to show his hand and give us his location."

**Thirty-two miles south of
Key West, Florida**

THE GIANT CONTAINER ship plowed through the increasingly rough storm that had tracked the vessel since its departure from Louisiana three days before. The *Kyoto Maru*, a ship with Japanese registry, was riding high as if the containers she carried on her decks were empty. With the storm-tossed seas there was little fear the United States Coast Guard would interfere in their crossing from the Gulf to the Atlantic.

Dmitri Sokol stood to the rear of the captain and watched Asmodius from a safe distance. The Grey seemed to be enjoying the rough seas as they passed just south of the Florida Keys. The wipers on the large and towering bridge structure were having difficulty keeping the flood of sea water from obscuring the view. Every time the giant ship dipped into a trough, Asmodius stabilized his strangely shaped legs and seemed to enjoy the ride back up. The captain and his crew watched nervously as the Grey turned toward them. The armed men of Asmodius' army stood watch on the frightened crew of the *Kyoto Maru.*

"You're not worried about your followers in those containers?" Sokol asked as the ship went into another depression.

Asmodius smiled, exposing its sharp and clear teeth. Most of the Japanese crew turned away as every time they had interaction with the Grey, they were tempted to throw themselves into the sea.

"They…sleep…they…prepare…They…and…their…ancestors… have…waited…many…life-times…for my…return."

Asmodius turned back to watch the seas ahead of the ship.

There had been times Sokol had tried to offer his help to Asmodius just for a promise from the Grey that its assistance would still be available in dealing with the Committee after the Grey's little war was completed, but all Asmodius had done was smile. The Grey hadn't been mentally aggressive since New Orleans, but Sokol feared that if he pushed the creature any further, he may not like the end result.

"Captain, we have an intermittent radar contact bearing three-four-seven," said the man at the radar console. The Japanese Captain moved and placed his face into the 'boot' of the scope and examined the contact. He looked up at Sokol and shook his head.

"Too big for a pleasure craft in this storm," he said. "Has to be the American Coast Guard."

"This is USCGC Endurance, calling container ship Kyoto Maru. We advise you alter course to three-six-seven degrees. The storm is worsening to the north. Come in Kyoto Maru."

The captain reached for the microphone, but it was suddenly jerked from his grasp. It floated in the air to the amazement of his crew and then it smashed into the radio console. Asmodius was smiling again. It slowly shook its head.

"Captain we have the vessel in sight. According to the computer, they are who they say they area. The *USCGC Endurance.* A two-hundred- and eighty-foot cutter out of Fort Lauderdale."

The Captain looked from his radar man to Sokol as if asking the Russian what he should do.

Asmodius turned away from the window and then moved to the large bridge hatchway to the outside bridge wing. Sokol hurriedly battened down the hatchway. With any luck whatsoever maybe Asmodius would be swept into the hard seas. Sokol watched from the drenched window as Asmodius turned in the direction of the Coast Guard Cutter.

"The *Endurance* has altered course and is on track to intercept us, Captain. She asks that we slow to one -third."

Sokol was still watching Asmodius as it stood on the elongated bridge wing of the *Kyoto Maru*. Then, as he had seen many times before, Asmodius raised its large hands to the black skies. It closed its yellow eyes to the view of the enormous waves. Sokol couldn't see but he did hear the seas grow louder. Asmodius stiffened and then clapped all eight fingers together just as lightning and thunder rent the air. It was so loud and full of power that every man on the bridge thought the *Kyoto Maru* had exploded.

"Captain! Rogue wave!" shouted the radar operator.

As Sokol turned to the many bridge windows, the darkness of the sky obscured his view. Then he saw it. The foam at the base of the wave highlighted the giant swell. It was tremendous in size as it rose to a height of half a mile. Then he saw the coast guard cutter as it vanished into its trough. Then the wave broke over the large cutter and that was when Sokol and the bridge crew saw the sleek vessel break in two as the wave totally covered its remains. Then they braced as the remnants of the rogue wave broke over the forward section of the *Kyoto Maru*, pushing her deep into the sea.

Sokol picked himself up after watching the death of so many American sailors happen without a whisper of a distress call going out. At least two hundred men had been snuffed out in less time than it took to take a drink of vodka. Every man on the bridge was turned to silence as the hatch door opened and a dripping wet Asmodius stepped inside. It turned to first Sokol, and then faced the captain.

"Follow...the...storm."

"Course?" the man stuttered in fear.

"Until the storm...dissipates...outside of...Boston."

"What happens when we arrive?" Sokol asked.

"War...happens. The battle...for the...world...I created many thousands of...years...ago."

Sokol and the rest of the crew that saw Asmodius that day would go to their graves remembering the absolute joyous smile on the Grey's scaly lips.

The Battle of Salem was at hand.

PART III

THE FATHER OF LIES

"Sometimes science is not, cannot, be the answer..."
~ Doctor Niles Compton,
Director, Department 5656

CHAPTER FOURTEEN

Cambridge, Massachusetts

C harles Hindershot Ellenshaw III walked in the back garden of one of the most beautiful estates he had ever been in. Even with the evening clouds starting to roll in over the skies of New England, Charlie was still amazed at the sense of peace the magnificent mansion brought to his state of mind. He was greeted by many young people who strolled the grounds the same as himself. Always polite, always cordial. It was almost as if he weren't being held against his will but an invited, respected guest.

Charlie spied a bench that had just been vacated by a large man in his early twenties that had been reading a book while the last of the sun vanished. As the man walked by, Ellenshaw saw that he was reading 'Paradise Lost.' The typical story of good versus evil and one that Charlie found relatable to the few words of explanation he received from staff and even Elsbeth Barlow. Charlie sat at the bench and watched the mansions staff roam here and there as they prepared for the new guests to arrive. Thus far he had counted over a hundred different people either lived, worked or studied at the estate. He figured he should have something to report to the Colonel when the expanded field team arrived.

Charlie relaxed and removed his wire-rimmed glasses and closed his eyes in thought as the smell of rain became more prominent. He heard movement to his left and opened his eyes. The blur was of two figures walking toward him. One medium and one extremely small. He replaced his glasses and then spied Elsbeth Barlow and walking beside her was Mahjtic Tilly. He watched. Matchstick was still disoriented and still had not spoken much since his revival from the grave. Although questioned lightly by him the small alien had not much to say. Sometimes when Ellenshaw spoke Matchstick would look at him as if he really didn't know who his old friend was. Late this afternoon when Matchstick was dozing in the wonderful prison Elsbeth claimed was their bedroom, he could have sworn Matchstick was crying in his sleep. He was concerned that the alien's memory of Gus and the many others that died with Matchstick that night came to him only in dream-like phases. Charlie worried about the mental strain that was being applied on an already taxed state. Charlie smiled and moved down the bench and then patted the wooden seat next to him, inviting Matchstick to sit. Elsbeth assisted him onto the bench. Then she gave the small alien a peanut butter cup.

"Well, Slim, have you been spying on my pupils enough to give your Colonel Collins a precise report?" She smiled and then eased her old body onto the bench beside Matchstick.

"Is that what you think we do, spy?"

Elsbeth cackled. It wasn't her normal laugh as it seemed to have a twinge of sadness to it. "Well, if I were in your shoes, I would be doing just that I imagine. But then you people have different priorities than we."

"Miss Barlow, how is it you know more about us than ninety-nine-point nine percent of the people in the country?"

Elsbeth rubbed her arthritic hands together and looked at Ellenshaw. "Well, Slim, old Elsbeth has been around for more years than this body likes to say. I know most of what happens around the world. Politicians really cannot keep secrets. Slim, do you think my kids here do nothing but cast spells and chant rhythmic tunes to alter the very properties of physics?"

"Well, yes, that's exactly what I think. You have admitted as much. Through demonstration and speech, you have told me so."

Elsbeth removed a small bottle from her flower-print house dress. She shook out two pills and swallowed them.

"When they are finished with their studies, they are sent out into the world."

"You set them free to alter normal people and their lives?"

"Slim, we live by a simple rule, we are never to change the course of human history for selfish purposes."

"That's why when we were losing the war with the Greys you didn't lift a finger to assist?"

"Oh, once the invasion was complete, we would have fought just as hard as anyone else. We all knew from past experience that there are some very good people in the world. Let's just say we bided our time." Elsbeth placed her pain medication in her dress pocket and then smiled over at Charlie while rubbing Matchsticks bald head. "After eight thousand years Slim, the doctors tell me I'm finally dying. I don't really know how to feel about that. Since the time of Rome, I thought I was ready to let go. Now I think I'm scared."

Charlie leaned forward as a freshening breeze washed over his stringy white hair. "Miss Barlow, *what* are you?"

"I think you've pretty much guessed I'm not one of you."

"Yeah, I only have a doctorate from Stanford, but I pretty much deduced that much."

Elsbeth reached over and pulled Matchstick onto her lap. Charlie could see that the arthritic pain medication was helping her. She again rubbed Matchstick's bulbous head. "To make a long story short, I was sent here by this little guy's race. Covertly. I wasn't of their world, but it was my people who, close to five hundred thousand years ago, taught my enemy everything he knows. Since then," she handed Matchstick another peanut butter cup, "it's been our duty to watch for his return." She looked past a chewing Matchstick and fixed Charlie with her blue eyes. "And Asmodius has indeed returned to place claim on a world the master of lies believes he created." She smiled at Matchstick. "Does your mind recall the tales my little friend as told by your people?"

Matchstick closed his almond shaped eyes as if in deep thought. He shook his head negatively.

"Well, when your friends arrive, we'll see what we can do to get you to remember the ancient times." She tapped his green head with a fingertip, making him flinch. "It's in there somewhere."

"If you and your power can't stop this Asmodius, what can little Matchstick do?"

Elsbeth helped Matchstick climb down from the bench. "You go wash up for our company, get some of that chocolate off your face."

Matchstick looked at Charlie and Ellenshaw nodded his head that he should go inside.

Elsbeth made sure Matchstick was out of hearing range. She turned to Charlie. "Slim, Matchstick and his kind are the only beings in the universe that cannot be mentally manipulated by the Greys. Matchstick and all of his ancestors have a built-in immunity to the games the Grey's play. This is why they could never be trusted and millions of years after they built the Grey's society, they were enslaved."

"And Matchstick, how did you know he wasn't dead?"

"I heard his faint heartbeat when it started up again. When I sleep, I wander the world. Not just this world, but also others. If I could explain it Slim I would. Needless to say, when I saw that our little onion headed friend was still alive, I knew we had a fighting chance at stopping Asmodius."

"Then why do you look so down?" Charlie asked.

"Matchstick's death experience has changed him. You can see it. I've watched you with him."

Charlie leaned back on the bench. "It's like a part of him didn't come back from the grave."

"Like Pet Sematary?" Elsbeth asked in all seriousness, and then cackled heartily when she saw Charlie's shocked expression. "I saw that movie. Written by a New Englander."

Charlie was shocked that someone like Elsbeth Barlow knew who Stephen King was, but decided to skip the subject of magical animals coming back from the dead. The Matchstick event was enough for him.

"Well, Slim, when your friends arrive, I hope we can go into that bulbous little green noggin' and see if we can't find what that boy lost while visiting the land of the dead. If not, Asmodius will take back what it thinks is his and his alone."

Elsbeth stood and started walking away. She stopped and turned. "I took the liberty of supplying you with a bit of formal wear for this evening, Slim, I hope it fits. Now, if you'll excuse me, I have to see if dinner is almost ready. I suspect your friends may be hungry after their travels. See you at dinner."

Charlie watched Elsbeth leave and continued sitting as the first raindrops started falling. He looked into the dark skies and he got the cold chills. When he shivered his gaze went up to the third-floor window where he and Matchstick shared a room. The small alien was watching him from the window. Then he was gone. Charlie was wondering if he had seen him at all. He stood up and as the rain started coming down harder his memory sharpened. He could have sworn he saw another form standing behind his friend. A large form. Ellenshaw shook his head knowing then that his mind was just playing tricks on him.

"Shouldn't have done all of that stuff in '69, I should have known it would catch up with me."

Jack was on his cell phone with Sarah as she gave her new husband a status report on Alice. Thus far the amazing Mrs. Hamilton was still comatose but alive. He tried to keep the conversation short and to the point as he felt Henri's eyes on him. Then Sarah offered up a worrisome addition to her report.

"Jack, we have a major problem."

Collins closed his eyes, not needing any additional distractions.

"Niles and I assume Master Chief Jenks is on his way to Boston.

We tried to stop him, but he threw a resignation letter at Niles and left the hospital after arriving from his field trip to France. We don't know how he got word about Virginia, but he did. We suspect Xavier may have dropped the ball."

"Why Doctor Morales?" Jack asked, rubbing his eyes as the pain began to creep into his temples.

"Because when he quit, he armed himself and then took Xavier and Anya with him. He may have gone insane over Virginia's murder. With Morales with him, he knows where your team is Jack."

"I hate to do this, but call Director Compton and let's get Wilkerson at the FBI to arrest the Master Chief. Make up a charge. Explain it's for his own safety, but we don't want him or his 'guests' hurt. Explain to agent Wilkerson that it wouldn't make me happy if something happened to them." Jack closed the cell phone and then turned his head. He saw Carl and explained.

"Shit, Jack, with Jenksy on the loose, that man could kill us all and we wouldn't even see him coming."

"One mess at a time," Collins said as his headache had increased tenfold.

"Well, here we are," Ryan said from behind the steering wheel of the large van as it pulled off the road.

The large entranceway looked as if it could have fronted any fancy New England boarding school. The cast-iron scrolling across the gate was more medieval than the three hundred years of the mansion's history could rightly explain. The trees lining that drive hid the sprawling grounds as Ryan pulled to the gate and stopped. On either side of the drive men appeared. Two on each. The men inside listened to the rhythmic beat of the windshield wipers as they cleared the glass of rainwater.

"We have concealed weapons," Carl said as he spied the two on the right. "Small automatics, probably Uzi's."

"Same here," Farbeaux echoed from the left.

"Henri, you're the resident bad guy here, smell a rat?" Jack asked, not kidding the Frenchman in the least.

"If I were to ambush an arriving party, I would have done it as we rounded the ten bends in the dense woods surrounding the property, not at my own front gate."

"Point taken," Jack said, somewhat relieved as he himself saw traps everywhere. But Henri was far more sensible in being bad.

"Does the fact that men with automatic weapons have our friends bother you much?" Mendenhall asked.

Jack saw Tram in the third row of seats back, flinch as he quickly scanned the area in the front of the closed gate.

"Colonel, the decorative rocks lining the drive just ahead."

"What about them Lieutenant?" Collins asked.

"Claymore mines."

"You see Will, there's always something more to be worried about."

"Yeah, the Claymores relax me far more," Mendenhall rolled his eyes.

Ryan rolled down the window as the first man, seemingly unaware of the drenching he and his fellow guards were taking, stepped up to the window.

"Which one is Collins?"

"That's Colonel Collins to you, Sparky," Ryan said as Jack shot the naval aviator an angry look.

"I'm Collins. Why the heavy artillery?"

"It's a big estate sir. We would rather be a little cautious than caught off guard. This is New England after all."

"Yeah, those Red Sox fans can be a handful."

Farbeaux glanced at Will. The Frenchman was starting to feel the vibes of revenge for Doctor Pollock's and the security men's murders, and Alice Hamilton's assault, starting to bleed through Collins and his men. He also knew that going into the unknown, this vengeance could get them all killed if these men didn't get their feelings under control.

"Gentlemen, may I suggest we all relax," Henri said.

"I believe we are expected," Collins said before anyone else could pop off.

"Yes, sir. Just follow the drive. I don't believe even you guys can miss the house."

"Why you son of a…"

"Commander!" Jack said to Ryan in warning.

"Name is Randall, Colonel. Just have your boy here follow the drive. My advice is not to stop until you reach the house."

Collins eyed Ryan until he turned away from the security man. Jason rolled up the window and fumed and cursed as the guard named Randall smiled.

The gate started to open and the van drove through.

"Tram, give me a count on any hidden surprises that you see."

Van Tram with his sharp eyes had already counted over forty Claymore mines disguised as decorative rocks.

"Whoever their enemy is, they have these people scared to death," Mendenhall said as his head was also on a swivel for the entire half a mile it took to reach the sprawling mansion.

"Okay, how can this place exist in New England without the property being on every television show the country over. Lifestyles of the Rich and Worthless," Ryan said as he bent down to see the five levels of house. Towers of masonry rose high above the ancient trees as they stood guard over the property. Gargoyles that looked as if they could have once adorned the steeples of Notre Dame watched the van roll to a stop underneath a portico that rivaled the great palaces of Europe.

Another man was waiting for them. This one wasn't armed as far as they could tell. He was dressed in a houseman's jacket and white gloves. As Ryan opened the door and stepped out, the man, who looked young enough to be a college student, greeted them. The young man was shocked when the woman, Millicent Krensky, the ex-navy pilot who had delivered the message to the Group, was thrust into the butler's arms. Jack stepped up to the man and woman.

"Here's your delivery girl," he said. "Now, we need to see Miss Barlow and we don't have much time for her flair of the dramatic."

"But that's what we do here, Colonel. It's much more exciting than getting straight to it. After all, we've been expecting this war for seven and a half thousand years."

Jack, Carl, Will, Henri, Tram, and Ryan looked up the large set of stone steps and the silver haired woman waiting at the top near the open doors of the mansion surrounded on either side by ten very large men in black tuxedos.

"Where is Doctor Ellenshaw and Matchstick?" Ryan asked, jumping the gun and not caring about the angered look from Collins.

Elsbeth Barlow turned to the man to her right. He whispered in her ear and she nodded.

"We have them boiling in a large pot at the moment." She crooked her arthritic fingers into claws and leaned forward at the group of guests. "Double, double, toil and trouble, fire burn and caldron bubble!" Elsbeth Barlow cackled like a mother hen laying an egg. "To quote Shakespeare anyway."

By the look on Jack's face Elsbeth knew the man wasn't amused by her small joke.

"For a man who will more than likely be dead in the next few days, you seem to be a serious kind of fella. I was just kidding, I wanted to set the mood. We witches have a reputation to adhere to. It's a union thing."

Millicent Krensky greeted Elsbeth with a hug and then turned and gave the men below a withering look.

"Glad to see they didn't take out my misdeeds on you, my dear."

"No, they were the models of decorum," the pilot said as she stepped inside the house. "Just firm believers in science, not fact."

"Colonel forgive me. I am a terrible host at times. Slim...or...uh, Professor Ellenshaw and Matchstick are dressing for dinner. Please, gentlemen, my kids will show you where you can wash-up. We have a nice selection of formal wear available. We like to dress for dinner."

"Kids?" Mendenhall said as he eyed the very large 'kids' standing next to Barlow as the new arrivals started up the massive steps.

"Ain't this the shit," Ryan said. "Welcome to Hogwarts School of Magic."

Ontario International Airport, Ontario, California

IN THE LATE AFTERNOON, the step van drove into the long-term parking lot of the smaller of the Los Angeles area airports. The kidnapping of Major Anya Korvesky and computer whiz Xavier Morales had been the easy part for Master Chief Jenks as he simply waited for the duo to leave the Event Group complex through gate number two when they signed out to visit Alice Hamilton in the hospital. Now, once out of Nevada and with surmising the entirety of the federal government was searching for them, the Master Chief knew the hard part was now getting them into the air. He waited behind the wheel for a very special engineering student to meet him in the out of the way airport.

"Master Chief, although we can't know how you feel and would never assume to, we empathize with you. We loved Virginia too. You know if anyone will bring whoever did this to justice, we will. The Colonel is working on it as we sit here."

The Master Chief was silent as he adjusted the rearview mirror to see a handcuffed Anya Korvesky. Next to her with his wheelchair chained to the sidewall of the step van was Xavier Morales who had the good sense to be silent as Anya pled their case. He was frightened because even though his reputation was one of arrogance, Xavier had also read the Master Chief's file and knew that this was the man responsible for training Captain Everett and numerous other extreme killers in the elite U.S. Navy SEALs.

"Master Chief, you know Virginia would never want this."

"Who said Virginia would want anything. This is me. Not her."

Anya exchanged looks with Xavier and both looks saw a man in the Master Chief who was slowly dying inside.

"I could kick your ass for telling Jenks to stay in Paris."

"Major, I thought I was helping," Xavier replied, knowing that the Master Chief was no fool. Quite the opposite as facts go. He may be a gruff cigar chomping navy man but was also one of the brightest mechanical engineers the military has ever produced. Morales knew he should have assumed Jenks would figure out something back home was wrong.

"You two need to be quiet now."

Anya looked up and saw the Master Chief's dark eyes watching them from the front of the van. His glare was withering. She knew the man's history as well as Xavier and knew he had a deep-down hatred for the federal government and had never fully trusted his own department. Every member in the Group knew the Master Chief tolerated 5656 because of his love of Virginia. Everyone knew it was Virginia who always calmed Jenks down and their relationship was more like beauty and the beast than true love. But whatever it was, Jenks was taking her loss personally and may go as far as blaming the hierarchy of the department for her murder.

"Jenks, would it help if I told you the Colonel and Mister Everett is meeting with what could turn out to be the people responsible for Virginia's murder?"

Jenks didn't say a word as he stood and squeezed his bulk between the console and passenger seat and went into the back of the van. He was silent as he pulled a strip of duct tape and placed it over Anya's mouth. He did the same to Xavier. He looked at them both.

"I like both you two. I respect what you're trying to do. But if you try to stop me from getting to the pukes that...that...," he choked up and they could see him struggle with his next words. "I won't hesitate going through you, the Colonel, or even Toad to do it. Now shut up."

They watched Jenks return to the front of the van. He started to light a cigar and then thought better of it and tossed it from the window. Anya remembered the last time she had seen Jenks and Virginia together. She had admonished him as she always did about his nasty habit of chewing on the cigar instead of smoking it. She was constantly teasing the Master Chief for using the cigar as a prop or a tool to scare people that intimidated him. Now she could see Jenks was feeling guilty about his bad habit. Anya felt the tears threaten to appear as it had several times since Jenks had snatched both of them from the Gold City Pawn Shop in downtown Las Vegas.

Jenks checked his watch and then seemed satisfied about something. He reached into the glove box to his right and brought out a Beretta nine-millimeter and chambered a round. He reached back and placed it in his pants as he started the van.

Unbeknownst to Jenks, Xavier had been working diligently and silently on his wheelchair. The spokes were made of steel wire and he had managed to pop free the top portion of one and had been working the steel back and forth and had finally managed to break the top six inches from it. He just prayed the Major was as good as her file said she was in the realm of survival, escape and evasion, as the Mossad was rumored to be. With his chair chained and his left hand cuffed to the chair, he lightly tapped on the wheel to get Anya's attention. She turned and saw the piece of steel and nodded as Xavier managed to drop into her free hand. Jenks was concentrating on the road as Anya received what she hoped would be their version of the old file in the cake escape plan.

Jenks spent the next five minutes negotiating the airport's private facilities. Making sure to avoid the many roving patrols by the uniformed security guards, he finally made it to the gate where his meeting with a young grad student from San Diego State University had been arranged. He relaxed when he saw the battered thirty-year old Camaro waiting. As he pulled up, he saw that the student's car was empty which was not according to his arrangements. Jenks strained his neck to see if he could view inside the new private departures area but could see nothing through the darkened windows of the terminal building.

"To hell with it," Anya and Xavier heard him mumble as he opened the van's rear door. He quickly ripped the tape from Xavier's mouth.

"Ow," Xavier said.

The Master Chief didn't give Xavier a rebuke other than place his index finger to his lips, shushing the kid. He turned and faced Anya. "I have your word that you won't scream?"

Anya eyed the Master Chief, and then reluctantly nodded her head. He pulled the duct tape from her mouth.

"This is where we part company. I'm sorry for how this had to happen, but I know the chief nerd boy and he would have never allowed me access to the bastards that hurt Virginia. This is the way I had to do things. Once in the air I'll contact the Group and tell them where they can find you. Tell Compton to let the Colonel and Toad know not to get in my way."

"Master Chief, I assume by your attitude your accomplice failed to show up. That means only one thing, either he's in custody or he crapped out on you. Either way that grounds you."

"After all of those years chasing bad guys, do you think I never learned to fly an aircraft? I designed half the airborne ships in service young lady." Jenks angrily placed the tape back on Anya's mouth. "Now I fully expect to never see you again in this lifetime, so, take care of yourselves." Jenks patted Anya on the knee and then jumped from the van and closed the doors.

"Mmm-um-mm," Anya said with arched eyebrows.

"Huh?" Xavier said, and then shook his head in self-rebuke and quickly pulled the tape from her mouth. "Sorry."

Anya was wriggling her hands and then suddenly the cuffs came free. She looked at Xavier. "The Master Chief doesn't know it yet but he's walking right into an FBI trap."

"How do you know?" Xavier asked.

Anya gave Morales a withering look. "Hello, ex-Mossad?"

"Right. Again, sorry."

"Look, I can get you out of the van, but I don't have time to get you to where we need to go, times too short."

"Wait, wait. What are we going to do?"

Anya jumped from the van and then pulled Xavier from the back, nearly spilling the large man onto the concrete.

"I haven't thought that far ahead yet!"

Xavier watched Anya turn and run for the small private terminal.

Doctor Xavier Morales who wasn't used to even being outside, used his powerful arms and started wheeling in the chase.

"Hey, wait for the overweight crippled guy!"

ONCE INSIDE THE terminal Jenks watched from a safe vantage point the comings and goings of people that could afford to skip the security lines at the airlines in lieu of private flights. To see any city police force in the area was a sure sign that Jenks was being watched. Thus far he had not seen any of Ontario's finest. He sat behind a newspaper near a small hamburger stand sipping coffee while his eyes roamed the spacious but mostly empty terminal. When he went to get another cup of coffee, he did notice the small Learjet chartered by his student from San Diego State. It wasn't tied down and looked to be pre-flighted. But thus far the Master Chief had not seen any sign of the young man who would pilot the craft to New England. He tossed the fresh cup of coffee in the trash and picked up his small bag. He wore a hat with a wide brim and his sunglasses would rival any pair Elvis had ever owned. He made for the double doors leading to the plane parking area in the front. He knew it was now or never and couldn't afford the delay in waiting for his young engineering student.

The sun was just starting to lower toward the sea only twenty-five miles away which was advantageous as the shift change with ground security was in its process. As he neared the small jet, he refused the urge to look around the area as small planes taxied and others pulled next to or inside hangars. When he was thirty feet from the aircraft, he at first felt relief and then apprehension as he saw a figure in the pilot's seat of the Lear. A hand came up and waved and that was when he saw that it was his student. Jenks didn't wave back. Thus far his prized pupil had failed to do everything that had been meticulously planned. He stopped walking after waving back and went to a knee to tie his shoe and as he did, he looked for where the FBI ambush would come from. He straightened and then started to turn around and return to the terminal when the stairs of the jet lowered and five FBI agents in their navy-blue windbreakers stormed from the aircraft.

Jenks knew his SEAL days were over, so instead of running, he simply stopped and glared at the agents rushing him with drawn service weapons. The Master Chief knew that if he had to, he could at least disable three of the five before they even got close. He reached behind him and tossed the nine-millimeter onto the tarmac.

"Master Chief Jenks, Director Compton sends his regards and requests that you come with us."

"Special Agent Wilkerson. Fancy seeing you here."

"Master Chief," Wilkerson said as he holstered his weapon and made the other four men lower theirs. "I presume we won't have any unpleasantness here?"

"Anytime I'm around Feds it's unpleasant."

"I was informed to prepare for your attitude toward the world in general. But due to the effort you put into the war with the Greys, I think we can handle your insults with mild applause as to your service."

Wilkerson didn't cuff the Master Chief out of respect. One of his agents allowed his apologetic engineering student to go free with no charges as Jenks was led away back inside the terminal. As the doors closed the agent and the others saw the objects of the kidnapping as they looked around the terminal. He waved Xavier and Anya over. Jenks, Anya, and Xavier were led into a private security office. Wilkerson excused the airport security man inside and offered them all a seat.

"As a courtesy we're going to hold the Master Chief here for a few hours until we can put his mean ass butt on a plane back to Nevada. Master Chief, I was at the crime scene a few days ago and am aware of the personal loss you..."

Wilkerson saw the slight shake of Anya's head warning him not to even go there. He stopped.

"Suffice it to say we are going to assist Colonel Collins all we can. That comes direct from the President."

Jenks remained silent as he watched the comings and goings outside of the office window. To Anya it was if the Master Chief were just a passenger with no more anger than a simple flight delay. She knew then that if she didn't do something drastic Jenks would do something that would be irreversible.

Wilkerson looked at his four men and then nodded. "Bring the cars around," and then he excused his men and they left the office.

Xavier saw Anya out of the corner of his eye move ever-so-slightly in her chair.

"Now, Master Chief," Wilkerson started to say when he saw the pistol aimed right at his right eye. Xavier felt his heart rate speed up as he watched Anya stand and pull the Master Chief to his feet.

"Jenks, you're going to have to help Doctor Morales to learn to fly," she said as Xavier's eyes went wider than before.

"What do you think you're doing?" Wilkerson asked as he started to lower his arms and hands. Anya frowned and shook her head.

"Agent Wilkerson, there's more ways to use this gun than just shooting you with it."

Wilkerson cleared his throat. "I uh, see your point."

Anya moved to the window without the stolen nine-millimeter moving an inch in either direction. The former Mossad Major unlocked the window and then slid it open.

"You don't have to do this Major. I can handle this myself," Jenks said as he started for the window.

"Yes, I can see that. You've done so well so far. Now assist Doctor Morales please. He may come in handy," she explained as she quickly and expertly cuffed the FBI agent who was shocked that Anya would go against her own boss in Nevada. She then used the same cuffs to cuff him to the large desk, knowing he would be free soon enough when his agents returned. She then pulled the phone cord from the wall and stomped on the connector. She then rummaged through Wilkerson's pockets and removed his cell phone. She angrily looked at Jenks. "Look, Special Agent Wilkerson is only going to give us a half hour to get over the desert as a head start and as a professional courtesy."

"I am?"

"Yes, you are. You said earlier you know how the Master Chief must feel. Now we'll see. I thought I knew how he felt also, now I see we both don't know what in the hell we're talking about."

Wilkerson lowered his head. Jenks nodded his thanks.

"Besides, you don't want the word to spread around Las Vegas that you were disarmed by a wheelchair-bound Doctor Morales, would you?"

"That's low."

Anya heard Xavier yell as Jenks unceremoniously tossed him from the window followed quickly by his backless wheelchair. Then Jenks leaped.

Anya patted Wilkerson on the back. "Thanks agent. For the head start that is."

"Don't mention it," he said embarrassingly.

CHAPTER FIFTEEN

Cambridge, Massachusetts

Jack and the others refused any offer to wash-up or change for dinner before they had a chance to confirm that Charlie and Matchstick were unharmed. As the group of six reached the top of the stairs they saw the long hallway. At least ten bedrooms lined the hall on either side.

"This is like the damn House of Usher," Mendenhall said as he eyed the medieval armor here and there and the crossed swords and axes. "Did they go out of their way to *make* this place creepy?"

Suddenly a door opened at the far end of the hallway and they watched as a small black-clad blur burst from the bedroom there. The head was bulbous and the eyes wide and large. Matchstick screamed as he ran toward the newcomers.

Collins, for the first time in years, choked up at the sight of the small alien as he went to a knee. Matchstick crashed into him and hugged Jack like there was no tomorrow. Mahjtic took turns hugging each. He gave Henri a curious look at first and then hugged his long legs. Tram, amazed at the sight of the small being in an even smaller dinner jacket and bowtie, bent over and introduced himself.

Then they saw Charlie Ellenshaw approach. Jack shook his hand as did the others.

"Is it true?" Charlie asked Collins.

Jack could only nod his head as he knew exactly what Ellenshaw was referring to. Charlie removed his glasses and dabbed at his eyes.

"Alice?" he asked.

"Barely hanging on was the last word from Niles. Sarah and he are with her as we speak. They'll let us know if anything changes, Doc."

Charlie placed his glasses back on and looked from Collins to Everett. "Without those two women the members of the Group would have ran me off years ago. I owe them everything."

Everett reached out and took Ellenshaw by the shoulder and squeezed.

"We going to get the bastards that did this?" Charlie asked, growing firm.

"So, you believe this crazy woman?" Jason asked as he picked up Matchstick and cradled him.

"I don't know how to explain it. I do know she reached out mentally and somehow chased this entity out of Nevada before it had a chance to kill Alice."

Jack grew silent as he took a few steps away. He turned. "We didn't come here for dinner parties. So, let's bypass the offer of clothing and go down and see for ourselves."

"Speak for yourself, Colonel," Henri said as he opened the first door to his right. "We just came from a most deplorable liaison with some rather shady and disgusting people. We need to wash before you go shooting everyone in this strange but beautiful house."

"Sorry to have to agree with Colonel Farbeaux here, but I do need to wash up," Will said as he relieved Ryan of Matchstick. "I missed you buddy." Matchstick hugged Will's neck tightly and when Jack saw that he relented.

"I guess we should all wash-up."

He looked at Henri as he started to walk into the first bedroom.

"Ryan, go with our friend here and make sure he keeps his hands off the antiques in this place."

"Colonel, you act as though I haven't mended my ways," Farbeaux said as he smiled.

"Maybe when it comes to material things, Henri. It's other precious valuables that concern me."

Farbeaux knew exactly to what precious valuables Jack was referencing.

Moscow, Russia

THE APARTMENT BUILDING sat just a few blocks from the glorious Christ the Savior Cathedral on Butikovsky Pereulok. The most recent sale reported by the Moscow Times stated an available apartment recently sold for thirty million American dollars. For the most part if you wanted to live anonymously in Moscow, the complex wasn't the best way to achieve it. With western-style doormen and twenty-four-hour services, most of the buyers were of influential stock. This included movie actors and film producers.

Regev Slivinski didn't live the affluent life. He lived across the street in a rundown shanty that was due to be demolished in favor of a new complex for the rich and famous Muscovites by the same conglomerate that owned the expensive high-rise across the way. As he eased into a chair at his rickety kitchen table, Slivinski unbuttoned the top of his light-brown colored tunic. On the shoulder-boards of the jacket was the three stars and double red stripes of a Russian army colonel. He watched the comings and goings of the rich men and women being allowed into the expensive apartments across the street. He heard movement behind him and relaxed when he saw the reflection of the young woman trying to sneak up on him from behind in the window's reflection. He turned suddenly in his chair and jumped up.

"Ahhh!" he yelled.

The young woman screamed and giggled as Slivinski picked her up and hugged her. She playfully slapped him on the chest, jingling the many medals adorned there.

"I can never sneak up on you!" she said laughing.

Slivinski put the small woman down. "If you could, that wouldn't make me a very good soldier would it?" he said smiling.

"Well, you're late for dinner. For that Mr. Colonel, I ought to deny you the pleasures of my company."

Slivinski looked at his daughter and smiled even wider than before. The Colonel was proud of her. She lived and made her way through life without a complaint as so many other young people did these days. He knew for a girl born out of wedlock the odds would always be against her in a world that frowned on the sins committed by the father.

"If you were to do that I would hurriedly volunteer for duty in North Korea and leave the Motherland forever."

She hurried into his arms and embraced him and hugged. "If you did that I would just die!"

He hugged her back and then turned her around. "If I don't get some supper in my belly I just might do exactly that."

Maleava Belka, the daughter produced years before by a brief liaison with a woman he loved but could never be with, saluted him playfully and turned back to the small kitchen separated by a shabby cloth divider. Slivinski kept his smile as he heard her preparing his dinner. He shook his head and finally turned away and sat once more at the table. His eyes went as they always did to the rich people across the street. His smile faltered as he watched. He wanted that very lifestyle for his daughter Maleava but knew as long as he wore the uniform of the Russian army, he could never give it to her without tongues wagging and higher-ranking officers judging him for his indiscretions. If they knew how guilty he felt about those indiscretions, they wouldn't be so hard on him. He truly loved the mistake of his life and would someday give Maleava the life she so richly deserved. His eyes sadly left the view from across the street.

The knock startled him.

"I'll get it. It's probably Pavel with his annoying American Facebook gabble."

Slivinski waited as the sounds of his illegitimate daughter opened the door echoed in the apartment.

"Father, this man said he would like to have few words with you."

"Father? How many times have I told you that no one can know…" He stopped his admonishment suddenly when he turned to see the portly man at the door.

"Even the oldest of friends?"

"Maleava," Slivinski reached into his coat and brought out a wad of Rubles and held it out to her, "Why don't you take the boy Pavel and go see that American superhero movie you've been wanting to see?"

"But you said for me not to waste my time on that drivel."

"Take the money and you go now, honey. I have to see this man."

"No introductions?" Number One asked as he removed the brown Fedora and admired the girl as she accepted the money.

"You go now, Maleava." Slivinski kissed her on the forehead. "I'll see you tomorrow. I'll lock up. Tell Pavel to keep his hormones in check!"

Maleava eased into her threadbare coat and looked Number One over. She had never once in her life seen her father frightened or concerned about anyone before this night. Number One smiled at her and with one last look at her father, she turned and left the rundown flat.

As soon as the door was closed Slivinski hurried over and locked it. He then placed the chain on and with one last look through the 'peephole,' he turned and faced Number One.

"May I sit, Regev?"

Without speaking, Slivinski gestured toward one of the two chairs at the table.

Number One dipped his head in thanks and placed the fedora down on the tabletop and then sat. "Are you going to offer me a drink?"

"I don't allow alcohol in the apartment. You know how young people can be."

"Forever the cautious one," Number One said smiling. "Sit Colonel, please."

Slivinski eyed the man for the briefest of moments and then placated him and sat. With hesitation the colonel buttoned his tunic all the way to the collar.

"I suppose you have heard that our army lost Lieutenant Colonel Leonid Petrolovich a few days ago," Number One said as he toyed with his fedora, spinning it in circles. Slivinski watched this movement with mild irritation.

"Army's have never been good at stemming the flow of unfavorable rumors."

"That is true. The only reason I mention it is because with the loss of Petrolovich and most of the Fifteenth Guards Brigade we...or I... have been placed in a rather tough spot."

"What does this have to do with me?" Slivinski asked, still watching the slowly spinning fedora.

"The Committee has a problem old friend. We need you."

Slivinski moved his eyes from the fedora and instead of talking he stopped the hat from turning by placing a hand on the brim. Number One looked at him with mild surprise.

"I don't do that work any longer."

"When you're the best at something, you never stop that which you love."

"I love my daughter. This is enough."

Number One leaned over and pulled back the small curtain in the kitchen window. He gestured outside. "Wouldn't it be nice to give your daughter what those fools have over there. What you and your daughter deserve far more than those leeches of our society?"

"We have enough."

Number One let go of the curtain and faced the colonel. "We on the Committee know we failed in showing our appreciation the last time we came to you. But now I am in a position to give you all of that," he gestured toward the window, "and so much more, Colonel. You are the only man that can do this. When you served under me many years ago you grew out of even my control to become the best at what you do. You pulled off the impossible in eliminating the entirety of the corrupt, western kowtowing government. It was you who placed a bullet in Putin's head. It was you who eventually created the new Russia. After this last mission, we can properly say that you deserve the highest honors of the new world."

"And now you want me to kill Putin's dolt twin brother here in Moscow, is that it?"

"If I wanted that done, I would get one of his cheap prostitutes to do it. No. This is entirely different. Regev, your nation needs you one last time. Then you and your daughter can write your own retirement orders for any spot in the world you wish to go."

Slivinski had done his duty, no matter how distasteful and low that duty had called for him to be. He had eliminated those the Army told him to eliminate and never once balked at an order. But since the birth of his daughter he knew that a portion of his soul had been lost because of his duty.

"It's time we settle some old business my friend. A man you know is in a position to hurt not only your country, but also your daughter."

Slivinski's head snapped up. "Who?"

Number One reached into his coat pocket and pulled out a packet. He offered the first photo to the Colonel. The picture was of a blading man with an eyepatch and glasses. A long scar ran from his forehead to his jawline. He placed the photo down onto the table.

"I don't know this face," Slivinski said as Number One gave him a second picture.

"How about this face?"

Slivinski looked down and saw the uniform and the stern features of a man he did recognize. The campaign ribbons on his chest were few and the silver first lieutenant's bars on his shoulders easily identified the man as a United States Army officer. He would never forget the eyes. This was a photo of the first man he had ever killed as a young officer in the old Soviet Army. After forty-six years it was still the man's eyes that gave Slivinski the cold chills.

Number One pulled another photo from the packet. He withheld it for the briefest of moments. "We both carry guilt for things we did as young men, Colonel. Now we are faced with something that can bring us both down. I could have possibly achieved this without calling on you by using the man you trained for operations such as this with Colonel Petrolovich, who is now dead, but I guess providence has brought us back to the very crossroads that placed us on the path we are both on." Number One handed the third photo to Slivinski.

The photo was almost a duplicate of the second one. This man wore his hair shorter and had small scars on his face as if he had spent many years in a rough profession Slivinski knew well. The uniform was also of the American army. This man had deep, penetrating blue eyes as did the first lieutenant in the second photo. He also wore the silver eagles of a full Colonel.

"Are you waiting to play guessing games with me?" Slivinski asked as his eyes roamed over the picture. "Who is this man?"

"The first man is Doctor Niles Compton. The fact he is a person the Committee needs eliminated has little to do with the second man other than the fact the two work together."

"Okay, so the second and third look like each other. What does that have to do with anything?"

"The third photo is Colonel Jack Collins. He is the son of the man you and I murdered in 1973. The Colonel has learned of our Committee. He is a danger."

Still, what has that to do with me?" Slivinski asked, holding Number One's eyes.

"He is the son of Lieutenant John C. Collins, missing in action during the summer of 1973."

The world Slivinski had come to know flashed before his eyes as he looked again at the face of the man whose father he and Number One had tortured to death in a small room in Hanoi.

"As I said Regev. I need you and you need me."

"What is it you want?"

Number One smiled and placed the fedora on his blading head and stood as he laid the package of orders on the table.

"What I want is the best assassin the world has ever seen. I want Colonel Regev Slivinski, the man our enemies know as, the Ghost."

Cambridge, Massachusetts

RANDALL MET the house guests in the upstairs area of the mansion. The giant of a man looked as if he was sent over from central casting with his villainous tuxedo and shaved head. The men of the Event Group had not changed clothing with the exception of Henri Farbeaux, Charlie Ellenshaw and little Matchstick. The later two out of necessity due to the kidnapping from a desert encircled lake in Nevada.

Randall led the group of seven guests down the long haul which afforded Jack a chance at gaining some information.

"How long have you been with Miss Barlow?" he asked.

The large man glanced at Collins as if he had expected to be grilled. He smiled. "I came to the estate at the age of thirteen. I was a runaway from an abusive home, and I made the mistake of trying to steal food from a pantry for the poor of which Granny supports." Randall slowed and then faced Jack and the others. "Needless to say, she tracked me down and made me see the error of my ways."

"How did she do that?" Ryan asked.

"She used her powers and sent me flying to the top of the Green Monster at Fenway. Left me there for five hours balanced on two legs of a chair. Let's just say I made an effort to listen to her rebuke about stealing. Then she took me home and fed me and gave me a place to live. After my days at Princeton, which was paid for by the foundation's scholarship, I stayed on to help with the estate and prepare."

"Prepare for what?" Jack pursued.

Randall didn't answer, he continued to the stairs.

"Is everyone here an orphan?" Mendenhall asked.

"For the most part. A few were criminals in another time of their lives. I would want to know how Granny changed them."

"Let's get down to the real question, shall we?" Ryan said as they started down the stairs. "How many of you nuts think you're actually witches?"

"We don't think Mister Ryan. Thinking sometimes gets in the way."

"Why do you call Miss Barlow Granny?" Charlie asked.

"What should we call her?"

The Group exchanged looks and it was Henri who asked the next question.

"How old is Granny?"

Randall laughed as he made the bottom riser of the stairs. "If you want to be turned into a frog or something else that crawls, you ask. I'm not."

As they moved from the foyer and into the dining room, they were amazed to see the long table filled with fine china and food piled so high it was hard to count the number of men and women at the table. Then it was jack who noticed many children dressed just as fine as the adults. At the head of the table Elsbeth Barlow stood. She was assisted to her feet by the pilot Millicent Krensky who was dressed in a formal gown.

"Gentlemen, thank you for joining us. Sorry for the formality but this dinner has been planned for quite some time. Please, sit and make your introductions." She smiled as the former military pilot helped her back into her chair. "None here bite—at least in their present form."

Jack and the others were amazed when this comment elicited laughter from all around the large table.

"Colonel Collins, please, sit next to me."

Jack looked at Will, Jason, Charlie, Tram, and Farbeaux and nodded that they should disburse and get to know the so-called coven. Collins himself took Matchstick by the hand and led him to the far end of the long table. Until he knew what was happening, he wanted Matchstick to stay as close to him as possible. He knew whatever was going on here the small alien was an important key. He excepted the offered chair and placed Matchstick in a chair next to him as an assistant placed a child's booster chair down. Matchstick's almost non-existent nose wrinkled at the plate of salad in front of him and looked up at Jack as if to ask, 'what am I supposed to do with this?'

"Colonel, before we begin with your interrogation regarding our actions and eventual intent, may I say I am so sorry for the loss of your friends and associates in Nevada." Elsbeth looked down the table until she spied Henri, Ryan, Mendenhall, and Tram. "To you gentlemen also. I never expected you to get so close. I'm afraid I was taken by surprise. It seems your Group is even more inventive than even I knew."

"It was our French friend who got us so close in New Orleans," Everett volunteered.

"Ah, Colonel Farbeaux. A most ingenious man of opportunity."

"Excuse me, but have we ever met before?" Henri asked as he accepted a glass of wine from one of Barlow's attendants.

"I can't know much about our friends in government service like the Event Group and not know about a man known as their greatest nemesis, who it now seems to be turning over a new leaf. An amazing turn of fortune." She looked at Jack and smirked almost knowingly. The look made Collins very uncomfortable.

"Thank you for your condolences about our friends. But that doesn't mean we believe anything you and your...your..."

"Cult, coven, whatever you wish to call it," Elsbeth said as the forty men, women and children all laughed.

"It doesn't mean we believe a word you've said, and it doesn't clear you of responsibility in regard to the murder of our people." Jack opened a napkin and placed it in his lap. "You should know when we find out this will not be handled through a court of law." He looked at the silent faces of his hosts. Then held his glass up for the red wine offered. His eyes returned to the old woman.

"Your friends here," Elsbeth nodded toward Ryan, Will, Tram, and Henri down the long table. "They saw the being responsible. Asmodius was prophesied thousands of years ago to return. He has." Elsbeth reached out and removed Matchstick's plate of salad and handed to an assistant and then the salad was replaced with a plate of frozen Hot Pockets. "That is why we need Mr. Stick."

"How did you know Matchstick was still alive?" Charlie Ellenshaw asked as he stood from his chair and placed a linen napkin in Matchstick's shirt.

"He told me of course."

"And how did he do that, Western Union?" Ryan asked with an angry look.

"Millicent said because of your naval aviator status you would be the short tempered one Mr. Ryan."

"Is that right?" Ryan asked as he took in the blonde woman who had found the Event Group Complex.

"She's the same way. Arrogant," Elsbeth said but took the woman's hand. "But we love her anyway."

Millicent smirked at Ryan and actually looked like she wanted to stick out her tongue. He returned the look with a silent snarl.

"In answer to your question Slim," she said looking down the table at Ellenshaw, "I have always had what you would call a mental connection with Mr. Stick and his kind." Elsbeth smiled at a chewing Matchstick. "They taught us most of what we know. That was before the Grey bastards turned on them of course and enslaved them. In essence Slim, Matchstick called me. Have you noticed that Matchstick has been a little...well...off?"

"Yes," Charlie said. "This is why it was a bad mistake to not allow our Group to check him out physically and mentally, but you took him before we could."

"Well, we here can help your Group with that. He doesn't seem right to you because part of him is still in the id."

"The id?" Jack asked.

"The plane between life and death. The Green's and Grey's are almost the same species. As you know both have two hearts and their brains are not unlike ours. They are compartmentalized."

"Thank you, Randall. Randall here is a brilliant astrophysicist that dabbles in alien biology as a hobby."

The guests looked at the giant of a man who managed to actually look embarrassed at the praise.

"Continue, Randall," Elsbeth said proudly.

"When injured, Matchstick went into a state we refer to as self-induced, coma-like reproduction. He has the ability to repair himself. An amazing species."

"We would have informed you, but even I have trouble penetrating your complex security at times."

Farbeaux raised his glass in Collins' direction when Elsbeth praised his security.

"Excuse me, but your cell phone will ring in two seconds Colonel. Someone on the other end will inform you that more assistance to our cause is in route I believe."

The house guests looked at Elsbeth, unbelieving, just as Jack's phone started buzzing. He removed it from his sports coat and answered.

"Did he hurt anyone?" Jack's eyes went to Carl. "Xavier too?"

"Damn it, who's dead now?" Mendenhall said as he angrily tossed his napkin on his plate full of untouched salad.

"Inform Agent Wilkerson we'll handle it if they make it this far." Jack closed the cell phone and looked at Everett. "Doctor Morales and Anya assisted Master Chief Jenks in escaping custody of the FBI and they're pretty sure they're on their way here."

"What?" was all Carl could say.

"Oh, I would so love to meet your computer man." Elsbeth leaned over and spoke in a conspirator's tone to Jack. "I think your Doctor Morales has a rather healthy love affair with someone named Europa."

Will Mendenhall leaned over toward Ryan. "Told you."

"Okay, enough of the mysterious school of witchcraft. What is this Asmodius?" Jack asked.

"He's a Grey that was sent here a very long time ago. He was one of many plans to place this world into submission without a major fight. Needless to say, Asmodius eventually ended up betraying his own kind. Asmodius is what we refer to as a necromancer. A Warlock. One of a kind Grey. Ancient ways produce ancient evil. Asmodius knows the science of witchcraft."

"Science?" Farbeaux asked.

"Yes, a science as real as Randall's astrophysics. A science of manipulation of an environment and nature through sound and motion. Magic. It was real once. Asmodius was imprisoned with the help of Matchstick's kind and with some assistance from us. We were once followers of the Grey known as Asmodius Modai. Then we learned he wasn't as he seemed. It convinced not only itself, but it's followers that he was the fallen angel mentioned in early scripture. This brought on the age of good and evil. We revolted and Asmodius has never forgotten." Elsbeth used the napkin and wiped Matchstick's chin frost from one of his Hot Pockets. "I need him. It was his ancestors that gave me the horrid gift of long life.

"How is that?" Jack asked.

"The way we defeated Asmodius," Elsbeth said. "The Green's had the knowledge but not the physical strength to stop a very much larger species in the Grey. They needed one of us to act as a conductor of sorts. Through me, the Greens used their science and we doubled the power needed to capture and restrain Asmodius. We need Matchstick to remember through the centuries past what his ancestors know."

"How do you plan on doing that?" Everett asked.

"I don't know. Randall and a few others think we can do this through some form of hypnosis. If Matchstick had not of been 'murdered', he would have the information about the ancient science readily available in his collective memory with his ancestors. But since he has been in stasis for so long, his memory is not functioning the way it should."

"You mean to say that you can mind-meld with Matchstick to double your power of witchcraft like Mr. Spock?" Ryan scoffed.

The children around the table laughed at Ryan's small and brutal insult.

"I mean exactly that. And we have very little time. Asmodius has help and I believe it may be connected to a group of evil men you may already be aware of."

"Are these men Russian by chance?" Everett asked.

"Not by chance Mister Everett, but by design."

"When is this Grey son of a bitch coming?" Mendenhall asked.

"I am having a hard time getting a fix on him through mental insight. But he draws close."

"Is it just him?" Jack asked.

"For seven thousand years me and mine have been keeping his followers at bay. A war has raged for many millennia right under the noses of regular society. But make no mistake Colonel, Asmodius is a coward deep down. He will bring that army with him."

"That means he can't fly, and he can't travel any conventional way with that many," Farbeaux added.

"Ship?" Charlie ventured.

"From New Orleans to Massachusetts by sea? Too long I would think. Too much could go wrong if he's transporting a lot of strange people," Henri corrected Charlie while eyeing the opposite side of strange around the table.

"If what they say is true, I will not underestimate a being that killed my friends from a thousand miles away."

Carl nodded at Jack's logic. "Now, as you say Miss Barlow, you fought him off before with your army of witches. Where is this army now?"

Elsbeth smiled. She stood with the help of Millicent. She spread her arms wide indicating the men, women and children sitting and eating dinner.

"My army." She cackled in her irritating way. "Small, but formidable."

Desert Springs Hospital,
Las Vegas, Nevada

NILES COMPTON STOOD at the window and watched as Sarah kept up a constant conversation with Alice Hamilton whose condition had not changed for the better in over five days. Niles had never professed to anyone concerning his religious leanings, but since the events on Flamingo Road he had caught himself being drawn back to his childhood and Sunday's at church with his parents. Scientifically speaking, Niles was fully aware that power of prayer was a form of a generated confidence made almost factual by the human condition. Niles had been praying off and on for five days.

"You two were pretty close?"

Niles turned and saw the Surgeon General standing behind him. He turned back and faced the I.C.U.

"The last time I received a phone call in the middle of the night from the President it was because of you."

Niles turned back, confused as to what the older man was saying.

"After the attack on you, the other world leaders, and the President at Camp David, the first thing he wanted to know after he awakened from his coma was the condition of you. Nothing else. Then I get a call from him concerning Mrs. Hamilton and for the first time in my life I was actually ordered to save a life. Evidently he favors that lady as much as you."

"Someday the world may find out just who Alice Hamilton was in American history." Niles tried to smile, but the attempt died a quick death. "Someday, maybe."

The Surgeon General placed a hand on Compton's shoulder. "We're doing our best."

Niles could only nod his head.

"I've got to check in with my offices back in D.C., it seems we have a small problem with a hurricane that seemed to have developed out of nowhere. One that's acting stranger than the experts say could be possible."

Niles turned back with a question itching to be asked.

"Oh, sorry, forgot you've been out of the loop for a while. It seems a small storm from the Gulf intensified and actually rounded the Florida Key's and gained strength. Storms just don't do that. It went from a tropical storm to a category three hurricane within two days. I have to make sure my people contact all of the emergency services people in the appropriate cities."

"What are the cities you're concerned with?" Niles asked.

"Well, right now it looks like it could come ashore anywhere from Richmond to Maine." The Surgeon General looked at his notes on a clipboard. "It seems more than likely it's going to strike Boston head on." The Doctor nodded at Niles and then turned and left.

Niles didn't like the coincidental fact that the targeted Boston area was exactly where Jack and his team were. With one last look at Sarah and Alice, he turned away to start making calls.

CHAPTER SIXTEEN

Cambridge Massachusetts

While Ryan, Mendenhall, Tram, and Randall toured the property looking over a possible defense, it was Ryan who stated the obvious when he placed a hand on the elbow of Randall and stopped him.

"If we know they're coming, why don't we just get the Massachusetts State Police or a Marine Combat team out here and wait for them?"

"Granny has contacted the appropriate authorities and without attracting much attention like your Marine combat team would do, the State Police can secure the roads enough around the estate. I also imagine Granny thinks the police and even your Marines have better things to do than die. Besides, with the weather we have rolling in the authorities will be having their hands full."

"Besides buddy, I don't think the world's quite ready to hear the Grey's are back in action." Mendenhall frowned at Ryan.

"Will Miss Barlow be able to get Matchstick's memory flowing again?" Ryan asked, making Will shy away with his glare.

"Gentlemen, it's not Matchstick's memory that needs to be

recovered. As you've seen yourself, he has no problem remembering you and your friends. It's his collective memory we need to recover. It's the moments from the past of his ancestors he carries that will provide the power inside of Granny that will defeat Asmodius. She can't do it alone."

"Are you going to live a long life like Miss Barlow?" Will asked as lightning flared across the treetops and rain started to pour in earnest.

"Thank goodness no. You see gentlemen, Granny may have been born on this world, but she hasn't been one of us for eons. She met her first Green when she was a just a child back in Babylonia. They trusted her. They trained her. They, in their own way, even loved her."

"We understand that part of it. When we lost Matchstick, it tore our guts out," Mendenhall added, and Ryan nodded his head in agreement.

"Well, we'll see in the next few hours if your small green friend can assist Granny or not. Right now, it doesn't look good."

"There's no way she can fight this asshole on her own?" Ryan asked as Randall produced two umbrellas.

"None."

"Then we just have to pump his Grey ass full of bullets," Ryan countered.

Randall laughed as he deployed the umbrella. "I wish we could just place your small sniper friend there into a tree and blow his brains out. However, Asmodius is a coward. He won't be anywhere near anything that can mortally wound him. His coven will try and take down our people with the skills he handed down through their ancestors thousands of years ago while the coward hides in a safe place."

"I don't understand how this coven could go through history without someone catching onto them," Mendenhall said.

"Major, many have caught onto them as you say. Battles the world remembers as glorious moments in warfare were more than likely instigated by his coven. Unlike our group who go through life as anonymously as possible, helping the world as we go. His people use events to prepare the killing ground for Asmodius and his return."

"For instance?" Tram said from behind.

Randall smiled and turned to look at his guests. "A man named Merlin Storm Foot fought his people in Northern Scotland over fourteen hundred years ago. Alexander the Great lost over two thousand men in Persia when he faced off against one of his followers. More recently an inside source guided Adolph Hitler in his supernatural leanings and quest for power."

"Not the Joseph Goebbels theory?" Tram said, surprising Will and Ryan with his knowledge.

"Not at all. That man was as dumb as a rock. But his wife Magda was quite an astute follower of Asmodius' teachings. Granny told us a horror story about the sacrifice of her own children in Hitler's bunker in '45. All because she thought that would bring the power of Asmodius back to the Third Reich."

"If they are all that stupid, why are they even considered a threat?" Ryan pushed.

"Do you think for the most part they're fools. Most use their power for personal gain and know as we do that if their secrets are spilled and widely accepted, their reign's as the most powerful and influential people in the world would come to an end. You would be surprised if you knew the celebrities and politicians involved. No, they have a lot to lose in the end. But our fear is they can't resist their true master when he comes calling, even if most have lost their ability to believe the legend." Randall stopped and faced the men. "And gentlemen, he's coming."

Ryan turned to see Will Mendenhall smile. "What are you so gleeful for?"

"For the first time in years someone who's trying to kill us is doing so without the use of a nuclear weapon someone misplaced. Now all we have to do is take on a horror story from a ridiculous book using Harry Potter's small army."

"If I remember right, old Harry and his army got their asses kicked."

Will looked frustrated as he never watched a Harry Potter movie.

"Now it makes me kind of miss the nuclear weapon thing."

THE LARGE DEN had been emptied as the coven within the mansion commenced preparations for its defense. The remaining men and women sat around a warm fire as the storm outside picked up in intensity. Jack and Carl stood by the fireplace as Collins spoke on the phone. Henri sat and drank wine as did Millicent. Elsbeth sat in a large chair with Matchstick and Charlie Ellenshaw facing her. All was silent except for the ticking of the large clock and its calming pendulum.

They watched as Jack moved to the far corner and turned on a large television. He adjusted the channel to the local Boston station.

"...the category four hurricane dubbed Lorraine has intensified ever since passing Cape Hatteras. At first it looked as if it would lose intensity and make landfall north of the capitol but instead headed back out to sea and is now projected to strike Boston head-on. The city is preparing all shelters and emergency services for this, the most erratic hurricane in recorded history to make war on the land...meanwhile..."

Jack switched off the television. "Niles doesn't think the storm is coincidental. The boys in the Comp Center think it's acting like it's on a guidance system." He turned and faced Millicent. "I take it you have a computer we can use to speak to Europa?"

"Yes," she said looking from Collins to Elsbeth.

"The Comp Center has pictures taken by the N.O.A.A. that show an object in the direct center of the eye. It's a ship."

"So, this guy is coming on like he doesn't care who knows," Charlie Ellenshaw asked.

Elsbeth looked away and closed her eyes. "This is why I couldn't see Asmodius. The power of the storm is blinding my third eye." She laughed. "I guess the Grey critter is learning. Not very good for us."

"Any naval assets in the general area?" Henri ventured. "It wouldn't be too hard for our mysterious visitor to suddenly vanish."

"And what if it's not them?" Carl asked. "Have a sub sink a commercial freighter?"

Henri replied by raising his right eyebrow as if to say, *oh well.*

Carl shook his head at the apparent coldness of the Frenchman. "Besides, the navy gets its ships in harbor clear of any hurricane. The ports will empty out."

"Great, the outlaws are coming, and the Marshal takes off in the other direction," Ellenshaw said.

"Elsbeth smiled at Matchstick. "I guess that leaves us Mr. Stick. Do you wish to try and remember?"

Matchstick took his time as he looked from Elsbeth, to Jack, to Carl and then over to Ellenshaw. His large eyes blinked twice. Then he slowly held up a minuscule thumb.

Jack looked at Carl. They could both see Matchstick was shaking.

"Have you gentlemen noticed that without even trying this Asmodius has succeeded in isolating us completely within a few miles of one of your largest cities?"

One thing the Event Group knew well was the singular fact that Colonel Henri Farbeaux knew his traps when he came across one.

"Well, I guess we can throw out the signal lamp crap. No one if by land, two if by sea," Carl quipped.

Charlie shook his head. "It's the sea then."

JACK AND CHARLIE were the only ones Elsbeth couldn't convince to leave the large study. The only light being cast was the flickering of the fire. All else had been extinguished. Once in a while lightning tore through the night sky but the thick drapes kept it at bay. Thunder was another problem altogether. Every time the room and seemingly the entire house shook as the coming terror intensified.

Elsbeth sat in the large chair and Matchstick sat on the carpet at her feet. There was no talking, only silence as their two sets of eyes met. As the study shook, as thunder boomed outside, Charlie Ellenshaw approached Jack as he watched for any falsity in Elsbeth's claims about Matchstick.

"I take it you're armed, Colonel?"

Jack raised his sports coat and Ellenshaw could see the nine-millimeter in his waistband.

"So, she worries you still?" Jack asked in a low voice.

Charlie removed his glasses and cleaned them. "It's not her. Don't you feel it, Colonel? It's like we're being watched. And it's not the good kind of observation. It has bite to it. Like evil is waiting our move."

Jack did feel oddly exposed for being secured in a large house with some of the best soldiers ever fielded just feet away if needed. It was something his mind picked up during combat. A sense of impending danger that no soldier the world over could ever explain.

"You look tired my friend," Elsbeth said as a mother would to a son. "It's been a long, strange road hasn't it?"

Matchstick just curled his nose as he listened to Elsbeth's soothing voice. Gone was the cackles. Gone was the brave way she faced danger and gone was the light way she had explained all to the visiting group. This was an Elsbeth that was world traveled and exceptional in her intelligence. She was the memory of the world.

"I need you to relax Matchstick. Your journey has rivaled the great explorers of the universe. You have traveled from your home world to this one and then from our plane of existence to the you we call death. Now you are here to save the world once again from a threat mankind doesn't even know is coming."

It was at that moment that Jack realized just what the world owed Matchstick and his race. He always knew the small being was responsible for the world being saved. But he never realized the fear he must have felt in doing it. In the years Jack had known Matchstick he never once saw or heard the alien complain or feel sorry for himself. He loved from Gus to everyone he met at the Event Group and it all was unconditional. If he could save anyone in this whacked out nightmare, it would be Matchstick. He deserved peace as a reward for his help.

"Tell me Matchstick, do you hear the pendulum on the clock as it ticks the evening away into night? How soothing is that sound?"

Matchstick's eyes slowly closed, and it looked to Jack and Charlie as if the small being was fighting to stay awake. Then thunder again crashed outside the window and his black obsidian eyes sprang open.

Elsbeth raised her left hand and that was when Jack and Charlie felt their ears pop as if they were in a plane climbing to altitude. Then the boom of thunder was cut off as easily as if someone suddenly lowered the volume on a stereo. Collins eyes widened as he looked at Charlie.

"Told you Colonel. This is some weird stuff. Now all we need is Black Sabbath playing the soundtrack."

"Now, think about your little bed in the desert. Remember laying there safe and warm? Remember how good it felt to feel the love of your friends and how comfortable you were?"

Matchstick's eyes closed again and this time when he tried to close his strange eyelids they faltered. His large and bulbous green head slowly went to his chest.

"Can you hear me little man?" Elsbeth asked.

"He hears."

Jack and Charlie exchanged startled looks. The voice coming from Matchstick's lips were not his words. They were Gus Tilly's. The old man who had saved Matchstick in the desert and became his best friend. Charlie wanted to say something but was stopped when Elsbeth held her index finger to her lips.

"Matchstick, we need you to remember the times of your forefathers. Can you help us do this?"

Matchstick was motionless.

"You know he's not alone in here, right old lady?" said the voice that used to be Gus Tilly's.

Elsbeth looked at Jack who nodded his head. He mouthed the words 'Gus Tilly.'

"Yes, that's very nice of you to get your friend Gus to speak for you."

"That's not who I mean, you old witch. I mean there's something in here with him. This thing is tracking you."

Charlie looked at Jack as the house started to shake and this time it wasn't because of the thunder. Elsbeth looked up.

"Asmodius is here."

DAVID L GOLEMON

237 Nautical Miles off
Montauk Point, Long Island

THE LARGE CONTAINER ship rode easily through the eye of Hurricane *Lorraine*. Dmitri Sokol knew something had attracted the attention of Asmodius when the Grey suddenly left his spot at the bridge windows. It seemed the closer they got to their destination the more influence the alien was receiving from its quarry. Now Asmodius stood at the very bow of the container ship staring at the wall of swirling air and sea. Sokol saw that the hurricane had increased in intensity since just a few hours before.

He went to the bridge wing and looked out at the distant figure of Asmodius as the alien stared out to sea with outstretched arms. It seemed even at that extreme distance the Russian could hear a soft chant emanating from the Grey. The unrecognizable words echoed across the calm waters of the eye and bounced around. Sokol could tell the creature was reaching out for information and a possible demonstration of his infinite power. He almost felt sorry for whoever was on the receiving end.

Sokol was just about to seek the shelter of the bridge when he noticed something on the surface of the sea. Bobbing to the surface on all sides of the ship, thousands of fish started to float to the surface. Hundreds of differing species and varieties. They seemingly just died and Sokol suspected it wasn't from the sudden change in the weather. He knew it was the poisonous thoughts of Asmodius Modai.

Cambridge, Massachusetts

ELSBETH WAS DEEP IN A TRANCE. Matchstick hadn't moved or spoken in over five minutes. Jack was beginning to worry about the safety of their small friend when the mansion shook once again. This time Jack had been looking out of the window and there had been no flash of lightning and no roar of thunder. It was if a giant being were walking the mansion's long halls.

He watched Elsbeth's lips move but no words came out. Then her eyes opened.

"The two rivers. The ancient city. You see don't you Matchstick? See through the eyes of your fathers and many others of your species. They keep the memories alive for them that follow. Do you see?"

"He sees," came the voice of Gus Tilly.

Charlie exchanged a nervous look at Jack as he returned from the window.

"Remember the tales of Asmodius Modai?" Elsbeth mumbled as her eyes once more slowly closed.

"The Fallen One."

"Yes. Gus will help you be brave. He will help you remember. Now I address Augustus Tilly. You are with your small friend, aren't you?"

"I'll always be with Matchstick. He's my boy. I am one with him and always will be. They shouldn't have done to him what they did. Never trust the outside world. They let my boy down."

Jack felt the shame in the statement even though he knew it wasn't really Gus talking. It was the memory Matchstick had of his father-like figure. This meant that the small alien had felt let down by the people outside of Gus that he most depended on. Him and the rest of the Event Group. Even Charlie felt the guilt slap him hard enough to feel real.

"Matchstick, can you help me stop Asmodius one last time? Together we can stop him from regaining that which he lost many years ago. If we don't, he will cause great harm to the people you love. The people I love."

Charlie nudged Jack as he nodded toward Matchstick. The tears flowed easily down his face as his eyes started to move rapidly.

"He say's he will try. But he knows Asmodius has grown stronger during his long sleep."

Suddenly the room exploded with light and sound. Wind struck from nowhere. The two large French doors were blown from their hinges and vanished into the storm outside. Rain washed in as Jack and Charlie tried desperately to avoid flying debris. Collins made Charlie lie on the floor as flames from the fireplace leaped from the grate and flew high over his and Ellenshaw's head. Jack then dove for Matchstick to cover him.

"Wake up, Matchstick!" Jack yelled as the double doors of the study burst open and Carl, Henri, and Randall burst in to be met by flying glass.

"It's not Matchstick!" The old woman screamed out.

Jack saw Elsbeth Barlow trying to stand, but the buttressing of the mighty wind threw her three feet away. Randall ran to assist but was blown from his feet and into the wall.

"Jesus Jack, look out!"

Jack heard Carl's shout of warning, but he was too late to stop the grandfather clock as it was thrown across the room, missing him by mere inches.

Then shots rang out as Ryan, Will, and Tram opened fire from the swinging, broken doors at something Jack failed to see. As suddenly as the assault had started it stopped. Lightning and thunder returned, and the house vibrated with energy. Jack helped Charlie up and pulled Matchstick into his arms. The alien was wide awake and wide-eyed. Then the room became preternaturally quiet. Jack stepped over the shattered remains of the grandfather clock and faced Ryan, Mendenhall and then Tram who stood just inside the study with eyes as wide as Matchstick's.

"What in the hell were you guy's shooting at?" Collins asked trying to get his own heartbeat under control.

"Oh, come on," Ryan said loudly. "You didn't see that ugly bastard?"

"He's right Colonel. The thing was standing right over Matchstick and looked like it was about to smash him into pulp. So, we fired."

Jack looked at Tram. The Vietnamese sniper simply nodded his head confirming what Ryan and Mendenhall had seen.

"Jack, I saw it too. The Grey threw the clock at you. First it was there and then it wasn't. Billy the Kid and his two sidekicks would have hit it, but the bullets passed right through it."

Collins turned and looked at the wall near the spot he had been standing. Six bullet holes were punched through the old plaster wall. All were at a height the Grey's head would have been.

Randall and Millicent helped Elsbeth into a chair. The old woman was haggard. Her hair windblown and scattered. Her forehead was bleeding. She lowered her head into her hands.

"He's much stronger than before." She looked at Randall and Millicent. "Inform everyone to leave. We can't win this."

Randall looked shocked and the woman pilot shook her head in disbelief.

"Go now."

"Noooo."

Jack knew it was Matchstick talking. He put the small alien down and went to a knee. "What did you say buddy?"

"Noooo run. Stay, fight."

Elsbeth managed to rise up from the chair. She stumbled and it was Henri Farbeaux who reacted first and caught her.

"Not if you cannot help," she said going to her knees next to Jack and leaning on him.

Matchstick looked from face to face.

"No more Greys. No more Grey master. Never again."

Will Mendenhall looked at Ryan and Tram. "I guess that means there's going to be a rumble."

Ryan placed his pistol in his belt.

"It's about time I got to shoot something."

Montreal, Canada

Colonel Regev Slivinski watched as the Canadian customs agent eyed his Russian passport. The agent compared his picture with the actual face standing before him.

"Your business in Montreal, sir?"

"Pleasure. I spent so long in military of Russia being lied to about the west, I thought it finally time to see for myself and confirm the lies we are told now that they retire me."

"Well, good for you."

Slivinski watched as the agent slammed the customs stamp down. "Enjoy your stay, sir."

"I'm sure I will."

Slivinski, in a nice but older suit, retrieved his suitcase and made his way from the international arrival's terminal. Once outside Slivinski eyed the cabs and finally spied the one with the flickering license plate light. He moved toward it.

The driver, a small man in a brown caddie's cap, jumped from the cab after popping his trunk. The driver held out a hand to take the suitcase.

"Good evening, eh."

"Good evening, young man."

"Long flight?"

"Very long and extremely bumpy."

The small man placed the luggage in the trunk and then opened the rear door for Slivinski. He resisted the temptation to look around especially after the correct response to his security challenge. The driver put the car in gear and started for the exit. Slivinski watched the passing cars as the driver made no excessive moves to speed off. This was a good sign. A few liaisons with younger officers had turned out differently in the past and he had to make corrections along the way. Maybe the highly recommended young man would be different.

"I am very honored to meet you, Colonel," the driver said, not giving into temptation by looking in his rearview mirror at his passenger. Missing was the practiced Canadian accent.

"I imagine your vehicle has been swept for listening devices?"

"Yes, sir, I performed the task myself. I never leave my fate in the hands of others when it comes to doing one's duty. Especially embassy security staff. I find they are a lazy lot."

"A wise precaution."

Slivinski had seen the young officer's credentials back in Moscow. Although not his personal choice, he was satisfied that the boy could do the job as laid out. According to his dossier the young Lieutenant had performed with high marks on three cases thus far in his young career. All three involved the fate of former committee members that went astray. High praise in the filed reports from his Canadian handlers. The boy's reward was to learn and work with Russia's premier assassin—Regev Slivinski—the Ghost."

"Have the arrangements progressed?"

The driver, Lieutenant Danie Mediskaya reached back and gave the Ghost a new passport and identity papers. "We will be crossing the border tomorrow and will arrive on schedule in Buffalo for our flight. As you can see you are an executive with the Canadian Gaming Commission on his way for meetings with your American counterparts in Las Vegas. I made the arrangements myself just in case there is a failure in the process."

Slivinski closed the passport and looked at the young man's eyes in the rearview mirror. "Just in case I fail?"

The boy laughed. "As I said, I like to be prepared for any contingency, sir. I don't expect to be acting in any capacity. I know the Ghost never fails to perform his duty."

Slivinski opened his wallet and pulled a photo of his daughter free of the plastic and looked at her smiling face.

"There is always a first time my young friend."

Boston, Massachusetts

THE STREETS of the city were nearly impassable even at this early stage as *Lorraine* powered toward the coast. Police cruisers had limited their patrols to the hotel and financial districts because of the downing of trees and power lines in the smaller neighborhoods. Even the seedier bars of the city were empty.

Logan and the other surrounding airports had been closed for the past six hours as flights backed up and hotels filled. Thus far the leading edge of the storm had dumped sixteen inches of water on the city.

Drake Airfield was a small landing strip near Cambridge. Rarely used because of no ground radar and sporadic upkeep, it was mostly leased out for the daylight testing of drones and other pilotless aircraft. Master Chief Jenks was one of the few in the nation who even knew the airstrip existed. As the executive Learjet approached, the craft was tossed twenty feet in each direction.

"Uh, excuse me Master Chief, but how long have you been flying?" Xavier Morales asked after he had parked his wheelchair in between the cockpit and the rear cabin as Jenks and Anya sat side by side up front.

Jenks risked it and looked at his watch. "Five hours, ten minutes."

Anya's eyes went from the storm outside the darkened windows to Jenks and then to Xavier.

"You lied to us Jenks," she said.

"Hey twinkle toes, you're the ones that decided to come along. All I ever said was that I've been around and designed most of the aircraft in the American inventory at one stage or another."

Anya turned away and saw her reflection in the side window with the aid of the console warning lights, which were flashing on and off on a terrifyingly regular basis. Her only thought was the fact she knew she would never see Carl again. She turned back when Jenks reduced power and the Learjet went slightly nose down.

"This crosswind's a royal bitch!" Jenks said as he fought the stick as one wing threatened to buckle and the other rip free.

"I better go and strap in somewhere," Morales said.

"Yeah, you do that Speed Racer."

Anya jumped when she heard the hydraulics of the ailerons deploy. She felt sick as she looked from Jenks to the darkness outside and the rain slamming into the windscreen. She saw no sign of the earth in any direction. Jenks was flying by instruments alone. Again, and again, the Learjet buffeted into and sideways of the powerful wind. The dips and valley's made Anya feel as if she were on a rollercoaster pieced together by two fly-by-night Carnies named Billy Bob and Pedro. She heard Xavier vomiting in the rear cabin.

Jenks shoved the remains of a cigar in his mouth as he gripped the wheel of the controls tighter than he had ever held any woman—his Virginia included.

"Not your cushy little computer center is it, Doc? Bet you won't bitch so much the next time the air-conditioning goes out, will ya?"

"Arghh," was the only sound from the back.

"Damn rear echelon bastard!" Jenks cursed. Jenks watched the altimeter as the Learjet fought its way toward the ground.

'Pull up...pull up...terrain...terrain...pull up.'

The computer warning made Anya close her eyes as the Learjet swayed left and then right, went down and then up.

"Damn it, that wasn't there two years ago!" Jenks yelled as he pulled back harshly on the wheel as the nose barely missed a small tower.

Anya felt the small plane bounce. Then it went into the air again and then Jenks fought the wheel and the jet hit the earth once more. The plane jinked left and then right as the crosswind threatened to capsize the speeding ship. Another powerful gust of wind and rain made the Learjet rise once more and this time Jenks yelled.

"Stay down, you worthless piece of shit!" The Master Chief slammed the control column all the way forward and the Learjet started swerving. Jenks used both feet and applied the brakes. Suddenly the right landing gear collapsed, and the Learjet started to slide out of control as it spun in an ever-widening circle.

Anya squeezed her eyes shut as her mind closed down waiting for the inevitable tree that lined every small airstrip in the world.

Finally, the plane stopped as the twin turbo charged engines started winding down. Anya opened her eyes just as Jenks peeled his hands from the control column. He clicked open his lighter and lit the stub of his cigar. The only sound was the ticking of the cooling engines, the rain pounding the fuselage and Doctor Xavier Morales continuing to vomit in the back.

"Welcome to Cambridge, ladies and gentlemen, I hope you fly Air Jenks again." He snorted laughter.

"I thought for sure we were going to explode," Anya said as Xavier wheeled himself to the cockpit door.

Jenks removed the cigar from his mouth and then used his finger to tap the fuel gauge.

"Nah, not a chance doll. You have to have fuel for that to happen."

"We were out of gas too?" Anya yelled.

"I didn't want to make you uneasy, Sparky."

Anya felt sick as Xavier started to vomit again.

"Come on kid, now's the time to get a backbone, we got people to kill."

Thirty miles South
of Boston

ASMODIUS STARED out of the bridge windows and ignored the Philippine Captain's curses as he assisted his wheelmen with controlling the giant container ship. It had been thirty minutes since the vessel eased out of the eye and started steaming directly for the coastline. Sokol, white from numerous runs to the head, watched Asmodius smiling as it spied the waves crashing over the bow of the ship. The outer wings of the hurricane were now battering the city with its full force as the eye had been pushed eastward through the concentration of Asmodius. Sokol shook his head knowing the giant ship was near to snapping into two pieces.

"It will do no good transporting all of these people to Boston if you drown them all before arriving. Anchor now and allow the hurricane to pass!" Sokol screamed at the Grey.

The Russian had already watched several containers housing his minions, cascade overboard when they were struck by a side wave out of nowhere. All Asmodius had done was smile at the death of so many. Sokol was beginning to understand his value in this plan. He had none.

"Outer marker!" the captain yelled as the bow of the ship actually ran over the signal buoy to the greater Boston harbor. Still, the lights of the great city had yet to peek out from the raging hurricane. "Slowing to one third!"

Asmodius lost its smile and turned on the Captain. He angrily stomped toward the helmsman and him and pushed them out of the way. Instead of physically slamming the throttles forward, the Grey used his right hand and waved it over the control console. The levers magically slammed forward until they hit their stops. Sokol heard the engines growl and felt the ship accelerate toward a meeting with the rocks outside of Boston harbor.

"If we survive this I am leaving once ashore!" Sokol screamed. "You're going to kill us all!"

Asmodius slowly turned and faced Sokol. Its head was tilted as if studying the Russian. Sokol backed off a step toward the companionway when he saw the smile slowly fade from the Grey. The alien turned away but with its left four-fingered hand simply gestured behind him and Sokol was taken by an invisible force as his body flew over the command console and into the large hand of Asmodius. The creature brought Sokol up to eye level. Again, it tilted its head as the yellow, flaming eyes studied the Russian Committee member. With its free hand he brought its fingers to Sokol's face and lightly caressed the chilled skin. It slowly shook its head. Suddenly Sokol jerked as his head was filled with the silent voice of the mental conversation Asmodius used when communicating with precision.

'You will lead the attack on the Ancient One and the Green. I will remain here. Do not fail me or I will make you believe in the power of the night.'

Sokol started to choke as the smile returned to the mouth of the Grey. Asmodius tossed him to the floor as if discarding a piece of trash.

Alarm bells started blaring as the hurricane sent the bow of the ship high into the air. Collision warnings flashed and Sokol watched as the Captain and his bridge crew dove for cover. Then Sokol was slammed into the closest bulkhead as the ship hit a rock filled barrier just outside of the harbor. It came to a grinding hull tearing stop as water cascaded in from numerous rips in the hull. Thirty-five containers flew free of their chains and vanished into the breakers smashing ashore. The mighty ship rolled right and then settled onto the empty stretch of beach ten miles from the city of Boston.

Lightning flashed and thunder boomed as if to announce that Armageddon had arrived, and the black angel of death had come to claim what it knew was his—the world.

CHAPTER SEVENTEEN

Cambridge, Massachusetts

J ack had spent the morning speaking with Sarah and getting his update on Alice Hamilton. He shook his head at Carl who was waiting anxiously for any word on Anya, Morales, and Jenks. Thus far there had been none and there would be no assistance from the State Police. They were busy with the hurricane which had suddenly stalled one hundred and five miles east of the coast. What was worrisome and unexplainable was the fact that the calm eye of *Lorraine* was actually shrinking as its outer edges became even more powerful. It was getting to be late afternoon when Ryan, Mendenhall, Randall, and Tram reported on the meager defenses of the mansion and property. Luckily Lieutenant Tram it said it shouldn't be too difficult seeing any advance by an unwanted force from the many high vantage points Tram could utilize. As for Elsbeth Barlow's forces, Randall had reported that for the most part the coven was scared, but ready.

Jack was at the window watching the wind driven rain when he was approached by Elsbeth, Matchstick and Charlie Ellenshaw. Collins turned.

"I guess you're waiting for an apology from me about doubting your abilities and claims?"

Elsbeth smiled and placed a firm hand on Jack's shoulder.

"Colonel if I held it against everyone who ever doubted the fact that witchcraft existed in the world, I would have lost my mind a thousand years ago. The only time the world ever believed was the time when they burned those that followed my teachings. Very disturbing time in world history, I assure you."

Jack looked down as Matchstick also patted him on the leg because he couldn't reach to his shoulder. Jack's brows furrowed as he caught the whiff of sympathy coming from the small alien.

"Well, I suspect pretty strongly I would have been one of the ones with the matches back then, because I just cannot get my military brain around the bull—the science of what you are."

"Well, let's hope you have a change of mind. I'm here to talk about something else, Colonel."

"What is it?" he asked looking at Charlie who seemed not able to hold Jack's penetrating eyes.

"When I was deep into Matchstick's head, I was picking up you, Randall, and Mister Everett by accident. Sorry, I wasn't eavesdropping. Sometimes mind baiting is rather random in its targeting. For instance, I know Mister Everett is concerned about a woman named Anya. Randall was concerned that young Millicent doesn't even know he exists," she leaned in with a smile. "It's love, I think," she gave a small cackle. "But you were different. After speaking with Slim here I learned that you recently married."

Jack shot a look at Ellenshaw who was staring at his shoes.

"I saw her by accident in your mind as I was speaking with Matchstick's memory. Three concerns Colonel. One, you may think the Frenchman is a threat to your love. Although yes, he does love your wife, it's more out of admiration and respect he has than true love. Confusing to a man such as him. But nothing threatening. Two, your hatred of Colonel Farbeaux is a falsity isn't it?"

Jack moved his eyes from Charlie, knowing he would have to have a talk with the Doc about keeping personal things zipped inside his mouth and brain. "What makes you say that?"

"I really don't know. As I said your thoughts crossed with Slim's here, suggests an admiration and maybe a little touch of guilt."

Jack remembered years back and the horrible way in which Henri's wife Dannielle had perished in the Amazon and one that Henri constantly reminds him of. He did feel a twinge of guilt, not that he caused her death, but like his lost soldiers it was the fact he couldn't bring her home as he did the others.

"Go on," he said instead of commenting.

"Now, this may be somewhat disturbing and it's the reason Slim opened up, so don't be too hard on him later when you got him cornered."

"Well see," Jack said, and Charlie frowned as Matchstick grimaced in sympathy.

"Colonel, for a reason I cannot explain, when I was picking up these random thoughts from you, for the first time I couldn't see your wife. Every time she started to appear, a dark shape clouded my view of her."

"Is that normal when you mentally eavesdrop on people?" Jack asked.

Elsbeth didn't answer, but Collins could see that she was concerned about something she had gathered from Jack's mind.

"Colonel, maybe it's your failure to see that after all of these years, from the loss of your father to the loss of your men in combat, you refuse to believe you can ever be happy and content. Like a self-imposed punishment. At least that's what I hope it was."

"If not?" he asked.

Elsbeth shook her head. "It worries me Colonel that I usually pick up a clean vision of the future. Sometimes murky and sometimes clear. But with your wife, Sarah, I don't see her because I have fears there is no future for her. That your thoughts may predicting a time of extreme loss."

Jack became furious deep inside. He forced himself to calm down as his look went from Elsbeth to Charlie and then back to the Witch Queen of Salem.

"I was beginning to believe that you may have some form of power that I never knew actually existed. But as it turns out you have no more ability that a reality show hack. From here forward if you have any vision concerning me and my wife, keep them to yourself."

Jack turned and left the smashed study.

"Jack's the kind of man that you really don't want to delve too far into his head, Miss Barlow. If you do you better be prepared to discover the man has dark thoughts and maybe even darker secrets. But one thing is for sure, he truly loves Sarah. Hell, we all do. If he lost her, I don't know what he would do."

"I suspect I know exactly what he would do if someone was responsible for the loss of her love." Elsbeth rubbed the top of Matchstick's head and smiled sadly. "That I'm afraid, was crystal clear in his thoughts last night." She started to leave.

"What do you mean?" Ellenshaw asked.

Elsbeth stopped and turned and placed the wrap she was wearing tighter around her as she felt the shivers creep up her spine.

"Colonel Collins won't be with you long, Slim. His destiny will lie elsewhere."

Matchstick watched Elsbeth leave the study and then looked up at a frightened Charlie Ellenshaw.

"Sarahhhhh, Doctor Charlie...Sarahhhh."

RYAN WATCHED the meager light vanish from the rain and lightning torn skies. He shook his head as Will approached. He was carrying a standard issue M-4 automatic rifle with a bandolier of ammunition. His rain gear was slick with rain and he looked absolutely miserable.

"Now I remember just why I don't miss regular duty. Why does it always seem to piss all over soldiers in the field? I think God hates us."

"God doesn't hate us, Will. He just hates you and the rest of us are collateral damage."

"Funny jet jockey." Mendenhall looked around at the darkening terrain and the trees that seemed to crowd every corner of the mansion's property. "Where's Tram?"

Ryan smirked as he pulled first one, and then a second Glock nine-millimeter from underneath his raincoat and chambered rounds into both. "I'm afraid we won't know that until the guy opens up on any intruder."

Will shook his head. "Well, I just hope he snipes the right people. It's damn dark out here."

"Come on, let's get to the driveway. Hopefully the dumb ass witches will stroll right in."

Mendenhall laughed for the first time in days.

"What?" Ryan inquired.

"Ten years ago, could you have imagined saying that about setting up a defense against witches?"

"Come on man, I'm a navy boy. Have you ever been to Seattle?"

Boston, Massachusetts

ASMODIUS HAD STEPPED off the container ship for the first time in six days. It looked around at the two hundred men and women of the ancient coven and for most it was the first time outside of Louisiana they had seen the Grey closeup. Many dropped to their knees in grateful glee that the stories they have always heard from their ancestors were actually true, while many others balked in fear. Those that chose to try and slink away were quickly caught by the true believers, stabbed to death, bitten to death or decapitated and were now floating in the rough surf. As the rain and wind pummeled the large gathering, Asmodius went amongst them.

Sokol watched as they crowded around the Grey and were trying to get a touch of his awful grey skin. Asmodius soaked it up and was actually gaining power from their worship. The Russian's attention was taken away from the sickening scene as he saw the streets flowing with rivers of water. Not one car was out and about. Even Boston's finest sought refuge and only ventured out when called upon by an emergency to do so. Sokol was hoping the weather created by Asmodius would also be its undoing. There was no way he could move these fools from here to Cambridge in this storm.

His hopes were dashed when he heard the grinding of gears and the whine of turbo-charged diesel engines as fifteen large dump trucks approached from the south side. As Sokol cursed he also noticed the men driving the trucks. They had been trusted worshipers sent out by Asmodius earlier. Sokol jumped on the runner of the first and peered inside. The man driving was large and covered in blood. They must have killed everyone inside the emergency services truck garage in acquiring the dump trucks. The man looked maniacal as he faced Sokol. The Russian jumped free and stood in the rain as truck after truck lined up to take on the Army of Asmodius Modai.

A long streak of lightning burst across the sky and waves the size of buildings washed into the flooded streets. Boston was isolated and Cambridge would be no better off and even worse.

The war of the Witches would start tonight at midnight—the witching hour.

United Airlines Flight 769
Over the Continental United States

THE RUSSIAN ARMY Lieutenant known as Danie Mediskaya excused himself from the second row of first-class seats sliding easily by Regev Slivinski. He moved toward the restroom. Once inside he adjusted the new tie while looking in the mirror. He then leaned over and opened the supposedly locked restroom supply cabinet. He used his fingers to probe the underside of the countertop and then pulled free the small yellow envelope. He made sure once more that the door was locked and then tore open the envelope. Inside was the short note from his handler in Montreal. His eyes went also to the signature under the handler's official title of military liaison. He swallowed when he read the name. Mediskaya had never met the second man but was aware of his status. The note contained only eleven words in code. The young lieutenant knew the security code by heart and was able to immediately transcribe the message. *'Insurance. In case our friend has doubts, show him what's at stake.'* There was something beneath the handwritten note. It was a picture of a smiling young woman. The same one as the very photo Colonel Slivinski had in his wallet.

"Hm, I wasn't aware the Colonel had a daughter."

The young assassin destroyed the note and then pocketed the photo in case he had to use it. Then he washed his hands and rejoined his superior to finish the flight to Las Vegas.

Cambridge, Massachusetts

WILL MENDENHALL WAS STARTING to wonder if it was possible for the skies over New England to ever run out of falling water. Enough electricity filled the air to light up every baseball and football stadium in the nation and didn't look to be letting up.

"We thought you two could use this," a voice said from behind them. Ryan was startled but over the years Will had gotten very used to Colonel Collins and Mister Everett sneaking up on him. Mendenhall admired Ryan for not jumping out of his skin.

Jack handed them a thermos of coffee. "Where's Tram, I have hot tea for him."

"Hell Colonel, every time we think we see him in his high-hide, we see him somewhere else. Then we realize neither spot was where he was really at." Will shook his head as he ducked when another snap of lightning burst right over them.

"Where are the white witches?" Carl asked shouldering his own M-4.

"White Witches?" Ryan asked.

"What in the hell else do we call them?" Everett asked.

"Oh, I don't know, how about whack-jobs?" Ryan smirked. "I don't know, they're bunched together somewhere. They don't know how to use the damn radios we gave them. I hope the screwy little witches have a plan if we get overrun by the wicked witches of the east."

"Well, don't underestimate anything or anyone," Jack said as he and Everett turned to leave.

"Colonel, where's the little guy and Doc Ellenshaw?" Mendenhall asked.

"With Miss Barlow. The bastards will have to get by her to get at 'em."

Will started to say something and then remained silent.

"You witch hunters take care. Don't let 'em turn you into frogs or chickens or something unnatural like that," Carl said as he walked away with the Colonel.

"Ha, ha, funny," Ryan said as he sipped the hot coffee.

"You have to admit buddy—the moniker has a ring to it."

"WHAT TIME IS IT?" Millicent Krensky asked.

Randall looked at his watch. "Five minutes to midnight."

As they sat behind a fallen tree a hundred yards from the mansion, Randall looked at the rain-soaked form of Millicent. He shook his head as he realized the former combat pilot looked like a drowned rat and could not have been more beautiful in the big man's eyes.

"Five minutes to midnight." She turned and looked at Randall. "Sounds damned ominous doesn't it?"

"Nothing you say could ever sound ominous."

"What?"

"Nothing."

Millicent gave Randall a sideways glance before turning back to face the dark woods to their front. "Anyway, did you ever think the stories were true?" She looked at him once more as lightning flashed overhead. "I mean really true?"

"Yes and no, I guess. You know I became more of a believer after the invasion of the Grey's wiped out a quarter of the world's population. Only then did I imagine that true evil was capable of being real. So, yeah, I guess I didn't always believe. But now, I think we may have little time to make amends to Granny for doubting her." Randall looked at the tomboyish face of Millicent. "How about you?"

"I always believed her. Ever since she taught me my first spell as a child. Even though I always thought it just a magician's trick, I knew somehow that she wasn't lying to me. She made me believe in myself. But you know what really convinced me?"

"What?" Randall asked.

"She told me that she would teach me witchcraft on one condition."

"That you never use it for self-benefit." Randall smiled. "She told me the same."

"I've helped so many people in my life, even throughout my career in the navy and you know, I'm a far better person for it."

"Millicent, would you ever consider a brute like me?"

Millicent, a veteran of forty-seven combat missions in Iraq and Afghanistan, knew her mouth had just fallen open. She looked at Randall and her heart wanted to melt. She was about to say something when lightning flared the woods to life casting shadows that resembled the disembodied head of a large Grey.

Just then a huge dump truck crashed through the main gate as others smashed into the outer perimeter fencing of the mansion.

It was twelve midnight.

ELSBETH BARLOW HELD Matchstick's small hand in her own as they waited with Charlie Ellenshaw inside the basement of the mansion. Crazy Charlie jumped at every boom of thunder and every flash of bright lightning that shown through the small basement window.

"Easy Slim, we have our forces out there. They know how to handle themselves."

"I imagine if Asmodius is as smart as you say he is, he may have anticipated that fact."

Charlie felt bad when he saw Matchstick's worried face. The small alien had been through so much he didn't realize that he may be close to the edge of sanity.

"Tell me if I'm way off base here Miss Barlow, but have you ever thought of attack instead of defense?"

Elsbeth looked at Ellenshaw and a thought struck her. She had never even thought of attempting to contact Asmodius directly.

"Slim, I'm beginning to think you've been learning tactics from your Colonel Collins."

"Believe me, the force of his personality rubs off on you in mysterious ways. Before he arrived at the Group we were separated by departments. He taught us to think as one."

"How is that, Charlie?"

Ellenshaw smiled at Matchstick. "That no ounce of knowledge was worth one innocent life."

"Told to you by a man who has lost many a boy. I know this Professor. Your Colonel Collins has not traversed his toughest road yet. He soon will."

Charlie didn't want to think about the meaning of Elsbeth's words. They had lost so much in the past two years that he knew that anymore would bring Department 5656 to near collapse.

"Slim, take Matchstick and hold on to him. The battle we've anticipated for thousands of years has started. There are more followers of Asmodius than I thought possible. We're out numbered two hundred to thirty. I have to leave you now. You're right about taking the battle to Asmodius. This has to end tonight."

"I'm not following," he said as Elsbeth handed Matchstick off.

"Asmodius is close, I can feel it. He's near, or on water. I told you the Grey is a coward and now is the time when he's vulnerable. He'll be reaching out mentally in an attempt to enjoy his victory. I can key on that when the bastard's not expecting it."

Charlie swallowed his fear. "Then go and get the son of a bitch."

Matchstick growled. "Gets the sons of a bitches bastards."

Elsbeth Barlow closed her eyes and went into one of the deepest trances in her existence.

RYAN SAW them coming through the trees. There were women in housecoats. Men in finery and teenagers that looked as if they just arrived from Hollywood Boulevard. Jason sighted in on a man who was wearing a tuxedo that was filthy. He tried to squeeze the trigger of the M-4 but his finger couldn't apply enough pressure because Ryan's heart wasn't really into killing civilians. Then the well-dressed man saw him behind the tree. Suddenly Ryan felt a wave of nausea strike him just as if he were in high, rolling sea. The seasickness struck him as if he were traversing through a rough storm. He cleared his vision as he saw the man was smiling with outstretched arms. He was looking right at Ryan. The falling rain was seemingly pushed out of the way by a force that wasn't visible to the naked eye. It was then that Jason realized he was being assaulted by witchcraft.

Ryan heard a loud 'pop' and the man lowered his arms and then went to his knees with a bullet hole appearing in the middle of his face just above his nose as a round ripped through him. Ryan turned and saw Will Mendenhall and a smoking M-4 he was just lowering.

"Are you a believer yet?"

Ryan didn't answer, but he was also firing wildly into the tree line not wanting to take a chance on being assaulted again.

TRAM SIGHTED his first target and hesitated for the first time in his life. He saw the woman, but she had the appearance of a normal housewife. He aimed but he could not force his finger to depress the trigger on his M-14. Then he saw that the woman waved her arms and several trees fell as if she had merely brushed off a filthy tablecloth. He aimed and fired. For the first time he missed, and the woman saw the muzzle flash. She saw Tram at the crook of a branch high up in a tree. Again, she waived her arm and Tram heard and felt the crack of wood and then the tree started to fall.

JACK AND CARL couldn't believe their eyes as men and women from both sides faced off in the area between the main gate and the mansion. Elsbeth's forces mowed down thirty followers of Asmodius with a combined fireball of power. It came at the intruders as if it were a flaming sun. It struck the members of the coven of Asmodius and the trees quickly burst into flames and was hot enough that even the force of the hurricane powered wind and rain couldn't dampen them.

Jack felt the surrounding air, water, and wind, change as if the magic being used sucked up the very molecules that made up the environment. At times it was hard to breathe as oxygen was depleted from the chants and spells being used as weapons. He was beginning to understand the dynamics of what Elsbeth Barlow had been trying to explain about the physical relationship between witchcraft and true science of the environment. All that was being used was what nature supplied and the audible use of certain words and phrases.

Lightning struck a nearby tree and it threw Jack to the ground. Several of the followers of Asmodius charged. As Jack tried to shake off the powerful blast, the first person to reach him was a large man in a set of farmer's coveralls. Stunned, he attempted to fend the man off but was quickly overpowered. Then the man collapsed with a bullet parting the left half of his forehead from his right. He was soon helped up by Carl.

"Damn Jack, I think we've been missing out on a better way of doing things!"

MILLICENT SAW the five men rushing her and Randall. She mumbled something and then brought her hands up as if warding off an attacker. Then a bright flash of light happened as her spell took control of a bolt of powerful lightning and directed it to the ground. The explosion of earth and shrubs tossed the men away as if they had been nothing more than ants in a strong wind.

"That was one of the first spells Granny taught me!" she said as she turned to face Randall.

He was lying in a heap behind the log where they had been hiding. She went to him and wiped the blood from his face. "Look out!" he managed to say weakly.

Millicent turned and saw a man as he jumped forty feet through the air and come down in front of her. The ex-naval officer allowed the man to get close. Then with a sorrowful look at a dying Randall, she placed both hands together and then pounded the wet earth in front of her. The ground cracked and the trees swayed as the world opened up beneath the intruder's feet. Then Millicent allowed her hands to part and she clapped them together one time. The ground closed up, crushing the warlock as he tried to free himself from the crevasse she had created. She turned and held a dying Randall and he smiled as his eyes closed.

TWO MORE DUMP trucks careened through the trees. Their drivers acting maniacal and caring little for the men and women they carried in the back. Men, women, and teens were thrown into trees and crushed on impact. One of the truck's rolled over and the centrifugal force tossed human bodies as if loose bits of paper into the storm. Ryan, Tram, and Mendenhall heard, even as the truck flipped, the driver screaming laughter as every single person in the vehicle were either crushed by the truck or smashed into the enormous oak trees. Women survivors were screaming for their husbands and husbands ran to and fro in search of a loved they would never see whole again. One young teen was thrown so far that her body flew over thirty yards, landing mere feet from Tram. The small Vietnamese slid through the mud and saw that the girl could have been no older than twelve. On a hunch Tram raised the sleeve of the girl's parochial school-type shirt. He raised her arm to show Ryan and Mendenhall. Through the driving rain and the flash of chain lightning they both were shocked to see the needle track marks on her young arm, Will felt like vomiting.

Ryan rolled to his left toward three bodies that they had brought down during the first phases of the assault. He had to use his knife to cut away a man's business jacket sleeve and shirt. He grimaced when he saw the same needle marks that Tram had discovered.

Ryan slid back into the small depression where Will and Tram were. Tram, probably the best trained sniper the men of the Event Group had ever seen, was now shooting to wound and not kill. Will and Jason caught on really quick. Ryan pulled his radio free of his belt and tossed it to Mendenhall.

"The Colonel needs to know!" he yelled above the boom of thunder and then fired three rounds from his Glock into the shins of a charging witch. His eyes widened when he saw that the woman was wearing a meter-maids uniform from the City of New Orleans.

Mendenhall clicked his field radio to life and called Collins.

"Go, Will, over," responded Jack as Will heard a burst of automatic fire from somewhere near.

"Colonel, look at the arms of the attackers!"

"Say again!"

"Look at the arms of the attackers!"

JACK TOSSED Carl the radio and belly crawled to the nearest fallen attacker. It was a man who was dressed as a mechanic with the name tag on his coveralls of 'Jimmy,' on his breast. Jack hurriedly rolled up his wet sleeve. The track marks were clear and abundant. He felt for a pulse on the man's neck and found his heart was still beating. He then raised his right eyelid and in the flash of lightning saw his pupil was dilated more than he had ever seen. He had seen many a soldier in field hospitals under a morphine drip and knew dilated eyes when he saw them. The man he was looking was so full of what was obviously heroin that he knew there would be no way he would ever have survived the night. He again looked at the track marks and immediately surmised the puncture marks were recent and not long term. He slammed his fist into the ground and back crawled to Everett. He picked up the radio.

"All mansion personnel, all mansion personnel. Stop shooting to kill, I repeat no more killing. Wound but not kill. I repeat these people are not responsible for their actions!"

"Jesus, Jack, what in the hell are we up against?" Carl asked as he adjusted aim with his M-4 and downed a crazily running older man in golf clothing. The man slid on the soaked earth and grabbed for both knees where the bullets struck.

"Elsbeth said Asmodius was a liar. I guess making your followers drug addled helps him explain his cause. The bastard's using these people as cannon fodder!"

DEEP INSIDE THE BASEMENT, Elsbeth opened her eyes as Matchstick and Charlie were startled by her sudden movement. Ellenshaw held a Glock in his shaking hand and was watching the stairs leading to the ground floor. Matchstick had a small baseball stadium give-away bat on his shoulder and looked ready to use it.

"Easy Slim. Don't shoot. And inform little Reggie there not to swing away just yet. Now, what did I miss?"

"The Colonel has ordered the killing stopped. Disable only. The son of a bitch is using drugs on his own followers!"

Elsbeth closed her eyes and slowly shook her head.

"You said he was the great deceiver. What creature is capable of that?"

"A Grey, Slim. As evil as its race is, he tops them all. It like a crazed animal who is starving. It knows no boundaries of right or wrong, child or adult. It kills and eats. That simple." Elsbeth stood and took a deep breath. "Slim, I found him. The cowards waiting for some man named Sokol to finish his attack. It's four miles outside of Boston on a ship that isn't going anywhere. He's as stuck as a rat in a trap."

"Sokol, who in the hell is that?"

"I'm a Sokol," said a voice from the stairs.

Charlie, Matchstick, and Elsbeth turned on the man who was leaning over the wooden railing of the basement steps and his pistol was pointed not at Charlie or Elsbeth, but the small alien who growled deep in his throat. Dmitri Sokol stepped aside and allowed five large men to pass him on the stairs and continue holding the three in their sights as he slowly descended and joined them.

"Miss Barlow. I know your powers. But you can't do anything fast enough to keep me from placing a bullet in the Green's brain. And as Asmodius explained it to me, you need his mind to get into Asmodius'.

Since you wanted to see the Grey so much, why not do just that? Professor Ellenshaw you're invited also."

It didn't take Charlie long to put the puzzle pieces together when he caught a hint of the Man's accent. He reached over and gently removed the small bat from Matchstick's hands who turned and gave Ellenshaw a sad and startled look. Charlie remembered the simple gesture that Will Mendenhall used on him many times when he himself was so frightened he was near to panic. He winked at the small alien and the trick seemed to work as Matchstick turned back to the four men and another deep throated growl escaped his throat. Ellenshaw threw his nine-millimeter and the bat down on the concrete floor as lightning illuminated the basement through the small windows.

"Wise move, Professor," Sokol said as he ordered one of his drug addled men to tie Elsbeth's hands behind her back. The man performed the task roughly. "Easy, have some respect for your elders. Apologies Miss Barlow, but if Asmodius fear's your power, I think it wise to treat you accordingly. No waving of hands," the man then placed duct tape over her mouth, "and no chants and spells." Sokol started to turn and then stopped. "I give you my word I will force Asmodius to make your demise quick and painless." His eyes went to Charlie and Matchstick. "All of you."

Charlie felt a pang of bravery and knew Will Mendenhall and Jason Ryan had truly rubbed off on him.

"You have that much pull with Asmodius, do you?"

"We have agreements," Sokol answered with a smirk.

Charlie laughed, really feeling the arrogance of the Russian. "Let me guess. The Committee, right? I may also guess that you're pretty low on the numbered order of this Committee. Because you have to be that dumb to think Asmodius will keep any agreement you've made."

Sokol took an angry step toward Ellenshaw and the Professor used every ounce of will power to stay his feet from backing away. Instead he doubled down and stuck out his chin in defiance.

"I have no use for the committee, Professor. They have no vision.

Just a bunch of old men who want to return to even older ways. Dreams of the past. Asmodius will give me the power to really bring my homeland into the future." He started to turn but stopped once again when he heard Elsbeth laughing under the tape. Instead of a rebuke he looked at two of his men. "There's a door to a garage. We need two vehicles."

The two men ran up the stairs.

"The storm's weakening," Charlie said. "I think your friend is also." Charlie dodged the man trying to place tape over his mouth. "Why don't you stick around Mr. Sokol. There's a man outside that's most anxious to meet you." The brute of a man grabbed Charlie's long white hair and slammed the tape over his mouth.

"Ah, Colonel Collins. Correct?"

Matchstick took an angry step forward and hissed. "Colonel Jaaaack!"

Sokol stepped back a foot and actually smiled at the small, brave alien.

"That is one problem that I won't have to face, Professor. His bleak future lies in the hands of others. That, as they say, is out of my control." Sokol gestured for his men to remove his captives to the first floor.

If he would have seen the relaxed look on Elsbeth Barlow's face Sokol would not have been so confident.

IT HAD TAKEN the three over an hour to find the mansion. If it weren't for the sporadic gunfire they would still be roaming in the woods and drowning under the rain filled skies. Xavier had been threatened by Master Chief Jenks several time about being left out in the wood if he got stuck in his wheelchair one more time. Jenks always relented and assisted Morales out of a hole or over a fallen tree. But Xavier knew the Master Chief's patience in helping him would soon be at an end the closer they got to the gunfire.

Jenks held up his hand when they came to an area where one of the many truck's had smashed through the cast-iron fences at the back of the property. In the blast of lightning overhead, he saw the spires of the tall chimney's rising above the trees.

"There's the house. That's where I'm headed."

"Jenks, the gunfire is coming from over in that direction. If there's gunfire, Jack and Carl are sure to be close by," Anya said with her black hair dripping water.

"I'm not after Jack and Toad, Doll. The bitch I want is right in there," he said pointing his nine-millimeter at the large mansion. "I don't think an old woman is out playing GI Joe with the boys."

"Master Chief think a minute," Xavier pleaded. "If you go in there, you're more than likely going to face a bunch of her people and get killed before you have a chance to...to, oh hell, avenge Virginia. Now I want to kill the bastards responsible as much...hell, maybe not as much, but..."

"Shut it, nerd boy, before I shoot out your tires," Jenks said. He turned and looked at both as the rain ran off and through his close-cropped hair. He angrily tossed the wet stub of his cigar away. "Okay Hansel and Gretel, you two take care of yourselves. And you," he pointed at Anya, "get Toad to settle down. Marry the asshole and save his life. God knows I should have made Virginia quit. Now it's too..."

"Good luck, Jenks." Anya almost choked up.

The Master Chief looked from Anya to Morales, then stood from his cover and ran for the dense tree line.

JACK AND CARL were hitting the remaining followers of Asmodius with a withering fire and they estimated that since the discover of massive amounts of drugs in their systems, had not killed any. Most would not be pain free walking from here forward, but as Jack saw it, it just may be a powerful lesson on not worshiping an alien Warlock named Asmodius Modai.

Suddenly Everett saw a blur of motion as a man sprinted toward the front of the Mansion. I the flash of lightning he saw it was a squat man that ran as if he knew what he was doing as far as assault tactics went. His heart stopped. He shook Collins next to him.

"Jack, it's Jenksy!" Carl didn't wait, he jumped up and started running for the mansion over a hundred yards away.

Jack realized that the Master Chief was under the false evidence that Elsbeth Barlow was behind the murder of Virginia and having Charlie and Matchstick in her company would do much to dissuade the Master Chief he was wrong in his assumptions. As he stood to follow, four large men crazed with heroin coursing through their veins jumped Jack. Three men forced him to the ground and a fourth held his filthy and mud-caked hands over his face. Collins felt the air being drawn from his lungs like the witch was using a straw to suck him dry. He tried to draw in an intake of air, but it was like breathing through wet cloth. Jack started to choke, and his mind was fuzzy, and then his vision started to tunnel.

Suddenly the weight on his arms were gone. His face was splattered with warm blood that was immediately washed away in the continuing downpour. Then his eyes fluttered open and he saw the Frenchman standing over him with a smoking and hissing Glock. He assisted Jack to his feet.

"Sorry to intervene, but that embrace didn't look all that loving and appropriate."

"Jenks is here and is going to kill Elsbeth!"

"You go, I'll cover!" Farbeaux said loading another clip into his Glock.

"Henri, shoot to wound, not kill."

"Colonel, I noticed that you like to take the fun out of everything," Henri fired two shots and brought down two women with thigh shots.

Jack didn't know if the Frenchman didn't kill them because of his orders or simply because they were women. The grin on his face was at the very least, confusing. He quickly turned and ran to follow Carl.

THE GARAGE WAS AMAZINGLY full of old and rusted relics. The newest model vehicle was a 1970 Dodge Challenger, canary yellow in color. The rest were station wagons and family-style touring cars.

Matchstick and Charlie were shoved into the very same Town and Country wagon they had come east in from Nevada along with two of Sokol's thugs. They had orders to run interference for the large 1972 Plymouth Fury that had the faded black and white color of a former police car. Both vehicles looked heavy enough to get the group to Boston. Elsbeth was shoved ruthlessly into the backseat of the Fury and Sokol piled in next to her. He slapped the driver's seat and told the two men in front to get moving. His sixth sense was telling him Collins was close by and that was one man he had no wish to meet in person.

JENKS SAW the automatic garage doors start to open and he ran in that direction just as the large Town and Country screeched out of the garage. The Master Chief stood his ground and took quick aim and fired at the speeding vehicle. Bullet holes smashed into the front window and the station wagon swerved and then fishtailed into a line of manicured hedges lining the drive.

Charlie Ellenshaw shook his head to clear it, after hitting his head on the side window. He looked at Matchstick and saw the small alien was alright, just frightened, and when he looked up he barely made out the form of a man running through the rain and then without one moment's hesitation the person placed two well-aimed shots into the front seat. The two men there were dead before they knew what had happened.

Matchstick jumped into Charlie's lap and pulled the tape from his mouth.

"Come on, let's get the hell out of here!"

THE PLYMOUTH FURY tore free of the large garage. The driver saw Jenks before Jenks could move. At the last moment he dove out of the way with the right front tire missing him by mere inches. As he rose and aimed, he saw an old woman's head pop up and look out of the rear window. He fired just as a hand pulled the woman back down.

The black and white Fury sped down the drive. Master Chief Jenks cursed his luck. He knew he had blown his chance of ending Elsbeth Barlow right then and there. He pocketed the Glock and ran inside of the garage. His eyes immediately saw the bright yellow Dodge Challenger. He ran for it and opened the door, but his hope faded when he saw no key. He hurriedly laid on the front bucket seat and started tearing at wires. He found the correct wires and then touched the two together. The engine roared to life and Jenks twisted the two together. He immediately jammed the manual transmission into first gear and the car fishtailed, striking two other cars as he sped from the garage.

JACK AND CARL saw the second car speed by them before they could react just as they saw Ellenshaw and Matchstick running towards them. Charlie was shouting something and pointing at the black and white car that had almost run them down. Ellenshaw slipped and fell and Matchstick hurriedly tried to help Charlie to his feet. Everett and Collins ran to help.

"A guy named Sokol took her Colonel. A damn Russian!"

"Essss, a dammmm Russssssian," Matchstick repeated.

Carl looked at Jack as the whole story of Asmodius may just be coming together.

The Dodge Challenger was heard before it was seen. There were no headlights as it nearly missed Everett. Carl aimed at the back window hoping for a lucky shot.

Suddenly he was struck from behind by a crazed woman who neck-tied her arms around his thick neck.

"No," was all he heard.

Carl tried his hardest to dislodge the wild animal and then he stopped when he recognized the voice. The woman finally relented in her ruthless hold on his neck. She dropped free just as Jack, Charlie, and Matchstick saw Xavier roll onto the drive. He tried to turn too quickly, and then his chair snagged in a rut and he was dumped onto the gravel. Jack ran to help.

"Carl, that's Jenks!"

"Damn it!" Everett said as he suddenly embraced Anya. "Are you okay?"

Anya said nothing as she received the emotion from Carl she had been waiting on for a full year. She squeezed as if he would blow away in the storm.

"You American's pick the strangest times for romance."

The hug was broken and they saw Henri Farbeaux standing in the drive.

"That was Jenks?" Charlie asked as he picked up Matchstick from the wet ground. "He tried to kill me and Matchstick!"

Matchstick was nodding his head up and down.

"Hey, we just saw Jenks in a Challenger. The asshole tried to run us over!" Mendenhall said as he, Tram, and Ryan came running from the front of the property.

"He must think we're still blaming Elsbeth for Virginia's murder," Jack said, looking through the rain at the remains of Elsbeth's army as they were now assisting the wounded of both sides.

"We better get after them Jack. This storm's dying down and some ass at Harvard is bound to report that there was some kind of major battle near campus," Carl said.

"Okay, Will, go round up two vehicles. Ryan help. Xavier, you stay and coordinate with Elsbeth's people. If the authorities do show up give them the code word 'Chicken Little.'

Xavier nodded his head. He knew that was code to all State authorities of a suspected terrorist attack. That should give Elsbeth's people the cover they need.

"Later, use Europa and erase this whole night from existence."

"Yes, Colonel. Can do."

"Good. Tram you ride with Carl, Matchstick, Charlie, and I. Number one, we stop Jenks from killing Elsbeth. Number two, Elsbeth needs Matchstick for her, hell, whatever it is. Number three, if she doesn't stop Asmodius, we do. All other considerations are secondary. Clear?"

Everyone knew what that meant. They were now all expendable.

"I expect you don't need my services any longer. So maybe this is where I bow out," Henri said.

"Are you kidding?" Jack said. "Henri, like it or not, you're now an official good guy."

Farbeaux looked sick. He kicked out at the gravel of the drive looking like a spoiled child who just got caught being bad.

"Let's go kill our last Grey, shall we?"

Boston, Massachusetts

ASMODIUS TURNED from the pier and looked at the damaged ship. His mind connection with Sokol and the others had just gone dark. He sensed the Russian was still alive but his ability to see his army was black. His mental embrace of Elsbeth Barlow was still intact and that could only mean one thing—his forces had failed him. The Philippine Captain and his crew were busy pumping out seawater and dumping cargo containers into the roiling sea that smashed the steel into the pier and rocks lining the coastline.

The captain grabbed his head as a riptide of pain shot through from his temples to the back of his skull. He bent at the waist as his crew watched in terror. Asmodius was standing only feet away.

'Prepare your vessel to leave these waters.'

The captain tried desperately to fight through the pain of Asmodius probing through his mind. He shook his head trying to say that the ship was no longer seaworthy. Asmodius hit him of another burst of searing, mind probing pain.

'Start the engines and steer south. We will acquire another vessel. Do it or die!'

The pain let up just as Asmodius commanded the giant engines to start. The captain felt the vibration as the ship shook because of its damaged spaces and the rumbling of the engines.

The large container ship would make a last run for the open sea.

THE BLACK AND white Plymouth Fury burst onto the rocky area lining the beach as the rain slowed to a more regular pattern and even the wind was dying down. The Fury bottomed out and tore the transmission free of the body and the car grounded to a halt. Sokol grabbed Elsbeth and forced the old woman from the car. Her eyes were closed in pain as sometime during the wild ride from Cambridge her body was starting to shut down. She knew her loss of strength wasn't natural. She knew then that her strength and that of Asmodius were somehow linked. The storm she saw was losing power as she was. The loss of his followers may also be affecting Asmodius just as the loss of hers was bringing her low. But she also knew that even with the loss of strength with Asmodius, she now didn't have Matchstick to counter the Grey's advantage.

"Come on bitch, I have a debt to settle!" Sokol cursed. He saw Elsbeth was having a hard time breathing and since he didn't want to lose his prime hostage, he removed the tape covering her mouth. He figure if she tried to use her chants and incantations on him, he would just let her fall into the raging sea. Then Sokol and the two men with him carried and dragged Elsbeth toward the ship that was trying to force its way off the rocks. Waves almost knocked the four people from their feet as they fought their way toward the tearing sounds of the container ship. "The bastard's trying to leave without us!" Sokol shouted.

"Hold it right there!"

Sokol and the other three stopped and turned. The rain obscured him momentarily, but they were soon able to make out the short man, and he had a gun aimed right at them.

"You killed the only thing in the world that ever loved me for who and what I am."

"I haven't killed anyone," Sokol said slowly raising his hands. "Her kind is responsible, not me," Sokol said through the dying storm. The Russian looked at his two companions and then gestured for them to release Elsbeth. She fell to her knees in the surf. "There, she's the one you want." Sokol started backing away just as his two men started to the same.

Jenks was torn between who he wanted to shoot first. His aim went from a struggling Elsbeth Barlow to the three men retreating.

The sound of a blaring horn got the Master Chief's attention. He ignored it as he heard a car screeching to a halt somewhere above him on the road. At the sound of the horn, the three men turned and ran in the direction of the container ship that fought to get off the rocks.

Jenks took two steps forward and placed the pistol a foot away from the old woman's head, he started to squeeze the trigger as Elsbeth was still trying to draw breath. With her head sagging Jenks aimed for the center of her wet, silver hair. He fired.

The bullet hit the Master Chief in the area just above his left thumb. Barely grazing it but was enough to send his shot wild as the gun flew free of his hand.

It was Everett and Ryan who got to him first.

JACK SLAPPED Tram on the back as the Vietnamese lieutenant ejected the only 7.76 round from the M-14.

"Thank God. Jenks is still on his feet. Mister Everett has him in custody." Mendenhall turned to Tram, Henri, and Jack with a worried Anya, her head down on the hood of the car praying. "Damn good shot buddy. Glad we kept you around."

WHEN THE OTHERS ARRIVED, Jenks was still fighting to get at Elsbeth. Carl shook the smaller man who looked at his old trainee with murder in his eyes as Jason assisted Elsbeth out of the cold surf. He was leading her to the rocks on the shoreline.

"Jenksy, Jenksy, stop it damn it!" Carl was screaming at him. "She didn't kill Virginia!" Everett forced Jenks' head around to face the slowly moving container ship. "That bastard out there did it with the help of the man you just let run away!" When Jenks didn't respond he felt something in his head. When he looked up the pain and anger were gone from his eyes. The Master Chief turned and saw in the distance the silver haired woman looking at him. He felt her thoughts in his head. He blinked and then his eyes looked at Carl.

"Toad?"

"That's right, you crazy ass bastard."

"It was a Grey?"

"It was that Grey son of a bitch all along Jenksy. She's been trying to bake that bastard's cookies for a very long time."

"Oh, God. Is she alright?" Jenks asked turned to see Elsbeth being held up by Ryan.

"We'll explain later Jenks. Right now, we have to figure how we're going to stop a thirty-two-thousand-ton ship from getting out of reach," Jack said.

"Send in your navy," Henri said.

"They're too far out and bedsides Asmodius would have an opportunity and strengthening power to sink anything that gets close. It'll be too late by the time the navy gets here."

"Right now, he's weak on power you say, same as the old lady?" Jenks asked as Anya wrapped his wounded thumb with a wet section of her shirt.

"That's the theory," Carl said.

"I can sink that ship and drown all aboard, even that Grey son of a bitch."

"How?" Jack asked

Jenks pointed out to sea about a thousand yards. They looked through the diminishing rainfall. As the closest wave fell it exposed another ship. It was a natural gas container ship. It was easily recognizable with its 'bubble' domes containing gas.

"Master Chief, that would possibly take out half of Boston if it's set off too close," Jack said.

"Besides, how in the hell would we get out there?" Mendenhall said. "If you've noticed that's why they anchored it so far out."

Suddenly they heard water rushing as if from a runaway waterfall. They looked at the spot the noise was coming from. A Boston Whaler fishing boat bobbed to the surface where it had been sent to the bottom by the rocks of the shoreline. They were all amazed as it rose from the sea with water falling free from the numerous holes created in its hull when it struck the rocks during the worst of the hurricane. The boat was hanging thirty feet in midair as everyone turned and saw Ryan supporting Elsbeth Barlow. With Matchstick's help while sitting on Charlie's shoulders, she was holding her arms out and slowly raising them into the air along with the boat. Matchstick was mimicking her every move.

"I'll be damned," Jenks said.

"Talented indeed," Henri quipped. "I would like to offer that woman work in another field of endeavor."

Most turned to look at Henri and his obvious reference to theft.

They all ducked when the boat flew over their heads and slammed back into the water. Leaking but still floating. They turned back and saw Ryan and Matchstick raise their thumbs at the group. Charlie tried to do the same but nearly bobbled Matchstick into the sea.

"Toad you drive. Colonel you assist," Jenks said angrily. "Let's go and blow us up an alien asshole!"

"I want to go too," Will said.

Jenks reached into his pocket and put a stub of cigar in his mouth but didn't try to light because it was too wet.

"Forget it Army man, these guys are expendable, but the nerds back at base need men like you to watch over 'em." Jenks winked and turned and ran for the boat as did Jack and Carl.

As long as Will Mendenhall had known the Master Chief, the comment was the first near complimentary thing Jenks had ever said to him. That was when Will knew the Master Chief was going to do something really stupid.

JACK WAS BAILING water with a bucket above deck and Carl below was working the pumps. The water was still coming in far faster than they could get it out. Jenks fought with the throttles sending the twin outboards to and then past the redline. The Boston whaler climbed and then shot over the high waves as it sped toward the gas container ship. The Master Chief aimed right for the boarding ladder on the starboard side.

"Okay Toad, get us there and skipper this thing."

Everett poked his head up and started arguing immediately on why it was to be Jenks who would ram the container ship and not him.

"And what if you have engine trouble Toad? You gonna' fix it? That things been anchored through a damn hurricane. Do you think there may be a little damage to her hull plates and pumps?"

"Yeah, I know all that Jenksy, but I'm a far better swimmer than you and you know you're going to have to jump off that damn thing before it hits!"

"Yeah, and that's why you'll be there to pick me up smartass."

Everett kicked a bucket overboard as Jenks powered down the engines.

"You got something to say, King Grunt?" Jenks asked Jack who stood rooted watching the container ship getting up its second steam and running faster. Collins just shook his head knowing that either man would have a hard time keeping the gas carrier on course in this weather. Jack knew his limitations.

Both men almost fell over when the bow of the Boston Whaler slammed into the hull of the carrier near the boarding ramp. The name painted in white was 'Ivy League.' It was out of Charleston.

"Jenks, what if there's a watch on board?"

The Master Chief looked at the Colonel and then pulled a nine-millimeter from his pocket. He chambered a round.

"Then I guess their watch is ended. I hope they know how to swim."

"Don't worry Jenksy, we'll pick 'em up," Carl said as he idled the twin motors.

"Good luck, Master Chief," Jack said as Jenks reached for the rope railing.

"Luck's for pussies, Colonel." Jenks swung easily onto the flimsy steps leading to the main deck.

Carl throttled the twin Johnson's until the boat was fifty feet from the carrier. The both he and Jack flinched when they heard two gunshots from above them. Then suddenly five men came flying over the side of the gas carrier. They hit the water and Carl slid the Boston Whaler over and Collins started to fish the crew out.

"Who is that crazy bastard?" one of the men asked Jack.

"Some escaped lunatic."

"He threatened to shoot my left nut off if we didn't jump."

"Then I take it you still have your nuts intact?"

The man exchanged looks with his crew mates knowing that not only had they been pirated by a nutcase; they had also been rescued by his buddies.

"Now grab a bucket and start baling!" Jack ordered with gun in hand.

WHEN THE BOSTON WHALER was a hundred yards off, they saw the gas carrier vessel 'Ivy League' get up to full power as black smoke poured from her twin funnels. Jenks had the giant moving. In the distance and riding low and slow was the container ship and Jenks main target for the largest civilian sea assault since pirates roamed the Caribbean three centuries before.

SOKOL and his men were pinned to the bulkhead with no visible restraints. The frightened captain and crew watched as first one, and then the second man was eviscerated by Asmodius. The knife he used came from the galley and the captain saw that instead of using magic on the men the Grey had decided to do it the old-fashioned way. It was sickening to all who was forced to watch the punishment for failure.

Dmitri Sokol tried with all of his remaining strength to power his way off the bulkhead, but it was a if a giant magnet held him in place and his skin was made of steel. Every time his hand and wrist would pull away, it would snap back.

The second man watched as his own entrails fell from his stomach to splatter onto the steel deck. The man was in shock and didn't feel the Grey angrily step on them as if stepping on trash. The man gurgled out blood and Asmodius reached up and simply sliced a fourteen-inch gap in the man's neck from one ear to the other. Sokol felt his gorge rise.

"Elsbeth Barlow is no longer a threat to you!" Sokol pleaded. The Green is helpless without her. You're free of them!" Spittle flew from the Russian's lips as he begged.

Asmodius stepped up to Sokol. The yellow eyes penetrated the man's worthless soul as he saw his fate in those eyes.

"She'll die soon, I swear!" Sokol started to cry. "Asmodius, Master, please!"

Asmodius placed his grey face right next to Sokol's and it hissed in his own words and not in the Russian's mind. "She's...already...dead!" Asmodius smiled. "So...what...do...I need...you for?"

The knife plunged deep into Sokol's stomach and he felt the blade twist as the Grey's final act of pleasure was to gut the man who thought he was dealing with a true God. The Grey smiled and tilted his head as if fascinated by the evisceration as Sokol's entrails slowly slid from his body. His eyes remained opened as his heart and lungs were the only organs remaining in his body. Asmodius turned away, intending to leave the Russian that was as an example to the remaining crew and followers.

"Master, we have company!" The captain called out loudly.

Asmodius turned to the radar screen and looked. The navigator felt the alien's excited breathing over his shoulder, and he closed his eyes and his body shuddered.

The blip was coming from them at four o'clock and coming fast, far faster than the damaged container ship could run. Asmodius threw the bloody knife away and roared in anger as the captain and crew hurriedly moved out of the way as the giant alien made for the bridge wing.

"Go, go, tell the rest of the crew to abandon ship!"

His men needn't be told twice as they vacated their stations and fled the bridge. Once outside in the weakening storm, they jumped even knowing some couldn't survive the fall. That death was far more desirable than what Asmodius would have for them. The captain was the last man to jump and he prayed that Asmodius would meet his just end.

JENKS STOOD at the large bridge windows of the *Ivy League* as his absconded ship plowed through the rough seas toward the slinking target dead ahead. The Master Chief had the bow aimed right amidship of the giant.

He felt a familiar pressure start in his head as if Elsbeth was once more inside. But after a moment he knew it wasn't the woman. He felt the Grey and Jenks smiled knowing he had the alien's attention. He closed his eyes and concentrated. For most people who ever met Jenks they thought him a brutish little man with not one mannerism worthy of a civilized man. But deep down inside that rough exterior, an exterior that only Virginia Pollock was ever able to breach with any success, was a man who was steeped in fellowship for those he respected. He had come to respect and admire the men and women of Department 5656 and now he would show them how much.

"Remember the woman you murdered in Las Vegas?" Jenks opened his eyes as he wanted to see the far-off Grey on his high perch on the container ship's bridge wing and wanted the bastard to know the words came from him. "I loved that woman. I LOVED HER!" he screamed wanting the world to know and at the same regretting that he had never told her to her face. Tears flowed down his gruff face as he managed to light a cigar. He puffed it to life as he saw his reflection in the window as the sun started to breach the skies in the east. Jenks remembered Virginia's face and he smiled.

"CARL, Jenks isn't slowing! We'll never catch him!" Jack yelled as the two ships were near to merging as one.

"Damn it!" Everett said as he spun the Boston Whaler to port so sharply, he almost lost two of the bailing crewmen.

"Hey man, if that ship collides with the *Ivy League*, we'll have an explosion that'll burn us to a crisp and anything else within a mile if he doesn't swing us around!" one of the men said to Jack in near panic.

"*Ivy League, Ivy League*, come in, this is Toad, over!" Carl yelled into the radio on the flying bridge of the boat. "Come on Jenks, answer damn it!"

"Hey, Toad boy," Jenks finally responded.

"Jenks slow down and I'll come alongside."

"Nah, can't do that Carl. All that Grey son of a bitch would do is use that big brain of his and swing this big ass baby right out of the way. Nah, I'll ride her to the end. Look, it's what I wanna' do. I've never been as good and as brave as you, son. I can't handle the loss as well as you did. I think I'll punch out and see what's out there. Maybe Ginny's waiting. One thing working with you assholes has taught me Toad, is that any damn thing is possible"

"Jenksy damn it, come on!"

Nothing but static was the return answer.

JENKS STOOD at the side window as he felt Asmodius delve deeper into his mind. At first it was difficult keeping his hands off the throttle and the helm, but as he thought of Virginia it became far easier. He watched as the Boston Whaler slowly turned away.

"Good for you Toad."

ASMODIUS SAW the gas container ship coming closer by the second. It fully suspected that its power would be enough to slow and turn the ship. But as he started to awaken to reality it grabbed the railing on the bridge wing and cursed the man that withstood its commands. With one final push it held out both hands and arms and slammed them down upon the railing. The bow of the *Ivy League* dug deep into the sea just as the sun broached the black storm clouds in the east. Asmodius then watched as the giant bow shook off seawater as it once more broached the surface, coming on after only losing two knots of speed. Asmodius roared in anger.

JENKS RETURNED to the windows at the front as in his mind he heard the fury of the Grey. He smiled and puffed on his cigar and then laid the burning stub on the window seal fully expecting to enjoy it later.

"This is for Ginny, you Grey son of a..."

JACK and the others felt the explosion before even hearing it. The two ships met and a split-second later the world that had been covered in rain lit up as if the sun had exploded. The Boston Whaler was lifted free of the sea and almost flipped over stern over bow but then righted itself.

Jack ran to the ladder and was about to climb up when he saw Carl was just steering and looking at the shoreline. He decided his friend didn't need the company.

In the east the sun rose as the weather started to mysteriously clear and it promised to be a beautiful day ahead.

CHAPTER EIGHTEEN

Desert Springs Hospital,
Las Vegas, Nevada

Sarah closed the cell phone and looked at Niles Compton. The director was looking even more worn than before. He refused every request made by his new Assistant Director to get some rest back at the complex. The news about the loss of Master Chief Jenks and the death of Elsbeth Barlow dug Niles' hole of depression even deeper. He toyed with the cup of coffee in front of him and kept his eyes lowered. Niles hadn't shaved in the full week he had been planted at the hospital and chose to even change clothes there. Sarah had covered for the missing personnel as best as she could under the circumstances, but it was nearing a time when the department needed its director back.

"How's Carl?"

"Jack said having Anya there with him has made it bearable. He lost the father figure he always had in the Master Chief." Sarah sighed. "First Virginia, and then Alice and the security men, we're all taking it pretty hard."

"You know, I always thought the Master Chief a bully. I never thought that maybe that's the only way he knew of teaching." Niles looked at Sarah and smiled for the first time in days. "And he *was* one hell of a teacher."

Sarah raised her coffee cup in a mock toast. "Amen."

"Where's Jack and the team now? We're kind of shorthanded around here."

"Just landed, he'll stop in in a few. He wants to visit with Alice."

"Do you mind if I join you?"

Sarah and Niles looked up and saw the Surgeon General smiling down at them. They both thought the smile was somewhat out of place but instead of saying anything Sarah gestured to an empty chair. He sat.

"When I'm gone, please pass on to whoever is in charge of general services here that their coffee is the worst I've tasted in the whole of the country."

The comment was met with silence from Niles and Sarah.

"You'll have to do it soon, because I'll be leaving here tomorrow." The Surgeon General watched their reaction but there was still nothing. Then Niles perked up, but the Surgeon General didn't know if it was in anger of just questioning his reason.

"Leaving?" he asked, exchanging looks with Sarah.

"Yes, my time here is done. They don't need me anymore. Hell, maybe never did. I told you Alice is one strong and determined lady."

Sarah suddenly stood. "You mean…"

The surgeon general looked at his wristwatch. "She's been awake now for twenty minutes."

"You bastard!" Sarah said as she turned and took a few steps. She stopped and turned to face the bearded navy man. "Sir!" She sprinted from the cafeteria.

"In Sarah-speak that means, thank you for everything," Niles said as he stood and then held out his hand.

The Surgeon General of the United States of America stood, smiled, and shook Niles Compton's hand. Then smiled wider when the mysterious director of a mysterious government entity followed Sarah out.

THE SMALL BAR was situated between the Rio Hotel and Casino and a small strip mall that had just been sold but had yet to chase off all of the tenants who had leases. The Rio waited anxiously for its destruction.

With the scorching sun outside, the air-conditioned dive was a blessing for Lieutenant Danie Mediskaya. His clothing was light and airy, but he had never seen such a scorching day outside of Afghanistan. He allowed his eyes to adjust and then he saw the man he was meeting sitting in a booth at the far end of the bar. Regev Slivinski was there with a tall glass of club soda. Mediskaya moved into the booth across from the colonel.

The female bartender came over and the younger man ordered a vodka on the rocks. The colonel offered no condemnation, but he wasn't pleased.

"I assumed you would be a drinking man, Colonel," he said as he settled in after the bartender left.

"Do you know what the Americans say in regard to assumption?"

"What?"

"That assuming is the mother of all fuck-ups."

"The Americans and their sayings. Witty at times, stupid at others."

The colonel sipped his club soda as the bartender delivered the lieutenants drink and left.

"What did you learn?" Slivinski asked.

"The Colonel has just arrived at McCarran and his Director Compton is still where he's been for that past week."

"The hospital?"

"Yes, sir. Surveillance says he hasn't left."

"This could be a problem."

"Why? I mean if Collins visits this woman in the hospital, they will both be in one place. I thought you would be pleased."

"Lieutenant, how many assignments have you had where you had to eliminate someone in a crowded, public setting?"

"None, sir. But I thought poison could be an applicable measure. I understand Kim Un-Jong uses it in public places quite successfully."

Slivinski was silent as he again sipped his drink. He looked at the boy closely and shook his head. "You've heard about my reputation. I don't poison targets, Lieutenant. Besides, and answer quickly, how much does Colonel Collins and Director Compton weigh?"

The young apprentice assassin looked confused. "I don't know, sir."

"I do. Collins is a big man. Compton a smaller man, but very robust. How much of this magical poison do you have on hand?"

"It can be supplied."

"And how much do you administer to each?"

"I don't know, sir."

"Exactly. Now, with their concern being in I.C.U. wouldn't you say they are watched closely by doctors and nurses?"

This time the lieutenant didn't answer. He knew Slivinski was teaching him something but for the life of him he could swear the 'give no quarter' attitude he had heard so much about was missing from the man they called the Ghost.

"Lieutenant, when you deal with a man such as Colonel Collins, you put him down by means you know for a fact are going to keep him down."

"A bullet."

Slivinski raised his glass. "With more risk, comes greater satisfaction."

"So?"

Slivinski lowered the tall glass and frowned. "With them getting ready to run to their underground lair, we have but one or two opportunities remaining. We can't guarantee any outside meeting because we just don't know their patterns. I'm concerned, but it has to be the hospital. And if my hunch is correct it will be tonight or tomorrow at the latest."

The information seemed to relieve the young lieutenant. His demeanor changed instantly.

"I need a full schematic of the hospital from our contacts. I need outside window locations. I need to know where their security is stationed."

"Right, I have everything in the hotel room," Mediskaya said as he downed his drink and held up his hand indicating another.

"I need them now, Lieutenant."

The boy immediately rose and with a disdainful look at the colonel, left the bar.

When he was gone, Slivinski removed the photo of his daughter from his wallet and looked once more at her smiling face. Then the smile vanished as fast as it had appeared. He turned and watched the young assassin drive off and he frowned. He knew as he replaced the photo that he couldn't do this work any longer. That not only would he lose his soul but curse his daughters also.

The Ghost knew he was finished.

Desert Spring Hospital,
Las Vegas, Nevada

THE HOSPITAL STAFF felt so confident about Alice's improving condition that they moved her to a private room two floors down. Jack and Sarah smiled and tried to not show how difficult things had been for everyone just to keep Alice's spirits from sagging. But they could tell that Alice had an intuition about her that was incomparable to anyone. Niles sat in a corner chair and was smiling steadily for the first time as he took in the reunion.

The door opened and Anya and Carl stepped in. Anya was the first to hug Alice and Carl second. As he bent over Alice locked her arms around him and hugged as hard as he's ever been hugged. No words needed to be said. Carl broke the embrace and then wrinkled his nose trying to force back his emotions.

"You look like you finally got some rest," he said smiling.

Alice smiled at Everett and Anya. "Yes, I'm ready to return to work if that ogre over there will let me," she said indicating Niles in the corner.

"I think we can scrape by a few more days without you. Besides, I need the rest also. You come back and the kickback days are over."

The room laughed as it was great to have Alice back again.

THE MEDICAL SUPPLY van drove slowly into the elevated parking area. The writing on the side of the large step van said *Golden Goose Medical*. As the van parked the lights shut off and the entire area was silent with the exception of the crickets.

"Are you sure this is where Collins parked?" Slivinski asked as he moved a large case onto his lap as he sat on the wheel well.

"Yes, sir. That's his puke green government sedan right over there. The Colonel and a lady drove in about an hour ago.

"Compton?" he asked as he screwed in the barrel of the specially redesigned Russian-made SVD semi-automatic sniper rifle and then did the same with the sound suppressor.

"So that's the famous *Ghost's Spear*."

Slivinski looked up. He was disgusted by the lieutenant's love of everything kill worthy and especially the nickname they had given his personal weapon.

"You've heard of it?"

"Who hasn't Colonel. You and it are like vodka and ice."

"Is that right?" Slivinski said as he placed the curved magazine of ten rounds of 7.62-millimeter rounds and then pulled the bolt back and left it open. He placed the PSO-1 optical sight on and adjusted it.

"I thought you would use one of the newer model scopes Colonel."

"This is a shorter-range weapon Lieutenant, any more power on the scope would just be heavier in weight and more than you need." He looked over at the eager boy. "Besides if you can't hit your target with this you need to find another profession."

The lieutenant's smile faltered.

"Okay, open the portal so I can sight in."

Mediskaya eased over and slid the portal that was disguised as the second letter 'O' in goose. The portal was just big enough for the muzzle and wide enough for the scope aperture to see properly. Slivinski was satisfied.

"Now we wait."

JACK, Sarah, Anya, Carl, and Niles needed to leave the room and let Alice get some rest. At least that's what a burly nurse recommended with a very serious frown. Alice had tears in her eyes, and all felt guilty about leaving her alone.

Once outside, the group relaxed and there was even some soft banter. Alice's recovery had made all feel re-energized like a shot of vitamin B-12. They remained at the entrance and spoke about going to get a well-deserved drink before heading back to the complex.

At the far end of the parking lot another green Chevy with U.S. Government plates on it drove past a large medical supply van and parked not far away. Three men climbed out and stretched.

"There's Jason, Will, Charlie and...what is that Charlie's carrying?" Sarah asked.

"Damn it, those idiots are trying to smuggle Matchstick in a blanket in to surprise Alice. We better turn them around before we have the National Enquirer reporting aliens in Vegas," Jack said smiling.

"Not that they haven't reported it before," Sarah said, and they all laughed as Ryan, Mendenhall and Charlie noticed them and waved.

"NOW COLONEL, you won't get a better shot. Both are right there."

Slivinski grated his teeth at the exuberance of the young assassin. The boy just irritated him to no end. In his old age anything concerning murder made him shy away further from the human race. To Danie Mediskaya's amazement, Slivinski lowered the rifle and pulled away from the portal.

"I can't do this anymore," he said with his head lowered.

"Have you told anyone else that Colonel?"

Slivinski looked up at the lieutenant. He shook his head 'no.'

"Oh, but I think you have, sir," he said as he handed the colonel a photo. "They told me this may happen, and I was told to remind you of the consequences of failure."

Slivinski saw the same photo of his daughter that he had in his wallet. His eyes flared brightly with anger as he looked back at Mediskaya who was holding a silenced Makarov semi-automatic pistol on him.

"I suggest you carry out your orders, Colonel. For all our sake."

Slivinski dropped the rifle and dove for the Makarov. The weapon discharged. Slivinski was hit in the chest and he fell forward into Mediskaya. The lieutenant quickly dropped the smoking pistol and picked up Slivinski's private weapon and pushed the colonel's still form out of his way. He quickly brought the rifle up and aimed through the portal.

"WELL, I'M PARKED OVER HERE," Niles said. "I'll see you people sometime tomorrow after eighteen hours of sleep." Niles waved and started to move off.

"Hey, you three, visiting hours are over!" Carl said loudly as Charlie, Ryan and Mendenhall stopped suddenly.

Carl saw Ryan push Charlie and Matchstick out of the way and both he and Will started running hurriedly toward them. Carl's eyes widened when he saw both men draw weapons.

"Get down!" Mendenhall shouted loudly.

That was when Anya looked over and saw Niles on the ground. He wasn't moving and blood was starting to spread across the asphalt of the parking lot. The blood was almost unrecognizable under the sodium lamp.

"Niles!" she shouted as they all turned.

DANIE MEDISKAYA WAS PLEASED to have hit Compton with the first shot of the ancient weapon. He used the bolt and ejected the spent round and chambered another. He sighted on his second target,

Colonel Jack Collins. He smiled as his finger started to put pressure on the trigger. He knew he was about to be known as the new Ghost. He squeezed the trigger.

"Get down!" Jack yelled and grabbed Sarah and pushed her as hard as he could as a second silenced shot went wild and smashed the window of a nearby car. Collins pulled his weapon at the same time as Carl and both advanced in the direction of the unknown assailant.

SLIVINSKI, with a bullet in his sternum dove for the weapon and struck the lieutenant just as he had pulled the trigger. The shot went wild. Mediskaya pushed the weakened colonel off of him and then started firing wildly at whatever moved outside.

RYAN WAS the first to see the barely perceptible muzzle flash of the rifle. He and Mendenhall started filling the step-van full of holes, but the shots from inside kept coming. Then Jack and Carl added their firepower to their defense. Soon the van was starting to burn but still the shots kept coming. Jack turned quickly as he reloaded and saw Sarah running with Anya toward Niles. He cursed her for not obeying his orders. He turned and started firing once more. Then the van exploded.

Ryan and Mendenhall dove for cover just as a man rolled out of the back doors of the step van. He was holding a pistol as another man jumped. The man with the pistol fired several rounds at the second and he went down and didn't move. The first rolled over and didn't attempt to rise. Ryan made it to him first and shielded his face from the intense blaze. Will kicked the pistol out of the still hand of the first man and then grabbed him by his shirt collar and drug him away just as Ryan leaned over and checked the second man. There were several holes in the man's face and Ryan said good riddance and moved away just as the van exploded for the last time.

Jack and Carl ran up and made sure Will and Jason weren't hurt. Then Jack leaned down and checked the first man's pulse. He was still alive but was bleeding out fast. The man's eyes suddenly opened and for a moment there was panic in them. Then he relaxed when he brought a crumpled picture to his eyes. He seemed content for the briefest of moments and then he saw who was leaning down next to him.

"Colo...nel...Collins...," the man reached up and pulled Jack close to his bloody lips. He whispered and Jack flinched. The man kept speaking, his words getting softer and softer, then he went silent. Jack angrily pulled the man's clenched fingers from his coat and let it go. He stood and his eyes told Carl, Ryan, and Will that he had been told something that put him into a blank rage. Then it passed and he looked at Will and Jason.

"You two alright?"

"Yeah, Matchstick and Charlie are over there," Will answered.

Just then, Ellenshaw and a blanket wrapped Matchstick hurried up to them.

"What the hell..." Charlie started to ask.

"Jack!"

Carl heard Anya's voice, and everyone sprinted back toward the entrance.

Carl was the first to see Anya with Niles in her arms. He was bleeding heavily from his left shoulder. But Anya was crying and pointing in another direction. Jack turned and saw Sarah sitting on the ground next to a car with a flat tire. She was looking at him. He saw the perfectly round hole in her chest. Niles was attempting to shake off Anya's hold and go to Sarah, but Carl moved in to help her keep the director still, but his eyes were on the scene in front of him.

Jack let the pistol he was holding drop to the ground as he hurried to Sarah's side. She tried to smile but blood started to drip from her mouth.

"I think...I tripped...Jack."

Collins saw the wound and he didn't know what to do. His eyes became blurry as his mind went to a state of incomprehension at what he was seeing.

Charlie, Matchstick, Ryan, and Will were frozen in time as they watched Jack cradle Sarah in his arms.

"Oh, short stuff, you're fine. Just clumsy."

"Jack...I think...I hurt...myself...," she said as her eyes started to close. They opened with difficulty. "Tell me about...tell me...about... our honeymoon."

Jack broke down as tears started to flow. He didn't hear it but Anya was wailing, and the others turned away. Carl went down to one knee and then lowered his head and started to sob.

"Oh, baby, it'll be great...I was thinking Tahiti...," Jack again lowered his head and brought Sarah close to him and hugged her.

"I think we...waited...too...long, Colonel."

Jack felt Sarah's head fall heavily into his chest as she died.

Will was crying as he walked up to a parked ambulance and started slamming his fist into the windows, shattering each one. Ryan finally had to pull him away as his hands were broken in several places.

Hospital personnel ran to the scene and started attending to Niles who was yelling and screaming for them to leave him alone and go to Sarah.

Anya stood with blood all over her clothing and helped Carl to his feet. When she saw Alice running out of the hospital doors with her I.V. drip dragging behind, both had to stop her from approaching.

Charlie Ellenshaw threw off his glasses. Then he turned and saw the Matchstick Man simply walking away. He ran to stop him. He picked him up and they both started walking and crying.

As for Jack, no one could get him to release Sarah. He held her in his arms for five straight hours. The hospital and police stopped trying to get Sarah's body free from his embrace but the cordon of Event Group security was far better armed than them, so with the encouragement of Special Agent Wilkerson of the FBI who had red eyes himself, the local police and sheriff's left them be.

EPILOGUE

ENDING OF A DREAM

Event Group Complex,
Nellis Air Force Base, Nevada

With only four months left in office, the President of the United States didn't have to hide much in visiting the complex as much as he had in the past as the world had stopped paying attention to him and began to devour the two men left in the presidential election. He sat across from Niles Compton who refused to stay in the hospital any longer than it took to stitch up his shoulder where the bullet had passed through. He was wearing another cast and sling as he stared at nothing as the President read the final report. When he finished he placed it softly on Compton's desk.

"What a nightmare. If this hadn't been you and this Group, I would swear I was reading a grade C movie script. A Grey? Witches? I can't fathom it."

Niles was silent as was Alice Hamilton who had escaped the hospital and dared anyone to stop her, and she had emphasized that fact with a pointed and cocked nine-millimeter pistol.

"Jack?" the president asked.

"No word. The last bit Europa and Xavier had was that he was spotted in the Ukraine. That's where the first five bodies were found. All Shadow Committee members, all shot in hiding. He's tracking them all down one at a time."

"How about Colonel Farbeaux?"

"Vanished."

"Jack's not going to show for Sarah's funeral?"

Compton just shook his head.

"Niles, we have to stop him."

Again, Niles didn't say anything.

"Interpol has warrants out and the FBI will take him in when he's caught. Jack's going to start a war."

Niles remained silent as did Alice.

"I'm sorry Niles, but I can't leave this mess for the next president. That means you have to have clean hands in this."

Silence.

"I wish I could stay old friend, but it would cause too much wild talk. I will fly to visit Sarah's mother and Virginia's family. The Master Chief's funeral I can attend. His headstone will be placed at Arlington, and Virginia's name will be right below his on the cross, I've seen to that."

The president stood. "Mrs. Hamilton, watch over things."

Alice gave a brief nod of her head.

"Niles, I am so sorry. This country owes you and your people more than they can ever..."

Compton stood suddenly and held out his hand.

"Have a safe journey home, Jim."

The president nodded his head at his oldest friend and took the directors hand. He nodded at Alice and then left the office.

The two sat in silence for five whole minutes. Then Niles smiled at Alice.

"Ready to go and pick up Mrs. McIntire at the airport?"

"Yes, I think I am," Alice said tossing her ever-present notebook on the desk.

Before they could leave, Carl Everett came in and handed Niles a sheet of paper. He turned and left without saying anything. Niles read what was written and simply nodded his head and then took Alice by the arm and they left the office.

NILES PULLED into the arrivals area at McCarran airport and parked. He had difficulty with his left arm in a cast but managed to get Alice and himself there in one piece. Instead of leaving the car he pulled out a cell phone and punched in a number that he had preprogrammed. He looked at Alice and gave her a weak smile as the phone on the other end was picked up. Alice took Niles hurt hand in her own and held it.

"Variable," he said and then waited for his code word to be answered correctly. "He was last seen in Siberia at 89 Catalan Street. He goes by the name of Lovesko. The name he used in 1973 was Stanovich. He was a Colonel in the KGB."

Niles listened.

"No, tomorrow afternoon. I will. Yes, she is." Niles looked at Alice and managed to squeeze her hand and smiled.

He listened.

"I'll let them know, but I'm sure I don't have to tell them that which they know so well." Niles started to lower the phone, but Alice took it before he could hang up. "You and Henri get the son of a bitch!" Alice listened for a moment. "Good luck, Jack."

Niles accepted the phone and tossed it out of the car window. He watched as the cell phone sizzled and burst into flame. It melted.

"Hm," he looked over at Alice. "Tell Doctor Morales his first secure phone worked."